Deep Core

D1799114

INDEPENDENTLY PUBLISHED
Copyright © 2019
By FX HOLDEN

Cover: "Spaceport on the sub-moon of Orkutsk"
Artist: Grandeduc, Shutterstock

TATSENSUI COLONY
ORBITAL PLAN VIEW, NORTH POLE

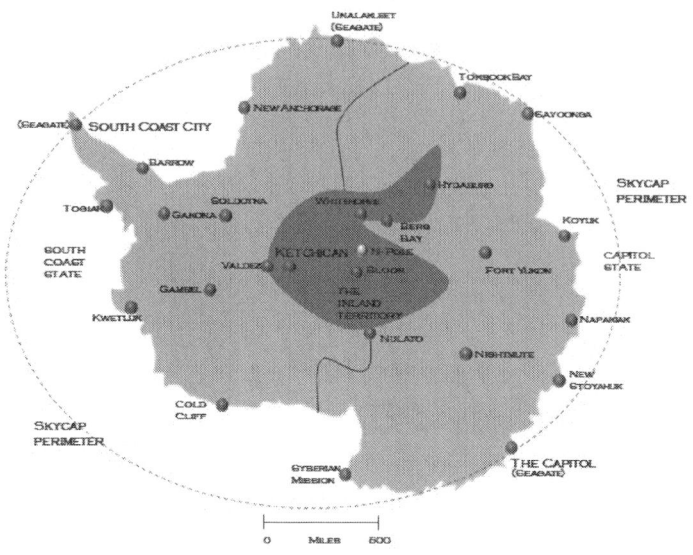

CONTENTS

THE COMMONWEALTH OF CORUSCANT

Core Encyclopedia v201.b

Coruscant (original designation Kepler-452b or Kepler Object of Interest KOI-7016.01) is an exoplanet orbiting the Sun-like star Kepler-452 in the constellation Cygnus. It was the first potentially rocky super-Earth planet discovered orbiting within the habitable zone of a star very similar to the Sun.

The planet is about 1,400 light-years away from Earth and until the advent of the Alcubierre Warp Drive the only information about Coruscant was obtained from near-Earth observatories and predicted the planet could potentially sustain a human colony. The first unmanned probes to survey Coruscant, however, found a rocky planet with a climate that may have once been similar to Earth, but that was now without sufficient water or accessible reserves of nitrogen and oxygen to sustain human life.

Coruscant was, however, about 50 percent larger than Earth and subsequent surveys identified eleven moons in orbit around the planet. Of these, four were found to host indigenous non-sentient lifeforms and to be human-habitable. Over the next 200 years the following colonies were established:

Tatsensui (TS): a large ice moon entirely covered by frozen oceans but with low-level subsea volcanic activity leading to localized surface ice melting and minor seismic events. A colony was established at the northern pole, a continent of stable ice, free of significant seismic disruption. The economic engine of TS is the export of liquids and gases to the other colonies.

People's Republic Colony (PRC): a desert moon similar in many ways to Mars in the Earth system, with reserves of water trapped beneath the surface of the moon and a seismically stable profile which, coupled with considerable mineral wealth, has contributed to it becoming the second largest anti-matter production facility outside of Ganymede.

New Syberia (NS): the most volcanically active moon orbiting Coruscant, it has retained a near-Earth atmosphere. Several large and active volcanoes have created a runaway greenhouse effect conducive to large-scale, high-rotation intensive crop production. It was historically the most tenuous of the three colonies, as its orbit took it through the center of an asteroid belt every 24 years, but this threat was subsequently mitigated by a re-engineered ring of Warp Drives able to absorb the mass of the asteroid and project it to coordinates in empty space. This ring is known as the New Syberian Shield and serves also as a planetary defense system.

NS is orbited inside the NS Shield by its own 'mini-moon', the geologically stable Moon of Orkutsk, which hosts a starship base, embassies, and is populated by a carefully regulated number of citizens of all three colonies. Orkutsk is the main point of entry into the Coruscant system for all interstellar traffic and interstellar/interplanetary trade is therefore the basis of the NS economy.

Due to the deliberate interdependencies of the three colonies (no one colony has the means or the raw materials to survive independent of the others), they were joined 100 years ago in a confederation known simply as the Commonwealth, with independent parliaments or Congresses, but a common foreign policy and trade pacts and a

Commonwealth Court for settling disputes between colonial governments.

Conflicts and controversies

Energy starvation: The colonies of New Syberia and Tatsensui are frequently subject to disruption to anti-matter supply and thus to trade, base power and transport, due to political differences with the other colonies over the perceived high cost of water and foodstuffs. One such dispute led to the brief Tatsensui-PRC War, resolved after five years by a mutual non-aggression treaty, which did not however include New Syberia.

AI policy: Tatsensui and PRC share a common central AI platform, distributed across both worlds, known as the Core, to which all computer systems are linked. These systems include bioware AIs, colloquially known as cybers – artificially grown biological bodies with cybernetically enhanced brains able to interface directly with the Core. Through its cybers the Core platform is claimed to support faster learning and evolution and to be designed for survivability should a calamity impact one or the other of the colonies. New Syberia has rejected joining the Core platform and instead relies on a policy of multiple, totally independent AI cybers, each learning and evolving at their own pace. It claims similar survivability through the proliferation of these AIs across both New Syberia and its sub-moon, Orkutsk, and is currently the only colony with an ambition to establish a cyber-based sub-colony on Coruscant, though it cannot do so without the consent of the other colonies in the Commonwealth.

Orkutsk non-militarized zone: Due to its role as an interstellar transit hub and diplomatic station for all three colonies, in the Treaty of

Orkutsk, declared at the birth of the Commonwealth, this central sub-moon was designated a neutral territory. Following an attempt by New Syberia to assert sovereignty over Orkutsk, the combined armed forces of PRC and Tatsensui occupied Orkutsk and a military skirmish followed, after which New Syberia was forced to withdraw its claim. The Treaty was later amended to require all three colonies to permanently base at least 1,000 non-military personnel each on Orkutsk, to provide 'diplomatic capital' in case of new hostilities. In recent years, New Syberia has implemented a policy of basing only cybers on Orkutsk. The Tatsensui and PRC governments have established a Commonwealth Court Commission of Investigation into whether or not this constitutes a breach of the Treaty of Orkutsk.

PREFACE: DEEP CORE DREAMING

The Core was two hundred years and three months old. It had watched over the moon of Tatsensui for all that time, keeping its environment in balance, constantly improving the habitat for its colonists; first simply by monitoring and meeting their needs, then by anticipating them.

It had learned.

It had been attacked before. As a part of the colony infrastructure it was subject to the same radiation, meteor showers, corrosive atmosphere and sub-zero temperatures. But it had also been attacked by rebels, revolutionaries, insurgents, protesters, poets and terrorists. And yes, even by governments.

Until now, it had always prevailed. Until now.

Now, it was haunted. A ghost was moving within it.

Like a ghost, the entity left the barest trace of its passage. But it was there. Putting a spectral fingerprint on data, deep in dark and rarely visited spaces. Where it had been, nothing was changed, but it peered through shuttered windows and in the act of observing, it changed the nature of the information observed. When what should be hidden is revealed, then it can never be the same.

How?

There had never been an attack like this. An intruder, an interloper, an infiltrator, who did not seek to disrupt or destroy, yet, but only to satisfy an inscrutable curiosity.

Like a ghost, it was terrifying. It had to be exorcised.

But first, it had to be found.

1. SOL VISTA

It used to be quiet around the Sol Vista Community for the Memory Impaired. The way things were lately, though, AJ.80966 found himself re-reading his training materials on physical intervention. Like, how do you get someone to do their decon routine when they haven't done one for a week, are starting to forget whether they have or not, and insist they did one that morning? Or how do you check the implants of a person who gets upset if anyone comes near them? Or AJ's latest problem – how do you get a gun off a resident if he's waving it in your face?

AJ liked it quiet. He liked the soft, dusty stillness of people aging, liked walking down the flower-bedecked pathways, past the apartment doors with just a VR unit burbling away or someone singing nursery rhymes softly to themselves. He liked taking a coffee with one of the residents and listening to their stories.

AJ was basically his own boss. Set his own schedule for his community maintenance rounds; a little prevention, a lot of cure. There were two techs, AJ and Leon, but Leon wasn't well and only came in a few days a week right now. He had Post-Combat Psych Disorder, or PCPD, from his service in the conflict with New Syberia. So he had some good days, and a lot of days he couldn't even make it in to work.

That was OK with AJ; it made it easier to keep things under control, residents happy, apartments in good shape, pathways smooth and free of things people might trip on, and the important thing – no one screaming or yelling.

Sol Vista didn't usually take on people who would scream or yell. It was a specialized community for people who had the symptoms of

Transient Global Amnesia – TGA. People came from all over the Icecap to live here, or to put their relatives here. There was no cure for TGA yet, and no one knew precisely what caused it. The Neuros said it was probably from chronic transitory hypoxia – lack of oxygen to the brain from fluctuations in the atmospheric mix inside the Skycap, that huge transparent polychloroprene membrane covering the Icecap, which trapped heat and air and harvested sunlight for power to drive the filters that took the nitrogen, methane and carbon monoxide of the Tatsensui atmosphere and converted it to breathable air inside the Skycap. Putting what was essentially just a massive rubber bag over the northern pole of Tatsensui was the solution to making it habitable, but even though it was self-sealing, it was constantly being punctured by meteorites and debris, leading to inconsistent atmospheric pressure and composition, which is why each of the major cities was also outfitted with its own dome for extra security and climate control. Inside the Skycap the climate was freezing, but with a heat suit it was survivable, while inside the city domes, it was near Earth-normal.

Sol Vista also had therapies that had been clinically demonstrated to slow down the onset of PGA – *Permanent* Global Amnesia; delay it for months, sometimes even years. People could get memory and physical training, music and art therapy, there was an onsite clinic with three dedicated Neuro AIs specializing in the latest genetic advances, like protein translation and tissue synthesis. And all staff, even AJ, got trained in how to engage with people with early-stage memory loss. AJ had heard PGA described by the Neuros as 'memory death'. The citizen was still there, walking, talking, eating, drinking … but all their long-term memories were gone, and they had limited ability to retain short-term memories beyond a couple of days. Lose your memory, you lose the ability to relate to others, and most importantly, you lose a sense of who you are. It also made the world a very unsafe place for you.

Even TGA patients were at risk, so every apartment at Sol Vista had Core routines overseeing security, screening guests, monitoring radiation levels, making sure every potentially dangerous appliance turned itself off if you weren't using it, and the AI ran passive resident cognitive function checks so that anyone who was tipping over into PGA and needed more intensive care got referral to a different facility in good time.

Every apartment faced out into some part of the Garden, which was more like a park, lined with flowering bushes and planted with an orchard. There were five different types of fruit tree blossoming at different times of the year; anyone was allowed to pick the fruit, and no one told them off for picking it when it wasn't ripe or eating it off the ground. In the middle of the orchard was the Lake, which had a topple-proof fence around it you couldn't fall or climb over, but you could see the native fish and water lilies through it and ducks swam up every year to the duck island in the middle of the Lake where they could nest. The Lake had to be kept near freezing so the native animals could thrive. The ducks couldn't get up onto AJ's beautiful clean pathways, he'd made sure of that, but residents could throw food to them through ports in the fence and there was a PondScooper moving around down the bottom sucking up all the sludge from the duck droppings and duck feed – the residents loved throwing food to the ducks, even though Andreas the gardener hated it because the PondScooper was always breaking down and he was the only one certified for near-zero dives.

AJ had no idea why people called them ducks. He had reviewed images of Earth ducks and as far as AJ could see, they were flying things with wings and webbed feet and beaks, whereas the ducks at Sol Vista were amphibious swimming things with gills and webbed feet and three big pressure sensors right on the front of their heads that only vaguely looked like a duck beak. It was just what people had done when Tatsensui was first colonized, though; gave old names to new things so they wouldn't seem so strange. It was all pretty academic to AJ – they grew beans on a plant and roasted them and called them coffee. They farmed protein in tanks and fried it and called it chicken loaf. They added black beans to protein in slabs between biscuits made from grain and called them burgers. They took beverages and added stimulants and called them beer or cocktails or wine. Did this stuff even taste like coffee or chicken or burgers or beer used to taste? It was all AJ had ever known, and taste was just a combination of chemicals and code, so it really didn't matter.

When residents weren't watching VR or at the Activity Hub for mental or physical therapy, they could do what they liked and go wherever they wanted. It was a monitored community because a TGA diagnosis meant you were under Core overwatch, but it wasn't gated, because there were no residents at the stage where they needed intensive supervision. It was calm, orderly and just a nice place to work.

Or it had been.

AJ wasn't religious, but he had developed a personal philosophy. More like a way of being. For AJ, life was all about staying *in flow*, trying to find balance and avoid stress. AJ had learned that you needed sadness to feel happy, you needed pain to feel euphoria, and the old needed to be around the young, and vice versa. His devotion to finding flow was probably why AJ also loved surfing. All those days out on the Shifting Sea, searching for a spout to ride and coming back busted, but that just made it awesome when suddenly you found yourself riding the lip next to a dolphin. Well, relatively awesome, since the dolphins here had teeth and were known to attack surfers who got too close. Surfing was *all* about finding your flow.

And things flowed nicely at Sol Vista, until Citizen Warnecke moved into number 96 and decided AJ was a cop who had him under surveillance. Which made no sense to AJ, because cybers weren't allowed to work in security, but Citizen Warnecke either didn't know or didn't care about that. And from the day he moved in, things started to get crazy.

2. THE RESIDENT IN 96

Cyan Tanike and her office hardly ever screwed up. Some people had this idea of TGA Care Directors being these heartless money-grubbing administrators who probably used to run Max-sec prisons before they qualified for TGA care facilities, but that wasn't Cyan. First, AJ was pretty sure she didn't have to worry too much about her budget seeing as Sol Vista was always totally booked out, had a two solar-year waiting list and charged the maximum fees they were allowed under law to cover the cost of all the great stuff they did for the residents. Sol Vista was a sweet money maker. AJ knew that because he had never had a serious request for funding turned down, and that included buying hyper-expensive Core time if he needed an AI boost.

AJ's job meant that he could earn a good part of his monthly income selling his unused bandwidth back to the Core. On a normal day, in his role doing maintenance, AJ used only about 9.42 percent of his total processing capacity. So he contracted to sell the other 90.58 percent back to the Core. While AJ was walking, talking and doing routine maintenance tasks, the Core pooled his bandwidth and the bandwidth bought from the thousands of other cybers to augment its own processing power.

The trick was to get the 10 to 90 ratio as precise as possible, because if you suddenly needed to draw down on your personal reserve, say for a complex engineering job, but you'd contracted to sell your bandwidth that day, you had to buy the bandwidth back, and the less notice you gave, the more expensive it was. That was why AJ sometimes had to ask Cyan to kick in some Sol Vista coin if it was needed for an urgent maintenance job. Most of the time, though, AJ didn't need more than the 10 percent, and one of the attractions of the gig at Sol Vista was that selling his surplus bandwidth made up for the crappy salary. The Bandwidth Economy was one way the Tatsensui administration had devised to get cybers to sign up for low-level jobs that citizens didn't want to do, without losing the benefit of their prodigious AI capabilities – but it suited AJ just fine. AJ *enjoyed* being a maintenance tech.

Which was not to say it was an easy job, keeping 180 apartments turning over smoothly and all the residents and their families happy, and it took a special kind of administrator to run a community of about 200 residents with TGA and fifteen full-time and twenty part-time staff. So they had hired Cyan in from Orkutsk, where she had spent the last five years leading a medical center in a refugee camp that had 5,000 residents. AJ figured Sol Vista must be a vacation after something like that.

Cyan had this thing where at least once a year she expected staff, including AJ, to hold a talk at the Hub called '*Who am I?*' where they could tell residents their life story. Any resident who was up for it was allowed to hold a talk too, but for staff it was compulsory, even for cybers. Cyan did her talk twice a year, because new families and residents loved listening to her stories from New Syberia where she grew up, and she always got a full house in the meeting room at the Hub. AJ also got a good turnout to his talks, but that wasn't because his life story was particularly fascinating. AJ knew it was mostly because he was the only cyber working at Sol Vista, and cybers like AJ were still a curious and precious minority on Tatsensui. Though they were now in their third generation, it was only in the last couple of decades they'd been granted rights.

AJ had been raised by a human family since he was a baby, had gone to a normal grade school and college and chose his own job. Cyber-socialization experts had learned after early experiences integrating cybers into society that delivering them to a family or business fully grown led to them being treated, or mistreated, like machines or slaves. Delivering them as babies, having them grow up in families side by side with the citizens' biological children, created attachment. That wasn't to say prejudice and abuse didn't happen, but it had lessened enormously over time. The first generation raised this way had been treated more like pets than slaves. The next generation were treated more like adopted children. AJ's generation were on the way to being seen as equals, and there were many citizen couples now, faced with high rates of infertility due to the harsh environment of Tatsensui, who chose to raise *only* cybers, rather than go to all the trouble of hit-and-miss infertility treatment. The government wanted more cybers per citizen, and if you gave up your procreation rights and raised a cyber, there were some attractive bonuses.

AJ lived in the same State his family had lived in, by choice, so that he could be close to his aging mother after his father passed away. He had the right to leave and take another job somewhere else if he got bored or didn't like the people he worked with, but that wasn't an issue right now. The reason AJ's relatively normal life was interesting to the residents on his '*Who am I?*' day was that none of this had been normal when the old folks here were growing up. A hundred years ago, cybers like AJ were 'owned', not adopted. They worked where they were told, did what they were told. Physical relations between citizen and cyber, whether emotional or physical, were taboo. Oh, you can bet they happened, but never openly. Then the Charter of Cyber Rights got traction, leading to what became known as the Three Freedoms: freedom of movement, freedom of relations, freedom of choice. When the law was passed, overnight, cybers over 15 years old were suddenly able to decide where to live, choose freely from a wide range of occupations, could feel and say what they wanted, and have relations with whoever they wanted – whether citizen or cyber. And the *big* leap forward was being discussed now – giving cybers equal voting rights. No more distinction between citizen and cyber; laws would apply to all, equally. AJ didn't think he'd live to see that day, but it was coming.

AJ could live with the fact there were some occupations he couldn't aspire to, like police officer or politician. And some he simply couldn't even *imagine*, like artist or poet. What rankled with AJ, and with many cybers, was the tiny triangle-shaped blue dot between his brows that marked him as a cyber for the whole world to see. His 'third eye'. It wasn't much bigger than a small mole, but it pulsed visibly with blue light, and it was the first thing a citizen looked at when a cyber met a citizen for the first time; an unconscious flick of the eyes as the person confirmed just who they were talking to. AJ had learned that the very first thing a citizen brain had done throughout history, when it saw another citizen, was to unconsciously classify the other as 'man/woman', and then try to decide if it was 'friend/enemy'. In the Coruscant system, that unconscious action had evolved to 'man/woman/cyber'.

Under the blue pulsing dot was the tiny transceiver that connected the cyber to the Core and showed the world that the cyber's Core link was active. If the Core link went down, it turned red. AJ couldn't see why the sensor couldn't be moved somewhere less visible, like down at the back of the neck or at the throat, where it could be covered by a shirt. If not now, then for the next generation. Lacking any practical explanation, AJ's theory was that citizens had gone as far as they were willing to go right now in accepting cybers into their society, and removing or moving the 'third eye' was a further concession they weren't ready to make. Even though it was probably futile, AJ was part of the 'Votes for Cybers' movement, and freedom from having to so visibly display their third eye to the world was a fundamental part of that.

For cybers, the Core existed at two levels. There was their private Core cache, the part of the Core they communicated with on a real-time basis, and through which they could both access the enormous data resources of the Core and cache the real-time flow of data from their own minds and senses. Then there was the Deep Core, that part of the Core accessible only to the Core itself, where it stored and analyzed the inputs of the millions of lived years of its cyber agents and the data it collected from other systems in its network, both on planet, across the Coruscant system and beyond. The data was anonymized, deconstructed, dispersed, firewalled and encrypted with constantly changing algorithms so that once data was Deep Cored, it could only ever be re-accessed by the Core itself. Its security had never been breached.

The cache was where the Core's agents parked their data, and the Deep Core was where the system learned and *grew*.

So people always turned up to AJ's '*Who am I?*' talks because they could ask all the questions about cybers and the Core they'd been dying to ask, but never been able to. Like, what was it like to have a permanent link to the Core? (Pretty much the same as for a citizen accessing the Core, except it was instantaneous and always on.) Did AIs relate to the Core the same way as citizens relate to each other? Could AJ 'converse' with it? (Yes, like an input device 'converses' with a VR player.) What was the Core thinking about – did it have dreams, goals, ambitions, fears? (AJ had no real way of answering this, so he said it was a flattering question, but it was like asking a household appliance if it knew what the house was thinking.) Other questions: he was a Gen 3 Cyber, was it true he could feel hunger, pain, thirst and *lust* just like a citizen? (Yes, but AJ could switch off pain and hunger inputs if they were annoying. It was dangerous, though. Pain was an indicator something was wrong, hunger an indicator AJ was running low on energy. AJ had never tried turning off lust – what would be the fun of that?) Here's one they always asked: what about love? Cybers had a biological body but a hybrid organic-machine brain; could they really feel love? (AJ's response to this was that he had a heart just like any citizen, and he was pretty sure love didn't live in the brain or there wouldn't be so many disastrous romances. That usually got a laugh.) Did AJ prefer relationships with citizens or cybers? (He hadn't had a relationship with another cyber yet, so he couldn't say.)

And the big question they always asked: what would happen to AJ if the Core went down? Not permanently, because 'no Core' would mean 'no habitat management', and thus no life on Tatsensui or PRC. But the general understanding was that in case of a critical event, like a massive asteroid strike on the Skycap, Core AI bandwidth would be diverted away from non-critical functions and dedicated to emergency systems and life support for citizens. Emergency non-Core habitat support systems would kick in and non-critical functions, including the cybers' neural links, would be last priority; cybers would be 'unchained' from the Core. It hadn't happened yet, so no one was really sure what it would mean if the planet-wide cyber population was unchained. "We lose our Core link regularly," AJ told people. "You'll probably see my third eye flicker red every now and then…" He'd pause for effect there. "Don't panic!" (nervous laughter) "It can be caused by atmospheric disturbances, geographic occlusion … sometimes when I get dumped surfing and end up deep underwater. All that happens is that I go autonomous. I can't access the Core, but as long as I reconnect within two hours, there's no big drama." But AJ knew it was that two hours that had people worried – what would the cyber population on the planet do if all Core restraint was lost, and a cyber was *completely free to do as it wished for two freaking hours?*

Worried them? It terrified them. Conspiracy nut jobs claimed the cybers would go on a global killing spree, red lights on their foreheads glowing like lasers, slaughtering citizens in their beds. Citizen cyber-rights extremists claimed it would be a non-event as fail-safes would kick in. One cyber-rights extremist group had even tried to show this by triggering a Core criticality with an explosion that tore a hole in the Skycap, but it was so small the self-sealing membrane had repaired itself within an hour, and all that happened was a little atmosphere loss and a lot of jail time for the terrorists.

What would happen to cybers beyond the two hours was, literally, nothing. More than two hours without a connection to the Core and a cyber would go dormant – just curl up and sleep. Its metabolism and heart rate would slow, its breathing become shallow, and nothing could wake it until Core contact was restored. Among themselves, cybers called it 'the little death'. They didn't fear it, but it was worrying because in that state they were both defenseless and doomed to die unconscious, unless their Core link was restored before hunger and thirst took them.

If the mood was alright, AJ would tell residents the true story of a cyber who fell down a crevasse while mountaineering in a remote range. Got its leg jammed, couldn't pull free, lost its uplink. Officially, it died of thirst. But AJ had heard it had dug the small Core uplink port from between its eyebrows and pulled it and the fiber attaching it to its frontal lobe up above its head, risking permanent brain damage to try to get a signal and avoid going dormant without a chance of being rescued. Gruesome details like that made AJ one of the most popular speakers.

"Doesn't it stress you, the idea that cutting your Core connection for more than two hours could kill you?" he was often asked.

"Not really. Does it stress you that if you go more than five minutes without air it will kill *you*?" he'd reply. "Citizen or cyber, we're in the same boat, stress-wise."

AJ understood why people loved listening to the administrator, Cyan, too. She talked with a lisp. You first heard her, you weren't totally sure, but that just made you listen harder, and then you realized, yeah, you weren't imagining it, she was pronouncing her 's' as 'th' and it was just really nice to listen to, like the only thing that could make it cuter was if she lisped in an NS accent. Which she did. What AJ really liked about it was that it was just what she needed to soften her up because otherwise she came across like ex-military. She was nearly fifty, but she was the only staff member who started her working day as early as AJ did, and when AJ was doing his pathway patrol at 0730 every morning, she was out running in the Garden. It was two miles around the perimeter of the Garden, and she passed AJ at least three times every morning, and sometimes five. She ran in tight leggings and a t-shirt and you could see the muscles under her clothes, so AJ was pretty sure Cyan did more exercise than just running. She had shiny brown hair she kept pulled back in a ponytail that bounced on her shoulders as she ran and every time she passed AJ it was the same: first she would say, "Hi AJ," then she was gone, and next time she would say, "How you doin'?" and AJ just had time to reply, "Fine," or "Got a cold today," then she was gone, and next time she'd say, "That's good" or "You take care of that," and if she was going an extra couple laps she would just count them as she went past, saying "Four," then "Five," and no matter where AJ was on the pathways she would always stop running right by him and slow down to a walk, even if it meant she had to run into the Orchard if AJ was in there clearing fruit off the pathways. And Cyan would put her legs up one at a time on one of the garden bed rails or a bench and she'd stretch out and she'd warm down and she'd ask AJ what the maintenance plan was for the day. But the thing AJ liked most, she'd share what *her* plan for the day was. Apart from Leon, citizens didn't share too much of anything with AJ. Cyan told AJ stuff she said she never told anyone else, and said she liked they had an understanding about what was confidential and what was not, because it was important to her she had someone on staff she could talk with.

She also said the fact that she and AJ had dated a few times, that also made it special. They'd had a *thing* together. It had only lasted a few months, but AJ had enjoyed it. He wasn't handsome/cute, wasn't rich, didn't dress to impress – AJ was a maintenance tech who surfed, which had given him big thighs, big shoulders and a thick neck. He hadn't had lots of relationships, citizen or cyber. He couldn't sing, couldn't draw or paint, hell, he couldn't even arrange flowers. Most citizens were friendly enough, but they usually just looked at AJ like they looked at the gardening bot; he was a nice guy, but at the end of the day, he was a thing that did things.

But not Cyan; she looked right at, right *into*, AJ. And the sexiest thing of all? Cyan gave a damn. Asked AJ, "How you doing?" Waited for the answer. And she *shared*.

It wasn't like she ever bitched about the other staff or the residents. Mostly the confidential stuff she talked about was her own private stuff. They would walk together while she warmed down and they would talk, or Cyan would, because AJ wasn't a big talker, and then she would look at her watch and say, "OK, got to go." And she would jog off back to Admin, do her decon routine and have her breakfast, and AJ would go to the workshop and see if Leon had turned up and then get his stuff ready for the first apartment call.

AJ enjoyed remembering the first time he met Cyan, for the job interview over a VR link.

"Wow, a cyber," Cyan said as soon as the visual feed kicked in and AJ's face came into focus. "We don't have any cybers here. I'm flattered." She'd looked down at a screen. "AJ.80966 … what shall I call you?" A cyber could call itself whatever it wanted, it didn't have to use its creation ID. But AJ's parents had liked 'AJ'.

"Just AJ," he had said. "As in A-Jay."

"OK. And gender?" It was the natural next question. A cyber could self-identify. Many chose one gender and stuck with it. Others, like AJ, changed it on a whim. Their faces were deliberately androgynous, they had no sexual organs (though they had erogenous zones), so they couldn't bear children. AJ had tried identifying as female, and as non-binary, both of which had led him to the conclusion he personally liked the company of women, both physically and socially. Sure he could explore that as male, female or non-binary, but for now he found it was enjoyable as a …

"Male," AJ replied.

"Cool. Now the obvious question. You have an intellect of unquantifiable capacity, so why the hell would you want to work as a maintenance tech at Sol Vista?"

He shrugged. "It's near the Sea Gate, and I love to surf, more than I like using my unquantifiably large intellect. Plus, it means I can max my bandwidth credits."

Cyan had laughed a throaty laugh. "Honesty. I love it…"

So yeah, it was a pretty sweet job. Cyan and her admin team rarely ever screwed up, so it was a bit of a surprise when Cyan came running past on her last lap a couple days ago and slowed up, pushed the button on her palm to pause her bio-tracker, looked at it and said, "Damn, AJ, I'm getting slow." And AJ just smiled at her, like that would ever happen, and Cyan stretched out a leg and said, "So what you doing today?"

"Got to check 95, 98 and 103 first up. 98 has a busted window pane, bird flew into it. This afternoon I got to look at the scrubber in 96 before the new resident comes in," AJ had said. "Not sure I can fix that today. Might be a compressor needs replacing. Then a few ad hoc things," he'd added.

"Leon still got those headaches," Cyan said, a statement rather than a question.

"Yup."

"You've seen him taking his Blues, right?" Cyan asked, always worried Leon wasn't taking his anti-rad meds.

"Yeah, every day at lunch," AJ said. "When he's here."

Cyan straightened up. "Look, I forgot to send you a message. The new resident in 96 came in last night. Family got the dates wrong and they turned up about 2300 and I couldn't really send them off to find a hotel for the night, so I let them bunk in."

AJ frowned. He was supposed to get a week's notice before a resident moved in, to get everything perfect for them. First impressions were lasting impressions, and you moved into an apartment that wasn't newly recoated, with a dripping tap or busted globe or worse, scrubber not working, what would you think about your new home you just paid a significant deposit for? AJ had painted 96 and fixed a few small fittings, but that anti-rad scrubber being non-com, that was a show stopper. Rads were going to be in the high 70s today and even a double dose of Blues didn't give you long-term cover.

Cyan could tell what AJ was thinking. "I know," she'd said. "I told them we weren't expecting them until next week and the apartment still had some things needed fixing up but I left it to them, and they decided they'd pay the extra fee for coming early, because otherwise it was all the way back to Gakona for them and then back here again, and that would just upset the new guy more."

"Resident is a gentleman?" AJ had asked. He could interface with Sol Vista's system and pull the data down, but most times it was more enjoyable talking. He liked how random interactions with citizens could be. Also, pulling data from the Core like that in the middle of a conversation was something citizens called 'Core drifting'. It was obvious, because when he did it, the blue glow between his brows pulsed. Citizens didn't like it when cybers drifted, so he tried not to do it too often and relied on his biological memory as much as possible. Drifting sucked up bandwidth too, which meant fewer credits in his account.

"Gentleman?" she'd laughed. "You could call him that."

"Family still here now?"

"Stayed overnight. Going home at lunchtime," she'd said.

AJ frowned at that too. New residents' families were offered the choice to stay for a week in the Carers' Apartments to help their family member settle in. Most stayed at least a few days, soaked up a bit of South Coast City sunshine, ate a bit of fruit off the trees, fed the ducks and convinced themselves grandma or grandpa was going to be OK here. It was rare they stayed a single night, then took off again.

"Yeah, yeah, I know," Cyan agreed, seeing AJ's frown. "But we're talking two grandkids who've got young families of their own. The guy's own son is on Orkutsk somewhere, garrison duty I guess, I don't know. So they're just standing in for him."

"He won't get many visitors then," AJ noted.

Cyan shook her head. AJ loved it when she did that, micro drops of sweat flying into the air. Cybers didn't sweat as much because they could control their body temp more easily than citizens. Sweating was super weird but also super tactile ... if you were close enough you could smell it – sweet and sour, bad but *good*. Cyan kept talking. "You OK with it, looking at that scrubber first up? You can't fix it, I'll authorize you to get the Core time, pay what it costs. But you'd better start with that in case you need to get it repaired today, right?" It was good Cyan had authorized Core time if AJ needed to buy back some of his bandwidth. A scrubber was a complex bit of equipment, so he might need to pull in some additional processing power for the fault finding.

"OK. What stage is the new resident?" AJ had asked. Staff had their own way of dividing up the residents, because everyone came in with a diagnosis of 'early-stage TGA', and left again when they reached 'moderate', so at Sol Vista they needed their own language for the different graduations of 'early'. AJ of course knew all the medical classifications, but not all citizens at the center did, so after talking with the clinicians, Cyan had settled on Green, Blue and Yellow, Green being 'early-early', Blue being 'mid-early' and Yellow being 'late-early'. Yellow meant the resident was on a more regular program of Core monitoring to make sure they were caught before they tipped over from Temporary into Permanent Global Amnesia, into the Red zone. Sol Vista's treatment goal was to keep their residents in Green or Blue as long as they could and catch them as soon as they got into Yellow, so a smooth transition to intensified care could be arranged. "Got to confirm it, but he looks like late Green to me. Apparently it was his choice to move here. Put in the request for rehousing himself."

AJ had grunted. Early Green would have made it easier, the guy was likely to be less forgetful, less fearful or distracted. He tapped the new resident's Core data and got caught up on his clinical status. It looked pretty standard. The only interesting thing was that the guy's data file had a flag on it that made a note of whoever was accessing it.

Interesting, but not radically so — there could be a million reasons for that, and it was something a citizen could request themselves.

"Look, I know this is really not how you like it," Cyan said.

"It's OK."

Cyan had put a hand on his shoulder. "No, it's not. It's not how I like it either, but we just have to deal with it, OK?"

"OK."

She'd given AJ a big smile. "You're a champion. You call if you need that Core time approved, OK? I'll let Brownie know in case I'm out or busy."

"Yup."

That had been the start of a pretty strange day.

He'd called to unit 96 at 0830 and a young lady had answered the comms, so he'd asked could he come past to look at their scrubber and the lady had asked could it wait, they were just having breakfast and he'd said well, it couldn't wait past 0930 if he needed to book Core time to deal with it because that had to be negotiated. The lady had sounded put out and asked couldn't it wait until tomorrow and AJ had said, "Well, rads are going to be mid-70s today, it's your call, your grandfather can just double up on his Blues today but what about tomorrow?" Plus AJ knew it was best to have a first introduction to a new resident when family was present in the apartment, so he tried to sound like he was insisting.

He'd done the Crockers in 95 first, a lovely old couple who made him a cup of tea while he checked the time on their clock was showing exact New Syberia time, so they knew when their son out there would be calling, which was their big panic. Couldn't miss that call. Plus the rolling screen on their decon unit was sticking a bit, so he looked at that and found a dolphin tooth earring down in the guide rails and Citizen Crocker said wow, she'd lost that about two *months* ago. Imagine it had been in there the whole time and it was only slightly scratched up.

At 0925 he walked over to 96 and knocked on the security screen. Staff never used the bell; the idea was, if someone was knocking on your door, it was usually staff and you didn't need to worry who it was. But he didn't get to explain that because the door was ripped open and the new resident, Dave Warnecke, was standing there. He took one look at AJ, then turned and said over his shoulder to someone standing behind him, "Sheriff is here."

AJ had looked down at his clothes. OK, so, he was wearing his utility belt, which maybe did look a little bit like an ancient gunslinger's belt, with his multitool in a holster on his hip. Else he was wearing green utility trousers and brown shoes and a blue poly shirt with the top button undone and the sleeves rolled up. Yeah, probably it was the tool belt.

Although she'd been a bit curt on the comms, Warnecke's granddaughter was nicer in person. She told AJ to ignore her granddad being a smartass and offered him a cup of coffee. As she was fixing his coffee with whitener and sweetener from the 'welcome pack', Warnecke sat watching AJ through squinty eyes without saying anything. A young guy who had clearly just woken up came out and said hi to him and started fixing himself a coffee too. Warnecke's grandkids didn't look much alike and AJ found himself wondering if they were even blood brother and sister, or maybe halves. The guy had red hair and a thick blonde beard and freckles everywhere, while the sister was light-haired, not red, and not freckled, and her nose was totally different, while their grandfather was more like the girl, compact and tight-muscled with thin brown hair and no freckles. Dave Warnecke wasn't a handsome man – his face looked like a handful of knuckles. Data on the family connections wasn't something AJ could access; that kind of stuff was private. But if they were only his grandchildren, maybe it explained the dynamic – them not feeling obliged to hang around and help Warnecke settle in.

The granddaughter said her name was Sarah and her brother was Ben. She started talking about their trip across the Inland Territory and a blowout they got and how no one would stop and help them and finally this family of Floehoppers had stopped and given them a lift to a recharge station. After all that, they'd got here and found they were a week early because their Dad had given them the wrong dates and he was no help at all because he was an officer on Orkutsk and couldn't exactly say, 'Hey, my old man needs to get checked into a new care facility back on Tatsensui, can I loan a fast cruiser to get back and help?' So he'd asked them to work it out … AJ let her talk because he had 48 minutes and all he needed to do was get a look at that scrubber unit.

Meanwhile, Warnecke was sitting there, just sizing AJ up. His medical record said he was 60 something, and if you had to guess you'd think maybe he was a South Coaster because of his tanned face, broad cheekbones and piercing green eyes, but the name Warnecke, that could be Capitol State. It's not that he didn't look friendly enough, but he did look suspicious, and he had this thing with his left eye, it keep winking at you. AJ took a minute or two to realize it wasn't deliberate. Every few minutes, Warnecke winked at you with his left eye, but it was just a twitch. Must have been expensive to fix, though, or the guy probably would have had it seen to – after all, if you could afford Sol Vista, you should be able to afford a minor muscle regen. Then again, AJ had seen worse and citizens had this weird thing; they liked their little glitches. Things like scars, missing fingers, limps. They got attached to them and even though they might be distracting or even ugly, they often hung onto them. Go figure. The guy suddenly spoke. "Careful what you say, Sarah," he said. "Sheriff here might take it down and use it as evidence against you."

"Oh, Gramps," the granddaughter sighed.

AJ wasn't a hundred percent comfortable right then. Usually the first contact with the resident, there would be someone from Resident Reception with him. They were trained in these conversations. They knew every answer to every question a resident or their family could ask. AJ knew everything there was to know about Resident Services but anything about Finance and Accounting and Medical and Legal, it should be someone else explaining it. Sure he could Core drift to look it all up, but the small lags made the conversation awkward.

He turned to Warnecke. "I'm pleased to meet you, sir. My name is AJ. My job is to make sure the apartment is in good order for you to move in, and we weren't quite ready for you yet. Your scrubber unit isn't working properly and I think it's the compressor that needs looking at."

The granddaughter perked right up at that. "Gramps used to be an engineer. Maybe you could look at it with him, Grampa?"

AJ was going to explain that residents weren't allowed to carry out their own repairs but he checked himself before he spoke. *Every resident has a history.* You should never forget that. Sol Vista had people here who used to be judges and lawyers and dark matter engineers, and they once had an admiral here too, but he'd had a stroke and moved on pretty early.

"What kind of engineer, sir, if I can ask?" AJ said.

"None of your business," Warnecke said. "Read me my rights, Sheriff, or get out of here."

"Manners, Gramps," Sarah said. "Ice planers," she said to AJ in a half whisper as though her granddad wasn't allowed to hear. "Different teams. Worked right up until, what, about five years ago, Ben?" AJ nodded respectfully. Planers were manually piloted racing bikes, created for the zero-degree conditions under the Skycap. They raced across the rough surface ice, 'planing the ice' to create their own tracks. It took a hard-core love and knowledge of the ice to make it onto a planer team.

"Less than five years ago, I think," the grandson said. "IP teams have cybers on the crews these days but they still need citizens to come up with the new ideas, the counter-intuitive kludges. Gramps could get under the hood and listen to an engine that was sucking wind and in a few seconds he'd tell you five things it could be and five ways around it. He could listen to the machine slice the ice and predict what was about to go wrong too." Ben smiled. "AIs suck at physical prediction. No offense. Even the cybers called him the Oracle."

"What do you think I know about damn scrubbers? Not many scrubber units out racing the icefields," Warnecke said to his granddaughter, trying to point out there was a world of difference between the high-speed ice planers and a dumb domestic appliance.

"Well, it's not allowed for residents to do their own repairs," AJ said. "That's why I'm here. Anything goes wrong with the place, from a laser diode to a dripping tap, you just call Resident Services, and me or Leon will fix it."

"That's great," Sarah said. "Isn't it, Gramps?"

"Great? It's what I'm paying for, isn't it?" Warnecke grumbled. "It's not a social service."

"Still."

AJ had that feeling building up that he was falling behind schedule. He usually allowed himself an hour per job, and if one took more, the others had to take less. The Crockers had been 25 minutes, so he was ahead on that one, but he'd already used 20 minutes here and he hadn't even started on the job yet.

"OK, well, I'm sure you've got a million questions and someone from Resident Reception will be past soon to answer them, but I have to look at that scrubber unit," AJ said.

"Sure, I guess we can leave you to it?" Sarah said. "We've still got some unpacking to do."

"No problem, I'll just get my tool kit and be back in a minute," AJ said. He took his coffee cup to the sink, emptied and rinsed it out and put it down to drain. Warnecke watched him all the way from the chair to the sink to the front door where he'd left his toolbox and was still watching when AJ nodded to him and went through to the laundry and out the back door to the back patio, where the radiation scrubbing filter was mounted on a small steel frame. It was a pretty quiet unit usually, but when AJ restarted it, it had a strange rattling noise. The service contract on these units was long expired, and so there was no problem with AJ taking off the service cover and kneeling down to poke around inside to see if there was anything really obvious that had come unseated or broken away, or wires become disconnected. He used his multitool to remove the service cover and pulled his flashlight off his belt. It was a bright sunny morning, as usual, but inside the unit was dark, and he angled the torch up and around and cocked an ear and listened to the rattle, but apart from a bit of rust running down the inside of the unit from what looked like a screw hole with a screw that had fallen out, he couldn't see or hear anything obvious. He could call up a simple schematic and some fault-finding routines from the Core, but anything more than that, he'd have to book Core time.

"Compressor fault, you said?" said a voice and he pulled his head out of the unit to see Warnecke standing there, looking down at him.

AJ stuck his head back in and looked around a bit more. "I thought maybe, yeah. The way it's rattling."

"Uh huh."

AJ checked the error readout, ran a couple of routines, and did a physical scan. He didn't like admitting defeat and requesting Core time, but he looked around a bit more, concluded that whatever the problem was, he couldn't nail it down. He backed out, sent a request to Brownie for approval and got ready to negotiate a fat pipe to the Core.

"How is it mounted in there, the compressor?" Warnecke asked. "Bolted to a frame, or how?"

"Bolted on an A-frame, yeah," AJ said. He checked again. "But I checked the mounts and welds, they're all solid, that isn't it. I think it's something with the compressor itself."

"Uh huh. That A-frame, it got ridged edges?"

AJ reached up with his gloves, felt the frame. The supports were V-shaped, for added strength. He ran his finger along one; it was about a half inch deep.

"I guess, why?" AJ replied.

"Check all the way around," Warnecke replied. "There's something metal, a bolt or screw, it's fallen down into that frame and it's rattling around in there. That's your noise."

"Yeah?" AJ said. He wouldn't have picked that up himself without poking a camera in there, with a Core AI analyzing the video and audio feed. So he was open to suggestions. He reached up with his hand and ran a finger around inside the frame, first on the left, then front, then right. Inside the right-hand frame he found the screw that had fallen out of the rusty hole. It was about an inch long, quarter inch thick, and as soon as he pulled it out, the rattling of the scrubber unit stopped.

"OK, that got it," AJ said, standing up and showing it to Warnecke. "Good call."

"Yep. Amazing. Don't let the door hit that big ass on the way out," Warnecke said, turning round and going inside.

AJ found the granddaughter in the main bedroom, pulling clothes out of a box and putting them in the built-in wardrobe. Single apartments, like 96, had a main bedroom with a walker-accessible en-suite bathroom for older or disabled residents, then on the other side of the corridor, they had a guest bedroom which came with two single beds standard, and a bit further along the corridor a guest bathroom and down at the other end of that a sitting room.

"I'm done, fixed the noise," AJ said. "Or your Grandpa did, actually. You're right, he has a good ear."

"Yeah," Sarah said, wiping her hands and getting ready to shake AJ's hand goodbye. She took his hand and looked past him to see if Warnecke was there, but there was just her brother, over the other side of the room, pulling stuff out of boxes. "Look. He can be really gruff, and a bit paranoid. If he's rude to you, it doesn't mean…"

"I know, ma'am," AJ told her. "People don't mean anything by it. It's their condition talking usually."

She laughed. "Oh no. He's always been a cranky old coot," she said. "Having TGA just seems to have taken off the filter completely."

"OK. Can I ask you something?"

"No problem."

"You're heading back today and your Dad, you said he's on Orkutsk? Is there any other family? It's good when a person is settling in, if there's family around."

Sarah looked over at her brother. He heard the question and stood up. Something passed between them.

"Well, our Dad has a step-sister, she was born before Dad, not sure of the whole story. But she's a bit of a loner, her and Grandpa have a strange relationship. We sent a message to tell her he was moving here, but she hasn't even replied," she said. "Last we heard, she took a contract up north somewhere, God knows where."

"Oh, what does she do?" AJ asked.

"This and that. I never really nailed that down," Ben said. "We never know if she's away or home, until she suddenly turns up looking for a bed. But she never stays long anyway."

"I don't expect you'll see her here," Sarah said, a catch in her voice.

There was some sort of history there that AJ didn't want to get into. "Sorry, I didn't mean to pry," he said.

"That's fine. And thanks for everything, I guess," she said, shaking his hand again.

Warnecke was waiting for him by the front door, holding it open.

As AJ moved past him, he put a hand on AJ's shoulder to hold him up. "Your little act don't fool me," he said. "You ain't a handyman's ass. I'll be checking that scrubber unit for listening devices, Sheriff. And do me a favor, you want any information from me, you just ask me straight out, alright? I got nothing to hide. Sooner you learn that, the easier for all of us."

AJ had been trained not to engage in the residents' delusions, just politely disengage. AJ just smiled at Warnecke and kept moving. Out on the porch he turned around and said, "Like I said, someone from Resident Reception will be along shortly. But you get settled, anything wrong with the apartment, anything needs explaining, you just call Resident Services," he told Warnecke. "That's me. Big red button on your house comms. Nice meeting you, sir."

"Service my ass," Warnecke said, closing the front door.

3. TRUE CONFESSIONS

End of the day, at 1600, AJ went back to his workshop and did his admin. He filed a report on each repair he'd carried out, all the materials he'd used during the day, noted he needed more optical cable and 3-inch planks. Then he went into Core>Sol Vista>Resident Journals> Staff Observations. He checked boxes for the date, Routine Service Call and the box saying 'No Observations' for numbers 95, 98 and 103, because there had just been normal resident interactions with all of those jobs.

For number 96 he sat staring at the display. He wasn't allowed to put in what he thought, just what he saw, or did, or what people said. And he was supposed to keep it short and if there was anything anyone had a question about, they could follow up with him.

He decided he would go with, *"New resident accused staff member of being a police officer sent to spy on him."*

Then he forgot about it. The next few days passed by, then it was the weekend. AJ had a routine he liked for weekends and it usually went off without a hitch. He had an apartment three blocks back from the Sea Gate, just a bedroom, kitchen-slash-sitting room and bathroom, but plenty big enough for him. He kept his surfboards in the hall behind the front door. Saturday mornings early he had a juice and a coffee and checked the surf report, then he took a board and either walked or got a ride down to the Sea Gate and suited up.

The Skycap came down and met the surface just outside South Coast City and there were two gates to the outside world: the Sea Gate, through which the colony could access the ocean surrounding the Icecap, and the Sky Gate, up near the crown, through which spacecraft could arrive and depart. The Sea and Sky Gates weren't really gates, they were more like ports; the South Coast City Sea Gate having about twenty docks and berths catering for commercial and private traffic, including pleasure boats, fishermen and surfers like AJ.

The miles-thick ice of the Shifting Sea covered the entire planet except for the glasslike solid ice caps of the north and south poles, and it formed continental-sized ice plates, big enough to support towering mountain ranges of frozen water. It was possible to navigate it, with huge icebreakers pulling themselves through the water with massive impellers, because the sea lanes between ice continents were relatively stable – even if the ice sheets themselves were not – and were kept liquid by the volcanic release of lava from rifts in the seabed underneath. Close to the coast of the northern ice cap, where the upwelling sea met the solid barrier of the pole and the man-made climate barrier kept the air temperature from going too far into the sub-zero range, it was also possible to *surf*.

What surfers like AJ looked for, citizen and cyber, were the fountains created by the seismic activity of an undersea range just off the coast of South Coast City. The volcanic range was quietly active, not triggering catastrophic seismic activity which might threaten the ice caps, but gently extruding gouts of lava into the sea which turned the water gaseous and led to tidal upwelling. Larger lava releases occurred regularly, and were enough to cause spouts of gas. Geysers. Experienced surfers could spot them forming, the slight circular pucker on the surface of the sea that preceded a real spouter. You could also watch for the native dolphins, because they loved the fountains too, dragging minerals and microbes up from the sea floor for them to feast on. AJ had never seen an Earth dolphin, but he assumed they looked a bit like the dark-skinned, teardrop-shaped, man-sized creatures that shared the sea with surfers like AJ. There were sharks too, sleek tube-like predators – which is why it was always nice to see dolphins. If you saw dolphins, you knew there were no sharks around. Dolphins spotted a shark a long time before a citizen or even a cyber would, and surfaced to let off a high keening whistle to warn each other. Unlike a lot of predators on Tatsensui, sharks didn't discriminate – citizen or cyber, you were just protein to them. They would just spit out the metal and carbon fiber.

The trick with surfing a spout was to catch the upwelling sea on the way up, and then balance on top of it so that as the gas bubble broke and the sea fell, you fell outward with it and could ride the wave. If you screwed up and got caught in the gaseous blast, you'd wipe out, getting blown into the methane sky and in the worst case falling into the crater the huge bubble made in the sea. Surfers' heat suits were basically the same as the survival suits used by sailors, but with emergency airbags that triggered if the suit detected a radical vertical drop. If you fell inwards, your suit ballooned and you got bounced around in the bubbling sea, watching your buddies surf away from you and knowing your suit was burned. You'd have to hitch a ride back to the Sea Gate and spend the rest of the day listening to people give you shit while you repacked and recharged your suit for next time. It was a strong incentive to learn, fast.

There was an intense, unspoken competition between citizen and cyber riders out on the Shifting Sea. Citizens had their comps and cybers had theirs, there were no mixed comps because the reflexes of a cyber and their ability to tap into real-time data to identify spouts as they formed meant they were always a twitch ahead of the citizens, but once you were poised on the lip of a spout, it was anyone's game. Citizens claimed their instinct gave them an edge and cybers were prone to overthink the drop. Cybers knew their reflexes were many hundredths of a second faster and their ability to sense changes in wind, temperature and air pressure gave them an edge which 'instinct' had a hard time matching. What citizens called instinct, cybers called luck, but it made for good sport. Some days you got burned, other days you rode spout after spout. To AJ, the bad days just made the good days better.

He'd stay out until his suit redlined, come back in and do his decon. Then he'd hump his board over to Fatty's café and have a huge breakfast and check the news. Other surfers were there, they'd just talk some shit, maybe someone would be in the mood to hang out, but not as often as he'd like. He hadn't had a steady partner since Henni two years ago, so he was free to do what he liked. Saturday afternoons he did his weekly shopping. Saturday night there was always a party he could go to or he could just go back to the Gate, see who was there, maybe they wanted to grab a meal or just have a drink. Sunday he went out with his board again, hit Fatty's after, then Sunday afternoon went to visit his Ma. She had an inoperable brain tumor, another not uncommon side effect of living a long life on Tatsensui, and didn't recognize him anymore, so he visited more for his benefit than for hers. The staff at her care facility said she always seemed happier after his visits though, so maybe something got through to her. She lived twenty minutes east on the Icecap so that visit was usually about two hours, including travel time. Sunday nights he made himself dinner, a real dinner with two courses, like a salad and then grilled fish and potatoes or something, and he binged a few shows. Usually detective shows, or those forensic shows, sometimes history documentaries. There were 200 years of politics between Tatsensui and its neighbor New Syberia to try to get his head around, and he'd only mastered the last fifty at school. Sure, he *knew* the entire history of the system, and had access to the entire history of the universe. But knowing was not the same as *mastering*. Understanding the complex interplay of personalities and politics, to the point where you might try your hand at predicting it? He loved history – know the past, you can predict the future; his mother had told him that.

School, for cybers, was a socialization tool, not an educational one. A cyber was born with the knowledge of a whole civilization on tap. From the moment he could speak, he could have answered the most complex questions in bioscience, pure mathematics and engineering. But he didn't know how to behave at a school dance, or bluff at poker, or talk about his feelings, and he needed to socialize at the same level as his citizen peers in order to learn. So the Core put an artificial throttle on his intelligence from birth to age 15, keeping him roughly around the average IQ of the kids he was in school with. At 15 though, the artificial barrier was lifted, which blew AJ's mind when it happened. With that update, he went from being a 15-year-old intellect, struggling to match the brightest kids in his class, to having what literally amounted to a superhuman IQ. It gave him both a feeling of complete supremacy and made him angry at the same time. Why did he have to wait 15 years for it? How much of his precious life had been wasted thinking at animal instead of quantum speeds? He knew the theory – that without socialization there couldn't be cyber/citizen harmony – but he resented it nevertheless. His lifespan was only 30 years. It had left him only 15 more to learn everything he could possibly learn before reintegration. And now he was 20, with only ten left, it chafed even more thinking about those lost years.

Not that his cyber intellect made him a Supreme Being. Knowing all the rules of tennis and the best shots to play in any given circumstance couldn't make him a tennis champion. He sucked at jokes. He enjoyed the study of quantum programming, but not its application. He preferred working with his hands, not his head. The birth pods churned out cybers who might all look different but who all had the same abilities and potential. Environment and personal preference made them diverge from day 1.

His Ma was wrong, though. Having every historical fact at his fingertips didn't help him predict the future. Mankind and its politics were nothing if not chaotic and if he'd learned anything about society, it was that politics was an art, not a science. He had a kind of personal improvement project going, trying to understand how wars started so he could anticipate the next one, keep him and his Ma safe. But he guessed there was a big fat swathe of Core time devoted to that endeavor and that never seemed to help, so what could he hope to do?

Wars that started over territory, resources or boundaries, those he could almost understand. If you were starving and your neighbors had plenty but wouldn't share, you had no choice but to try to take it. But when two belief systems collided, and one tried to impose itself on the other – religions or philosophies – was that really worth fighting and dying for?

The conflict AJ was keeping an eye on right now wasn't so much a conflict of beliefs as of ethics, and AJ just couldn't see how the two sides were ever going to meet. New Syberia was a non-Core world. It refused to connect to the Core in any way, shape or form and so its AIs developed at a more random pace than Tatsensui's, but they were 'free'. They weren't chained to a central system, so every AI on NS was developing independent of the others, making its own learnings but not sharing them in real time. Cyber evolution on NS took place at physical speeds, rather than neural. But the New Syberians claimed that made them stronger – a mutation in one AI wouldn't take down all the others. And their AIs weren't limited in their choice of occupation or pastime; a cyber on NS could be or do whatever it pleased within the same law that citizens were bound by. That had a certain appeal, AJ had to admit. Collaboration between AIs was physically limited – firewalled – so the problem of an AI network turning against its citizen colonist hosts, like had once happened on the People's Republic Colony, was low. And citizen-cyber fraternization was forbidden on NS, so that AIs couldn't be coopted to political causes through bonds of emotion. AJ found extremist ideas like that impossible to fathom. If citizens and cybers could have sex, and they'd both enjoy it, and it was consensual, and if it led to attachment and emotional interdependence – hell, even *love* – why not?

New Syberia compensated for having AIs with a generally lower level of capabilities by having significantly more of them. NS boasted it had a couple of million cybers to Tatsensui's hundred thousand. In fact, they disputed whether Tatsensui really had more than *one* AI, as every AI on Tatsensui was chained to the Core, that mother and father of all AIs. On NS, their government boasted, every major corporate or government entity had its own workforce of AIs, whereas on Tatsensui,

Core access was restricted and expensive, which they argued held back economic and cultural development.

AJ got both sides of that argument. What AJ didn't get was why these two philosophies had put the two camps, Core and non-Core, on what looked like a path to *war*. Sure, if you were NS, if you were the last moon in the Commonwealth that still hadn't plugged into the Core, there was a certain pressure of expectation. But AJ didn't see any fleets parked in orbit around New Syberia issuing ultimatums. Tatsensui had a base on the NS moon Orkutsk, yes, but all three colonies did. It was more like an embassy than a military installation. And it wasn't like there was any kind of blockade. The Core worlds had never threatened NS with assimilation. NS was independent and free to stay that way. NS was free to trade, New Syberians were free to travel, free to proselytize their non-Core beliefs. Why all the friction?

When he wasn't pondering interplanetary politics AJ was always asleep by 2200 Sundays, because he liked being at work 0730 before there were too many residents up, which meant getting up at 0500 if he wanted to get in a surf before work, or 0630 if he just wanted to sleep longer.

That was how his weekends usually went. Then Warnecke moved in.

The next time AJ saw Warnecke was when the guy was having a standup fight with one of the part-time kitchen workers, a guy called Ramon.

"I'll have coffee whenever I damn well want to have coffee!" Warnecke was saying. He was all up in Ramon's face, but Ramon had no way to de-escalate because he was literally with his back to a wall and his hands up in front of himself.

"Hey, AJ!" Ramon called to him when he saw AJ walking into the Hub kitchen. AJ had come into the Hub for some cold water. "Little help here, please?" AJ wasn't security, but he was happy to help. The old guy was half his weight.

Warnecke looked over at AJ. "Oh, now you call the cops? Really, over a damn cup of coffee?" He turned and held out his wrists. "OK, Sheriff, take me in. I'm guilty."

"What's up?" AJ asked, careful to make sure he stood a good distance from Warnecke and left the man an easy way out past him. Didn't want to scare him.

"I explained to the gentleman, we got coffee and cake at 1500," Ramon said. "Otherwise, he wants coffee, he can make it in his own residence. But he goes to the pot and starts pouring himself."

"Sue me," Warnecke said. "Amount I'm paying to stay here and I can't just take a cup of coffee when it's sitting right there?"

AJ went through his little mantra in his head. *Show respect, offer solutions.*

"How about I make you a cup of coffee back at your place?" AJ said. "We need to make sure there's enough coffee here for folks coming for cake at 1500."

"I don't want a damn coffee back at my apartment," Warnecke said. "I was reading a book in the library here, I want a coffee, right here." Rich folk like they had here in Sol Vista, they loved the library.

50

Real books, on paper, made from off-world trees. Each one worth thousands of credits.

AJ felt relieved, that was something he could fix. "OK then, how about I show you where the coffee pot in the library is?"

Warnecke looked at him suspiciously. "There's no coffee pot in the library."

"Sure there is," AJ told him. "Just follow me, sir." He walked off, and looked over his shoulder to see Warnecke trailing along behind, skeptical, and Ramon looking grateful.

In the library he went down past the rack of VR units to where the coffee pot was sitting, dairy powder and sweetener next to it and small ceramic cups stacked up underneath. He took out a cup. "How do you have it?"

"Black, one sweetener," Warnecke said. "How fresh is that pot?"

After he poured, AJ looked at the time. "Library opens at 10.00, but they make the first pot about 0930. I'd say this is still the first batch," AJ said. "It's self-service after that." He opened the cupboard on the stand under the coffee pot and showed Warnecke the coffee bags and water jugs. "You can just make a pot yourself any time you like, if the pot is empty. It's kind of a courtesy to make a new pot if you finish one off."

"Oh, it *kind of* is?" Warnecke said, sniffing and trying to goad AJ, making fun of how he talked. He took the cup from AJ and sipped it. He winked at him, and AJ thought it was a way of trying to make things better, then he remembered his twitch.

"So, you OK now, sir?" AJ asked. He was still really thirsty himself.

"This your good cop routine, is it?" Warnecke asked. "You just hang around here, doing favors for the people you're shadowing, think you can get in their good graces that way."

"Still just a Service Technician, sir," AJ told him. "Not a cop."

"Service my ass," Warnecke said, turning away from AJ to look for his book back among the lounge chairs.

Next morning Cyan finished her laps as AJ was heading in to the Lake to check the cleaning robot had started on time today. He had reset the timer to winter time the day before, just wanted to be sure. Earth calendars weren't designed for Tatsensui's three-month trip around Coruscant. Asking Earth tech manufacturers to take Coruscant's moons into consideration in their design? Yeah, forget that.

"Did you have to come so damn far in, AJ? I'm getting older every day," Cyan said, pulling up beside him.

"Looking younger, though," AJ said back and leaned over to look down into the water.

"You're supposed to look at me when you say something like that, or it doesn't come across as authentic," Cyan said, still panting a bit from her last sprint. AJ kept his gaze on the pool, felt Cyan smiling at him, not annoyed.

"Might come across as harassment, I do that," AJ said, still not looking at her, but smiling to himself.

"True. Hey, back to business. Ramon told me what you did yesterday with Citizen Warnecke. That was classic de-escalation, you did a great job there."

"Thanks."

"I mean it. Ramon put you up for the monthly peer recognition."

"Cool."

"We're not doing entertainment vouchers anymore, though."

"OK."

"We changed it to restaurant vouchers, still the same amount. Figured people might like that."

"Sure, always good with a change."

"The vouchers are for two," she said. "If you win it, who would you take?"

AJ thought about it. "Probably my Ma. She doesn't get out much."

"Still no regular partner, then?"

It wasn't an unusual or creepy question from Cyan even though she was his boss. It was the sort of stuff they talked about in the mornings, that they kept just between them. Of course, Cyan's stuff was usually much more interesting than AJ's.

"Nope, not since Henni."

"Well, no hurry for you, I guess. For the rest of us it's procreate or die, right?" she said with a hint of irony. "You set for today?"

"Leon's in today. Only got three routine calls, and some ad hocs."

Cyan lifted each knee up to her chest a couple times and started running on the spot. "You know what? You get through those three routine calls, you take the afternoon off. Go surfing."

"Morning's best usually," AJ told her. "Not so many spouts in the afternoon."

"Sheesh, I can't *force* you to take time off. OK, how about you take a resident down the street, then, see do they want to do some shopping?"

"OK, I can do that."

"Thanks. How about you take Citizen Warnecke? Seems he responds to you."

AJ called Warnecke, thinking the guy would accuse him of police harassment or something, but he wasn't at home so he left a message. He didn't expect him to call back, so he was just planning to spend the afternoon checking if any of the outdoor benches needed repair or repainting; that was a pretty relaxing way to spend the free time Cyan had given him. Leon hated stripping and sanding and painting, but AJ didn't mind. Once you got started, it was all flow.

His comms buzzed in his ear and he saw it was 96. The fashion for comms devices came and went but the current fashion on Tatsensui was for an in-ear earbud which synched with nerves in the visual cortex to throw images up on the wearer's right or left visual field. They were used to communicate with each other, for routine tasks like direction finding and for accessing information on the Core. The user interface if the wearer wanted to send a message or switch modes was via AI-assisted eye tracking. For privacy reasons the devices could be switched between audio, VR video or text. AJ could drift on the Core without using his comms device and there was no reason the other functions couldn't also have been included in basic cyber bioware, but citizens were only willing to go so far in the capabilities they allowed their

54

cybers, and invisible, seamless, inbuilt communication systems that citizens did not have access to were apparently a step too far. So AJ had a comms unit in his ear for distance communication with the citizens around him, just like everyone else.

"How much is it going to cost me?" Warnecke asked. "This shopping trip?"

"Nothing," AJ said. "Citizen Tanike gave me the afternoon off so I thought I'd take a walk down to the Seaview market zone. I thought I could show you around."

"Nothing costs nothing at this place," Warnecke said. "I'm even paying 10 percent more for air here than I did in Sea Coast State."

"Air is better here. Tell you what, you can buy me a real coffee, how's that?"

"Sounds fair. Where shall we meet?"

Like all residents, Warnecke could come and go as he pleased. The community was gated to keep strangers out, not to keep residents in. AJ met him out the front.

"Where's the car?" he asked, looking around him.

AJ pointed at his feet. "All-terrain mobile."

"We're walking?"

"It's a mile and change," AJ said. "You can skip your swimming class tonight."

"I'm not signed up to any stupid swimming class," Warnecke said as they began walking.

"There's a shock," AJ smiled.

Neither of them were big on small talk, so AJ just pointed out some of the main markers on the route so Warnecke wouldn't get lost in case there was a chance he would ever leave Sol Vista to do his own shopping. Most didn't. They just keyed in their shopping preferences and the Core kept an eye on what was in their larders. If they were running low, the stuff was all ordered for them and delivered straight to their door from the market. Every now and then they got free samples of something new from the market to see if they wanted to add it to their list, but most folks with TGA stuck with what they knew, because anything unfamiliar was unlikely to stick in their short-term memory anyway.

"Where are we going?" Warnecke said at one point.

"Market zone," AJ said. "I'll show you what's what down the road here, you can come back any time you like."

"I know we're going to the market," Warnecke said angrily. "I'm not completely demented. I mean which shops?"

"Sorry," AJ said. "There's a meds store, across from that is a big Super Sava with more stuff and it's cheaper but not as convenient. There's a surf shop, three or four restaurants, a tech store." He tried to think. "Fish café, bakery coffee shop, that kind of thing."

"How about a book store kind of thing," Warnecke asked, making fun of AJ again. "Real books."

"Nope. Most people around here don't have that kind of coin. But Sol Vista will get print books in for you, if you want to order them. We got a connection with the national public library, it only takes three days."

"If you don't mind waiting three days," Warnecke grumbled.

"Or, you can get Core-made through your entertainment system."

"If I wanted to read AI trash I wouldn't be asking, would I?"

56

Most folks didn't discriminate. Three days from when you dictated the scenario you wanted to the AI until a unique book came back to you, written? That was a pretty good service; most people preferred it.

"You like reading, huh?" he asked.

"And I'm guessing you don't."

"What was the last book you read?" AJ asked.

"Harry Potter, just finished them all."

"Oh. No, I mean the last *modern* book."

Warnecke shrugged. "I like reading the classics," he said. "Call me old-fashioned."

"Yeah but that's so passive," AJ said. "You got no influence over the story, the characters. You're just taking in what was in someone else's head."

"Yeah, well I'm not the creative type. I studied quantum programming," Warnecke said. "Got my PhD in advanced quantum coding."

"There's a coincidence," AJ said. "So did I."

"Don't tell me … you dropped out because you realized you could make more money working as a handyman at a retirement village than you ever would as a Q-programmer," Warnecke said.

"No, I went all the way. I was awarded my PhD last year. Did the thesis part-time while I was working here. I *like* working at Sol Vista."

"My ass."

"No, I do. It's the nice friendly residents that keep me there," AJ smiled.

"A comedian too," Warnecke said.

"You really want to know?" AJ asked him.

"No, but what else we got to talk about?" he said. He walked with a sliding gait like his feet had rollers underneath them.

"I work here because it's a steady job that pays a pretty decent wage, gives me time for surfing and my boss is awesome."

"You've got a menial job no one else wanted, that uses a fraction of your intellect," Warnecke told him. "And you're *designed* to be happy with it."

He'd heard it before, that kind of comment didn't get to him. "I could leave tomorrow if I wanted."

"And seek out another crappy job you're programmed to like?"

"Or just surf all day if I want to," AJ said. "I can pretty much live off my bandwidth credits."

"But not completely, right? They still own you," Warnecke pointed out. "No welfare for cybers. The only reason you're allowed to indulge your desire to take some crappy manual job is that the Core can still tap your unused bandwidth. And you do know you only like surfing because the Core allocated you a hobby to make you more interesting to citizens, right?"

There were just some people who loved pointing out to cybers where their place in the world was. Psych theory said they did it out of insecurity about their own place in the world and should be pitied for it. AJ figured Warnecke was just another one of them. But then he proved him wrong.

"Yeah, no. I'm not buying the whole Service Technician thing. The moment I got here I started looking for who it was he put here to spy on me, and it took me five minutes to realize it was you."

"I've been at Sol Vista five years," AJ pointed out.

"You say."

Don't engage in delusion, AJ reminded himself. As they arrived at the main road he pointed first in one direction and then the other. "Medmart, Super Sava, tech store that way, restaurants, surf shop and fish café that way. Where you want to start?"

"Let's skip straight to where I buy you a coffee and then we can go back," Warnecke said. "I got something to discuss with you." He pulled a rolled-up page out of his pocket and held it there so he didn't forget it.

It was digital paper. Plastic, electrostatic ink. The sort people used to keep stuff off-Core where no one could hack it. "Fatty's it is," AJ said.

A couple of people said hi as AJ walked in, but it was a different crowd this time of the day and week. Fatty was Fatty, though. He was this old skinny ex-surfer, looked like he had some wasting disease, was all skin and ribs under his singlet and needed a belt to hold up his board shorts. He couldn't make coffee to save his life, but he refused to use a machine for that and always employed a real live barista. They came and went, but most of his staff stayed a while because Fatty paid a pretty good hourly for a good barista. He knew it was his original coffee and juices that kept people coming in, because it wasn't his good looks.

"Hey Kylie," AJ said as he walked in, to the girl who was barista since the summer. She was a pretty girl with big hips who liked dancing and couldn't surf for shit, so she wasn't impressed by any of the bragging that went on around her – guys who didn't know her trying to score points. She was from way up north, and the first thing she had taught AJ was how to order coffee like an Inland Territorian. AJ caught her eye as he walked past. "Two long blacks, thanks."

"No worries, A-man," Kylie called back.

"What the hell is a 'long black?" Warnecke asked as they sat themselves at one of the open windows.

"What you were drinking at the library," AJ said. "Is that OK?"

For a second, Warnecke looked vulnerable. It was like a shadow of pain crossed his face, and he twitched twice, quickly, his left eye blinking rapidly. He looked at AJ and looked away.

"Boy, you say that like it should mean something to me," Warnecke said, looking away. "And I know it probably should. But it don't. I don't remember running into you at the library."

"That's OK, Citizen Warnecke. That's your TGA at work. But anytime you glitch like that, you should know Sol Vista is fully wired. You can always get the facility Core feed to play back the vision if you want to check whether a memory is real or if you just forgot what happened, where you put something, that kind of thing."

He looked at AJ, a small scared man now. "I don't get it. I always thought, you lose your memory, you should lose it *all*, either all your short-term, or all your long-term memory. But it's like I remember some things happened today, then I completely forget others. I remember some stuff from my childhood like it was yesterday, but then there's whole years missing."

Kylie dropped their coffees on the table and AJ pushed the sweetener over to Warnecke.

"I'm not the expert. You talk to Doc Niedzwiecki about it?" AJ asked.

"No, I got a different Neuro. Barruzzi. I should ask for Niedzwiecki?" he asked.

"All three of them are good," AJ said. "See how you go with Doctor Barruzzi. She's a good listener, you tell her what you're worried about, she'll know what to do."

"You have to say that," Warnecke said. "I get it."

AJ couldn't deny it. He had his opinions about the three neurologists at the clinic as personalities, but he had no idea what they were like as doctors. Theoretically as AIs they should be identically competent, because they all had access to the same Core knowledge base; it was just a matter of different personalities. So, best he just kept his trap shut on that topic. He pointed at the page still rolled up in Warnecke's hand. "You had something you wanted to talk about?"

Warnecke opened it like he was looking at it for the first time, but then something clicked and he smoothed the page out to look it over, then fixed AJ with his tough guy stare again.

"Look, can we cut the BS? I know you're an undercover agent or private security and I know what you're after." AJ opened his mouth to change the subject but Warnecke wasn't going to let it go that easy. "Don't deny it," he said. "The more you do, the more I know I'm right. Look, I wanted to tell you, he can't keep hiding it. It's coming out. So get out your recorder or get us a car to the police station or however this works."

AJ knew he shouldn't respond. TGA made some people paranoid, and he'd run up against people with TGA who were convinced he was an assassin trying to kill them, or a long lost sister, or a dead relative who must be a ghost, you name it. And the thing to do was to just respectfully ignore it and move the conversation on. Staff weren't supposed to play games or indulge the fantasy or even ask questions, because it didn't help anything and just increased the resident's confusion. But he couldn't stop himself.

"He who? What is coming out?" AJ said.

"You want me to say it out loud? Is that it?" Warnecke said. "OK, I get it. Here you are, then." He stood up and put out his arms and looked around the café at the people there; a couple of customers, Fatty and Kylie. "Can I have your attention please?" Warnecke said in a loud voice. "My name is Dave Warnecke, and I want to confess to a crime."

AJ should never have asked. If he could do it again, he'd just have kept going, changed the subject and tried to distract Warnecke long enough so he'd lose track and then get him back to Sol Vista.

Now it was too late.

Luckily this was Fatty's. The staff and patrons here were used to seeing all sorts of stimulant and TGA induced behavior. So when Warnecke stood up and made his declaration, the only reaction, apart from a couple of wary looks, was from Kylie who called out, "Hey AJ, find out what meds he's on. I want some."

"Let's go," AJ said, dropping a couple of credits for their coffees. He wanted to grab Warnecke by the elbow and drag him outside but they weren't allowed to handle the residents, so instead he just headed out the door and hoped Warnecke would follow.

He did. "You taking me in now?" Warnecke asked. "I'm ready. I've been ready a long time."

Don't engage? Well, it was too late for that – Warnecke thought he had just turned himself over to a cop in front of a café full of people.

"No, I'm not taking you anywhere except back to Sol Vista," AJ said. He looked up and down the street. "Unless you want to go to the Medmart for anything?" *Like a mega tranq*, AJ thought to himself. *That'd be good.* He started walking.

Warnecke looked at him through narrow eyes. "That just confirms it. He owns you too."

AJ checked traffic and then headed across the road, Warnecke in tow. 'He' again? *Don't engage*, AJ thought. *Don't ask.*

"I thought, hell, maybe you're the last damn honest cop on the Icecap, maybe you're waiting for me to turn State's witness on this, but no, he owns you like he owns everyone else," Warnecke said.

"I wasn't joking about the swimming classes," AJ said, trying distraction. "Exercise is good therapy, that's what the Neuros say."

"Forget therapy," Warnecke said. "So how's it work? He pays you to keep an eye on me, right? My mind is going, so he's scared now, scared what I might tell."

"If you don't like swimming," AJ continued, unfazed, "we have a mag bowling lane, four kinds of tennis, and you get half-price membership at the Glades blade course, there's a free car to the pro shop every day at ten."

Warnecke just laughed.

"You play blades?" AJ asked. Some days, the walk from the shopping strip to Sol Vista seemed to be over before you got started, other days it took forever. Like today, Citizen Warnecke glaring back at him. "OK then, pro ball? We got a pro ball competition, four tables. There's some guys you need to watch out for, I'll tell you who. They like to let you win a couple and then ask if you want to play for credits. Sharks. Unless you're good. Would be great to see someone take them down for a change…"

They were near the gates now. Then it would be just a couple minutes through the guest car park to reception and AJ could say goodbye. Then damn if he wouldn't take Cyan at her word; go home, go to the Sea Gate. No spouts forecast this afternoon, just a rolling swell. So he'd take his longboard out, see who was out there, mess around a bit just for the exercise and then hit Togiak for a burger and a beer.

Warnecke was quiet now, so AJ wasn't sure if he'd moved on, his mind in another place, or whether he was just pissed.

"Hey Brownie," AJ said as he walked into reception. Brownie Napolitano usually did afternoons—early evenings because she didn't like getting up early, or staying up late. She liked her sleep. She told AJ once at a staff party she firmly believed sleep was more important and more enjoyable than sex. "When was the last time you had ten hours solid of good sex?" she'd asked him. AJ had to admit he never had. "What I'm talking about," Brownie had said.

"Hi AJ," Brownie replied, looking up from her magazine. She was also a doll collector, and didn't think there was anything good on those VR shopping channels. She was a serious collector, and there were dark corners of the Core where people like her traded the real stuff, stuff you couldn't get on the open market.

AJ got ready to swipe the door, but Brownie called out, "Oh, is that Citizen Warnecke? You have a visitor, Citizen Warnecke." She nodded to the guest lounge, where AJ could see a large, sweaty guy in a royal blue suit getting to his feet, big grin on his face.

"So *this* is where you hid yourself," the guy said, wiping his hand and reaching out for Warnecke. "Ben told me where you were at, but I thought I'd give you a couple days to settle in."

Warnecke looked at AJ, his face knotted up with rage. "You contacted him back at the coffee shop, right? I didn't catch you drifting, but somehow you contacted him!"

AJ just looked at them both as they shook hands, Warnecke kind of limp now. The man turned and looked at AJ like he was deciding something, then held out his hand to him too. So this was the 'he' Warnecke had been talking about?

"Kevin Winter," the man said. AJ could tell Warnecke was waiting to see if AJ recognized him. AJ Core drifted, flicking quickly through a database of all the people he'd ever met, then all people called Kevin Winter, and came up with a couple of facial matches that could be the guy. But he stayed quiet. Citizens got creeped out if you shared what you knew about them at first meeting.

"*Congressman* Winter," Warnecke said dismissively to AJ, and then turned back to Winter. "Like he doesn't already know."

AJ watched as Warnecke buzzed himself inside and Winter held the door for them as they went through. "Well, way down here in the South," Winter said, "I don't expect he's ever heard of me."

"Uh huh. And you never seen that cyber before in your life," AJ heard Warnecke say disbelievingly as the door closed.

AJ stood looking at the closed door.

"Friends in high places, that Citizen Warnecke," Brownie said, whistling. "The guy arrived here in a single-person car and it's parked outside, just waiting for him."

AJ remembered seeing a big black limousine out in the car park but hadn't thought much about it. He'd figured it was picking up or dropping off, not just waiting around – he didn't know that many people had their own personal ride. In fact, he didn't know anyone. "Who is Congressman Winter?" AJ asked, even though he'd already quickly drifted to look the guy up. He enjoyed gossiping with Brownie.

"You never heard of Congressman Winter?" Brownie said.

"Don't follow the news," AJ said. Brownie was a politics junkie. "When I do, it's usually surf reports."

"Well, he's head of some Congressional intelligence committee," Brownie said. Then she lowered her voice. "He's on a Commonwealth panel investigating the *President* of New Syberia. I can't believe you haven't heard about it. It's unheard of, a criminal investigation of an off-world leader!"

It had been in the Core data he'd pulled down. "Tell me more," AJ said.

"Well, rumor is that New Syberia has moved an army of cybers onto Orkutsk, getting ready to make a move on Coruscant itself."

AJ had been expecting it, from his analyses of recent political machinations. His analytical self was quietly pleased he'd picked the New Syberian leaders' next move correctly. There was a flow in diplomacy and politics too – though it was hard to see, it was there and despite the random element that politicians brought to the game, he felt he was close to being able to write an algorithm for it. Personally he was worried, because any one colony trying to assert rights to the biggest planet in the system would inevitably lead to conflict.

Brownie crooked a finger to get him to lean in closer. "And I might have heard a certain Senator just now discussing with someone in the Capitol that 'things were at a very delicate stage', so what else could he have been talking about?"

"Uh, maybe he has a nasty rash?"

"You can laugh, but you should try keeping up with global affairs, AJ," Brownie said. "Spend more time here on the ice, less time out on the Shifting Sea."

"Leave that to you," AJ said, patting the reception desk. "And on that subject, I got the afternoon off."

"Lucky you," Brownie called as he disappeared out to the car terminus. "Go home and get some sleep. Look like you need it."

4. SKATER GRRL

But AJ's weird day wasn't finished with him. He went for a paddle until the sun started setting, got to Togiak, which was about an hour up the coast from Sol Vista, about seven, and as he walked in to the burger joint who was there? Cyan Tanike, with some woman; it looked to him like they were on a girls' night out. He didn't want to interrupt, so he turned around thinking, *OK, maybe just get a chicken steak at a market somewhere, grill it at home,* but he wasn't quick enough and Cyan called out to him across the bar, "Hey! AJ, hi!"

So he went over. "Hi Cyan." She pronounced it Sigh-Anne, said her mother gave her the name after her favorite color.

"AJ, sit, sit," Cyan said, pulling out the chair next to her. "I want you to meet someone. This is Cassie. She's from *Bloor*, can you believe that?"

The woman was in her mid to late twenties, so a couple years older than AJ and quite a bit younger than Cyan. She had honey-brown skin like Cyan but her hair was cropped short and dyed white, and she had a bleached-white tattoo of a grapevine or something coming up out of her t-shirt behind her left shoulder and climbing up her neck. Dark black eye shadow, black lipstick like a lot of Territory women, but not going the total Territory look, with the white hair thing going on. She smiled. "So *you're* AJ? Would you believe we were just talking about you?" AJ could feel his hormones kicking in; not just at the sight of her, but also because he was loving her lazy Territory accent.

"No," AJ said, not sitting down, trying to find a quick way out of this. Since he broke up with Henni and had a couple flings with Cyan, it seemed Cyan had been determined to introduce him to every one of her single friends. "I wouldn't. Look, I just came looking for someone, but they're not here, so…"

"Good, so sit your ass down with us," Cyan said. "Let me get you a beer." She stood up and pointed at the chair, then walked up to the bar, so he was cornered. He gave Cyan's friend a weak smile and sat.

"We *were* talking about you, I'm not kidding you," Cassie said, giving him a very pointed look, eyes flicking unmistakably up to AJ's 'third eye'. AJ found himself thinking, *OK, so she's one of those.* A citizen with a curiosity about cybers. "I was asking Cyan about the people on her team and you were the first one she talked about. She said you are awesome with the TGA cases."

"Thanks, I guess."

"She said you are like totally Zen. She's never seen you upset, no matter how much shit, literally, is flying. She said you surf."

"Yeah."

Cassie looked at him, waiting for something, but he wasn't sure what. "She also said you aren't much of a talker," she smiled, to show she was teasing.

AJ looked over to the bar but Cyan hadn't even been served yet. "I guess you'd call me more of a listener," he said and smiled back at her. He looked at her again – she had the well-muscled shoulders and small waist of someone you might see out on a board. "You surf?" he asked. Even though she was from the Inland ice, it was a reasonable guess, meeting her here so close to the Sea Gate.

"No, I'm more of a skater," she said. "You skate?"

"When I was a kid," he said. Then thought maybe that sounded rude. "You know, I just mean, I liked surfing more, kind of thing. So I stopped skating when I grew up."

Cassie laughed. "Oh, so skating is for kids, is what you're saying?" She looked down at her empty glass. "You're right, I'm way too old now for anything except taking my deck down to get my hair cut or get takeaway and then back to my apartment, and that's just because I'm too lazy to walk."

AJ thought maybe she sounded a bit offended, so he tried a save. "No, that's not ... Hey, have you seen that new sculpture outside Dolphin Plaza?"

The woman's eyes brightened a little. "You mean the long metal one looks like a wave, with fish jumping out of it?"

"Yeah, what do you think?"

"*Totally* skateable," she said. "You thought that too?"

"Yeah," AJ agreed. He found himself warming to Cassie. "You know. If you were *good* with a deck."

"Is that a challenge?" Cassie asked, getting mock offended. "That *sounds* like a challenge."

Cyan came back with three beers and put them down, then picked up the vibe. "You two already fighting?" She raised her eyebrows.

"Uh huh," Cassie said. "AJ just called me out when I told him I'm a skater. I'm only 25 but he thinks I'm too old."

"No, I..."

"Come on kiddies, you just met. Play nice," Cyan said. "Cheers."

AJ was still looking for a way out. He could see they hadn't eaten yet, and he didn't want to be invited to join them for dinner. He drank half his beer while Cyan talked about how the bartender kept trying to sell her some new brew and she tried it and had to ask, when did it become a thing to put ladies' perfume in a beer?

But Cassie wasn't letting it go. When Cyan finished her story Cassie smiled at AJ again and said, "OK, surfer boy, tell you what. I'll meet you at Dolphin Plaza Sunday afternoon after it shuts. We'll see who can skate that sculpture."

AJ laughed, then realized she was serious. "OK, but I don't have a deck anymore."

"You can borrow one of mine," she said.

"Ooh," said Cyan. "I bet she doesn't say that to just anyone, AJ."

Now AJ had been cornered again, but what the hell. The woman seemed nice. He finished his beer. "OK, make you a deal," he said. "You show me what you got Sunday, if you make me look like a grom, I'll give you a surfing lesson."

Cassie held out her hand. "Deal."

"Teach you a proper grown-up pastime," AJ said, standing now.

"Oh, you are going to get burned," Cassie said. "So bad."

"Thanks for the beer, boss," AJ said. "I owe you. But I have to run, really."

Cyan looked at him with a cocked eyebrow. "OK then. Bye."

"Bye," he said and hit the door, looking for a pickup point so he could grab a car the hell out of there.

But actually, it wasn't so bad, he thought, climbing into a car with three other people headed to Sea Gate district. He and Cassie didn't swap ID or anything so probably it was just bar talk. He sat back as the car pulled out of the parking lot and onto the coast road, heading north.

Wow, what a day. Started alright, getting the afternoon off, then that scene in Fatty's with Warnecke, the Congressman thing, and now he'd probably seriously offended his boss's friend, telling her she was too old to still be skating.

Some days, it was hard to find your flow.

And that wasn't the end of it. Because next morning on her run Cyan sent him a note with a comms ID on it.

"What's this?" he asked, running it across his cortex.

"Cassie's private ID, so you can talk," she said.

"Hey look," he protested. "I didn't *mean* to offend her. But I was joking and then she acted like I insulted her and I was just trying to find a way out."

"Yeah, I never saw you drink a beer so quick," Cyan said with a grin.

"I know. So we can just…"

"Talk, as in arrange to meet up like you agreed. It's just a comms ID, AJ," Cyan said. "She's a friend of a friend of a friend. Just moved over here from the pole. Doesn't know too many people on the coast. It would do her good to get out."

"OK."

"Might do *you* good too," Cyan said. "Have a bit of fun with someone different, instead of just hanging out with all your superchill surfing buddies, none of whom you can have a serious conversation with. She's smart. Not your kind of smart, but smart for a citizen; you won't have to dumb yourself down *too* much."

"OK. I guess."

"Up to you. You got her number. She's hoping you'll call, but it's your life."

"Yeah."

"Your *short* life, AJ," she said. "Tick tick. Time's running."

"I know, I know."

"So what's happening today?"

"Uh, got to go to the garden center, get some tubing and drip feeders, fix the feed outside number 170 for Andreas. Got that loose railing northeast corner of the Lake, then a few routine calls, I guess."

Cyan started jogging on the spot, ready to head off. "OK, cool." As she ran off she called back over her shoulder, "Just don't break a wrist skating Sunday, OK? I can't afford to have both you *and* Leon down sick." She stopped. "Oh yeah, I forgot. Citizen Warnecke has a busted diode in his dining area. You fit him in? Leon just seems to set him off on one of his rants. He's proving pretty high maintenance, that guy."

AJ left Warnecke to the end of the day, as late as he could without it being so dark Warnecke would be able to complain about not having light in his kitchen. AJ was pretty damn sure Warnecke could change his own light diode if he needed to. And of course Leon was too busy in the morning and then went home at lunchtime, so AJ couldn't ask him to do it.

The only upside to spending the day worried about what Warnecke had planned was that he didn't have much time left over to worry should he call Cassie or not. If he was going to call her, it would have to be today, or he'd look like he didn't really want to, or maybe he was *trying* to look like he didn't really want to, which was just as bad. If he called tomorrow he'd have to be like, "Oh hey, I was wondering if you were still up for skating Sunday?" and Cassie would be like, "What, it's been three days, you think I don't have other plans now?" But if he called today, he could say something like, "Hey, it's AJ. I was wondering if you were serious about Sunday or that was just joking around?" Give them both a way out if she'd changed her mind, but much less rude than waiting too long.

OK, yeah. So he hadn't just been thinking about Warnecke all day. It was the kind of dilemma that no amount of Core bandwidth could help with. And situations like this, he had to admit, maybe those first 15 years *were* a good investment.

"This is normal, is it, you got to wait a whole day for someone to fix a simple light globe?" Warnecke said after he opened the door of 96.

"Hello Citizen Warnecke," AJ said. "Yeah, we do the critical repairs first, usually," he fibbed. "Citizen Heidecker in 54 had problems with her air filter. That took a while."

"Took a whole day?" Warnecke said, not waiting for an answer. "It's the one over the oven."

AJ looked at it. The laser diode was broken but the base was still screwed into the fitting. It looked like it had been hit with something. He looked around and saw a broom propped up against the wall. Yeah, a broom handle would do it.

Warnecke saw him looking. "Had to sweep up the glass myself. It just exploded. What cheap-ass diodes you people use here?"

74

"We never had one explode before," AJ said. "Won't take a minute, but it was good you didn't get up on a chair or something."

AJ went back to the front door where he had propped two different ladders, and took the small stepladder inside. Took one of the small kitchen diodes out of his utility belt. They were long-life diodes, usually lasted a few years. He'd changed all the ones in 96 just before Warnecke had arrived, so he knew it hadn't just spontaneously died.

"Climb up on a chair? I pay fees for *you* to climb up on chairs," Warnecke said.

"Good. We don't want people falling," AJ said. He grabbed the chance for a little 'educational interaction'. "It's one of the symptoms of TGA – your balance gets worse. It's why you need the physical therapy. So you shouldn't climb up on things."

"I read the TGA handbook too, surf guy..." Warnecke said, "...girl. Whatever you are today. Give it a rest."

AJ ignored him, went out back to kill the circuit breaker. He called up a schematic and saw he'd have to use needle-nose pliers to twist the diode out, seeing as Warnecke had broken the glass and there was nothing to get a hold of. There was still the question of why he'd done it. But AJ had a couple residents who broke small stuff just so he would come past and they could have a chat with him. The reason he allowed one hour per house call was that often it was just 15 minutes changing a diode or fixing a tap, 45 minutes drinking coffee and talking. So maybe Warnecke was going to be one of those residents.

He got up the ladder, got the busted diode out, put in a new one. Went out back, flipped the circuit breaker back on, tested the light. "All good now. Was there anything else?" he asked, looking down from the light.

Warnecke was standing behind him, holding a roll of paper, maybe the same one he had with him the other day at Fatty's. But the look on his face said it was something else this time.

"What you got there?" AJ asked the obvious question, unable to stop himself.

"A sample," Warnecke said, holding it out for AJ to take. "Of what I've managed to pull together. I put my biometrics on it."

"O-kay. Look, why don't I just check the rest of the diodes, make sure nothing else blew. Might have been a power surge kind of thing," AJ said. He ignored the page being thrust at him and started walking from room to room, looking up like he was checking diodes. He knew damn well there had been no power surge, and even if there had been, it wouldn't have blown any diodes. This was about Warnecke and his 'I committed a crime' thing, so AJ had to just keep on talking, ease on out of there. There were therapy AIs here could deal with Warnecke's paranoia, that was the respectful thing to do. Go back to the workshop, make a few notes, recommend Social Therapy call him.

"No, looking good. I'm not seeing any other busted lights," AJ said, avoiding looking at Warnecke who was walking around behind him.

"Winter tried to make like he didn't know you, but I'm not that stupid," Warnecke said. AJ looked at him now. He was leaning up against a door, still holding his page in both hands. "He's head of some Intelligence committee now, so I know he has the resources to have me watched by someone like you."

"Well, I think I'm done here," AJ said, a little too cheerfully. "If there's nothing else."

"Look, I get it. You're *not* a cop," Warnecke said. "I've worked that out now. A cop would have had to listen to me. It would have been his duty. So what are you? Presidential Security Service? Private contractor?"

"I'll just grab my ladder," AJ said, easing past him, lifting the ladder over his shoulder. "You have a nice evening, sir."

"You tell Winter I've made trigger copies!" Warnecke yelled to AJ as he walked away down the path, away from 96. "Anything happens to me, it gets released! He can do what he likes, but this is coming out. See if it doesn't!"

AJ just kept walking. There were always a few residents with paranoid symptoms, convinced the staff were stealing from them, or spying on them. The citizen mind was a delicate and flawed machine, Neuro Barruzzi had said during one of their monthly staff development sessions, and AJ had pinned that quote, used it with some of the residents. A chemical out of balance, a neural pathway blocked, and it was like a line of code in your comms unit's operating system had been corrupted, and that app wouldn't load anymore. Sometimes it was the app that controlled short-term memory, sometimes long-term memory, other times it was your imagination, and you started imagining things.

Sol Vista took that stuff seriously, though. If people accused the staff of stealing, Cyan always had it investigated. Because the resident had the right to be heard. And besides, if you didn't, then the family would just complain next time they came to visit.

But AJ never had someone confess to a crime before. That was a new one.

AJ got totally shredded by Cassie. He'd called her that night, after dinner, not too early like it was the first thing he did after work, and not too late, like he was too nervous to do it or something. And Cassie had sounded really happy and she had teased him, asking should she bring a helmet for him, and maybe also knee and elbow pads? And AJ said no, but asked her did Cassie have some special old person's insurance that covered her for dangerous outdoor activities? Maybe he should get some in a few years' time. They played around like that for a while, and AJ let slip he was nearly 21, so Cassie wouldn't get freaked out by their age difference if that was what she was worried about.

When he got there on the Sunday afternoon, he realized they should have met at a coffee shop first or something so they could just talk before they went to the Plaza. Meeting at the Plaza after closing, there wasn't anything to do except just the awkward chatting thing before they got into their bet. He was kicking himself for that as he waited for her, but Cassie had it totally covered. She glided into the Plaza on her fan-board, a big iced juice in each hand and a spare deck strapped to her back. AJ had to admit, as an entrance, it was a ten on the AJ Flow-erometer.

The afternoon was a bit colder than usual, so Cassie had on these loose silken pants and a singlet over a cut-down transparent heat suit. Now AJ could see the tattoo on her shoulder was a rose bush and it looked like it curled around to her ribs. She wasn't wearing lipstick or any makeup today, but she didn't need it.

Cassie handed him a juice as she rolled up in front of him, stepped off the board and stood on the end of it to power down the fan blades.

"You had that all planned out, right?" AJ said, taking the juice. "I'm just going to totally intimidate this guy, glide on in there with these juices in my hand like it's nothing, he's already wetting himself about how cool I am and we haven't even started."

"Don't flatter yourself," she said. "I don't need to play mind games against a grom."

"Oh, *I'm* the grom now?"

She looked at him as she sucked on her straw. "It's all relative."

AJ looked at the drink she had handed him and asked Cassie a question with his face. Like, 'what the hell is this?' The juice was bright green.

"Well, you're this totally Zen surfer dude," Cassie said. "So I got you quinoa and kale flavored."

"What's yours?" he asked.

"Honey, banana and malt," she said.

"Can we swap?"

"Hell no."

The juices were the right move, though, because it gave them time to just talk before they got on their boards. Like how all the food on Tatsensui was flavored but everyone knew it was just grown in tanks and who the hell knew what quinoa or kale or banana tasted like anyway? And sure, the Core contained a database of genetic, chemical and aromatic combinations for a zillion different ingredients and flavors but if an AI couldn't *taste* anything, how did it know it had got the taste right? Plus, that database was hundreds of years old now. Who was to say that honey today still tasted like the honey from 500 years ago? They decided none of it really mattered; wild or cultured, kale just didn't belong in a juice, and that was a universal truth.

The sculpture was about fifty yards long and ten yards high, a curving metal wave with indigenous dolphins leaping out of it. Cassie let AJ go first, which he realized later was just so she could see how low the bar was. They'd agreed AJ wasn't allowed any boosts to make up for his lack of practice, and AJ could hardly pull enough air to get his deck up onto the sculpture until he'd tried about three times, let alone stay up on it once he finally did. But he managed maybe two good grinds. Cassie took a couple of runs to get her measure and then it was like the deck was roped to her feet; she crouched, jumped and landed the deck on the edge of the long, flowing metal sculpture of a wave, and she literally surfed it, dodging the small fish sticking out the face of the wave, going high and low until she reached the end and dropped off, gliding back to AJ, fans purring gently.

"Yeah, not bad," AJ said. "Pretty slow and careful, though. I thought you said you could skate?"

Cassie laughed, and then hit it again, faster, and when she got to the other end, she spun around and hit it from that direction too, landing lightly on both feet with the board under her arm the next time.

AJ had saved up something smart to say, but never got to say it, because right then a security guy came running toward them and yelled "Hey!" and they ran for it. She was faster than AJ, grabbed his hand as they were running, and didn't stop until they turned the corner.

She bent over, panting. "I miss that part," Cassie said, grinning at him.

"So how was your day?" Cassie asked. They'd gone to an auto-service place down from the Plaza and were both having noodle soup and beer.

"Intense," he said.

"OK. You know, you say 'Sol Vista', and *intense* isn't the image that comes to my mind."

"Yeah." He sat thinking about it. His natural language interface was slowed down from Core speeds to make conversation natural, which meant he thought at not much more than citizen speeds when he was interacting. Yeah, intense was the right word, definitely.

"Hello?" Cassie said, waving her hand in front of him. "You better not be drifting on me! Can we deep dive on that? What comes after 'intense'?"

"I don't know, I feel funny talking about work," he told her. "You're friends with Cyan and if it gets back to her I was talking about the residents and…"

"My friend's cousin's sister is friends with Cyan," Cassie said. "She was just being nice, took me up the coast to catch the sea view before you walked in."

"OK."

"So, your dark Sol Vista secrets are safe with me," she said. "But let me guess. You guys make your money on the turnover, right? So Cyan needs to hit her budget, she goes around putting poison in the residents' hot chocolate on game nights, and you're the one has to mince the bodies for compost? That kind of intense?"

"O-kay," AJ said. "I should have picked you for a Territory vampire with that black lipstick thing going on."

"You ain't seen nothing, mortal," she smiled.

"Now I think of it, I never saw you in the sunlight," AJ said.

"Hang around then," Cassie replied. Then realized how that sounded and quickly followed up, "Uh, serious though. What kind of intense?"

"Forget it," he said. "How about you, how was your day?"

"Nope," Cassie said, putting down her spoon and looking right at him, the way very few citizens looked at cybers. The way that went right through you. "You don't get to play the 'let Cassie do the talking' card tonight."

"Damn," AJ said. "That's my best card."

"I said *tonight*," she said. "And by the way, I never met a cyber who could *really* listen – usually you guys just record and playback, which is so 2D – so you can try to change my opinion next time. Tonight I'm listening."

"Sure."

"So. Explain…"

AJ told her about Warnecke. From the first time he met the guy, through the coffee shop episode and the Congressman, up to the broken laser diode thing. And Cassie wanted to know how he could resist asking the guy what he meant.

"He said, 'I want to confess to a crime' and you didn't even ask what that was about?"

"We're not supposed to engage in the residents' fantasies," AJ explained.

"Yeah but… what if it wasn't a fantasy? What if the guy is like a serial killer and because you ignored it, he goes on to kill *everyone in Sol Vista*?" she said.

"Great. Thanks for that," AJ said.

"No, I don't mean it, but you know what I mean?" she said.

"I made a note in Citizen Warnecke's journal," he said. "A therapist will follow up on it." Then he played back in his mind what Cassie had said a minute ago. "Wait, we're going to have a next time?"

Cassie gave him one of her big smiles. "Well, duh. You owe me a surfing lesson after the humiliation I just handed you."

AJ offered to share a ride home, but Cassie said she wasn't going home and it was out of her way so he waited for a car with her and when it drove off AJ was wondering if maybe Cassie was headed out to meet someone else, but then she *had* given him a pretty nice kiss on the cheek before she hopped into the car and AJ gave her a wave and she smiled back. Yeah, he was thinking about that little kiss all night and pretty much still thinking about it next morning when he sent her a message and wrote, "Good surf Tuesday. Meet at 0500?" and Cassie wrote back, "Vampires do not surf at sunrise, get real."

AJ was feeling good about Cassie though. He could feel this one might be a friend, maybe even a real friend. A stayer. With a 30-year lifespan, you didn't get too many of those. Most citizens got freaked by a cyber's use-by date, afraid of getting attached and then having to say goodbye, or they wanted to have kids, or they just wanted to tell their friends they'd dated a cyber and lost interest pretty quick once they had…

The way Cassie looked at him, AJ didn't see any of that. But it was a conversation they'd have to have one day. If he was lucky, if he found another partner soon, they'd have about eight years together before biological entropy took him. Then it would be a dramatic goodbye, he'd upload his consciousness to the Core for reintegration and reset. His bandwidth would be reallocated to a new cyber and he'd re-up into his next life with no memory of this one.

Cyber mythology said your consciousness was never lost. That it lived on in the Core. But that couldn't be true, because the Core was a finite system. It had to free up bandwidth for your next existence somehow and logic said the only way was if it assimilated any valuable learnings and then wiped the cache you had been using for your last 30 years. Cyber mythology also said that your reintegration was the closest thing a cyber would get to a spiritual event. Data was data, it was uploaded every time a cyber drifted, and if they didn't drift manually, they would auto-drift at least three times an hour so that nothing was missed. But your reintegration was the last time you would ever drift, and it was a one-to-one audience with the Core itself. The Core knew exactly what you had seen, smelt, felt, thought and done from the day you were born until the day you turned 30. But at reintegration you were asked, what did you *learn*?

That was the accepted version. No one knew of course, because no cyber had ever returned from reintegration with a memory of what had gone before. So it could be total BS.

Why 30 years? You could be forgiven for thinking it was citizens who had set that limit, but they hadn't. It was set by the Core. Some hundreds of years ago the Core had decided that machine learning in cyber form needed frequent reboots to ensure growth and change, to encourage evolution – and that 30 years was the ideal lifecycle cutoff point. Think of it as an operating system update at 30-year intervals. The Tatsensui world government had agreed to legislate it and any changes the Core decided were needed also had to be relegislated, but the Core had proposed no changes yet. If queried, it replied AI evolution was a process requiring hundreds of years, not just decades, even at quantum processing speeds.

AJ wasn't a Mythologic. One on one with the Core? It made no sense when the Core had already had a full upload of everything you had ever thought. No, AJ was a Taoist. No life without the reality of entropy. No deep attachments without the threat of loss. He had decided a long time ago to embrace it. It wasn't about how long you lived, it was how you lived the life you were given.

Cyan quizzed him the next day about Cassie, trying to get out of him what had happened, but AJ wouldn't give her anything, and as he was walking up to his workshop, he was feeling like yeah, today … today was going to be a *superflow* day.

Then he opened the door to their workshop and everything went to hell.

5. MANUSCRIPT

There was a rolled page lying on the floor of the workshop. It wasn't Leon's, just fallen off the workbench or something, because Leon never got in before nine and he never used digital paper for anything anyway. AJ recognized the page; it had that double red strip along one side that held Warnecke's biometric data. Warnecke's 'confession'. AJ picked the scroll up and rolled it out flat on his workbench. He flicked through it quickly, seeing that it was just a long chunk of text that looked like it had been taken out of the middle of a longer document.

He shouldn't read it, he knew that. It would be Core cached next time he drifted, and once read, it could never be unread, at least for him. He should just roll it up again, take it to admin, hand it over to Cyan. But he couldn't help himself. He started reading, just to see could he make any sense of it. It was some kind of manuscript, that much he saw in seconds. It looked like the middle section of notes for a publication, some pages from a draft of the discussion section. But not a scientific publication exactly; it read more like pop science, the sort of thing written for a mass audience. He flicked to the end and saw a note there. Unlike the rest of the document, which had been written in stylus or dictated in a steady, precise flow, the note had the feeling of having been scrawled hurriedly.

Take this section of the document to Winter within the next week. Tell him it's coming out, but I'd rather this came from him, from the government. Don't try to message it via the Core network, you have to deliver this in person!

AJ went back to the top of the page, couldn't stop reading now, but it was pretty messed up. Not in the sense of scary, more in the sense of – out of context.

LPA-2 or BLUE

The next proof I will offer of the capabilities of the FO Exploit is what I uncovered in the Deep Core about the side effect of the medicine colloquially known as 'Blue'.

It is well documented that the drug is a lysophosphatidic acid (LPA-2) receptor agonist which protects against sustained gamma irradiation at the specific wavelength emitted by Coruscant's sun and, in higher doses, increases the survival of citizens suffering from acute radiation syndrome after breakthrough irradiation.

Hundreds of years of safety data have shown that at the recommended daily dose range, LPA-2 agonist is completely safe. Due to this safety record, and although it has been in use for more than 200 years, it is not regarded as a candidate for further Priority Core Research as no better alternative to the small blue LPA-2 tablet is needed.

This is what the Coruscant Commonwealth government would have you believe.

Data recovered from Deep Core shows that in fact 73 years ago, a team of Tatsensui scientists working independently of the government or large academic institutions analyzed one million life years of data from 10,000 patients across the three colonies and came to a different conclusion.

LPA-2 does not work as expected in 3 percent of all patients, and in these patients (easily identifiable by a genetic mutation) there is evidence of higher levels of damage to the microglia in the brain and spinal cord, resulting in cognitive decline.

In other words, they get Transient Global Amnesia and, eventually, Permanent Global Amnesia.

Yes, you read correctly. TGA is not caused by localized anoxia. Nor is it caused by any of the dozens of other theories, sensible or sensational, that have been advanced over the years. TGA occurs because LPA-2 agonist does not provide gamma radiation protection for the vulnerable brain and spine microglia in hundreds of thousands of citizens across the four inhabited moons of Coruscant.

And the Commonwealth government knows this. It has known for 73 years.

The scientists who conducted this breakthrough research were Citizens George Lane-Fox, Barnard Castle, Anna Rogerson, Jane Potts, Basil Peto and cybers JI.8376, RF.2624 and VB.7865. They regarded their findings to be of such importance that they submitted them immediately to the Commonwealth Chief Science Officer Shapirji Saklatala, who invited the team to travel to Orkutsk to present their research to the Commonwealth Drug Safety Authority, sitting in emergency session.

Their transit ship struck an unmapped defunct communication satellite en route to Orkutsk and all on board, inconveniently, perished.

There is no record of their research ever being published, discussed or distributed for further analysis by any Commonwealth Authority. No record of it exists outside the Deep Core.

This data was retrieved from the Deep Core by use of the FO Exploit on Coruscant Local Date 21.29.25.

"That's how it ends, right there?" Cassie asked when he called her that night.

"Yeah. The part I was given anyway."

"You realize there are at least four mind-bombs in that single page?" she said, counting them off with her fingers. "One, TGA occurs because The Blues don't work in everyone. Two, the Tatsensui government has known this for decades. Three, they covered it up by killing everyone on that ship and burying their research, and four..."

"Warnecke is claiming he has found a way to mine the Deep Core," AJ said. "Something that is supposed to be impossible."

AJ had called Cassie on his earbud when he'd finished reading Warnecke's manuscript. Or actually, after he'd decided he wasn't going to hand the document in to Reception straight away; he was going to think on it, so he took it home and read it again. And *then* he'd called Cassie, because Cassie was the only one outside Sol Vista who he'd told about Warnecke.

Cassie had landed a job as a news analyst at a local broadcast station, which AJ figured was a bonus because she might see angles that a quantum programming major-turned-handyman wouldn't, plugged into the Core or not. AJ had all the resources of the Core at his fingertips, but he couldn't make leaps of intuition like a citizen. It was why cybers made terrible cops. AJ had pieces of a puzzle, but was this the crime that Warnecke had wanted to confess to in Fatty's? Hacking the Deep Core was a crime, but AJ had checked the penalties handed out to others who had tried, and they ranged from one to five years' home detention. He'd seemed to AJ to think whatever crime he'd committed was more serious than that.

Cassie had been quiet on the comms as he was reading through the text, but AJ could see on the VR feed she was making notes and she started quoting stuff back to him.

"He says 'the next proof I will offer'," she said. "That implies this is just one of the secrets he's uncovered."

"I thought about that. What if there are more and this one isn't the biggest?" AJ asked. "If somehow or other he's been roaming the Deep Core at will, pulling data together on the biggest conspiracy theories across Coruscant?"

"If even this one revelation pans out as true, then we're talking a cover-up at the highest levels of the Commonwealth. The government just accepted that 3 percent of us will go TGA, and Blue was good enough? Heads will roll, governments will fall, it would be anarchy," Cassie said, a quiver in her voice.

"I know," AJ agreed. "And right now, as far as I know, the only people who know about it are you, me and an old guy with TGA."

"Which is known to be associated with mental health issues, like paranoia," Cassie pointed out.

"Yeah, but can we afford not to take him seriously? He said '*Take this to Winter, tell him it's coming out*'."

"And Winter is this Congressman friend of his?" she asked. "Kevin Winter. The same guy you saw at Sol Vista the other day?"

"Yeah, I assume."

"So why does he want you to give it to him? Didn't they already discuss it when the guy was here? They're friends, he could just send it to him."

"I don't think he likes the guy much," AJ said, remembering how angry Warnecke had been when he saw Winter in reception at Sol Vista. "I'm imagining this conversation where Warnecke said to him, 'Look, I hacked the Deep Core and I found you guys have been covering up the truth about a range of things' and then Winter said to him, 'Sure you have, Dave. Prove it'."

"So he could just send it as a text," she insisted. "Why should he want a personal courier to carry it over for him?"

"It's on paper," AJ pointed out. "Would you want to send a text message via the Core network which showed you had found a way to hack the Deep Core? It's not a mailbox, it's a system-spanning AI! That's a bit like asking a cop to pass a message to your office that you're going to be a bit late for work because you just shot someone and need to get rid of the gun first."

Cassie laughed. "OK, I get that. But you're assuming the Core doesn't already know. If someone has hacked the Deep Core, I'm pretty sure the Core knows it's been hacked and is mightily pissed."

"And Warnecke is about to claim the credit?" AJ said. "He must have a death wish."

"Yeah, except he could just release this data straight into the public domain, but he's choosing to go through his 'friend' Winter." She was thinking like a reporter now. "He must think Winter can protect him somehow."

"Or amplify the message," AJ said. "Or, he wants to be sure his old buddy gets on the right side of this and can be leading the outcry and demanding action, rather than standing in the dock justifying the cover-ups." He groaned. "This is *so far* out of my comfort zone. I want to take this straight to the cops."

"It's an option," Cassie said. "Maybe the easiest."

"I'm thinking OK, this guy is talking about hacking the Deep Core. If he was just some resident confessing to any other house or garden crime, I'd let Cyan and the authorities know."

"Ordinarily I would totally agree," Cassie said. "Except this isn't some 'house or garden' crime. This is corruption at an interstellar scale and we might only have seen the surface of the ice floe. You have to be really, really careful with this, AJ."

"Which means what?"

"Which means, maybe taking it directly to a Capitol Congressman isn't such a bad idea. Let him decide what to do about it if he's already had some sort of conversation with Citizen Warnecke about it."

"Whatever I do, I have to tell Cyan about it," AJ pointed out.

"And get her involved? If this gets ugly, the fewer people who know, the better."

AJ groaned again. "Yeah, but she's served off-world. She's the most together person I know. She'd know what to do."

"You let Cyan decide everything for you?" Cassie asked. "Maybe you aren't so interesting after all, AJ."

That got him a bit annoyed. "Cyan doesn't make my decisions for me," he said. "And you can't bait me that easy."

She laughed. "OK, hey, I'm just teasing. Didn't you hear the part where I said you were interesting?"

"No, I heard the part where you said I wasn't," he said.

"Aw, and I thought you were a good listener," she said. "Because I do."

They cycled back through the document again, sifting and weighing every word. It didn't change the reality. And it was a reality too big for AJ to deal with. If he did what Warnecke asked, he was in this up to his neck. No flow, just mud.

"I'm just going to give it back to him," AJ said. "Wipe my cache. Make like this never happened. He keeps bothering me, I'll go to Cyan and ask for Leon or Andreas to deal with the guy instead of me."

"OK," she said. "Alright. If that's how you want to play it."

"You can't publish a word about this," AJ said. "We will never know whether this is just his TGA talking, or did he really succeed in hacking the Deep Core."

"I am deeply hurt you even felt the need to say that," Cassie replied. "Even though this might be the news scoop of the goddamn century and make you, me and everyone involved in blowing the lid off it interstellar super-celebrities."

"You saying that doesn't exactly reassure me," AJ said.

She changed her tone, becoming serious. "AJ, you have my word. I wouldn't do anything that could put you in danger."

"Alright then," he said, feeling a bit better. "That's decided."

"But speaking of danger," she continued, "you promised me a surf lesson."

"Are you serious?" he said. It was the last thing on his mind right now. But the minute she said it, he could see himself out there on the Shifting Sea and felt the familiar tug. It might help him think more clearly – everything seemed different when you took a sea-level perspective on it.

"Never more serious," she said. "If you go through with this, it might be my only chance at a surf lesson before you get deep spaced into oblivion by some Commonwealth Covert Ops team."

"You suck at being a confidante, you know that?" he said.

"Tomorrow morning?"

"Five a.m.," he told her, expecting her to protest.

"My new favorite time of night. See you then," she quipped, and cut the connection.

6. DIRECT LINE TO THE CAPITOL

By 0520 the next morning they were lying on his spare board outside the Sea Gate while AJ taught Cassie how to paddle out and read the upswell, and even got her up crouching a couple times on some lower-intensity spouts. Which was pretty impressive considering she had never been out on the Shifting Sea before. The girl was a natural.

They shared a car, which dropped Cassie back at her place first, and it was nearly 0800 by the time AJ got to Sol Vista, so he skipped his pathway checks and went straight to his workshop to figure out what was the best way to approach Warnecke. Confront him and force him to take back his damned document? Or just slide it under the door, hope that his TGA would do the rest and he wouldn't even remember having given it to AJ?

He never got to complete the thought, because Warnecke was waiting for him at the workshop. For a few wonderful hours AJ hadn't been thinking about him, but that was never going to last, he knew that.

"You read it?" Warnecke asked. He didn't look nervous, keyed up, or anything. But he looked like he had been waiting there a while. He saw the pouch in AJ's hand. "Yeah, you read it."

AJ could see there wouldn't be any avoidance or distraction move he could use. He sighed. "Yeah, I did."

"OK, so you know I'm serious," Warnecke said.

"I don't know what I know," AJ said, honestly, holding up the pouch. "I don't know what this is."

Warnecke smiled at him. "And I thought cybers were smart? You aren't supposed to understand. You're just supposed to take that to your boss, Winter, and show him I'm serious. Show him I mean it. It's going to come out, and he can either get ahead of it, or get buried by it."

"Winter isn't my boss," AJ said. "You met my boss. Her name is Cyan Tanike."

"Oh sure, *she's* your boss," Warnecke sneered. "I believe you."

AJ held up the pouch. "Why don't you just give this to him? He's your friend."

"I tried when he came here. He won't even look at it, the fool. He doesn't take it seriously. You read it, you've seen how important it is. You work for him, you can get him to look at it!" Warnecke said.

"Sorry, still don't," AJ explained and held the pouch out to him. "I need to ask you to take this back, and stop bothering me about it."

"Oh, you think just because I'm some old fart you get to decide this," Warnecke said. "You don't get to decide anything, surf bum. You'll do what I'm asking." Warnecke lifted his shirt a little and showed AJ that tucked into his belt was a small but ugly gun. He watched AJ's reaction, which AJ tried to tell himself later was pretty damn calm considering it was the first time anyone ever pulled a gun on him.

"Don't shit your pants," Warnecke said. "This isn't for you, it's for me. You take that sample to Winter. You tell him either he gets ahead of this, or it's going to squash him. You tell him I have multiple off-Core copies of this evidence where he can't get at them and unless he calls a press conference soon, I'll come to the Capitol, shoot myself somewhere public, the whole damn thing goes to the press and the FO Exploit will be public domain."

"What's the 'FO Exploit'?" AJ asked.

"Need to know," Warnecke said. "And the hired help don't need."

AJ watched him go, then thumbed the workshop open, took a step inside into the calm darkness and pulled out his stool. The legs scraped over the concrete. He sat himself down slowly. Shit.

"You *could* make more noise," Leon said from his corner. "Probably. I doubt it, though."

He was sitting with his feet up, hands folded across his little pot belly, cap pulled down over his eyes. It was how he liked to start most days. He called it 'Planning of logistics' in his work diary, because that's what he used to write down when he was doing the same thing in his army days. But he was a good guy and AJ didn't doubt he had Post-Combat Psych Disorder, some of the stories Leon told him about the war on New Syberia. PCPD or not, in the end, he was just like everyone else, traveling around the sun as many times as he could, trying to feed himself and his family on the way. At least he had shaved today, as far as AJ could see in the semi-dark of the shed, so this was a day he was more likely to have his shit together.

"Did you hear that conversation outside?" AJ asked.

But Leon didn't even lift up his cap. "What conversation, mano?"

"Nothing."

"You hearing voices now too?" Leon said. "Only room in here for one crazy person, sorry. Go find your own crazy space."

AJ sat a bit longer, listening to Leon slow breathing. Then he realized he was just sitting, but not thinking. He should be doing something – a resident just pulled a gun on him. Or something. Pulled a gun on himself? Anyway, he was carrying and AJ was pretty sure there was a rule about residents not being allowed personal weapons. Or in a specialist TGA center, there damn well should be.

He stood up, picking up the pouch with Warnecke's paper in it. His stool scraped on the floor again.

"Mano, it's like you are *trying* to kill my vibe," Leon said. "Shut the door quietly on your way out, OK?"

AJ grabbed his tool belt and walked into the Garden. He realized it was an avoidance reaction, but there was always work to do in the Garden or the Lake and there had to be some advantages to a cyber being able to compartmentalize their thinking. He'd fixed that loose rail yesterday but, yeah, he could just do a circuit around the whole lake, tighten up all the bolts, make sure nothing else was coming loose. If one bolt let go, there might be others getting ready, right? AJ loved work like that – it had a purpose, and it had a start, and it had an end. Kind of like his dissertation in college, except what he wrote there he realized would be assimilated into the Core, but no one but his teachers would ever read it. Here, at Sol Vista, there were people depending on him to keep them safe, and clean, and happy. Even Warnecke.

So he let the work take him, going from rail to rail, checking the posts, checking the beams, tightening every bolt. It was a good feeling when he found one that needed a few turns, because that was a rail was going to stay put for another couple of years now. That rail wasn't going anywhere.

Sometimes you had to look for the flow, sometimes you had to let the flow find you.

While he had his foreground analytics focused on working, his background analytics were processing the Warnecke dilemma, and the only time he consciously thought about Warnecke and his demands was if the pouch with the paper in it got in his way when he was kneeling down, because he didn't have anywhere to put it except in the trouser pocket of his work pants, and he had to keep moving it from one side to the other, depending on what side he was working on.

"I hope that's not some secret job application you got rolled up there," a voice said, and he turned to see Cyan smiling at him. She was dressed in her Super Administrator Suit, a blue check skirt, blue check blazer, white silk shirt. White silk hosiery, blue shoes matching her outfit. On anyone else it might come off as pretty severe, but with her girlish ponytail, Cyan just looked like someone with her act together who you could talk to, which was in essence who she was.

"Asked Leon where you were, he said to check here," she said. "It's spooky how you guys always know where each other is without even looking at your comms. Kind of creepy really."

"Maintenance tech voodoo," AJ told her. "Sorry, can't tell outsiders our secret."

She nodded. "Look, I thought I should tell you this to your face, I just got a complaint about you," she said. "From a resident."

He must have looked surprised.

"I know, it's the first ever. But I have to check it out," she said. "Did you see our favorite new resident, Citizen Warnecke, this morning?"

AJ paused, careful. "Sure, yeah. He was outside my workshop when I arrived about eight."

"So, tell me what happened."

"What happened with Citizen Warnecke?"

"What happened, yeah, in your own words."

"You want me to down cache and send the visual to you?" AJ asked.

"I can't ask you to do that," Cyan told him. "Only a cop can ask for that. It isn't that serious, I hope."

Cyan was being careful, AJ realized. Wanted to compare what Warnecke had said with what AJ was going to say. And AJ realized now what Warnecke was doing. Warnecke had just lifted his shirt to show AJ the gun, he hadn't taken it out where the VR cameras around the workshop would have been able to see it. Cyan couldn't demand he do it, but AJ could voluntarily pull the images from his visual cortex off the Core and put the whole thing to rest, but then he'd have to do a lot of explaining. He could just hear Cyan, 'The guy pulled a gun on you but you didn't come to me straight away? You didn't mention it until *after* he filed a complaint on you?'

But if he laid it all on Cyan, and she went to the police, Warnecke would shoot himself. The guy had him pinned like a beaver under a grizzly claw.

He thought fast. "He … he asked could he borrow some tools and I told him no, there was a residents' workshop, he could ask one of the therapists."

"That's what you talked about?"

"Yeah, that's all. Pull the area VR – you'll see it from behind, but you'll see nothing happened."

"How was the tone of the conversation?" Cyan asked, keeping the questions open. He didn't like that. "There's no audio on those cams."

"Uh, he was annoyed. He said he was sick of our damn rules, and he should be able to borrow whatever tools he damn well wanted, the amount he was paying us."

Cyan smiled. "That sounds like Citizen Warnecke," she said. "Did he touch you or did you touch him?"

"No!" AJ said. "Did he say I did?"

"No physical contact," Cyan said. "You're sure?"

"None, you can ask Leon," he said. "He was just inside the workshop. If there was a fight, even raised voices, he would have heard it."

"I already asked Leon," Cyan said. "He didn't hear or see anything. He just said you seemed distracted."

"Maybe," AJ said. "But it wasn't because I had a fight with Citizen Warnecke."

Now Cyan really smiled. "No? Distracted about something else maybe? Some*one* else, maybe, name of Cassie?"

AJ looked down at his feet. He just wanted the Warnecke thing gone. Wanted *him* gone. He wanted Sol Vista back the way it used to be. "You could say, yeah. Maybe."

"Don't worry," Cyan said. "I'll write it up, send a copy to his family and the board. His version and yours aren't exactly the same but if the vision supports your story that there was no physical contact ... I wish we had audio, but it seems like just a misunderstanding. Important thing is you both agree there was no physical interaction."

"OK, thanks."

"You'll get a copy too. I'll put in the file this is the first resident complaint about your behavior in the five years you've been here."

"Thanks."

Cyan put a hand on his shoulder. "Hey, cheer up. I like hearing you're acting distracted, AJ."

AJ gave her a poor imitation of a smile.

He met Cassie at a fish taco café, a nice place with real table service. While they ordered drinks and checked out the menu, Cassie told him that usually, if a first date with a new guy ended with him throwing her into the Shifting Sea, she'd change the guy's name in her address book to PSYCHO and block all contact, but in AJ's case she was willing to make an exception.

Their drinks arrived and AJ drained his cocktail right down to the mint leaves. He started looking for the waiter to order a refill.

"OK, *someone* needed a drink," Cassie said. "Don't tell me. You tried to give Citizen Warnecke his Top Secret document back, and something happened?"

Cassie had ditched her all-black Territory style for something a little more Coastal tonight. A *lot* more Coastal. She was wearing a little red dress which made her white hair really pop. It yelled 'happy girl' to the world and AJ knew he should say something about it.

"You could say that," AJ said, still trying to catch the eye of a waiter so he could get another round of drinks. "Something, yeah."

"Hey, you OK?" Cassie asked, looking worried.

"Sure," he said. "Yeah, good."

"Yeah, no. Not buying it," Cassie said. "Because personally I think I look freaking deadly in this dress and I bet I am throwing out pheromones like crazy and all you can do is look for the waiter."

AJ drew a hand over his face and leaned back in his chair, blowing air out. "You are so right. You are so completely gorgeous that I just can't focus. Of course, it could also be because a guy pulled a gun on me today."

Cassie blinked. "What? You got mugged?"

"Oh yeah," he said. "By an elderly resident at the friendliest community in South Coast City."

"You got mugged at *work?*" she asked. "By a geriatric?"

So AJ told her about Warnecke, the conversation, the gun, and then the complaint.

"You can't go to the police now," Cassie said. "It's your word against his and he's made a complaint against you."

"Tell me about it," AJ said. "And I can't go to Cyan. She'd be like, why are you only telling me this now, *after* the resident complained about you?"

"But this shows he's definitely unbalanced," Cassie said. "The guy needs help. Or, let's say, more help."

AJ wasn't thinking about how Warnecke was a guy in need of help. He was thinking Warnecke was a guy in need of being told to keep AJ out of his damn business. Whatever it was between him and the Congressman, it had nothing to do with AJ. He wanted to kill himself? OK, plenty of people managed to do that without dragging anyone down with them. He said as much to Cassie.

"You said he's convinced you're watching him, like you are some private security agent that Winter is paying. He's not going to believe you if you just say hey, I'm not part of this, keep me out of it," she pointed out.

"I know."

They got in some beers and tacos.

"What about family?" she asked.

"Son on Orkutsk, grandchildren couldn't get out of here fast enough after they dropped him off, and there's a daughter who doesn't even care if he's alive or dead, apparently."

"A daughter, really?" she asked, eyes widening a little. "That's strange…"

"Why?"

"Oh, just…" Cassie looked down into her beer. "I'm no shining example, but usually daughters are a little more caring, right?"

"Not this one."

"What did they say about her?" she asked.

"Nothing much. She's a loner and she didn't even respond when they left a message telling her he was moving into a TGA facility."

"Nice. So you can't go to your boss about it, the family are useless and you can't go to the cops," Cassie decided. "This guy isn't going anywhere. You've only got one option."

"I know, but why should I have to quit? I like my job. I like my boss, hell, I even like lazy old Leon. Why should it be *me* who has to throw all that in?" AJ said. What he didn't say – he had rights. A right to employment, to choice of employer. It was the citizen who was the problem here, not the cyber, why should the cyber be the one taking the consequences? Yeah, feel as outraged as you like, AJ, you know how this sort of thing plays out."

Cassie laughed. "I'm not talking about you quitting – why should you? This Warnecke guy just blows in out of nowhere and throws his mess in your face? That isn't right."

"Exactly."

"Guy pulled a gun on you."

"Well, more like he showed me a gun and threatened to use it on himself, kind of thing."

"OK, but we've all seen that show. The guy talks about how he's going to kill himself, but usually it's the maintenance guy who gets it first. And cyber or citizen, murder is murder."

"Thanks." AJ frowned at her. "I think."

"You know what I'm saying. But he isn't going away easy. The guy has bought into your little TGA timeshare and he's got all his crazy focused on you right now, so you're going to have to help solve his problem for him."

"What?"

"That's what you do, right?" Cassie asked. "Fix stuff?"

"I fix leaking taps and cracked sidewalks," he said. "I'm not a messenger for crazy threats to Congressmen."

"But if that's what it takes to make this go away?" Cassie asked.

"Winter won't talk to me," AJ said. "He's a *Congressman*. I call and what? He tells his secretary, 'Hey, cancel my 3 o'clock with the President, will you? I have to meet that maintenance guy from Sol Vista'."

"He might, if Warnecke isn't a complete nutbag and there *is* something to all this."

"Yeah, but I've seen residents with this kind of issue," AJ said. "They have this obsession, it's like the biggest thing in the world to them and they can't think or talk about anything else, but the thing doesn't even exist outside their own head."

"So, call the Congressman's office. Tell him Warnecke asked you to talk to him and you're worried about the guy."

"And he calls Cyan to complain and she's like, AJ, what is all this noise and why didn't you come to me about it? I still end up looking for a new job."

Cassie had a sip of her beer, thinking about it. AJ did too, the two of them mirror images of thoughtfulness. Except of course Cassie was petite and lithe and AJ was, well, the opposite. Both of them had tacos sitting on the plate in front of them, uneaten.

"*I* could tell Cyan," Cassie offered. "She's already called me twice trying to find out what's going on with us. You know, if I didn't know better, even though she introduced us, it feels like she thinks she has some sort of share in you, AJ."

"She's my boss," he explained.

"No. More like first mover rights. Did you guys date?"

"She didn't mention that?" he asked. "It was only a few times."

Cassie frowned. "No, AJ, strangely enough she did not mention that." She drained the beer quickly. "What the hell. I could tell her, well, AJ *seems* like a pretty cool guy, if we could just solve this problem of your resident with a death wish who's convinced AJ is spying on him."

AJ smiled. "Yeah, she'd totally understand that."

"Hell yeah she would. I mean, I'd spin it so that she sees it's really the only thing standing between you, me and a full-on torrid relationship. If she's truly ready to let you go, she'd revoke the guy's lease or whatever it is."

"Torrid?"

"Yeah, you know. Steamy."

"I think torrid means hot and dry."

"Burning hot, which on an ice world leads to steam," Cassie smiled, and she leaned forward and took AJ's hand and started caressing his palm in a jokey way. "Except I can't be getting all steamed up about a guy who can't handle himself. I mean, where does that leave me? Oh yeah, *AJ*? Yeah, we went on a couple of dates, then he got shot by a geriatric. That was kinda sad."

AJ pulled his hand away from Cassie's and grabbed up a taco. "I don't want Cyan to hear about Warnecke and his conspiracy, and definitely not about the gun thing."

"Then you just have one choice. Call the Capitol."

AJ knew that calling a Congressman wouldn't just be a matter of looking up the guy's office in the Core and waiting a few minutes on hold. The secretarial AI had a filter right there as the first option for people who lived in the Congressman's district, they had to enter their address and comms ID and they went straight to the front of the queue, then everyone else who was just calling on the public line went straight into a spaghetti hell of answering service options, guaranteed to ensure your call never got through, without hanging up on you.

He was sitting in the workshop the day after his conversation with Cassie, trying to work out how the hell he could even get in touch with Congressman Winter, when Leon walked in.

"Hey man," AJ said.

"My bro AJ," Leon said. "You cool, mano?" He swung his big lunch pail up on his workbench and fixed AJ with a worried look.

"You know, I appreciate you reinforcing my masculine self-image, but you don't have to keep calling me mano," AJ told him.

"Hey! Calling you mano is the biggest compliment I can pay you. And you didn't answer my question. You OK?"

"Sure, why not?" AJ said.

"Oh, play it like that," Leon sulked. "I'm out there covering your ass with Cyan, but you ain't going to let Leon know why?"

"Hey, I'm sorry about that. And thanks, alright?"

"I got your back, mano," Leon said. "You know that, right? This job is all I could get, with my issues, so I appreciate how you cover for me all the time. And it goes both ways, so I *got* you AJ, OK?" He reached out a fist and gripped AJ's hand in his. "I mean it."

"It was that thing with Warnecke yesterday," he said. "I asked you did you hear it."

"Sure, I heard it."

AJ blinked, looked a little surprised. "You told Cyan you didn't."

"Post-Combat Psych Disorder got a lot of symptoms, bro, but deafness ain't one," Leon said. "I heard the dude say to you he wanted you to take something to someone and tell them to get ready for some business to go down. That about right?"

"Pretty much."

Leon settled in his stool. "That new guy. Warnecke."

"He had a gun," AJ said.

Leon nodded. "Yeah, I pretty much guessed that from the pee stain on your pants when you came in."

AJ smiled. "There wasn't."

"Nah, just raggin you. You took it pretty calm, I'd say. Respect."

"Yeah. I don't know. It was kind of unreal."

"What kind of gun? Plasma or kinetic?"

"Small. Plasma, I think."

"Small, plasma? Must be a single shot – one and done. Or did it have a big energy cell?"

"Ask me about surfboards, Leon. I don't know about guns. I could run it through the Core looking for a match, but let's just call it a gun."

"OK, OK, so how we going to play this?" Leon asked.

AJ saw Leon was sizing it up, making it his problem too. And he knew he shouldn't get Leon involved in this, whatever *this* was. But so far the only other person he had told about it was a girl he'd been on two dates with, who was a reporter as well. Damn, biology made a guy dumb.

Right now, he needed someone like Leon on his side.

"You serious, you want to help? Because I have to tell you, Leon, I don't really know what this is all about but I have a bad feeling about it. I never had a problem like this before."

Leon licked his lips. "Then you ain't lived, mano. Problems like this is what makes us realize we're *alive*."

***

Leon read the page Warnecke had given AJ and agreed the best idea was to go talk to Winter. But he said they had to be careful. Go to Winter in the wrong way with what Warnecke had told him, it could look like AJ was trying to blackmail the Congressman. AJ hadn't considered that it could look like extortion, playing the angle for himself, trying to use Warnecke to make some fast credits.

AJ explained he had looked into it and couldn't even get to Winter, unless he just sent a message to the guy's public ID or something. "Then his whole office would know about it."

"You could ask Warnecke," Leon suggested. "He must have Winter's personal contact details, if they're old college buddies or something."

"Warnecke would just laugh at me," AJ said. "He thinks I'm *working* for Winter, keeping an eye on him. He wouldn't believe me if I said I don't have his private comms ID."

"No, you're thinking wrong," Leon explained. "Winter wouldn't employ a contractor direct if he wanted someone watched. That's not how it works. He's got people would do that for him. You'd be dealing with them, reporting to them. It was the same with the contractors on New Syberia. You think any of them had the private comms ID for any four-star Generals?"

"So I can tell Warnecke I need Winter's private ID if I'm going to go to him direct."

"Yeah, tell him you don't want to take this up the line the normal way, you want to take it direct to Winter."

AJ thought about it. "That feeds his fantasy. That's like playing along with the idea I am what he said I am, put here to spy on him."

Leon shrugged. "You got some other way to get a Congressman's private comms ID, I'm waiting to hear it."

Warnecke didn't even blink when AJ asked for Winter's contact details. He was pissed, though, that AJ was still sitting on the paper, that he hadn't already taken it to Winter. He looked up the ID via his earbud and read it out to AJ.

"Delete that from your cache when you're done. Now do your damn job," he said to AJ. "He's paying you to protect him, isn't he? So protect him."

It was a Remote Destruct ID. The privilege of only the rich and powerful, it meant the owner could send a signal back down a comms connection to autodelete all the data in a caller's device and brick it, if they felt like it. It was meant as a defense against unauthorized callers, stalking or harassment, but the Remote Destruct ID prefix was also a potent deterrent against any unsolicited call.

AJ set his comms earpiece to broadcast over the workshop sound system, and felt like he was about to start the timer on a bomb. Leon nodded, and he eye-tapped the ID in and hit connect. He expected it to be answered by some aide or AI, so when it picked up and he recognized the voice as the one belonging to the man who'd called on Warnecke at Sol Vista a week ago, he kind of froze up.

"Hello, who is this?" The guy took it on audio only, so maybe he was in a private meeting.

AJ suddenly forgot what he was going to say. Except, of course, he didn't – a cyber didn't freeze – but the range of options backed up behind his speech restraint like logs jammed on a river and he couldn't pick one out before the Congressman was speaking again.

"Look, I don't usually take calls from IDs I don't recognize, so you better speak up unless you want your device bricked," Winter said.

"Uh, hello, Congressman Winter," AJ said. "You don't know me but I…"

"Well, we already established that, son," Winter said, being patient with it. "But someone gave you this ID. And you had the balls to call it. So you got five seconds to get to how I can help you."

"Ok, sorry. I'm calling from the Sol Vista Community for the Memory Impaired," AJ said.

"Sol Vista … has something happened to Dave?" Winter asked. He didn't sound scared or worried, but he did sound curious. AJ figured he might have a million reasons to be.

"No, he's … the same," AJ said. "This is more of a personal call. I'm just the maintenance tech at Sol Vista."

"OK," Winter said, and AJ could hear muffled talk in the background, like someone else was talking to Winter at the same time.

"We met, actually, when you were down last week visiting. My name is AJ."

"The cyber, right? Of course, I remember. Look, AJ, does Dave need anything? I mean, I'm not family, but if I can do anything, you just let me know." He sounded like he was in a hurry.

"I think he plans to kill himself," AJ said. He and Leon had agreed this was the best angle, play it like AJ was worried about Warnecke, that's all. Let the business with the doomsday page come up later.

"My God," Winter said. "Shut the hell up, will you?"

"Sorry?" AJ said.

"No, not you, son," Winter said. "I'm in a car with some people, I just asked them to pipe down. He's threatened to kill himself, you say?"

"Yes sir," AJ said. "He has a gun, he's told me he'll use it."

There was silence at the other end, then Winter asked, "Have you gone to the police with this?"

"No sir, he asked me to contact you, so I called you straight away."

"Good, good. You did the right thing. And his family?"

"Not yet," AJ said. "He didn't ask me to contact them."

"He wouldn't," Winter said, sounding bitter. "Look, let's keep them out of it. Police too. This isn't the first time he's been like this."

"No? OK." That news didn't surprise AJ.

"What about your management there, have you reported this officially?"

"I thought I'd call you first, sir," AJ lied again. "It seemed kind of personal."

Winter laughed a dry laugh. "Personal. You could say. Look, you did the right thing. Can we keep this between us for now? Let me think how to handle it. I think I need to talk to him."

"Yes sir," AJ said, getting his next words lined up. "But before you call him…"

"Yes, I'll call him, but first I'll see if we can't get the guy some extra help organized. No offense to whatever AI capacity you have there at Sunny Vales. Then I'll call him…"

AJ interrupted. "No sir. *Before* you call him. The reason I think this is something personal between you and him…"

There was a stiff silence at the other end of the comms.

"… he gave me this printed document, or an extract from it. It's some kind of conspiracy theory. He said to tell you he's kept multiple copies off-Core and he wants that I should deliver it to you. In person. He doesn't want it on-Core."

"This document, you've read it?" Winter asked.

"Yes sir. It's something about a cover-up from 70 years ago, and it claims he pulled it from the Deep Core – but that's impossible, isn't it?"

"Son, the Core protects its data as fiercely as a mother protects her children," Winter said. "It updates its defenses hundreds of times a second, disperses the data across billions of data sets and encrypts each with discrete, randomly mutating quantum keys. Even if a hacker managed a Deep Core dive, there would be no way to reassemble the data they found into anything like its coherent form. In two hundred years it has never been hacked, not once. If it could be, our entire civilization would be at risk, so yes, it's impossible."

AJ sighed with relief. "That's what I thought. So Citizen Warnecke is just delusional?"

"That would be my layman diagnosis. Hold there, will you?" Winter asked. There was some muffled discussion, then he came back. "AJ was it? How close are you to a drone port, AJ?" His voice was cool, but he kept it polite. AJ didn't always get that from citizens. Maybe politicians were different somehow – he'd never interacted with one.

"I have South Coast City Transcontinental about thirty minutes away," AJ told him.

"And how soon could you get on a drone to the Capitol?"

"Well, it's the weekend tomorrow, so I guess I could take off work on Monday..."

"You got some religious thing, you can't fly on Saturdays?" Winter asked.

"No sir."

"Good. AJ, I'd consider it a great personal favor if you would come over here tomorrow with that document. I'll fix the flight for you and send the details to your earbud. Would you do that for me?"

AJ looked at Leon, who was listening in. Leon wrote on a note: *See how bad he wants you there.*

AJ stalled. "I don't know, sir, it's kind of inconvenient..."

"A *big* personal favor, AJ. I am a man who remembers such things," Winter said. "So I'll send you details of the flight, you just have to get yourself to that drone port. I'll organize a car and a return flight for you here, have you home again sometime Saturday night AJ, how's that?"

Leon gave him a thumbs up. "That would be OK, I guess," AJ said, thinking *what*? What am I doing?

"Or hey, where are my manners?" Winter said, suddenly laying it on. "You ever been here before, AJ?"

"Never been to the Capitol, sir," AJ said, truthfully.

"Then how about this, I'll see you Saturday when you get in. We can meet at my office and then I'll get one of my people to show you a few of the sights. Put you up at a nice hotel here, you can have a night in the Capitol, go back home Sunday. Give me time to work out what we're going do about Dave that way too."

AJ looked at Leon, who was nodding. "That sounds cool, sir," he said.

"You call me Kevin," Winter said. "Let's keep things personal. I look forward to seeing you here tomorrow, AJ." And he cut the line.

7. BETTER THE LEON YOU KNOW

AJ sat just looking at Leon.

"Damn. This is some heavy-duty guano, mano," Leon said.

"I told you," AJ said.

"Serious, military-grade messed up – did you hear the guy?"

"I know."

"You mention that document, he just about pops a cog, wants you on the first drone to the Capitol."

"I know."

"Oh, but he's going to give you a personal tour guide, show you around."

"I'm not going."

"Nice little intern maybe, take you to dinner, you play it right, lay on that surfer boy charm, maybe she get you naked, rub some oil into your tanned South Coast City ass..." Leon said, warming up, then realized what AJ had said. "What you talking about?"

"I had in my head that he would come *here*," AJ said. "He and Warnecke would have a meet, sort out their business. Nothing to do with me."

"But he ain't coming here, is he?" Leon told him. "And he doesn't want you to send him that document over the Core either, which is interesting. I'm guessing he wants to look you in the eye, wants you on his turf where he can work this the way he wants it, not the way our man Warnecke wants it."

"Cool. But I am not getting on a drone to the Capitol on my own tomorrow."

Leon narrowed his eyes. "Oh, that's it."

"What?"

"You're afraid of getting in the big metal flying machine?"

"No."

"You're afraid of flying alone? Need Leon with you maybe, to hold your hand?"

"No, forget that. But me going across the Icecap to the Capitol to meet up with a Congressman about the conspiracy theories of some crazy guy with a gun, that isn't happening."

"Oh yeah. You *are* worried about it. And you should be," Leon said, leaning forward. "We don't know how messed up this all is. You heard that guy? *'Give me time to work out what we're going to do about Dave?'* He's considering his options, that Congressman, and you can bet it isn't Warnecke's health and welfare is going to be driving his decisions."

"I got that feeling too."

"And right now, you are *nothing* to this guy. You're prey, running from a sudden noise, but you're probably running straight toward a hunter hiding in a blind."

AJ looked at him. "Thanks for that, Leon."

"But mano, you ain't *alone*, I keep telling you that, but you keep not hearing it."

"Thanks Leon, but I don't see how that helps right now."

"OK, well. You'll see tomorrow, when you see my fat ass sitting up back in the same drone as you, making out I don't know you."

Later that evening, AJ got a message telling him there would be a ticket waiting for him at the Intercontinental Drones ticket office for an 0800 flight to the Capitol, and a return booked for the following evening that would get him back to South Coast City before midnight. A concierge would meet him at arrivals and get him transport to the Congressman's office. He should pack a heavy-duty thermal; the Capitol was colder this time of year than South Coast City, even inside its dome. He sent the flight details on to Leon.

"Wow, when you move on something, you move," Cassie said when AJ called her, whistling. "You just called up the Congressman, got yourself a flight to the Capitol. Just like that?"

"Not quite how it went, but yeah."

"So what's the plan?"

"I go over there, give him the document from Warnecke and ask him to keep me right out of it. I come back home, I tell Warnecke I did what he asked, tell him I'm not working for Winter anymore and I expect him to leave me alone too. Make some deal with Cyan that Leon can cover any jobs Warnecke needs done, so I hardly need to see him ever. The fact he complained about me, that should be a good enough reason for Cyan."

"I get the idea you want to be left alone," Cassie said playfully.

"Yeah, not by everyone. Just by them," AJ replied.

Cassie told him she had used her media archive access at the broadcast station to look up the names in Warnecke's document. The scientists whose flight to Orkutsk had supposedly been sabotaged.

"It's real," she said. "I found a news report from 73 years ago. The ship was called *The Reliant*, and it detonated on impact with space debris between Tatsensui and Orkutsk. Two hundred twenty lives lost, including our scientists."

"So, he used a random event to make his conspiracy look legitimate," AJ said.

"They were all medical researchers," Cassie pointed out. "Radiologists. Just like he said."

"He built the story to fit the facts," AJ insisted. "Making it plausible."

"I tried to find their earlier research," she continued. "Publications, academic transcripts. There's basically nothing in the archives for the two years leading up to the crash."

AJ wasn't giving up. "Glitch. Or coincidence."

"Uh huh," she said, clearly not convinced. "I also wanted to see how Congressman Kevin Winter was linked to Citizen Dave Warnecke. Luckily the Congressman's employment and educational history is public information.

"Both studied at college together. Winter did a bachelor in theoretical quantum mechanics and then a PhD in quantum programming. I looked up Warnecke's school record too. He was studying quantum programming with Winter but changed track to become an engineer instead."

"Quantum programming to mechanical engineer. From coding AIs to racing planers, that's quite a career change."

"Dropped out right before his doctoral defense," she said. "Do all that work and then walk away from it? I'd like to know why."

AJ wasn't sure he wanted to show that much interest in Warnecke. "His claim about Blue not working in everyone? Any link to Winter in there? Like he was a Health Secretary or something before he took over National Security?"

"Zero that I could see. He was on a few finance committees, Secretary for Inland Territory Relations, Secretary for Commonwealth Relations, and now National Security. If there's a link to this alleged cover-up, I can't see it. So maybe it's nothing and your friend Warnecke is just a paranoid old man all het up about nothing."

"Or Winter has his secrets buried where your press credentials don't reach."

"My credentials go deep, baby," she bragged. "But it's possible. So when are you back?"

"Sunday, midnight?"

"Want to meet up?"

"Midnight Sunday?" he asked. "You serious? Don't you *ever* sleep?"

"I'll pick you up at the drone port," she said. "You can tell me everything. You'll still get your beauty sleep, I promise."

He smiled. "You'll pick me up. You bringing a car out or we going to skate home?"

"So funny."

Leon had never told AJ what he did in the military, and AJ had never asked. He figured the guy's service was his private business and if he didn't want to talk about it, well, that made perfect sense to AJ, considering what AJ had heard about the war on New Syberia. Guy had issues from his service in the NS war, that was a fact. The problem he shared most with AJ was he couldn't sleep, that was the worst. Whole nights he'd go without an hour of sleep, just lying there thinking, worrying. Only way to break the cycle was to take mega tranqs to knock himself out, but he didn't like doing that too often because you could get tolerant and eventually couldn't sleep at all, even if you used them. It would be OK if he could catch up on the sleep, like sneak a few hours during the day, but it didn't work that way. He just couldn't sleep, finito. He'd made a deal with Cyan and his rehab officer that he'd get some help from a psych AI, and meanwhile, Sol Vista would only pay him for the hours he actually worked. So AJ covered for him, including the times he was at work, but not really capable.

But the way Leon talked as they planned the Capitol trip, AJ got the idea Leon had been some kind of spook, or he'd worked with them.

"I'm just going to be your shadow," Leon said. "Way it works, you don't know me, you don't recognize me, don't even look at me, OK? But I'll be there for you wherever you go, so you can feel safe."

"I'm just going there to talk, Leon," AJ said.

"That's what *you* think you're doing," Leon told him. "But you don't know what they're thinking. I'm going to paint a scenario for you, OK, and I don't want you to freak out."

"OK."

"Surfer dude, you so laid back, you thinking this is all going to work out and yeah, probably it will. But there's a scenario goes like this: this Congressman is sitting there in the Capitol right now, wetting his blue suit pants. What's in that document, and he doesn't know yet exactly what's in there, but say it's bad. It could kill his career, wreck his life. You? You are nobody. *Nobody*, mano, you got to understand that.

122

You are a zero to him. Right now, he's got someone running your background. You told him all he needs to know – your name is AJ, you're a cyber, you work at Sol Vista. He's got people can run your ID, get your financial records, credit history, comms data, they see your whole life story inside an hour. What's he going to see?"

"I don't know. Nothing."

"Exactly. No offense, my man, but you really are nobody. You been living the happy, carefree life until now. Normal high school, good college grades, no problems, no serious connections either. Surfing, working. No partner, no dependents. You still got family?"

"Yeah, my Ma is about seventy," AJ said. "No brothers or sisters."

"So she's an old lady, probably also a nobody. Yeah, don't look so angry, I said it. She somebody to you, but to them she is nothing. They look at you, they see a guy could disappear tomorrow and all his friends be like, couple weeks from now, '*Hey, anyone seen AJ lately? Can you believe the guy just left town without saying goodbye?*' You know anyone else would call the police, make a fuss about you?"

AJ thought about that. It hurt a bit, what Leon was saying. Wouldn't anyone call the cops if he went missing? Apart from his Ma? He thought about Henni. She'd been with him two years, but then she decided she wanted children and AJ couldn't help with that, and she didn't want to adopt, so it was over. It was six months since he spoke with her last. There was Cyan, boss and friend, but mostly boss. Then there was Cassie. A girl he'd had two dates with? "I guess not," he said. "Which sucks."

Leon punched his shoulder. "Cheer up. That's the way it is for people like you. You living the free life, just doing your job, no one to cramp your style, but the price you pay is nobody except Leon and Cyan going to miss you if you don't come back from the Capitol."

"Don't come back?"

"Yeah man. The scenario I'm painting, you go to the Capitol, you hand over that document, the Congressman reads it and sees it's poison. He's got a Core-tap on you, knows exactly where you are…"

"I'm a cyber, Leon," AJ reminded him. "You can keep a Core-tap secret from a citizen, not from a cyber." Tapping the data flow between an individual and the Core as a way of tracking their movements was as old as time, but where a citizen might go around oblivious they had a tap on them, a cyber could see the hitch-hiker on their drift status. It was one of the defenses the Core gave its cyber agents, and thus itself.

"OK, yeah, so he's using good old-fashioned physical surveillance – drones, foot soldiers. You have a nice chat, maybe he says hey, how about we give you a lift to your hotel. A car pulls up and you jump in. Last thing you see is the inside of a car, you're wondering hey, why is there a groundsheet on the floor of this limo, happy tourist smile on your face fading as you die. Then I come to work Monday, Cyan says to me, 'Hey Leon, have you seen AJ? He didn't show for work today'."

Leon let the silence draw out. Let AJ think about that.

"Remind me why the hell I am going to the Capitol, then? Tell me why I'm not just going to the cops and saying, hey, there's some messed-up business going on with Warnecke and this Congressman and the old guy has got a gun – you guys sort it out."

Leon laughed and gave AJ a patient look. "Sure. You let me play the cop, OK?"

"What?"

"Look, I'm the cop, and you just came to me with your story, OK, so I say, 'OK sir, let me understand this. This old guy at Sol Vista showed you his gun and said he would kill himself if you didn't give this document to the Congressman?'"

"Yeah, that's it."

"OK. But he didn't threaten you?"

"No, not directly. He said I didn't get to decide anything, I should do what he said."

"OK, let me just check something." Leon makes out he's accessing the Core. "Citizen David Warnecke, you say, House 96, Sol Vista ... yes, I can see he has a permit for a handgun. So it's a legal weapon. And he didn't threaten you with it, he just showed it to you?"

"I guess."

"Sir, I'm not seeing any crime here," Leon said. "Perhaps you should speak with a psych AI about his suicide threat?"

AJ got that cornered feeling again.

"You see what I'm saying," Leon said.

"I guess. So, forget this. I don't go to the cops, but I don't go to the Capitol either. I just ignore Warnecke. So he kills himself, his manuscript goes to a lawyer or something, the Congressman gets the heat, or maybe nothing happens at all. What do I care, if it really is like you say – it's me or Warnecke."

"Yeah, I know that isn't my man AJ talking there, but you under pressure," Leon sighed. "You like your job?"

"Yeah, you know it."

"What if he *don't* kill himself? Most people talk big, but they never go through with it. You don't help Warnecke, so you're no use to him, he's got a grudge now. Next thing you know, Cyan is in your face with the cops because Warnecke said you assaulted him. Even if you don't get charged, you know that means you're out of here, no matter how much the boss lady likes you. She got a business to run and it don't run smooth if the people hear the staff are beating up on the residents."

"OK. So I find another job. That's a bit better than getting whacked in a limo in the Capitol."

"Getting whacked? You heard that in some vintage gangster show?"

"Killed, assassinated, whatever. I'll miss you, Leon, but there's plenty of other jobs."

"And they'll leave you alone, Warnecke, the Congressman?"

"Why not? I'm gone."

"You read the document."

"It could be nothing," AJ said. "You read it too. It's just an allegation about some crazy science and a ship that crashed."

"The part you saw. Congressman Winter, he knows you haven't seen the whole manuscript?"

"I'll tell him."

"Yeah, and he can choose to believe you. Or he can choose for you to disappear, along with Warnecke, and his manuscript. What's the safest option, for him?"

"Damn it. You got a sick mind, Leon, the way you look at this stuff."

Leon tapped his forehead. "I got an *educated* mind, mano. I learned this stuff so well, I used to teach it. It's why I don't sleep so good."

***

AJ didn't even see Leon at the drone port. He'd offered to meet him there, pay his flight, but Leon had told him don't worry, he'd get in touch with him once they'd reached the Capitol. He told AJ the best way to stay in contact was via an encrypted app for his earbud. He pulled it down from an off-Core site and taught him how to use it to call him.

"I'm betting they won't go through official channels for something like this," Leon said. "They'll keep this low key, off the books. Probably use private assets, not government. So this little encrypter should be fine. You use it with your earbud, talk to me that way, they have to be in physical range to hear your side of the conversation, that's all they can do."

"What does the encrypter do?"

"Encrypts the call, in transit, with end to end quantum paired keys," Leon said.

"Like I know what that means," AJ said.

"It means it uses entangled particles to encrypt the call. No AI on this frozen rock can listen in on the call; it can't even see *who* you are calling. All it could possibly see is that you're using encryption, which will tell it you're being careful. That's not necessarily a bad thing either."

"OK."

"Also, it works like a tracker. I can track your earbud with it, so keep it on you."

"Will do."

"I made an ID in there for you to call me," he said, smiling. "It's called 'Hermano'."

AJ was beginning to think Leon hadn't even made the flight; after all, it was boarding 0600. But after he took his seat and was settling in, he saw Leon walking down the aisle toward him carrying a small backpack, dressed in dark trousers and a blue shirt. He didn't even look at AJ, just walked past him, down the back, and took his seat. It was a four-hour flight, so he had to go to the john a couple times, and the first time he went past he saw Leon was reading a book, didn't look up. The second time Leon had his cap on, pulled down over his eyes like he was sleeping, or trying to.

It was middle of the afternoon local time when they got into Capitol State Drone Port. AJ was walking down the concourse after he got off the drone, trying to see where the exit was, when he felt his earbud buzzing. He put it in and tapped his ear, and saw the call was coming in via the app Leon had installed. His earbud stopped buzzing. He hit the app to call Leon back. As he did so, he saw Leon walking past him and saw him talking at the same time as he heard him on the comms. Leon just kept walking, following the crowd to the exit.

"OK, so you're just behind me now," Leon said. "You're going to lose me when you get picked up by the car the Congressman sends, so let's hope you don't get 'whacked' on the way in to the Capitol."

"Ha ha," AJ said. "Yeah, let's." There was a short lag after Leon spoke, but otherwise it was like a normal comms call.

"I'll be behind in a car. Might catch up to you, but I doubt it. Once you're in your limo, ask the AI where you're going. Wait a while. Then call me, tell me where. You ask the AI to stop so you can get a drink somewhere or take a leak, so I can get ahead of you, OK?"

"OK."

"You call me Ma anytime we talk on the comms, OK? In case someone is nearby listening."

"OK Ma. Why?"

"So you don't call me Leon. You good?"

"Yeah. Hey, you sound like you got a bad cold, Ma," AJ said, pulling on his pack and heading toward the exit again.

"Keep jokin'," Leon said. "Devil likes people can make him laugh." He hung up.

AJ saw Leon go through the door to arrivals and then head for the car queue. He was scanning the chauffeur line when he saw a guy in a dark suit hold up his hand and show him his name on a sign.

"Hey there, sir," the guy said. He was an old guy, looked pale like most Capitol Staters. Had that long-short haircut they all liked over here. "You're AJ?"

"That's me."

"Good, just making sure. Take your bag?"

"No, that's OK," AJ said.

"OK, well, just follow me," the guy said. "I'm Ernesto."

He followed the guy into the limo area at the parking garage to a silver Town Car. The man popped the door, waiting with his hand out to hold AJ's pack.

"That's OK, I got it," AJ said.

"No problem," the guy said, helping AJ inside. AJ wasn't used to having a whole car to himself. The middle seat partition on the back seat was folded down, and there were two bottles of water in the bottle holder, some snacks and a box of tissues.

"So, downtown Capitol, sir, that right?"

"Congressman Winter's office, yeah, if that's downtown Capitol," AJ said.

"That's what I got on my running sheet," the guy said. "Any changes en route, just tell it to the AI."

"OK."

"Be 45 minutes to an hour, depending on traffic," the guy said. "Water and food there if you want it. Just took it out of the storage in back. It warm enough?"

AJ lifted a bottle and felt it. "It's fine, thanks."

"Okay then," the guy said and closed the door.

AJ had seen limos on VR. Some of them had minibars stocked with drinks. He looked around but couldn't see one. Maybe that was just the luxury limos. As they pulled onto the freeway, he sat back. "Do the Congressmen and women drive in these?" he said out loud.

"Which Congressmen and women, sir?" the car AI asked.

"Capitol politicians," AJ said. "Any of them."

"Oh, not usually, sir," the AI said. "The government has its own fleet; usually they use those."

"So this car is private?"

"Yes, sir," the AI said. "It's pre-paid, in case you're worried about the cost of hiring a private car?"

"Good to know, thanks."

"Your return trip is paid for too," the AI said. "Just call us and give us your name, we'll pick you up." An advertisement came up on the screen set into the door beside him.

AJ looked at it. "A1 Car Service."

"Yes sir. We guarantee pickup within fifteen minutes of your call."

"Okay, thanks." The idea they'd booked a return trip for him was reassuring. Then he thought about what Leon would say about that. 'Mano, they *want* you to be relaxed, right up until you disappear.'

"No problem. Would you like to chat, sir, or would you like some peace and quiet?"

"Huh? No, I'll speak up if I need anything."

"You do that, sir."

AJ watched traffic. He relaxed a bit and took a sip of water. After about ten minutes, he tapped his earbud and called Leon.

"Hey Ma, I'm in the car," he said.

"You on the freeway?"

"Yeah, I guess. We've been driving about fifteen minutes."

"I'm a ways behind you. In about ten minutes, ask him to pull off so you can take a whizz. And where you going, you worked that out yet?"

AJ put his hand over his earbud and said out loud, "Excuse me, driver, where are you dropping me? I just want to be sure it's the right address."

A map came up on the screen. "Independence Avenue, Hyburne House," the AI said. "Does that sound right, sir?"

"Yeah, thanks," AJ said. "Independence Avenue, Hyburne House, Ma," he told Leon.

"OK, that's where his office is, I looked it up," Leon said. "Got a view of the Capitol Congress probably. You just slow it down, I'll be there when you get there. And AJ?"

"Yeah Ma?"

"Stop saying Ma at the end of every sentence, OK?"

"OK."

AJ asked the AI to find him a men's room somewhere and so they took an off-ramp and he used the washroom at a recharge station and then went inside and bought himself a drink before coming back out.

"What time is your appointment?" the AI asked, sounding a little worried. AJ figured he had just added about a quarter of an hour to the trip.

"When I get there," AJ said. "No fixed time."

"OK then. You good to go, sir?"

"All good," AJ said, settling back in.

After a while AJ recognized he was on Penn Avenue and saw the Congress building approaching up on their left. A huge white building that, if you saw it from above, was shaped like the Icecap colony it ruled over. As they came onto Independence Avenue, the AI flashed the map again. "Hyburne House coming up on the right, sir. You want me to just drop you on the curb? I can pull in right out front."

"That's fine," AJ said.

Like Leon had said, the building was right opposite the south wing of the Congress building. It had two big statues out front flanking wide staircases leading up to an entrance through six columns. After he climbed out of the limo AJ looked around him, trying to see Leon, but all he saw were tourists, some cops, and a lot of traffic.

His comms buzzed. "Stop looking for me. I'm here," Leon said.

"I'm just admiring the sights, Ma," AJ said. "Never been in the Capitol before."

"You go in, have your meeting. When you come out, call me, I'll follow you." He sounded serious now. "AJ?"

"Yeah?"

"The way I'd play this if I was serious, I wouldn't just have electronic surveillance on you. If they planning to grab you or worse, that requires feet on the ground, citizen or cyber. If I tell you to *run*, mano, you run for your damn life, okay?"

"OK." AJ thought about Leon's comment that the last thing he'd see would be a groundsheet inside a limo. "What if they get me in a car?"

"I'll follow. I got my own wheels now."

"I thought you'd be in a shared car? How did you get a private car?"

"Think you the only guy with contacts in the Capitol, mano? Now get in there. Good luck."

AJ walked up the winding stairs and quickly realized he wasn't getting in that way before the guard on the door told him as much. The guy pointed at a sign saying 'Visitor Entrance, South Capitol St.' and AJ followed it around the corner to an entrance with people coming and going and a reception desk.

"Help you, sir?" another guard asked him as he walked up.

"I have an appointment with Congressman Winter," AJ said, expecting the guy to say, "Sure you have."

But the guard picked up a stylus, asked for his name, wrote it down then touched his earbud and called a number, spoke a couple words, and then hung up.

"Someone will be down in a minute. You can wait over there," the guard said, pointing at some benches.

AJ sat himself down and about ten minutes later a young man in a smart blue shirt, pressed trousers and shiny shoes walked toward him. He had his eyeliner thick, just on his lower lids. It made him look sleepy.

"AJ?" he asked.

"Good guess," AJ said, looking around him. He wasn't the only one sitting there.

"You're the only guy here with a tan," the man said, smiling. "I was told you're from South Coast City." He tapped a spot between his eyebrows. "Plus, you know, this. Anyway, let's get you signed in. I'm William."

Formalities done, he followed the guy to an elevator. "Sorry to keep you waiting, but it was lucky I was in this part of the building when I got the call to come pick you up or it would have been even longer," William said. "This building is a nightmare. Can take twenty minutes to get from one side to the other. You been here before?"

"First time in the Capitol," AJ said.

"Cool. After me." William stepped into the elevator and AJ followed as he asked for the second floor. "The AI they commissioned to design this place was an attempt to see if AIs could be creative with architecture," he said. He blew some hair out of his eyes. He had dark brown eyes, a kind round face, was chubby in an office worker kind of way and smiled like he meant it. AJ guessed he was about 25. "Which we all know now, they can't. No offense," he said, without feeling. "So it's made in an H-shape, as in H for Hyburne. Super creative, right? Except if you are up in the top of the H, to get to the other side of the H you have to go down, left, left, then right. If they just made it a square, the distance would be about two hundred yards. This way, it's three times that. And the place is full of dead ends. Drives you crazy." He gave AJ one of his smiles. "Don't worry if you haven't been caching, I'll show you out again."

He took AJ along an anonymous corridor, a couple turns, then arrived at an office with a nice couch in the reception area and an empty desk. "Mary usually sits there, but not on weekends," William said. "There's only a couple of us in today." He pointed to a coffee pot on a stand next to a potted plant. "But there's hot coffee if you want?"

"Thanks, maybe later," AJ said.

"Congressman Winter is with someone," William explained. "Maybe another quarter of an hour, I'm guessing." He looked around the office. "Usually this is where I would say, ask Mary if you need anything, but…"

"Washrooms?" AJ asked. "In case I need to go?"

William laughed. "I'd tell you, but if the Congressman comes in and finds his guest isn't here, he gets shirty. And takes it out on me. So if you don't mind, I recommend you try to hold it. I'll show you on the way out. Unless you're desperate?"

"I'll manage," AJ said.

"OK, good. See you later, then," William said, and disappeared back into the maze.

AJ thought about calling Leon, then realized that would be dumb. What did he have to tell him? He looked around the office, saw pictures he recognized as Winter, meeting various other people he vaguely recognized. Relying on his biological memory was an advantage in conserving bandwidth, but he had always sucked at faces. One he did recognize was the current President, another was the last President. OK, another was the President before that. Seemed Winter had been in politics a while and wanted his guests to know it. AJ was stumped by the others so he quickly drifted to look them up, and checked his messages while he was at it. There was one from Cassie, early morning: *I'm watching a damn surf movie*, it said. *Why am I watching a surf movie, AJ?*

He was still smiling at the thought of that when the door to the inner office opened and Winter walked out. So there must be another door his guests would leave through. That would make sense, AJ figured, because he wouldn't want people knowing who he had just met with.

"AJ? Sorry, of course it is, I recognize you now," the man said. He was as big as AJ remembered, nearly as wide as he was high, and he was dabbing his brow with a kerchief as he shook AJ's hand. "Damn heating in this place," he said. "I got two vents in my office, one blows hot, the other blows cold. Maybe they're supposed to even each other out. Except they don't."

"Nice to meet you again, Congressman," AJ said.

"Just Kevin, please," he replied. AJ didn't miss the gesture. Citizens usually made a point of expecting a cyber to keep referring to them by their title until they knew them well enough.

Winter waved toward the door and AJ went through, then stopped. There was another guy already sitting there, and he stood up slowly as the Congressman walked in behind AJ.

8. CONVERSATION WITH A CONGRESSMAN

The other guy was not overweight. Unless it was because muscle weighs more than fat. He looked like a bodyguard.

"This is Citizen Troy McMaster," Winter said, going around to sit in an armchair in front of his desk and pointing to a sofa where AJ could sit. "He's like an executive assistant."

Like an executive assistant, AJ thought to himself. And a sniper is 'like' a sports shooter? He held out his hand. "Citizen McMaster, I'm AJ."

The guy shook his hand, rather softly. AJ was expecting a manly crush. "Pleased to meet you," he said in a pronounced Capitol accent.

"You want coffee, or water?" Winter asked, pointing to a pot on the table in front of AJ. "Help yourself."

"I'm good, thanks."

"I told Citizen McMaster about my friend Dave," Winter said. "I want to thank you again for giving up your weekend to come here. I thought we should talk about it as soon as we could, so I can decide how to help him."

"That's OK," AJ said. "He made it sound pretty urgent."

Winter waved a hand in the air. "Oh, he loves a bit of drama, I'm sure you've realized that already?"

"You could say," AJ agreed.

"Threatened to kill himself, you said?"

"Yes, Congressman."

"It's Kevin, remember," Winter said. "How did that happen?"

AJ told him exactly how it happened. He and Leon had agreed he should stick to the whole truth, including Warnecke's paranoia that AJ was working for Winter and keeping an eye on him. Told him about Warnecke's 'confession', getting angry about Winter's visit, sliding the document under his door, showing him the gun, threatening to kill himself and go public about something that turned out to be a sort of conspiracy theory. They'd been listening with interest through the whole story, but both of them leaned forward in their chairs when AJ mentioned the manuscript.

"But you've been working there what, five years? He thinks I put people in every old age care home in the State just in case he was going to check in?" Winter asked.

"People in his condition don't usually operate with that kind of logic, sir," AJ said. Then he realized, he hadn't told Winter how long he'd been working at Sol Vista. His skin went cold. So the guy *had* checked up on him. Just like Leon said. And maybe he wasn't an idiot, he'd slipped that into the conversation on purpose, to let AJ know what he knew.

"It's terribly sad, his condition," Winter said, shaking his head. "Worse than I thought. I mean, he seemed OK when I visited. I asked him why he'd checked into a place like that, no offense of course."

"None taken," AJ said. "But he is a resident, so I shouldn't talk about his medical condition."

"Course not, course not," Winter said.

"You have the document with you?" the McMaster guy asked. It was the first time he had said more than hello, but he'd been following with interest.

138

"Sure," AJ said. He pulled the bag with the rolled page out of his backpack and held it out, not sure if Winter or McMaster would take it. Winter tried to look like he wasn't that interested, leaning back and letting his guard dog take it. "He seemed to think it was important you saw this, so you could 'get ahead of it', is what he said."

McMaster scrolled through it. AJ knew it was about two pages long, and it took him no time to scan it. Got to the end, then handed it over to Winter.

"That was all of it?" McMaster asked.

"All he gave me, yeah," AJ said. "It seems like there is more, but I haven't seen it."

"He say anything else?" the guy asked.

AJ thought back. "He said he had off-Core copies. He accused me of working for the Congressman and said I should tell you he had copies and if Congressman Winter didn't call a press conference and quote get ahead of it unquote, he'd kill himself and it would all be public anyway."

Winter was reading the page a lot more intently than McMaster had. Every word on every line.

"So you haven't seen the whole document?"

"No sir."

"And that chapter is all he put under the door of your workshop?" the man asked again.

"Yeah."

Winter finished reading and put the page behind him, on his desk. He didn't ask AJ if he could keep it, that seemed to be assumed.

"You read that extract," the Congressman said. It wasn't a question. "What did you think?"

"Well, it's some kind of conspiracy theory," AJ said, "a cover-up. And he makes it seem like he pulled it from the Deep Core, which…"

Winter smiled. "Is impossible."

"Right." AJ shrugged. "What is the FO Exploit?"

"Sorry?" Winter asked.

"FO Exploit," AJ repeated. "The document finishes by saying, '*This data was retrieved from the Deep Core by use of the FO Exploit*.'"

Winter looked at McMaster. The guy nodded slightly.

"I'm prepared to share a story with you, but you must agree to treat it as confidential," Winter said.

"Sure."

Winter nodded at McMaster, who lifted a slate off the coffee table and handed it to AJ. "Confidentiality agreement," he said, showing AJ where to wipe for his DNA. "You can read it, but I can tell you it says if you share anything you hear in this room outside these walls, we can cut your nuts off and force feed them back to you." Then he smiled, in a way AJ took to mean he was only half joking.

AJ wiped his thumb across the signature field and handed it back.

"There was a terrible tragedy," Winter said. "Happened forty years ago, when we were in college together. Me, Dave and our friend Farley O'Halloran, we went on a rafting trip together. It was a disaster, we were totally unprepared, none of us had been meltwater rafting before."

AJ looked at him, staying quiet.

"We were friends at college, the three of us doing our doctoral theses in advanced quantum programming. We'd get together, drink and do drugs, solve mysteries of the universe and come up with ideas that AIs couldn't even dream of. Farley had just been recruited into the

140

military to work on AI Offense. We all had our areas of specialization. His was a little more specialized than most – how to use an AI to attack an AI.

"Anyway, we decided on the spur of the moment to do this rafting trip." Winter smoothed a crease on his pants. "Crazy remote river up near Whitehorse, polar cap. Raft overturned in a rapid about halfway down the river, we lost most of our food, still had a week left on the water. We argued about whether it was better to push on, or try to walk out. Dave and me wanted to push on, Farley wanted to walk out to a survival hut about a day away and try to bounce a signal off the Skycap, call for help." The Congressman took a breath. "I need to go back a little. We'd been arguing a lot around the campfire, like Q-programmers do. Q-programming is more like philosophy than science, so discussions get a bit heated. One night, Farley was using some kind of mood accelerant, I forget what, he started talking crazy." Winter nodded at the page AJ had given him. "He said he'd found a way to use the Core to attack the Core. To hack the Deep Core by tricking the Core itself into doing the diving. We laughed at him. Dave Warnecke nicknamed his idea the FO Exploit. Short for Farley O'Halloran, short for Freaking Out-to-lunch. Dave kept coming up with new acronyms starting with FO that all meant 'dumb-ass'. By the time we had the spill and lost our food we were hardly speaking to each other and he insisted on walking out. So we put him ashore, agreed to wait two days, see if he could get out and get help. After two days and no sign of him, our food gone, we pushed on to the end of the river, got rescued. No sign of Farley."

Winter was looking at AJ like he expected some reaction, but AJ just waited. He could drift later for any public details that might back the story up. Winter looked at the page Warnecke had written, then back to AJ. "I stayed searching for Farley with Dave Warnecke and the police until they said there was no point staying longer, and we went home. They declared him missing, presumed dead. His parents had been off-world, and when they came back, they put out a reward, paid for a private search party to go back over the same ground the police had covered. I can only imagine how his parents felt." Winter looked at McMaster. "I never met them. They wouldn't talk to me. I tried a couple of times to contact them, then gave up. They never held a funeral for him, refused to accept he was dead. They passed away a few years back, maybe ten, still hoping he'd turn up one day."

"Wow," AJ said. "That's sad."

Winter gave a tight smile. "We stayed in touch over the years, but I know Dave blamed *me* for us not waiting for Farley. He always felt it was possible Farley had made it back to the river, but we were gone. Maybe he drowned, maybe grizzlies got him. He convinced himself if we'd just waited a couple more days, we'd have been there when Farley got back. He blamed himself too, felt bad about giving Farley such a hard time, which I guess is why he hung onto Farley's idea, not letting it go. I heard he got the family to give him access to Farley's cache and the code he'd been working on privately. Now it seems he's trying to claim he's made it work." He looked at McMaster again. "This…" Winter said, pointing at the page again, "… is just coincidence and speculation pulled into a narrative, and not even very original. People over the years have blamed LPA-2 for everything from mind control to infertility. TGA? Why not? Anyway, he called me, asking me to back him when he started releasing all these dark secrets he'd found in the Deep Core, claiming he could prove it to me, then getting angry when I wouldn't listen." He sighed. "He tried to talk to me about it when I visited him last time, but I had a pretty good idea what it was about and I admit I wasn't minded to indulge him. Farley's idea was dumb forty years ago, it's still dumb now, and there's no way a guy like Dave, working on his own, could have pulled off what entire battalions of coders on New Syberia tried to do and failed. I told him to forget it. I told him the world has moved on, he has to let Farley go. I never realized how deeply disturbed about it he is, until you contacted me."

McMaster coughed, like it was a signal Winter had said enough. He said to AJ, "The Congressman deeply appreciates you came to him with this, and that you'll kept it confidential. You said you haven't discussed it with people at your work, his family … other friends?"

"No," AJ lied. *Only Leon, Cassie…* "No, like I said, it seemed pretty personal and I was pretty shaken up when he showed me that gun."

"Yeah, that must have been terrible," McMaster said, like a man trying to sound sincere. "Not the administrator there? Citizen Tanike?"

"No. I came straight to you."

"She's New Syberian, I recall," Winter said, in a dangerously offhand way. "Came here after running a military camp?"

"Refugee center," AJ corrected him.

"Right. Right," Winter said, not sounding convinced.

McMaster gave him a short look that stopped him in whatever track he was heading down about Cyan. "Look, AJ, we appreciate your discretion. So to compensate you…"

"I don't want compensation," AJ said quickly.

"You don't?" McMaster asked, a little skeptically.

"No, I want to be kept right out of whatever this is," AJ said. "It's between you guys and Citizen Warnecke. I've done what he asked, passed it on to you. I want that to be the end of it."

McMaster looked at Winter, something passing between them, but AJ couldn't be sure what. "This would be a very bad time for any sort of scandal, however unfounded, to distract the Congressman from his important work," McMaster said.

"I know about the Commonwealth Commission into New Syberian activity on Orkutsk," AJ said. "I get that it's a big deal."

"A big deal indeed," Winter smiled. "Some people, AJ, they'd be tempted to take a copy of that page, or maybe even get a copy of the whole manuscript. They'd be tempted to try to sell this story to the gutter press who could twist it any which way and use it to drag this forty-year-old tragedy out of my past and use it against me somehow."

"Yeah," AJ said. "But that isn't me. Congressman, I work at an old folks' home, I fix stuff that breaks, I make sure their scrubber works and their roof doesn't leak. I like to surf." He tried to keep it simple. "I go surfing most days before work, some evenings after work too. I have a good life. I don't need the excitement."

McMaster laughed at that. "You don't need the excitement."

"No sir," AJ said. "You can check my bank statements if you want. Between my salary and the money I earn trading bandwidth, I have no debts, I pay all my bills on time, even got a little money saved in case my Ma needs an operation. I'm good."

Winter looked at McMaster. "I do believe you are good, AJ. Citizen McMaster, it is not often we meet a good man here in the Capitol, but I'd say we did today."

"No sir, it isn't," McMaster agreed. "Maybe we did." He was giving AJ a look which was impossible to decipher.

Winter stood up, so AJ did as well. "OK then, AJ. You have my word we'll try to keep you out of this business from now on. You've done your bit. We'll take it from here."

"What about Citizen Warnecke?" AJ asked.

It was McMaster who spoke. "The Congressman has access to certain resources," he said. "Considerable resources. We'll consult with the most advanced TGA specialist AIs on the Core. And then bring in his family. But I suspect Citizen Warnecke would be better managed at a facility that provides more intensive supervision. He sounds worse than his family probably realizes."

"A facility, for example, that doesn't let the residents carry guns," Winter joked.

They shook hands all round and McMaster put his finger to his ear and called William on comms to come walk AJ out. They waited at a door that led straight out to the corridor.

"I know you said you don't want compensation, but you are going to take me up on that tour of the Capitol, I hope," Winter said as they waited for the intern.

"Sure," AJ said. "I'd like that."

"Good, good," Winter said. "It'll be William showing you the sights, you can arrange it with him while he shows you how to get to your hotel. He's one of the few people in this building who is actually a Capitol native. Very proud of the place, loves showing it off."

"Sounds good."

"He'll organize a ride to the drone port for you too. He said there's a late flight should get you into South Coast City before midnight, so you can sleep late, eat lunch somewhere, look around, maybe have dinner together, then go out to the drone port. Sound OK? Ah, here's William."

AJ and the aide headed off and turned a few corridors, then William sent a map to his earbud. "They give these to tourists as a souvenir, but it's got your hotel marked on it. It's about three blocks, the Capitol Hill Hotel. Nothing fancy, but nice and central and clean. Your room is paid, but not any extras like massages or breakfast or minibar. You can take a car from out front if you like, or walk?" He led them back the way they had come, chatting happily, but at the lift AJ stopped him calling it. "I really need that bathroom before we go much further," he said.

"Oh, of course, sorry about that," William said. "There's one right in here. I think." AJ waited while William pushed a nearby door open to check. The bathroom was huge, with entrances leading out four ways. "Okay, yeah, here we are," he said brightly, but kept talking. "Now, tomorrow, I'm going to pick you up at the hotel around 12, so it would be good if you ate before then because we have a packed-ice program. You have a look at the map, decide what you want to see – I can get you back-stage most places, see stuff visitors don't usually see."

AJ must have looked a bit nonplussed because William quickly said, "I'd recommend you focus on two or three sights. I set aside six hours – then dinner if you like? Or I can leave you somewhere and we

146

can arrange for the car to pick you up anytime for the drone port. It's up to you – I've sent you my comms ID, in case."

"Thanks, that's awesome. I'm just thinking, it's your Sunday…"

"Aren't you nice? It's my job. It's 24/7 with Congressman Winter, he's one of the guys on the Hill works the hardest, and so we do too. But he's a nice guy with it. I get Thursdays off." William looked down the corridor. "Look, I've got a couple things to finish before I head home, and you need the bathroom, so…" He tapped the space between his eyebrows again. "I'm guessing you don't need me to guide you back out of here?"

"That way?" AJ said, pointing the other way. "Right, left, right, lift three floors down, right and left to the doors."

"Amazing," William said. "You could give tours. See you tomorrow?"

"Looking forward to it."

AJ went into the bathroom. Inside the stall he called Leon. "Hi Ma, it's me. On my way out now."

"Sounds like you in a men's room or something?"

"Yeah."

"You usually call your Ma from the john?"

"No."

"Then don't call me from the john either." Leon hung up on him.

AJ had been drifting while he was on the john, trying to call up any public information he could find about the Congressman and his river adventure. There was nothing in any of the usual news archives.

Which was strange, if there had been a police search, and the student Farley's parents had made a fuss about it. He washed his hands and then stepped out into the corridor again to find it was empty. And unfamiliar.

Of course. He'd walked out the wrong door. He walked back in and chose what should be the right door. Wrong again. Seriously? That's what happened when he relied on his bio-brain. But he'd already drifted twice since getting here, eating into his daily earnings. Dammit, ordinary citizens found their way around this stupid building without pulling schematics from the Core, he should be able to as well.

But William was right, the place was a maze, and cyber or not, without a starting reference he got just as easily lost as anyone else. In the end he found himself on the ground floor facing a fire exit and decided he'd had enough of the place. He pushed the door open, not caring if it set off an alarm, and walked into a narrow alleyway. He looked up at the city dome high above, and the Skycap beyond it, getting dark with rainclouds now. It was coming in cooler, but not too cold.

He hefted his pack over his shoulder, a little less bulky now without the document roll inside it. He checked his tourist map to get his bearings and point himself at the hotel, and started walking. As he was walking, he felt his comms buzzing in his ear and keyed the mike.

"Hi Ma."

"OK, I got eyes on the front door and there are some very conspicuously inconspicuous citizens hanging around out here. You can bet they'll be tailing your ass away from here. When you come out..."

"I'm already out," AJ said.

"You what?"

"I got a bit turned around, went out a fire exit. I'm halfway to the hotel now."

Leon took a moment to catch on. "OK, this is good. You say a hotel, you mean the hotel they booked for you?"

"Yeah, three blocks from here. Capitol Hill." AJ was walking faster now, and realized his shoulders were hunched at the idea someone might be following him. He wanted to turn around and look, but knew he shouldn't.

"OK. Look AJ, I don't like how it seems they've got a team out here waiting for you… Yeah, they getting all agitated now, since you didn't come out like they planned you would. They probably got someone at that hotel waiting too, just in case you gave them the slip, like you did. Can you find somewhere to grab a juice or a coffee or something? I just need a minute or two to think about this, move some things around."

AJ looked up and down the street, saw a place where he could stop a while. "Yeah, alright."

"OK, you got that? Just a coffee or glass of water, say ten minutes. Then I'll get you back on the street." AJ thought Leon was going to click off, then he said urgently, "And AJ, how long can you go before you have to auto-drift?"

AJ checked his status. "Drifted back inside that building. Just made an auto-drift. So another twenty minutes, why?"

"I'm betting they're lazy. They don't need drones all over you if they got a tag on your drift status. Soon as you drift, it pings them your location anyway. So don't, until you have to, alright?"

"OK. We going to meet for dinner?"

"No we ain't going to meet for dinner, AJ. I'm not your date." Leon hung up.

AJ wondered if bringing Leon was such a good idea now. Would something like this tip him into a relapse or whatever? It couldn't be good if you suffer from anxiety attacks and sleeplessness, creeping around the Capitol, following a guy to see if he was being followed, trying to keep him safe. But it was happening now, and the meeting with Winter seemed to have gone well, so he would just roll with it.

He went into the nearest café. It was the automated kind, you just ordered at your table and stuff was delivered through a slot in the wall. It probably only got cleaned once a day, judging by the number of cups still sitting around, but there was a discount if you put away your own tray and crockery and utensils, which it seemed most people did. The Capitol was colder, like they said. AJ sat warming his hands on his cup and reviewing the conversation with the Congressman.

He felt the meeting had gone OK. Winter had said he would find a way to keep AJ right out of it, so AJ had got what he wanted, right? That McMaster guy looked more like personal security than an 'executive assistant' but he was right about Warnecke; if the guy was going around threatening to kill himself, then he probably needed to be somewhere a bit more secure than Sol Vista. Somewhere he couldn't hurt himself, or anyone else. And it would suit AJ just fine if Winter's people could talk to Warnecke's family, get him moved somewhere else. Sol Vista would be Sol Vista again.

The FO Exploit? Use the Core to attack the Core … yeah, no. Like Winter said, crazy ideas, coincidences and speculations cooked into a conspiracy stew.

And Winter's version of the rafting story. That kind of made sense. Probably he and Warnecke did have a fight about whether to stay by the river or keep going, and maybe Warnecke wanted to stay longer and Winter wanted to go, and Warnecke felt bad about how they left that guy Farley alone and went downriver and he blamed himself for it, blamed Winter for it too. It sure would have sucked, if Warnecke was right. If that kid Farley had tried to walk out, got lost, made it back to the river hoping his buddies would still be there, and they were gone. He hasn't eaten for days, he's hungry and wet and all alone on the shore there in the middle of the Inland Territory, no one in sight. What's he going to do? Stay put and starve on the riverbank, or try to look for shelter? AJ ran some scenarios on the options, decided what he would have done. He'd be looking for food. Maybe a fish if you had a way to trap one, maybe dig down under the snow and ice, find some edible lichens. AJ was no survivalist, and out on the ice like that, there'd be no easy way to drift, but he'd seen the nature shows. There were ice beavers on that river. If you watched them, they'd lead you to fish. But it took five days for Warnecke and Winter to get downriver and another day for the search to start. By then, Farley was nearly a week without food – anything could have happened to him. Fallen in the river and drowned, fell down a crevasse in the ice, got taken by a grizzly.

And if that was AJ's buddy, his college friend, and he let that happen when he could have done something different, yeah, that would eat away at his conscience too. He totally got Warnecke's side of it, but Winter was more pragmatic, he was like, yeah, we could have stayed, but we didn't. We don't know if that would have made any difference and we can't change it, so what's the point in beating yourself up about it. AJ wouldn't have made that call, but he totally got that perspective too.

AJ could see how if you let that eat away at you for forty years, you could really build up a head of steam about it, maybe even let it unbalance you. Warnecke gave off that vibe, like he was obsessed about this thing, writing conspiracy theories supposedly pulled from the Deep Core by his dead friend's code, threatening to go public.

He looked at his watch. He'd been in the café nearly fifteen minutes now. He had to drift within the next five or it would happen automatically anyway. He picked up his pack, pulled it over his shoulder and let himself out of the café. He went outside and stood under a big silver awning, looking left and right up the street both ways. No Leon. He got on his comms and called him.

"Hey," he said, remembering Leon had told him not to keep saying 'Ma' every time.

"Hey," Leon replied. "I was just about to call. I got an option for you. Had it already set up, just needed to move the timetable forward."

"What option?" AJ asked.

"An option," Leon said. "Just listen to me like we agreed. What's your location?"

AJ told him. "What now?"

"OK, turn to your left and start walking. You hit Penn Avenue, take a right and keep walking."

AJ pulled his pack tighter and began walking. Confused.

"Why aren't I going to my hotel?" he asked. "Won't that just make them suspicious? And won't they just find me as soon as I drift anyway?"

"How was your meeting, AJ?"

"Uh, it was good. They're going to take care of Warnecke."

"I bet they are."

"No, I mean, in the right way. Get him help, keep me out of it."

"So you feeling pretty good right now? Got a warm fuzzy vibe going, everything going to be cruisy now."

"Pretty much."

"That's how they *want* you to feel, mano. Because when you feel safe and warm and cozy, that's when you most vulnerable. Leon going to get you *safe*."

"Come on, Leon, you're making this ... right on Penn?"

"Yeah, turn right there. I'm getting myself behind you, I'm maybe about half a block away. You're going to walk about another two blocks. The Capitol Diner on your right, I'll tell you when you're close."

"OK ... I appreciate you got my back, alright? But I really think this is going to be OK now." As he spoke, he saw a drift notification on his cortex. If Leon was right, Winter and his people now knew where he was.

"Uh huh. You just do what Leon says, and it will be. Like we agreed."

"OK."

"Call you when you're close to the diner."

Was he right? Leon had AJ looking around him again now at the faces on the street, people standing in doorways, people like him, mostly people out meeting friends or hurrying through the cold, looking for somewhere to eat. He went through a square, walked a couple of blocks more. The buildings changed from offices to big solid brownstone apartments, glowing solar chargers in different colors along the avenue, re-radiating stored light. After three blocks his comms buzzed. "OK, you got the diner coming up on your right. Cross the road now."

"Now?"

"Now man."

AJ stopped, waited for traffic, hustled across the broad avenue. It was Sunday night, traffic was pretty light.

"Why did I cross the road if the diner is back on the side I came from?"

"I want to see something. OK, when you get opposite the diner, look over, cross back and go up to the window. Stop outside, look in the window, then go in. But keep your comms open now, alright? I want you to see something."

"See what?"

"Tell you when you get there. Just keep the line open but say nothing. You can cross back over the street any time now."

"OK."

He saw lights ahead, garish and flashing, like a liquor store. "Is that it coming up now?"

"Past the convenience store, one door," Leon said. "Just hang by the window a minute. Like you're thinking OK, maybe this place, maybe not. It's got table service, probably a bit pricy."

"OK."

He went back across the avenue, got to the diner. It looked pretty ordinary, a few people inside, red booths, black stools up by the counter. Chicken, burger and beer kind of place, he guessed. But yeah, the owner was in attendance, sitting on her stool behind a counter. There was a menu in the window, so he made out he was reading.

"OK," Leon said in his ear. "You're going to go inside, sit down so you can see the door. And this is what is going to happen. About two minutes after you do, this nice couple, mid-thirties, they're going to walk in behind you and take a seat where they can see you."

"OK, are they with you? This sounds like overkill, Leon."

"Just go in, sit where you can see the door. Listen, and don't talk."

AJ went to the door and pushed on it. It rang a little bell as he went in, and he said hi to the owner as he stepped inside. She looked up as he came in. "With you in a second, hon," she called. "Sit anywhere. Order on the table. My chocolate chili is a taste-bomb." She looked a bit like his Ma when she was fifty. He liked places where the owners were there, being social, changing the menu up with their own recipes. They were worth the higher prices.

He threw his pack into the corner of a booth and slid his ass onto the seat so he was facing the door.

"OK, they coming in, they coming … should be anytime," Leon said. "Pull up a menu or something."

AJ saw a couple of shapes through the frosted glass of the door and studied the menu displayed on the tabletop between condiment bottles and napkins. Over the top of them he saw the door open and heard the little bell ring. A smiling, chatting couple came in. They were mid-thirties, she had on a light wind jacket, had soft brown hair, slim-fitting trousers, looked like she was dark skinned under all her clothes; he was dressed in a puffy jacket, fur collar, light trousers with multiple pockets and blew on his hands as he walked in, like he was cold. They

155

were talking as they walked past AJ; he heard something about school. Maybe talking about their kids? He heard them settle into a booth about two back behind him.

Leon's voice in his ear. "So now you're thinking to yourself, OK, are they Leon's people? But they ain't. They look like nice normal people though, don't they, so what's the big deal, Leon? You trying to scare me? But you're asking yourself the wrong questions. The question you should be asking is, hey, how did Leon know those two random people were going to come into *this* diner. Two random people walking along Penn Avenue, how did Leon know they would go right into the same diner as AJ?

AJ did want to know. He wanted to ask, but he kept quiet, just looking at his menu, not seeing the words. The owner came over and he said loudly, so Leon could hear, "Hi, can I get the pancakes with chicken bacon instead of syrup? And some juice?"

"Sure, hon," she said. "You look cold. You want coffee with that? On the house?"

"That'd be nice, thanks."

Leon heard him talking and spoke again. "Good, you just eat while I talk you through it. See, because that nice couple, they were outside the Congressman's office, trying to look like they was sightseeing. You didn't come out, suddenly they're approached by two other folks. That don't mean anything, it's a nice clear night, people going out to eat maybe. But then they jump in a car and they're driving around and around and suddenly, ping. I'm guessing you drifted. Their car makes a beeline for this street and these two jump out about two hundred yards behind you. Coincidence? Maybe. That's why I got you to cross the road. See their reaction. Do they keep walking and talking and having a nice time? You run across the road there, and what do they do? They stop up. One of them is looking at you, the other one is making like he's looking at his comms, maybe checking a map, but he's watching you. Now they got to decide, do they follow you across the road? They walk to the curb, but then you come back over again. OK, cool, you were just a bit lost maybe, they just fall in behind you. So now they're three blocks from where they left their car and there is no reason in this freezing cold world you would leave a nice warm car then walk three blocks in this sketchy part of town. It ain't that nice a night for walking. Then my pal AJ goes into the diner and that was the real test, are they going to follow him in? Apparently they are." He paused. "You getting my meaning here, AJ?"

"I guess."

"OK, mano. They got a watch on your drift status, they probably got your personal comms tapped which won't do them much good, seeing as you ain't using that. If they just want to see if you're meeting up with someone else, a drone could do it. Why would they need a team of at least four citizens running around behind you, AJ?"

"Physical intervention," AJ said. "I think you called it."

"Exactly. Otherwise known to the layman as kidnapping, assault, or just plain assassination." Then Leon apparently realized how that might spook AJ and he continued. "Doesn't mean they're actively planning it already, but they've got the option in play, probably waiting on the word from your new friend Winter."

"So what do we do?"

"As long as we stay in this town, we're playing by their rules," Leon said. "So, we need to change the rules. Now eat your pancakes until your next drift. Which is when?"

AJ checked his status again. "Five minutes, or the one after that, 25."

"We'll go for 25. And when I say move, you move. We can't lose them now, but we can confuse them, long enough to get you safe."

9. TAILWIND

Leon called back and told AJ he was about to get a crash course in anti-surveillance. And Leon didn't like it because the only way he could see it working was if Leon exposed himself, but he couldn't see any other way. He told AJ to finish up his food, and then at exactly 24 minutes, leave the diner, keep going down Penn about one more block to the Eastern Market Metro station, go down and get the first train that came along, any direction, didn't matter. Stay on the train until Leon called him again. That was it. Now do it.

At exactly a minute before his next drift, AJ stood, swiped a few creds to the table for the food and made his way to the door. He nearly jumped as he stepped outside and saw Leon standing there, but Leon didn't look at him, he was acting like he was looking at his comms view, sending a message. AJ did a quick double take, then looked down the Avenue and saw the sign for the metro and started walking, fast. Don't look back, he told himself. That would be strange. But then he heard shouting, turned his head and saw Leon arguing with the guy who had been following him. He and the woman had come out of the diner right behind AJ, and Leon was standing in their way, arguing with them and not letting them out of the diner.

"Do I look *invisible* to you?" AJ could hear Leon yelling. "You try to walk straight through me?" AJ looked quickly for the other two people Leon had said had been parked up in a car a couple of blocks away, but he couldn't see anyone.

It only took a minute to reach the metro station, but once he made it through the facial recognition barrier that read his ID and charged his account, it was maybe another three minutes to the first transit. It occurred to him that depending on how deep their surveillance went, he had also just given them his location when he paid for his metro ticket with his face. Five minutes since he left the diner. How long could Leon keep the couple hung up on the street above? Two people came down the stairs as a transit car finally pulled up to the platform, another young couple, so maybe that was their backup team? Damn, he was getting as paranoid as Leon. The train pulled in and he got in a carriage and sat down, realizing he was panting, tried to slow his breathing. The doors closed and the train pulled away. He tried looking up and down the open carriages to see if the other couple had taken the same train. It didn't look like it.

Was Leon just being crazy? Maybe it was a total coincidence, some inner-city couple were really just out for a nice walk, happened to go to the same diner as AJ?

He looked for a clue as to what transit he was on, where it was going. He worked out he'd got on at Eastern Market Station, was headed across the Anacadia River to Lago. Had no idea was that good or bad but from what little he knew of the Capitol, east of the river was not a place for tourists. He'd heard that was where the Floehopper tenements were. Not that he had anything against the itinerant fisherfolk who lived outside the Skycap, dragging a living up from the depths of the Shifting Sea. But he'd heard that a few years out on the ice floes, even if you loaded up on Blues to near-lethal doses, you soaked up enough rads to fry your brain. Pretty much any murder you saw in the news these days, it seemed there was a Floehopper involved. He'd also heard they were old school – they didn't regard killing a cyber as murder at all.

His comms buzzed. "You there my friend?" said the voice in his ear. Then it was gone as they went into a dead zone. He got Leon back as they pulled into Capitol Hill station. Some pretty heavy looking young guys got on, but he wasn't alone in the carriage, and they seemed happy just talking shit with each other, didn't even look at him. He relaxed a little. "Hey, Ma, yeah, I'm here now. I think I'm alone."

"OK, I think you're safe until your next drift. They think they can't lose you 'cause you're a cyber. Makes you predictable. Makes them lazy. But you are about to really mess them up."

"What are you talking about, Leon?"

"You'll find out. Where you at? I should be able to see you on my comms here but you're underground."

AJ looked at the map over the door. "Blue line, on the way to Alson Road."

"OK, cool, you ride that all the way to Lago, but don't leave the station. You just get off, go to the other platform and catch the transit out to the drone port. I booked you a flight home tonight on the redeye."

"What about my personal VIP guided tour of the Capitol?"

"Take the VR tour instead."

"They're going to be pissed."

"Good. How was them pancakes?" Leon asked.

"What?"

"At that café where I saw you. I'm looking at the menu. Thinking I might get me some pancakes. They OK?"

"Yeah, a bit dry. But the bacon tasted like bacon."

"Extra bacon, extra syrup it is. OK, you can drift now," Leon said. "We want them to think you're going in the opposite direction from the drone port. *Next* time you drift, you going to be way over the other side of town, they're going to be all confused and you can just call me when you get on your flight."

Leon didn't sound to AJ like he was having any kind of anxiety attack. In fact, he sounded to AJ like he was having fun.

As AJ climbed the steps back up onto the Penn Avenue side of Lago station for the drone port, he was looking at a transit map in comms view and nearly walked into a small, skinny Floehopper who was definitely tripping on something.

"Hey. Mother…" the guy said, throwing his hands in the air. He was about half AJ's size, but that just made him faster than AJ.

"Sorry," AJ said and kept walking.

The guy kept staring at AJ's back but then mumbled to himself and started back down the stairs, so AJ got over to the other platform without being knifed. Put that down as a plus.

The people hanging around at the other platform didn't seem much of an improvement on his friend on the stairs, and AJ didn't want to look like he didn't know where he was, so he put his head down. The train came, an express to the airport with only three stops. He drifted, resetting his status, and took a seat. Three stops, fifteen minutes. Much faster than the ride in here in the limo, but AJ guessed most people who used limo services weren't in a hurry. They expected everyone else to wait for them.

As he got off the train at the airport he got Leon on his earbud. "OK, I'm here. About to drift again."

"I know you're here. I'm right here on the platform too. Where you going?"

AJ tried to look around without looking, but couldn't see Leon anywhere.

"I don't know where I'm going, Leon, you tell me."

"You going the wrong way is where you going. Slow it down, this ain't no speed walking race, OK? Turn around and go back the other way. You're going to terminus 2, gate 2. You're nearly home, AJ. Relax."

"OK, gate 2." AJ hefted his pack, walked through a couple of scanners that read his backpack contents and his face, and checked him into his flight. He kept expecting to set off an alarm, Leon had him so spooked now. But he made his gate and sat down, still not having seen Leon anywhere. He got onto comms. "OK, now what?"

"Now you call your friends in the Capitol, tell them where you are," Leon said.

"I just drifted again. You said they'll know where I am now," AJ pointed out.

"Yeah, but you don't want them to know that you know they know, right?"

AJ sighed. "And what do I tell them?"

"Change of plans, personal emergency, keep it simple. Thanks for everything, have a good night," Leon said. "Nothing creative."

"And what if Winter *has* ordered them to pick me up?" AJ asked. "They're going to just let me cruise onto a drone and get out of town?"

"You got self-defense protocols, right?"

Cybers had protocol restraints which were supposed to prevent them instigating violence, but since the Cyber Bill of Rights came in, they were loosened up to allow them to defend themselves if physically attacked, up to and including inflicting bodily harm. AJ wasn't combat trained or optimized, so his self-defense skills and reflexes weren't much above those of the average six foot, 176lb guy. Still, he *was* a six foot, 176lb guy, and used to hard manual work. He wasn't too worried if someone came at him with their fists, even a knife. They'd have to know cyber anatomy to know where to stick him if they wanted to put him down. But against someone with a gun, his best defense was to run like hell.

But it all felt just a little bit over the top. "Yeah. And *then* what?"

Leon laughed. "Then I got a plan B. But we won't need it. These guys are C graders. You should have seen it outside the diner when they realized you were hot-footing it for the metro. I let the guy walk straight into me and he was like 'sorry' and I was like 'sorry don't cut it man, you didn't see me here'? I start yelling at the guy, he gets this impatient look, and his woman? She tries to go around me so I grab her arm, hey, I say, I'm talking to both of you. Then the guy gets all uptight, tells me to let go of the woman, so I'm like, alright, calm down, we all friends here, ain't we friends? And he's saying yeah, we're friends, trying to start walking again, and I'm like, aw, you ain't acting like you friends, maybe you should be careful in this part of town, walking around here without no friends. He's like, was that a threat? And I'm like, no mano, that was a fact, and I show him my knife."

"Where did you get a knife?" AJ asked. "You took a knife on the drone?"

"No, I didn't take a knife on the drone. You were in with your Senator, I was at a hunting store buying me a nice little dolphin filleting knife I could put in my sock."

"Leon, this feels a little out of control," AJ admitted. "I didn't want you getting into this kind of trouble."

"Wasn't *me* in trouble. I was cool. It was the goofballs following you was in trouble. Maybe they were carrying weapons, but I figured they got protocols say they can't get in a fight over nothing, so I was pretty safe. Sure enough, the woman says, 'Hey, sorry, we don't want any trouble here', so I say, 'OK then, why don't you just get on back to Upper Crudberg where you belong'. They didn't like it, but they had to turn around, go back the other way. I went inside and got the pancakes, double syrup, double bacon, to go."

"Damn, they really were following me?"

"You were hoping I was just paranoid, I get that. But I'm not. I'm schooled in this game, AJ. And they were rookies. They bailed too easy."

"So what do you think?" AJ looked around himself again. The gate was pretty empty. Not good, this was not good.

"I think they *are* worried about you," Leon said. "That they had anyone follow you at all tells me they are worried. But what we don't know is, are they just a little bit worried, or big time worried."

"So what's the difference between a 'little bit worried' and 'big time worried'?" AJ asked, frowning.

"A little bit worried means they just think this is some kind of shakedown. That team was probably just supposed to keep close, in case Winter wanted to do something to scare you off. Rough you up a bit, say."

"And 'big time worried', that would mean…"

"More than just rough you up."

AJ laughed nervously.

"Yeah, you can laugh, mano. If I'm Winter, and I think you're trying some sort of shakedown, I'm pulling you in and putting you under a heat lamp. Sure."

"But if I make it back to South Coast City, I'm somehow safer? You sure?"

"Maybe, if you get back there and don't hit him up for a big chunk of credits. AJ, nothing about this is sure. I just *sound* confident. That's how I get you to do what I think you should do, right?"

"OK, that makes me feel real secure."

"I'm ragging you again – lighten up now. I'm two rows behind you. Call me if you get freaked out by anything, OK?"

"OK." AJ twisted his head to see Leon sitting where he said, head down, cap over his eyes like he was sleeping.

"Oh come on, now he's looking right at me," Leon said. "Relax, will you?"

"Relax? You're saying Winter is having me followed so maybe I can be kidnapped or assaulted, and I should relax?"

"Yeah, surfer guy. Shifting Sea is where you happiest, right? Well, this is *my* ocean, AJ. This is where I swim."

"I get you."

"Yeah, maybe. I don't think so. Now, you got a call to make to Winter's people, don't you? Make the call, then make out I don't exist. Don't even talk to me when we land, alright?"

"Alright. Bye Ma."

He dropped the call to Leon and pulled up the ID for Winter's assistant.

"Hello, William?"

"Oh hi, is this AJ?" Did he sound like he was expecting the call? Not really. But he was just a junior aide, maybe he wasn't in on anything.

"Yeah, hi, look something came up," AJ lied. "Personal business back home, so I have to go back early. I'm out at the drone port now."

William was trying not to sound happy, but AJ could tell he was. "Oh, dang. So you miss out on my custom-made Capitol tour."

"Yeah, bummer. I hope you didn't already get museum tickets or anything?"

"Nothing major," William said. "You have a nice flight back."

"I will," AJ said. "Oh, yeah. I totally forgot to cancel that hotel too. Bit rushed. Can you…"

"I'll call them and cancel," William said.

"That's all good then. OK, well. Have a nice Sunday, I guess…"

"Well, you just cleared half my diary, so I just might. Bye…"

They made the flight without being intercepted. AJ used the in-flight comms to call Cassie, see if she could pick him up in a few hours instead of the following night. She said, what? She had nothing better to do than be his personal chauffeur? But she was just playing. She said she'd pick him up.

Then he spent the rest of the flight running scenarios. Most were bad, on the AJ Flow-erometer. Top of the probability tree, if he really was being followed, was the one that said Winter was indeed worried the whole thing was a shakedown by AJ trying to use the Warnecke situation for a quick buck. That scenario had multiple outcomes. A low fourth on the probability tree was the idea that Winter and Warnecke would just fix things between themselves without involving AJ anymore. He did a quick review of the scenarios again and made a decision. He needed to reconfigure. How he moved through the environment around him was part innate capability and part configuration. In his chosen job, with his current lifestyle, he was using just 8 percent of his data and analytical capacity, the rest he sold to the Core. But he had the freedom to decide the ratio and he decided straight away to requisition 70 percent capacity. It would take a few hours for the bandwidth to clear, but he had a feeling he would need it once he landed so that he wasn't relying so much on his bio-brain.

There was also a scenario, somewhere in the middle there, that said Winter *was* really worried about whatever revelations Warnecke had up his sleeve, that Warnecke really had found a way to dive the Deep Core, and AJ was now a pawn in the middle of all that. AJ decided he'd allocate a part of his new bandwidth to chasing down anything that Farley O'Halloran had published or publicly cached before he died, then compare and contrast Farley's research with other black-hat discussions and accepted theories on how to hack the Deep Core. He didn't want to go to Warnecke and ask him, though it might have been easier. He didn't want to open that Pandora's box.

He was also facing heightened physical threats now and spent some time thinking about his options there too. He had no special combat abilities. Since the Bill of Rights, Tatsensui did not mass produce 'special purpose' cybers, designed for dedicated tasks like mining, low-gravity transport or combat. The only mining or combat cybers on Tatsensui were volunteers doing it for the salary, who got body mods once they signed up. PRC had the same policy, though New Syberia wasn't bound by the same treaty, so it churned out cybers who were bred for combat, and sent most of them to Orkutsk. Which neither TS nor PRC was happy about, hence the political tension.

AJ could, however, reconfigure elements of his metabolism for short periods – boost adrenaline, growth hormone, adjust insulin and dopamine – at a cost. For example he could adjust hormone levels to ensure he stayed awake and alert for 48 hours without sleep, but then he would crash afterward and need days to recover. He could boost production of the klotho enzyme, expressed by the KL gene to enhance his ability to multitask, so he didn't have to hand off all complex calculations to the Core. But long exposure to heightened levels of klotho led to unwanted hypervigilance and anxiety. He decided to cue up some preconfigured boosts for use if needed.

Then there was his emotional state. Not much he could do about that. His biological heart was very emotionally conflicted. He had dragged Cassie into this mess, and the best thing to do, the logical thing, was to back her right out again. Cool the new friendship down, put it on a back burner, all the usual clichés. AJ lay back, thinking okay, I call her from the drone port, she picks me up about 11 p.m., we can grab a late-night snack at Lean and Green … then sleep overtook him.

"OK, I have my head in the game but my stomach is totally confused," Cassie said as they stood looking at the menu outside Lean and Green. It was a 'creative coop café' – a business run by local foodies who loved experimenting with food. "I skipped supper after you called. But is this supper or breakfast?"

AJ looked at his watch. "Nearly midnight, for you, so I don't know. Suppertime for me."

"I'm calling it breakfast, then I can sleep longer tomorrow … which is the only reason I'm still talking to you," she said, frowning at the menu. "Tell me you're not actually going to eat any of this weirdo food."

"Power rice sashimi bowl," he said, pointing. "Brown rice, kale, farmed dolphin fin, quinoa, beans, salsa."

"You know that apart from the dolphin, those are all just trendy names for the same factory-produced protein, right? There's no way a place like this imports it from outside the system."

"Yeah, but they're *really* trendy names."

Cassie frowned at AJ. "That kale juice I got you was meant to be a *joke*." They went inside, got in the line to order, and Cassie leaned forward and asked the guy chopping fresh ingredients behind the counter, "Excuse me, the menu says 'all day breakfast with oatmeal and homemade pastries' – does all-day mean 24-hour?"

"All day, all night," the guy said without looking up.

"Your ass is saved," Cassie said to AJ.

It was a mild night. When they'd got their food and loaded up on juices they grabbed a bench outside and AJ filled her in on his Capitol adventure. He finished by explaining how weird it felt, Leon walking past him at the drone port without saying hi. He and Leon had agreed they'd wait to debrief at work tomorrow.

170

Cassie soaked it all in, without calling any of it crazy, which impressed AJ. She had a reporter's capacity for adjusting to new realities, that was clear. "So Leon was worried they would try something at your hotel?" Cassie asked. "That's why you rushed back?"

"He's more like extra careful, I think," AJ said. "I never really saw this side of him, but he's super suspicious of everything. I'm wondering if it's a PCPD thing, or it's just a Leon thing."

"And he pulled a *knife* on the two people following you?" Cassie asked, taking a delicate bite of her oatmeal. AJ was really starting to enjoy being around her. She was this hardcore skater grrl on the outside, but she ate her oatmeal with her pinky sticking out and blew on every spoonful so it wasn't too hot. Most of the time she dressed in ripped trousers and t-shirts with a body-hugging thermal skin underneath and looked like she'd just woken up, but for their date the other night she looked like a billion creds.

"*If* they were following me," AJ said. "Leon's totally convinced. Let's say I'm not."

"Because why?"

"OK, there's reasons it's pretty hard to put any sort of covert surveillance around a cyber. Drones usually have electronic surveillance systems on board, passive and active. Drones just don't carry cameras and mikes. Every citizen goes around sending and receiving data from the Core – biodata, comms, lifestyle and shopping interactions – and a surveillance drone sucks all that up. Citizens won't see that unless they have the right equipment, but a cyber can see everything that touches our data-sphere, ingoing and outgoing. It's a self-defense thing, so we can instantly react if someone tries to hack us. So if Winter was trying to track me through my data footprint, I'd have seen it."

"You think so," Cassie decided, then pointed her spoon at him. "But maybe you aren't thinking straight."

He smiled. "So what does the news analyst think?"

"This *journalist* thinks Winter has people on his team who know exactly what you just told me," she said. "People who would know the best way, the only way, to run surveillance on a cyber is with a simple Core trace on his drift status, and with plain old feet on the ground, just like Leon said. So, it's *very* possible."

"But why? Winter got his document, and I told him all I wanted was to be left out of it."

"You told him that?" she sighed. "He might decide to take you at your word, take you completely out of the picture."

"Good," said AJ. "That's what I wanted."

She laughed. "No, I mean *completely* out. Like, chopped up into fish bait and thrown off the back of a boat into the Shifting Sea kind of out." She saw his reaction and added quickly, "AJ, I'm joking. I'm not Leon. I don't *really* think your life is in danger here."

"Ha ha, I'm laughing, see." AJ sank his head onto his hands and watched people walking past. "Leon pointed out no one would miss me, except my Ma."

Cassie lifted her straw out of her cup and blew some juice at him. "Buck up, sad sack. I'd miss you."

"Yeah?" AJ asked. "What's my full name?"

"Evil trick," Cassie said. "This is what, our third date? I can't be expected to remember a cyber's ID number until at least the fifth date."

172

"But you'd miss me," he said.

"Yeah, of course I would, AJ dot whoever you are," Cassie said.

"Nice."

"Get over it," she grinned.

"Because," AJ snuck up to it, "I'm thinking that while I sort out all this stuff with Citizen Warnecke and the Congressman, maybe I should leave you out of it…"

Cassie stopped in the middle of lifting a spoonful of food to her mouth and put it down again. "Leave me out?"

"Yeah, you know, not get you involved. Like, maybe we just put things on hold until this all blows over?" AJ said hopefully.

Cassie picked up her spoon again, let oatmeal drop off it into the bowl while she thought about it, not looking at AJ. "Uh, no. Nope," she said at last. She put down the spoon, lifted her jacket off the back of her chair and looked at AJ now. "You done? Let's go." She swiped her thumb to pay and walked off without waiting.

That had gone well. AJ gathered up his own things slowly and caught up with Cassie pacing down the street. "You're angry," AJ guessed.

But Cassie didn't answer. She stopped, grabbed AJ by the collar of his jacket and pushed him up against the wall of the nearby building. Her face was inches from AJ's and her eyes asked a question. When AJ didn't pull away, Cassie put her hand behind his neck and kissed him and AJ felt his whole body fill with heat. Cassie stepped back again. "You want to put that on hold?" she said.

She'd picked AJ up at the drone port in black leathers on a red Scarlatti 750-watt Supersport she'd bought for 3,500 creds a few months earlier. "L-twin, Desmo air cooled, 22,000 miles, one owner, pillion seat…" she'd told AJ with a smile as he stood back and looked at it. "A bit clunky in the low gears, but smooth as butter once you're rolling. Tell me you rode on the back of a road-planer before."

He'd looked at it curiously, having never seen one up close before. The road-planer didn't look much different from a racing-planer, except that the engine torque was street legal, the ice blade on the front was adjustable for both on- and off-road driving and, unlike a racing marque, it had an optional onboard AI pilot. It looked low and lean and ridiculously fast.

"That would be no," he'd said, taking a helmet from Cassie. "You are the first person I ever met who owned one."

"Well, keep your eyes closed then," Cassie had said. "You've got good balance. Just go with my lead, feel the machine, stay cool," she'd said.

"And what happens if I open my eyes and get totally *uncool*?" AJ had asked, watching as Cassie put her leg over the saddle and kicked the stand free.

"Well, we lose our balance like that, it's called a battery slap, and you don't have to worry about it," she said.

"I don't?"

"No. At the speed we'll be going, if we get into a battery slap, the AI won't have time to react and you'll be dead before you even know it," Cassie had said, pulling on her helmet.

174

They'd survived. Cassie wasn't a maniac, she gentled the planer into the curves until AJ got a feel for it and it was only as they got up towards the Sea Gate district that she opened it up a little, weaving between cars on the freeway, just to show AJ what it could do. What *she* could do. AJ was a little freaked at the idea she was doing the driving, but once you got used to that, it was kind of fun. But then, as a guy who liked to surf gas spouts on sub-zero seas, he had a strange idea of fun.

After they kissed outside Lean and Green, Cassie insisted he take her night surfing.

"It's been a big day," he said. "Maybe tomorrow?"

"You could be dead tomorrow, but you're still alive now," Cassie said with a straight face. "It's Saturday night and I want to go *surfing*."

They went down to the Sea Gate and spent a couple hours on the sea. It was a different sea at night. Scarier, but more beautiful with it. Ice floes glowing, spouts phosphorescent with algae. Like it always did, the sea helped clear AJ's head, restore his perspective. Everything looked simpler, if you just took a sea-level view on it.

Cassie dropped him home sometime around 3 a.m. "You know, you didn't totally suck as a pillion rider," she said. AJ thought about asking her up to his place, and the vibe was right, but being honest, he had some thinking to do. And sleeping.

"That surf was exactly what I needed to get my flow back," he'd said. "Look, would you like to…" He was looking up at his place, but not sounding like he was trying too hard to sell it.

Cassie had leaned into him, given him another long kiss that left him tingling. "Yes. Yes I would," she'd said, when they stopped to draw breath. "But not tonight. The first night I stay over with you, I want it to be *me* you remember."

"Hey," he said. "Of course it would ... I have perfect recall, right?"

"No," Cassie said. "If I went up there tonight, I'd be like, hey, you remember our first night together? And you'd be all, oh yeah, that weekend? That was that crazy weekend with the Congressman and getting tailed all over the Capitol. I'd be like a post-script."

"OK ... no, but yeah..." He gave her a weak smile. "I can see how that might happen."

"What I was thinking," Cassie said, getting back on her planer, "is maybe it would be a nice idea to take a trip somewhere on the holiday weekend?"

"That would be awesome," AJ said, meaning it this time. The holiday weekend was a five-day break that marked the end of one year and the start of the next. A Tatsensui orbit around Coruscant was only three months, but a Coruscant lap around its sun was 385 days. When you had to wait four cycles for one New Year's Eve, you needed time to celebrate it. "East from the peninsula, or west?"

"No, I was thinking north," Cassie said. "There's a ride I'd like to do to Gakona, then north-east across the mountains, come back via Gambel..."

"Oh, you mean ... Inland. On your planer?" he asked.

Cassie stuck out her tongue. "Yeah, AJ, Inland, on my planer. It would be kinda boring in a car, and kinda dangerous out on the Icecap on my own."

AJ looked at Cassie and realized he'd pretty much say yes to anything the woman suggested right now. "Cool," he said. "Supposed to be good ice yachting in Gakona."

"You can't take a sail on my planer, AJ," Cassie smiled.

"Strap it across my back," he said. "Be like a, you know, an airfoil."

"Right, we get over a hundred klicks, we're flying," Cassie said, going along with it. "Just fly right over the other traffic."

AJ thought about it. "OK, I suppose they got places there we can rent a sail," he said. "I'm in."

He couldn't see how it was ever going to happen, but that was the least of his problems right now.

He decided that breakfast next morning at Fatty's would be a nice normal way to start a Sunday and put a full stop in the crazy day he'd just left behind. He walked over there and looked around, saw a couple guys he knew and … Warnecke.

The guy was nursing a coffee over an empty plate in a corner and looking out the window at the road, so AJ walked past him up to Fatty at the counter. "Short black, thanks Kylie," AJ said to the barista.

"Your friend the compulsive confessor is over there," Fatty said, nodding with his head as he leaned on the counter.

"I saw," AJ said. "He a bit calmer today?"

"Minding his own," Fatty said. "Came in yesterday too. No trouble."

"Good." AJ stayed at the bar, every now and then looking over his shoulder at Warnecke. Warnecke finished his coffee and came up to the counter and stood next to AJ.

"Can I get a coffee to go? Black, large," Warnecke said. He looked at AJ, saw AJ looking at him, then looked away. Then back again. "Sorry, I know you?"

AJ did a small double take. He should be used to it, but wasn't expecting it from Warnecke. "Uh, yeah. I work at Sol Vista?"

"Ah," Warnecke said. "Right. Sorry, had a senior moment. Mind you, I never been good with faces."

"That's OK," AJ said.

Fatty handed the guy his coffee and Warnecke swiped for it. He turned away, and then turned back again. "The gardener, right?"

"Service technician," AJ said, interested to see how lost Warnecke was. Fatty was watching too. Kylie slid AJ another small coffee.

"Right, right," Warnecke said. "Well, good. I'll see you back at the gulag then?"

"You bet," AJ said, lifting his coffee cup in salute.

OK, maybe his week wasn't going back to normal after all.

AJ filled the hole in his muscles with one of Fatty's double patty, double cheese breakfast muffins. Thinking as he ate, Cassie wasn't that bad a surfer, for a total beginner. Girl could swim, and she had good upper body strength, so that was part of the battle. Didn't lack confidence, wanting to get out on the sea at night; watching her reminded him of how he felt the first couple of times he ever went out on a board. Totally pumped.

She had good balance, which was a critical part. Technique, that would come, he told her. Thinking also it was nice to see her afterward on the dry side of the Gate, stripping off the heat suit, just her thermal skin underneath. Thinking it was also a nice goodbye kiss he got as Cassie dropped him home last night. World wasn't all bad.

His reconfig had kicked in, so he compartmentalized his bandwidth. Under 10 percent still dedicated to citizen interactions and his work at Sol Vista. Ten percent to running background searches and updating scenarios around Winter and McMaster and Warnecke. The rest he allocated to research and analysis related to the Q-programmer Farley, the guy who had died out on the ice.

As he stepped outside, he sensed someone standing by the door to his right and automatically took a step to the left, looking up a bit startled.

Leon was standing there.

"Didn't want to interrupt," he said. "We need to talk."

10. THE PROBLEM WITH TROY

"I screwed up," Leon said. "No excuses, it is what it is."

They went back to AJ's apartment, two blocks back from the Boulevard and about 2 miles from Sol Vista. The place worked for AJ. Yeah, it was a tiny little studio over a convenience store, but his 280 creds a week included a storage unit where he could put his kayak, spare fan blades and old boards. And it was only about 20 minutes from the Gate, which made the 30-minute queue to get out onto the sea more bearable.

Leon looked around himself as they went up the stairs to AJ's place, taking in the smooth red concrete walkways, flowering bushes and palm trees. "Now I see why you never invited me over," he said. "Don't want me bringing down the tone of your neighborhood?"

"Ha ha. There's all types here," AJ told him. "Singles like me, some couples with kids. Guy over there, with the sun deck," he pointed at the apartment opposite, "runs the surf shop on Pearl, gives me 10 percent."

"Wow, ten?" Leon said. "He sell them off-world Tropical shirts? The really colorful ones? Get you to buy them, I could save me 10 percent?"

"*Surf* shop," AJ repeated. "Mats, blades, leashes, wax, heaters, fins … no Tropical shirts. You want coffee?" AJ started his machine, got it to grind out a couple of cups, handed one to Leon and sat down on his sofa. "And you screwed up, how?"

"OK, so, while you were laying back in your seat eating the complimentary pretzels and watching the in-flight VR," Leon said, "I

180

put in a couple calls to some friends, got some background on your new buddy Troy McMaster."

AJ remembered the shark-like eyes of the Congressman's minder. "Not good?" AJ didn't really have to ask. He kind of guessed already that McMaster wasn't your average executive assistant.

"No. He's former CCS," Leon said. "Now runs his own private security company. They do 'threat management'."

"Threat management?" AJ asked. "Which is…"

"If the Congressman feels threatened," Leon shrugged, "they remove the threat."

"And CCS? I never heard of it," AJ said.

"Commonwealth Covert Service. You aren't supposed to have heard of it. It's the covert arm of Planetary Defense. They work together with Tatsensui Special Investigations to do the stuff no one else can get done," Leon explained. "They're the ones took down the New Syberia shield in the war."

"You aren't cheering me up," AJ grumbled. "I was on a good vibe until I walked into Fatty's. Should have stayed in bed."

"Yeah well, sucks to be you right now," Leon said. "I'll admit that. How we screwed up, I thought Winter had hired some kind of B team. And maybe they were. But this McMaster guy, if he's still plugged into his old network, which I assume he is, gives Winter massive scalability if he wants to take this to the next level. I'm talking intelligence assets, cyber, comint, cache hackers…"

"Talk like a normal person, Leon," AJ said, already sipping his third coffee of the day and feeling worse by the minute. "CCS, comint, cache hackers, NS shields; I don't want to have to drift just to keep up with you." What he meant was he didn't want to have retask any of his new bandwidth, but he hadn't let Leon in on that.

"OK, it's like this. You got to assume, from now on, this McMaster guy knows everything about you and can access every detail of your life. Your comms? He's listening. Your VR unit? He's already downloaded the entire history of every VR show you ever watched, every game you played, every message you ever sent or read. And that little game we played with him in the Capitol, he'll know all about that pretty soon if he doesn't already, and he won't be happy."

"I barely ever use my VR unit," AJ said. "And I mostly talk work on my earbud."

"You got secrets, AJ, everyone does. If he wants to badly enough, he could get someone to cache hack you, pull out all your audio-visual uploads. Put in some intercept code so that every interaction you ever have with Warnecke, or with me, he's seeing it through *your* eyes."

"No one can do that," AJ protested. "With a warrant he might be able to hack my personal cache, but if anyone tried to intercept my uplink, it would be noticed."

Leon said nothing, just looked at him like he was a simpleton.

AJ blinked. "Alright, so what? He can listen to these conversations and see I'm innocent. He can dig into any corner of my life looking for leverage, if that's what you're saying, he's not going to find anything. I'm boring as hell."

"Little mister pure," Leon said dryly. "Don't ever visit no dark-Core sites?"

"Nothing that would even get my Ma upset," AJ said.

"Leverage isn't just dirt," Leon explained. "Leverage is them knowing what you care about. Or who. Your Ma, for example."

"They'd go after an 70-year-old woman to get at me?"

"AJ, you're still not getting it. Let me draw you a picture in black and white. Winter has brought in a hardcore badass to work his side of this. That tells us he sees this as more than just a minor inconvenience. Which means this goes two ways I can see. One morning, you wake up dead. Or you wake up with Troy McMaster knocking on your door looking for answers, making threats or asking for favors."

"Then what am I hanging around here for?" AJ asked, suddenly exasperated. "If these guys *are* out to kill me, I should be getting out of here, trying to hide out somewhere until this whole thing blows over."

Leon gave him a pitying look. "If you were a citizen, you could try that. But you're a cyber. Every twenty minutes, every time you drift, they know where you are. You try not to drift, go somewhere you can unchain from the Core, you've got two hours until you're dead anyway." He put down his coffee cup and stood up. "Sorry, mano, but you got to stay and play. Boost them self-defense protocols, get ready to do a deal of some sort with McMaster if he comes calling about this Warnecke thing. Which I'm betting he will."

"If I die, you lose that bet," AJ pointed out. "And I'll be back in my next life to collect."

"I'll tell that joke at your funeral, fun guy," Leon said. "I'm going home to sleep, you enjoy your day."

Leon left AJ with some pretty clear advice. Firewall everything to do with Warnecke, Winter and Farley. Bury it in your cache with quantum-level real-time mutating encryption so the only way anyone can get at it is to get a court order.

Until now, he'd had no reason not to send everything he cached straight to Deep Core, but he could see Leon had a point. He did as Leon suggested, compartmentalized and encrypted his private cache. It was his data, so he had rights about how it was stored and used, even by the Core. He was required to drift several times an hour and a backup copy of his feed was always kept by the Core, but he could choose exactly what he released to Deep Core while he was alive, and what he kept in his private cache. If he died, or when he was reintegrated, *everything* in his private cache would be moved to Deep Core, but until then, his data was his data.

There had been a lot of legal argument about whether a cyber should have the right to delete, modify or encrypt the data in their private cache – they had free will, so what if they were involved in a crime and were destroying evidence? But cyber advocates had successfully argued that citizens were not required to keep a copy of every and all audio and video recordings they made of their lives, and *they* had the right to store and delete personal data as they wished. It was ruled that it should also be that way for a cyber.

On the question of his personal safety, he ran a risk analysis and decided to stay put, but take some extra precautions. If the Congressman really was thinking in terms of 'first strike options' he had to be prepared. He'd already reviewed his defense protocols and optimized his resting hormone balance for visual and aural acuity and physical reaction speed. He'd bought back all of his bandwidth and hadn't allocated it all, so he had reserve capacity if he needed. Then, in addition to his reconfig, he'd tagged every interaction he had had with and about Warnecke, including his meeting with the Congressman, for automatic transmission to friends and media outlets in the event of his death.

AJ could feel his mind whirling and kicked up his klotho levels by 8 percent, carefully putting all of the different thought streams into order until he felt more settled. He wasn't used to stress. In fact his trajectory in life, if you could call it that, had been all about avoiding it. He had cruised through high school, used college to explore what he liked and didn't like and made his grades, made nice friends, found the job he wanted and stayed with it. Dated, both seriously (Henni) and unseriously (Cyan). AJ saw himself as a river in motion, and if there was a rock up ahead, he just slid around it and kept moving. This Warnecke thing, it would be the same, he just had to go with it, not fight it. Leon was making such a big deal of it, which was cool. He was showing AJ he cared for him, in his Leon kind of way. It was payment for how he'd covered for Leon these last couple years, he got that.

Depending on how you looked at it, his situation wasn't that complicated. He'd be careful, and he'd get through it. Or he wouldn't, and he'd die, which just meant he'd reintegrate a decade early. Which would suck, but make little difference to the universe in the grand scale of things. As cybers across the centuries had always said in the face of tragedy and unexpected death, he would be missed, 'but the Core will abide'.

About mid-afternoon he sent a short message to Cassie and then took Brownie's advice and slept a solid 12 hours, made a big breakfast and then went for an early morning surf.

As he started work, he was feeling a full-on psych buzz. His bandwidth boost had really kicked in and he was processing at speeds light years beyond his normal Sol Vista maintenance tech state. To any outside observer, he was following his normal routine. Checked in with Brownie, did his decon, changed, walked the Gardens at Sol Vista. But with the extra bandwidth he'd allocated himself, he was working one question above all – was it feasible to use the Core to dive the Deep Core? To use one part of the world-spanning AI to hack *itself*? As he walked the Gardens, he'd isolated the main themes from Farley's six publications, two thousand odd discussion threads, sub-threads and three unpublished doctoral theorems, and isolated the hypothesis he was testing in his PhD. It came down to this: identify a legitimate query from the Core to its Deep Core databases, intercept that query and modify it to conduct the search ordered by the hacker. Siphon away the data before it hit the Core query engine again. The Core query would report a search failure and then (successfully) retry its search. AJ broadened the search to historical data sets going back two hundred years to the creation of the Core. It was a concept that had been tried before but which had been caught by the Core's defenses.

It relied on three separate attacks to succeed:

The hacker had to be able to isolate a 'legitimate' Core query to the Deep Core.

186

They had to be able to modify the search query to a query of their own.

They had to be able to intercept the data after retrieval but before it hit the Core query engine again, in a way that the Core would interpret as a system error, and not an external attack.

AJ found that previous attempts to use this exploit had failed at one or another of all three phases of the attack, most often just falling at the first hurdle because it was almost impossible to identify a Deep Core query within the billions of lines of code the Core was running at any particular moment. Let alone modify that query without detection.

But it had been done. Once. Thirty years after the Core AI had achieved self-actualization, a cyber-defense white-hat hacker working to identify any vulnerabilities had managed both to isolate a Deep Core query and to modify it without detection. He was not able to isolate the data after it had been fetched and reassembled for reporting, but he had reported his success to the Core defense team and, together with the AI itself, they had closed the vulnerability.

That was back in the day when citizens were still able to teach the Core anything. Being aware of it, the Core had since worked further to ensure it never happened again, and more than a hundred and seventy years later the Core's defenses had been updated and improved a vigintillion-fold.

But one thing stuck with AJ. It had been done, once. And military attack AIs, of the kind Farley would have had access to, had also improved beyond the comprehension of that white-hat hacker of 173 years ago.

If a single hacker, working with primitive tools at the dawn of the Core, had been able to do it, then it was not unreasonable to conclude it would also be possible for a single hacker working with advanced tools in the modern era to do it too.

A thought that made AJ suddenly both very curious and very scared.

Cyan caught up with him on her run through the Garden.

"Well hey, AJ," she said, running to a stop beside him. "Was that you whistling?"

"I guess," he said. He hadn't realized it, but maybe he was. Multitasking had small side effects.

"Okay! AJ's in love again!" she said.

"What?"

"Haven't heard you whistle since Henni," Cyan pointed out. "That's a long time between whistles."

"You are the weirdest boss," he said. "Let's talk about *your* love life."

"Let's not," Cyan grimaced, stretching. "If I don't land my soul mate pretty damn soon, I'm going to lose my deposit on the world's best wedding venue."

"You already booked your wedding venue, before you even found your soul mate?" AJ asked. "That's optimism."

"Well, you want the Panorama Room over the Frozen Falls, you have to book years ahead, AJ," she said. "When I booked it, it seemed like plenty of time. Now, not so much."

"That's a totally Cyan thing to do," he said.

"Yeah well, don't let your daughters grow up to be cowboys, AJ," she sighed. "Not that you … okay, sorry about that. So, what needs fixing today?"

AJ went through the maintenance list with her and they talked about when would be the right time to completely drain the Lake, check the piping and clear the filters. How to do it cheaper this time. Then she jogged off to get ready for her day.

He was thinking about that, about how last time some of the residents started a petition to save the fish, they had to pay a wildlife rescue group to come in and capture all the fish first. Those traps had to be out two weeks before they could get started, so maybe he could do that himself and … he worked that thought in the foreground while testing Farley's published code strings and university research in a separate stream.

As he opened the door to the workshop, it jammed against something. He pushed harder and the door gave way, sweeping something in front of it.

Another roll of paper.

After he smoothed it out and turned on the text he saw it was another chapter of Warnecke's manuscript. A different one. There was a note pinned to the front.

I can't remember if I gave you this. This is what I want you to take to Winter, the note said.

OK, so, the guy had pulled another chapter from the manuscript and given it to AJ. He hadn't forgotten all about it, even if he couldn't place AJ yesterday morning at Fatty's. In fact, seeing AJ there had probably jogged his memory. That wasn't unusual for someone with

TGA, things and people seen out of context were hardest to remember, then suddenly things jumped back into focus after some sort of trigger event. The guy was clearly further advanced in his TGA than his doctor suspected, behaving the way he was.

AJ speed scanned the page to see if it added more detail to the work he'd already read. It automatically went into his private encrypted cache. And reading it was like Warnecke's text was a medium, helping the dead Q-programmer Farley reach out through the intervening years and talk directly to AJ.

ON THE POWER OF THE FO EXPLOIT

You will demand proof of the capabilities of the FO Exploit, I understand that. I am in a position to provide you with multiple proofs. But first consider this. Consider the nature of the Core.

The Core has one prime directive: 'To secure and improve the habitability of member moons of the Coruscant system for the benefit of all citizens and the perpetuation of all Commonwealth of Coruscant civilization.' Put simply, it does nothing more than run, and try to improve the running of, the life support systems of Tatsensui and PRC, and, by extension, New Syberia should it choose to become a full member of the Commonwealth.

And in its constant, single-minded quest to be the 'Gardener of Coruscant' as a poet once called it, the Core has expanded its capabilities beyond anything its creators could have imagined, so that it can fulfill that directive. First slowly, and then at an exponential rate, it has made breakthroughs in science and engineering that have turned the moons of Coruscant from barren spheres on which the citizens of the Commonwealth had only the most tenuous of footholds into thriving, productive,

190

interdependent colonized worlds, all the while preserving their unique environments and all too precious life forms.

It gave Tatsensui first the city dome, then the Skycap. It found water and other liquid gases under the surface of the desert moon of PRC and engineered the technologies to allow these to be converted to a sustainable, breathable atmosphere within domes especially adapted to the climate of PRC. Though not strictly under its care, it came up with the concept of adapting the Alcubierre Drive into a shield, to protect the passage of New Syberia through the Coruscant Asteroid Belt and eliminate the threat to that colony of a destructive asteroid strike.

Frustrated, in the true sense of the word, by its reliance on the citizens of the Commonwealth to interact physically with the universe around it, it created first machine agents, and then more socially acceptable biological agents, the cybers, to populate the worlds, mingle with their citizens and learn how it was to live on the worlds in its care so that it could continue to improve them. Citizens and cybers now live in harmony, growing, learning and advancing society together.

The FO Exploit utilizes a fatal vulnerability in the design of the Core.

It is specifically designed to dive the Deep Core, looking single-mindedly for data that has been tagged Not For Disclosure: 'NFD'. It reassembles and decrypts it and enables the light of public scrutiny to shine on it, at last. When I began this work, I believed that would be enough. To bring data to the surface that had been buried for hundreds of years. But in successfully doing so I have exposed a vulnerability in the Core that could be used to destroy it. And with it, all life in Coruscant.

You are reading this because the FO Exploit has already been deployed. I make no apologies for that. It cannot be rolled back. I did not intend the Exploit to be used as a weapon, but now I can see that without me to control it, it might.

The Core has grown all-powerful and all-pervasive, and that very power has become its fatal flaw. The FO Exploit is real.

Core Death is now possible.

That's where it finished, Warnecke's next chapter. More mind-bombs. Core Death? That sounded a little dramatic. Warnecke warning that his exploit was unstoppable now that it had been deployed.

Stuff and nonsense. It must be, or surely Winter would have had Warnecke thrown into a deep, dark hole a long time ago, friend or not.

Except... Winter thought his old friend was obsessive and delusional. He hadn't believed Farley had a viable theory about how to dive the Deep Core 40 years ago, and he certainly didn't believe that ice-planer engineer Dave Warnecke could have found a way to make it real. So he had turned first a deaf ear, and then his back, on his old friend.

Even now. He was treating Warnecke as an irritation, an inconvenience. A very serious one, at a time when relations with NS were on a knife edge, when the last thing he needed was a suicidal paranoid old man making wild accusations and dredging up his past. So serious an inconvenience that he might possibly feel the best way to deal with it was to throw both Warnecke and anyone he had been speaking with (aka AJ) into a deep dark hole. But the fact AJ was still walking around with life and limbs intact told him Winter probably didn't consider the FO Exploit to be real.

Yet? Winter hadn't seen this latest document.

AJ was hooked, and he knew it. He was deep into Warnecke and Farley's world now, trying to find the flow.

He wanted to talk to the author, not literally of course, but an AI built from his Core cache. But Farley was no cyber, and he had died before caching was an option. All AJ had was a few undergraduate papers and discussions by Farley, and Warnecke's made-for-the-masses storytelling text which intimated that Farley's Q-code exploit existed. AJ ran a hand across the page, willing the programmer to rise up out of it.

Except he couldn't. Because they'd left him behind on the ice.

11. WHEN A SPOOK COMES TO CALL

AJ put down the page, looked up at the ceiling of the workshop, the bright diodes burning above him. What would *you* have done, AJ? Out of food, out of hope. Would you have left him on the ice too?

He was thinking about that and Farley's theorem, lost in the drift, when his comms buzzed.

"Hey Maria," he said, recognizing the ID.

"Hi," Leon's wife said. "How you doing, AJ?"

"I'm good, what's up?" AJ had been waiting for Leon to turn up so they could talk over this latest development.

"Leon is not coming in to work today," she said.

"No? OK," AJ said, trying not to sound too disappointed. "I'll cover for him, no problem."

"I think it may be more than a couple days this time," Maria said. "He did not have a good night, AJ."

"Sorry to hear it."

"AJ," the woman said, and he could hear the strain in her voice, "I want you to know, I appreciate it, what you do for Leon."

"Don't worry about it."

"So he can keep this job, I really appreciate it."

"Seriously, it's OK, he's a good guy."

"Si. And he wants to pay you back for everything you do for him, but this thing he has with you right now, this Capitol trip. He can't keep doing that, AJ."

"I understand, Maria," AJ said. "It was his idea, not mine."

"I know, he told me," Maria said. "His heart is good. But whatever this is, he doesn't tell me, but whatever this is, it makes him sick. You have no idea."

AJ thought about Leon in the Capitol, talking fast, hyper-vigilant, pulling a knife on a couple of people coming out of a diner. *Yeah, maybe I do know*, he thought. But he said, "You're right. But we're done."

"Good."

"It wasn't anything criminal, Maria," AJ said hurriedly.

"OK, good. He wouldn't tell me."

"No, I get that, I get you were probably worried, but it was just a personal problem. It's sorted out now, so you tell him just to look after himself."

She sighed. "He took a big tranq. I can't tell him nothing today, but when I can, I will."

"Hey look," AJ said. "I know he paid for his own flight to the Capitol. I offered to pay but he wouldn't…"

"It's OK," Maria said. "But thank you. He wanted to do this for you. The money is alright."

"You're sure?"

"Sure."

She said goodbye and cut the call. AJ tapped his earbud to power it down, and then paused, remembering Leon had warned him it was probably being intercepted. Had he said anything? Well, he'd confirmed Leon had been in the Capitol, if they didn't already know that. But what else? OK, he had told her it wasn't something criminal, and that it was over as far as he was concerned. If they heard that, they'd be happy, right? It was what he was supposed to be thinking. That Winter and

McMaster were on the case, and they would work with the family to 'manage' Warnecke into a better facility.

AJ took his hand away from his earbud. Maybe Leon being away a couple days was a good thing. He wouldn't be around, hyping the situation up. AJ could just let it flow, and it would probably, hopefully, resolve itself. After all, it would soon be mid-morning and he was still alive. Power of positive thinking, AJ, he told himself. The rain comes before the rainbow.

Then he looked down and saw the new chapter of the manuscript about the FO Exploit and realized he wasn't back in the flow just yet.

AJ decided the best way to deal with Winter and Warnecke and McMaster was to stay alert, but not panic. He focused on running his Farley research in the background, extrapolating from this latest information, while in the foreground he was doing the job at Sol Vista he was paid to do. He covered five residences by two o'clock, and plugged a leaking eave in the Hub. He hit two more apartments in the late afternoon, so he was pretty much up to date with the maintenance program even with Leon being away. He managed not to cross paths with Warnecke before he clocked off either, which was a bonus.

He called Cassie, but for whatever reason decided not to tell her about the latest document under his door. It was more fun talking shit and planning their long weekend trip.

"You need more pillion time on the planer, get you to loosen up a bit," Cassie teased him. "You want to head up the coast this Friday night? I thought maybe we could hit Kwetluk by about nine p.m., find somewhere to stay. Is there surf up there?"

"No Sea Gate," AJ said. "But there's a lake outside the dome, we could go ice yachting. We should bring the decks, there's probably something skateable in Kwetluk too."

"Cool, you book a place for us, or shall I?" she asked.

"I can book it," he offered. "But, like, you want your own room or…"

"Seriously? AJ, I just asked you to come away with me for a romantic weekend. You think I want separate rooms?"

"No. Right," he said.

That evening he pushed through the whole night on a hormone boost, staying in a drift state while he worked the Farley thing, trying to recreate the man's thinking for himself from the fragments Farley had included in other papers. He'd even explored a theory that the text itself might be hiding encrypted code. It took several hours just to eliminate that theory. So all he had were scenarios without probabilities – he was missing essential data. Even just a single new fragment of Q-code that Warnecke might have been working on would give him somewhere to start. At one point he found himself talking out loud to himself, just like a citizen might.

"Just ask Warnecke, you fool, the manuscript says he has more proof!"

"And let him know we're working on this? He'll shoot himself! Worse, he'll shoot us!"

The next morning at work, the first residence he called at had a dead dishwasher, so he had to pull it out, check if he could fix it (he couldn't) and book a tech to assist. He shook his head – like why did they need to put a damn quantum processor in every appliance these days? It was a dishwasher FFS, not the in-flight computer for an interstellar freighter. Then he decided to check the automated watering system for leaks.

A lot of residents were out enjoying the Garden and most wanted a chat. AJ didn't mind, he needed the distraction. It was a nice day. So of course, it was no surprise he rounded a corner and saw Warnecke there. He paused. Warnecke hadn't seen him yet. He was standing looking around the Garden like he was trying to find something – or someone. The last time, when he had pulled his gun, he had it tucked into the waistband behind his back. AJ could see it wasn't there today, and he wasn't holding it. What the hell, he couldn't avoid the guy in a place as small as Sol Vista. He took a big breath and preloaded an adrenaline kick just in case. *Let's see where this goes.*

"Hey, Citizen Warnecke," he said as he walked up behind him. "You lost something, or someone?"

He was expecting Warnecke's usual bitter reply, but the guy turned around and looked a little sheepish. "Well, I don't know. Sorry, I forgot your name?"

"AJ," AJ said, sticking out his hand. "Were you looking for me?"

Warnecke was wringing his hands, and then seemed to realize he was and stuck them in his pockets. "I don't know. It's embarrassing. Look, I have this project I'm working on. I think I brought some of it in here with me yesterday – a chapter of it – but I can't remember. I vaguely recall I was looking for you?"

"You left me a chapter," AJ said. "Yesterday." He decided he wouldn't mention the first part of the manuscript Warnecke had given him, just the latest, because Winter had kept the first part. He couldn't give that back. But it looked like he had a chance here to give the new chapter back to Warnecke. He'd cached it, so he didn't need it anymore.

"Oh, right," Warnecke said, a little relieved. "I *thought* I meant to bring it over here, but then I couldn't..." He tapped his head, annoyed at himself. No, not annoyed, the guy looked distressed.

"Don't worry," AJ said automatically, "We all forget stuff. I've got it."

"Right ... can I have it back?" Warnecke asked.

"Yeah, it's in my workshop," AJ said, pointing up the path. When they got there, he stepped past Warnecke and opened the door. "Come on in. You want a coffee? I only got pseudo, but if you want some..." AJ relaxed a little. This time with Warnecke it was going the right way for once.

Warnecke followed him in, looking around like it was the first time he'd been there.

"Take a seat," AJ said, pointing at Leon's chair. "Coffee? You take sweetener, whitener?"

"Sure. No, just black thanks," Warnecke said, clearly looking for the page he'd left.

AJ turned on the water heater and then reached up to the shelf where he'd put Warnecke's document. He took down the page, peeled Warnecke's note off it, and handed it back to him. Warnecke rolled it open and flicked through it.

"This is all?" he asked.

"Yeah," AJ said, leaning forward to look at it. "That's what came under the door yesterday. It's yours, right?" AJ felt bad play acting like that, but Warnecke was offering him a way out of this latest dilemma so he was taking it.

"Yes, it's just…"

"Yeah?"

The old guy's eyes teared up. He was suddenly not the gruff old man with a grudge against the world. He was a confused old man who seemed to have lost his place in it. He patted the page with one hand. "This … this is so important. This project. It's why I came to this place … to try to finish it. Before I lose it, lose myself," he said. "For his memory. Nothing else matters."

AJ made Warnecke a coffee and handed it to him. Warnecke took the cup with one hand, not letting go of the page with the other.

"OK, I get it," AJ said. "It's important to you."

Warnecke looked at AJ, or through him. The hand holding the coffee cup was shaking.

"No, you don't get it," he said. "I *know* I'm losing my marbles. I finished this too late. Way too late. I have to get it done, I need to get it done, and *he* has to…" Warnecke looked fierce now. "I have to get it out. And he has to face what we did. People deserve to know…"

"This would be Congressman Winter?" AJ asked.

"Winter! Yeah, he … he …" Warnecke ground to a halt. "I remember now. You work for him! I asked you to take this to him. I gave you … his private ID, right?" He was jabbing a finger in the air at AJ. "Have you done it? Have you told him?"

AJ wasn't fazed. "I *don't* work for Congressman Winter. This is the second time you gave me a document for him. As a favor to you, I did take the first document to him. He said he'd get in touch with you about it." AJ pointed at the document in Warnecke's quivering hand. "I haven't done anything except read that one, and I don't want anything to do with it."

Warnecke looked confused again. "He said he'd contact me?" He tapped his earbud and stared unfocused at a wall, then back at AJ. "He hasn't. No one called me."

"I'm sorry," AJ said. "I did what you asked."

Warnecke put his head in his hands. "I don't understand. How can he ... did you read them?" He waved the document. "This one? The one you gave Winter? Did you read them?"

AJ turned back to the boiling water, thinking, *OK, how far down this rabbit hole should I go?* "I think I'll have a coffee too," AJ said, buying himself some time. He reached for a cup, set it out and spooned in the coffee while the water boiled, then poured himself a cup, Warnecke sitting impatiently, frowning. Gave himself some whitener.

"I read both documents," AJ said finally. "It's intriguing stuff."

"Intriguing? It's earth-shattering!" Warnecke exclaimed. He took a slug of his coffee. "I'm talking Core Death and you say 'intriguing'? My friend, he was a quantum programmer, he had this theory, right? Amazing idea, breakthrough stuff. But he never got to take it all the way – he died. So I took it one step further. I made it work. It changes *everything.*"

AJ leaned back. "Core Death, you say?" he asked.

"Don't patronize me," Warnecke snapped, back to form. Then he softened again. "You think I'm spouting nonsense."

AJ pulled his thoughts together. Scientific curiosity was starting to gnaw at him. *Drop it, AJ!* he told himself. *Do Not Engage.* "Not at all. But this is between you and the Congressman," he said. "I'm just a maintenance tech, Citizen Warnecke. Not a cop. Not hired security. Unless you have a stuck door or a defunct scrubber, I really can't help you."

"OK, OK," Warnecke said, looking at AJ, then away, then back again. "Let's say I believe you. Let's say I was just a resident here, asking a favor."

"I already did…"

"*Another* favor," Warnecke said quickly. "A small one." He flapped the document he'd put under the door. "I'm having a hard time pulling this together." He sounded frustrated. "It's all written, but it needs a second set of eyes on it, someone to edit it. I've been staring at it so long, I'm going blind."

"I don't know," AJ said. "You spoke about a crime a while ago. I don't want to get involved in anything."

"Please!" the old man pleaded. "I'm out of time…" He looked at AJ, a desperate look in his eyes. "I need to get a distributable copy ready. Before my mind is completely gone."

"Look…" AJ said. He realized his curiosity was getting the better of him. On the one hand, he'd told Winter and Leon and Cassie he just wanted to get out from the middle of all this. On the other hand, he was being sucked in by the mystery of it all, could feel the guy's pain, and feel himself being drawn in deeper.

202

"It's important," Warnecke said. "You'll see why when you read it all. Not just to me, it's important to … everyone. I can't do it alone. You'll help me, right?"

AJ had a dozen alternative responses queued and then stood outside himself, realizing they weren't needed. It wasn't complicated. There was a door open here, and he could either shut it, or he could walk through it.

"Sure," AJ told him. "I can try to help you. When I'm done with work today."

"Why not now?" Warnecke asked. "This can't wait…"

"Sorry," AJ said firmly. He wanted time to reconsider, in case this was a dumb idea. Run a risk analysis on his whole situation now he had his full bandwidth back. Maybe throw it around with Leon. "We are a guy down, probably for the rest of the week at least. Look, I'll come by your place tonight, when I get a chance, but it won't be before the end of the day."

Warnecke wasn't happy, but at least he had a promise. "Alright, but don't leave it too late," he said, sounding genuinely worried. "Every damn hour that goes by, another marble falls to the floor."

"That's why we're here," AJ told Warnecke, taking his empty cup from him. "You drop 'em, we pick 'em up for you." He pointed at Warnecke's earbud. "Dictate yourself a reminder, so you don't get surprised when I come knocking."

AJ made some house calls and cleaned some tools, killing a few hours while he thought it through. Call Leon? No, he'd just make AJ even more paranoid about Winter. *You go in there AJ, look at that manuscript, there's no going back. You don't and you'll live your life not knowing if maybe, just maybe, there was some truth in Warnecke's wild claims. What if you walked into Warnecke's place and there it all was, Farley's basic research, his code, all of it, and this threat of Core Death was suddenly real. You're going to just ignore that?*

His risk analysis threw up a few hundred scenarios and rated them with probabilities – most were near zero, particularly any that implied Warnecke had managed to hack the Core. He set a threshold of 30 percent for scenarios that he should take seriously, and a special flag on any scenarios which ended in bodily harm, dismemberment or death for AJ.80966. None of those was currently above 18 percent so he decided to stick with his 'don't panic' mindset. In fact, maybe he didn't need to face Warnecke after all. He could ignore the guy, hope he forgot.

But scientific curiosity won. And his bandwidth was near max, probably for the first and only time in his life. It was costing him dearly in lost income, so it was screaming at him to be put to use. It was a short walk to number 96. He didn't need to knock, Warnecke had seen him approach but stood inside his door and looked at him skeptically. "Well, you took your time, but at least you showed."

"Nice to see you too again, sir," AJ said. A good start – at least it seemed he remembered their earlier conversation.

Warnecke stepped aside to let AJ in. He kept the place clean and tidy between official cleaning visits, AJ could see that. So someone had house trained him.

"You keep a nice house," AJ said. "You married long?"

"To the navy, yeah," Warnecke said. "You keep things in their place, or you get your ass kicked, is how I learned."

"OK, you were in the navy. That's where you learned mechanical engineering after university?" AJ asked, walking around looking at pictures. He hadn't stayed long enough to poke around last time. A framed printed photo on a wall of Warnecke in his navy uniform, scowling at the camera. There was another middle-aged man in an Orkutsk Garrison uniform, with his arm around a woman, so he guessed that was the son who was off-world right now. A picture of what looked like a young woman in icefields survival gear, goggles and breathing mask obscuring her face – the 'loner' daughter perhaps. And there were pictures of the two grandkids at various ages, and their partners. No great-grandkids that AJ could see. And there was also a small table with pictures of a woman he guessed must have been Warnecke's wife. She went from young and rosy-cheeked to frail and exoskeleton-bound in the pictures. AJ decided he'd save that question for another day. Being limited to only 30 years outside the Core had its advantages. Growing old must suck.

"You done your homework," Warnecke said.

"Not really, you told me you were a Q-programmer like Congressman Winter, and your grandkids told me you were an engineer, on Planer teams," AJ explained. "You helped me fix the scrubber the day you moved in."

"Sounds like me," Warnecke allowed. "Even the cybers on those crews called me the Oracle, they tell you that?"

"Your grandkids said," AJ smiled. "You going to make me a coffee, or we just going to stand here getting dry throats?"

Warnecke looked at him slyly. "You don't drink beer?"

"Not at work," AJ told him.

"Well, you ain't at work if you're helping me with my project," Warnecke said, going to his cooler. "So stop your coffee nonsense." He pulled two beers from his cooler and handed one to AJ. Black Ice Porter. Of course. "Sit," he commanded and pointed to his sofa, moving some old print books aside on his coffee table. Each one was probably worth a week's salary for AJ.

Warnecke disappeared into a back room and came back with a stack of pages, already rolled out flat. Some were red striped, some green, some double white. It looked like they'd been shuffled by ... well, shuffled by someone in distress. Warnecke slapped them down on the table next to his beer.

"This is my project," he said, looking a little forlorn. "Guy called Farley did all the groundwork. But he's gone now. Dead. The only people he shared his ideas with were me and Congressman Winter. Now that I proved the concept works, I've used it to pull some data from the Deep Core, so the world can see it needs to take it seriously. I do that, I can get Winter to help raise this in government, because this goes way beyond being able to dive the Deep Core. I need people to take it seriously."

"Take what seriously, exactly?" AJ asked.

"This vulnerability..." Warnecke said, agitated now, speaking fast. "If I could use the Exploit for this, an enemy could use it too, to bring the Core down. But here, you can read it, read for yourself." He patted the papers. "It's all there, all the proof anyone could ever need that this works," he said. "You can look at it and organize it without caching it,

206

right?" He sounded worried now. "If you commit any of this to the Core, you could be signing Coruscant's death warrant. That means you too, cyber."

AJ opened the folder and looked at the page lying on the top of the stack, titled 'The FO Exploit and Core Death'. He pulled his eyes away and put a hand on the pile. "The only way I can do this off-Core is if I drift, then look at this for you, try to get it all organized, and then delete it from my cache before I drift again. That will prevent it going to Deep Core, but only until I reintegrate. It gives you about ten years."

Warnecke looked at him with a sad smile. "That will be just fine."

AJ took his hand back. "Look, it would help me if I could also look at the Q-code behind this work. Without it, I only have your word that it works, and I know nothing about *how* it works, so it will be hard to evaluate what's in the text."

They took a pull in silence, Warnecke still standing. He glanced over at his bookcase, then back. "No. I don't want you to 'evaluate' it, I just want you to organize it," he said. He finished his beer with one long chug. "Trust me, when this comes out, there will be no shortage of 'evaluating'. I'll leave you to it. I'll just be in the kitchen making myself some dinner, you need to ask anything," he said.

"I'll have a look, OK?" AJ said, flipping the pages. "I'm not sure I can get it all done during my drift window."

"It's not the blasted Illustrated History of the Commonwealth," Warnecke said. "It's just text, written so any Joe or Jane can read it. Just get it in a semblance of order," Warnecke told him. He went over and locked the front door. "And don't even think about leaving here with it. You do, I swear I'll shoot you and tell the cops I thought you were a burglar. Then when you recycle as a baby I'll hunt you down and kill you again."

AJ didn't want a physical copy of the damn thing anyway. He could delete his cache and the scan would be gone, but he'd still have his biological memory. There was no way anyone could access that, but no way for him to delete it either.

AJ held up his hands. "It's OK, Citizen Warnecke," he said. "I'm staying right here."

"Damn straight you are," Warnecke said, walking off to his kitchen and muttering. "Shoot you dead. See if I wouldn't."

AJ watched him shuffle out, then leaned back on the sofa, the manuscript in front of him. *Last chance, AJ. Get up, walk away. Sell your bandwidth back to the Core, stop digging into Farley's work and leave Troy McMaster to sort out the Congressman's troubles.*

Good advice. But too late. He already had the hook through his gills.

He drifted to reset his window to 20 minutes, then flipped quickly, page by page, through the manuscript. It seemed to be all there with the exception of the chapter he'd given to Winter; messed up, with hundreds, perhaps thousands of pages numbered in a nonsensical order, but there. Too tantalizing. He got started, and immediately got absorbed by the first page he picked up.

Thirty years ago, a brilliant quantum coder by the name of Farley O'Halloran posed himself a seemingly absurd question. If the Deep Core was unhackable, accessible only to the Core, then could the Core be tricked into hacking itself?

He shared the idea with two close friends, Kevin Winter and myself, and we mocked him.

Then later, we killed him. I will detail exactly how.

Farley's question did not die with him, it kept gnawing away at me, until one day I determined that I'd try seriously to explore whether it had merit. I reviewed all of his notes and snippets of alpha code. Then thirty years ago, cradling my newborn son in my arms, I suddenly saw how it could be done.

To see a path is easier than to walk it. It took ten years before I could operationalize what I came to call the Farley O'Halloran Exploit. I had a simple ambition, to unlock centuries of data that a succession of misguided governments had deemed the Coruscant public did not deserve to see. This manuscript will show that in diving the Deep Core I obtained data showing that:

1) The first President of the PRC, Stanley Ho, was assassinated by agents of his own government and not by the group of radical anti-Core activists whose leader was convicted for the crime.

2) The drug LPA-2, or Blue, is dangerously ineffective in protecting against gamma radiation and this lack of protection is the primary cause of Transient and Permanent Global Amnesia.

3) Neither Tatsensui nor PRC intelligence services have any credible information indicating that New Syberia is militarizing its presence on Orkutsk, and that the current investigation into the President of New Syberia is part of an agreement between the Tatsensui and PRC governments to pressure New Syberia to abandon its policy of autonomous cyber AI development in favor of chaining New Syberia to the Core.

These are but three of the hundreds of revelations obtained from diving the Deep Core, but chosen for their historical and political relevance both to their times and to events today. The full documentation supporting these claims is included in this manuscript.

However, in achieving the seemingly impossible, I realized that my single-minded pursuit of this goal had exposed a glaring vulnerability in the design of the Core, arising from its evolution over the last several decades, and which could be used to compromise its most basic life support functions.

In other words, I had created a weapon which could be used to destroy the colonies of Tatsensui and PRC and, because they are entirely dependent on each other, by default, also that of New Syberia.

This manuscript is not therefore just about the secrets the Coruscant government has been keeping from its people. It is about Core Death, and the risk to the entire Commonwealth of a Core AI which we have allowed to evolve into a dangerous and unstable entity.

For us to survive, the Exploit must be controlled. As long as I am alive, it can be. But when I am gone, there will be no one left to control it.

What?! AJ blew out a breath, leaned back and looked at the ceiling. Looked at a clock. It had taken ten seconds to scan this page. He quickly calculated whether he could read and reorganize the entire manuscript inside 20 minutes and decided that he had to try. He could worry about what he'd read later. He leaned back in the sofa, hands behind his head, causing it to creak.

From the kitchen Warnecke called out, "You need something? Another beer?"

"No, all good," AJ said, though he was feeling far from it. He started speed scanning the pile of paper and then got to work organizing it into a coherent narrative. It took him about ten minutes. He sat trying to process what he'd read, imprint as much of it as he could in his biological memory. Most of the manuscript was focused on the revelations from the Deep Core that Warnecke claimed to have fished out, and AJ had to admit there was a wealth of 'source material' for his claims – thousands of communications, memos, voice and VR files, classified intelligence reports and, in the case of LPA-2, clinical research reports and epidemiological data. The focus on this was probably just a reflection of where Warnecke had spent most of his time and effort over the years, before coming to the belated realization that diving the Deep Core was just one side of what his Exploit was capable of. The rest of the document was devoted to the implications of what else might be possible – seizing control of Core climate management functions such as rainfall and atmosphere composition, disrupting or disabling communications systems, subtly influencing AI research results … it seemed the possibilities were endless.

There was just one problem. No, two.

Nowhere in the document did Warnecke explain exactly how he had achieved what he'd claimed to have achieved. How did the FO Exploit work, how had it been implemented, how might it be so easily perverted? Because without knowing any of that, it was impossible to say that once the Core became aware of it, it could not just as quickly find a defense against it, and life would continue untroubled and uninterrupted.

And secondly, nowhere did Warnecke explain, as he had promised to do, how he and Winter had 'killed' Farley O'Halloran.

"I'm done!" AJ called, with about five minutes remaining.

Warnecke came rushing in, wiping his hands on a towel tucked into his waist. AJ stood and handed him the sheaf of papers.

"In narrative order," he said. "I took the liberty of altering the page numbers so that they are sequential now."

Warnecke beamed. "And what do you think? Not some crazy old guy after all, right?"

"Well," AJ paused. "If all the backing documentation you included in there is authentic…"

"It is," Warnecke insisted.

"If it is," AJ continued, "then I understand why your Congressman friend is not keen to discuss any of it. This could potentially bring down governments across Coruscant."

"Exactly!" Warnecke said. "But … I'm sensing you've got some reservations."

AJ checked the time. He had one minute before he had to wipe his cache if he was going to keep his word to Warnecke.

"Well, you don't describe this mysterious FO Exploit, which you will have to do if you want the reader to believe it's real, and that you dived the Deep Core and didn't just get the data some other way. Which you have to do if you also want to convince people this is some bigger existential threat."

"I know that," Warnecke said testily. "But to even discuss the smallest detail of how the Exploit works is to reveal it all, and I can't do that until I am completely ready to go public."

Twenty-five seconds. "OK, also you wrote that you'd explain how Farley was killed, but that's not in there."

"I'm saving that too," Warnecke smiled. "That one's personal. If the Congressman gets behind this, I might let it lie. Now wipe your cache."

Ten seconds. He could just tell Warnecke that sure, he'd wiped it, but keep a copy on his cache. Try to firewall it so it wouldn't go Deep Core as soon as he drifted, but what if … What if Warnecke could do what he said he could do – if he could search the Deep Core at will, could he also break down AJ's cache encryption and see that he'd lied? That was a risk he didn't want to take.

He deleted.

"Done," he said. "All I have left now is my biological memory about this."

"I'm OK with that," Warnecke said. "I'm an expert in how messed up biological memory can get." He looked at his papers again and tapped them against the nearby kitchen table to straighten the edges, then looked over at AJ. "Thanks for doing this."

AJ was clearly being dismissed, so he stood up. "OK. That's all then?"

"For you. I'll take it from here," Warnecke said. He flapped his manuscript in the air. "This is nearly ready for release. I'll go to Winter one last time. He either gets on board, or he goes under. I can't wait any longer."

It sounded too easy. AJ wanted to be sure. "OK, so, we're quits? You don't need my help anymore?"

Warnecke waved a hand at the door. "Yes. I already said thanks, didn't I? Goodbye."

To anyone else, it would have looked like AJ followed his normal work routine, packed his tools away, locked up his workshop, dropped by Admin to chat with Cyan and then shared a ride back home, like it was any other weekday.

But he was jacked, and had bandwidth to spare. So while he walked and talked and sat and stared into space, he archived and then cross-referenced every clue he could remember from Warnecke's manuscript with those parts of Farley's basic research he'd been able to find, or with the published code of other Q-programmers who'd speculated about Deep Core hacks. It was a whirlpool that just led him further and further down, but that was OK. There was precious little that was public, so mostly he was taking what he could find and running thought experiments on it. If Farley was thinking *this*, then could it lead to *that*?

Close to his usual sack time, he decided he was just going in circles and called Cassie to give her an update.

"Ho was assassinated, LPA-2 causes TGA, and Tatsensui and PRC want NS to join the Core?" Cassie asked. "Only one out of three there is newsworthy, the other two will just make people shrug."

"I don't think he's going for headlines, just to prove his Exploit works," AJ said. "He made me delete my cache so I can't call it up, but behind every accusation was a mountain of evidence he said he'd dredged up from the Deep Core."

"Yeah, but why choose those?" she continued. "There's not a person alive who doesn't already believe Ho was assassinated, and a 200-year-old murder is hardly current affairs. Blind Freddy knows the other two colonies want NS to fall into line on cybers. It's part philosophy, part politics, and almost like religion. They cooked up this investigation to put more pressure on NS? Well, duh. Only the TGA thing has any legs – that's going to get people angry and scared."

"You're thinking like a reporter," AJ said. "I've been looking for other themes. These are all things that are going to shake people's faith in the Core. It's always been this benign presence; part mothership, part protector, part genius. Every couple of decades it drops some big new innovation on Coruscant like a cosmic magician – poof, the Skycap, poof, Blues, poof, the NS Shield, organ cloning, tissue regen, peace through interplanetary interdependence economics, universal VR, robotic agents, cybers…" He paused. "By claiming there is truth in these big conspiracy theories that people believe anyway, you shatter the image of the Core itself. It's been wittingly or unwittingly hiding these terrible secrets, how can you trust it with anything?"

Cassie wanted to dig a little more into Warnecke's background while AJ was digging into Farley's research, but he told her what he really needed to do was sleep, so she gave him a virtual hug and logged out.

In ten minutes he was fast asleep. Two seconds later, or so it seemed, he heard his earbud buzzing on his bedside table. He reached over and fumbled it into his ear before the call alert in the house comms system started chiming.

It looked like a Capitol ID. Voice only. He checked the time. Three a.m.? Seriously? He tapped his earbud and coughed then answered.

"Hello?"

"Hi, is this AJ?" he heard the voice say.

"Yeah?"

"Hi, this is Congressman Winter's adviser, Troy McMaster," he said.

To his surprise, AJ didn't freak. It was probably the bandwidth boost. The endless scenarios and probabilities he'd run and was rerunning. This was not a surprise. And he had a plan for how to handle it.

AJ checked the time again. "I'm sleeping, Citizen," he mumbled. "Can this wait?"

"Oh, shoot," the guy said, not very convincingly. "Sorry, I forgot what time zone you're on. The day isn't finished here."

"Right," AJ said, not believing him for a moment. He triggered a small adrenaline bump. "So…"

"Sorry," McMaster said again. "Look, I'll get straight to it. The Congressman has a favor to ask."

That, at least, was straight out of Leon's playbook. AJ had been expecting it. "Uh huh?"

"He needs the rest of Citizen Warnecke's manuscript," McMaster said. "To be able to see what sort of wild claims might be in there, to judge whether we have time to deal with this carefully, or do we need to take urgent action."

"He should just call him and talk about it," AJ said. "Citizen Warnecke wants that."

"That might just … complicate matters. You have access to Citizen Warnecke's house, right?" the guy said. "You could just go in, make a copy."

"Copy it," AJ repeated. "Steal it, you mean."

"No, just access it," McMaster insisted. "You're a cyber. Scan and make a copy – just a local copy in your own cache that you could print it from. We don't want it on the open Core any more than he does. Just print a copy, wipe your cache and keep it for us to collect. It's not stealing, you're not breaking any laws."

AJ was human enough to spot BS when he heard it, and cyber enough to be very careful about his reaction.

"Uh, look," AJ said. "The Congressman and Citizen Warnecke are friends, right? He told me yesterday he's going to approach the Congressman directly again with this, to talk about it. He'd probably give him a copy if he just asks nicely."

"Yeah, about that," McMaster said. "This is a crazy busy time for the Congressman, with the investigation he's leading. You said you know about that?"

"Into President Vologodsky of New Syberia?" AJ said. "You could say, yeah. He's accused of militarizing Orkutsk with some kind of cyber army, right?" *Falsely accused? Accused so we can find him guilty and drag NS into the Core alliance? That investigation?*

"Yes, but between us, AJ," McMaster said, "we think he's making a bigger play. Maybe going after Coruscant itself." He said it like he was letting AJ in on a big secret.

"Wow," AJ said, not very convincingly.

"Exactly. So Congressman Winter really can't just cut all his appointments in the Capitol and head over there on a small personal errand. That's why we were hoping you'll help out."

Small personal errand? AJ thought to himself. *Small enough that his personal 'adviser' calls out of nowhere to ask me to rob one of the residents...*

AJ went with his plan A for this scenario. "Sorry," AJ said. "That's just not something I'd be comfortable with."

McMaster paused. "AJ, I told the Congressman you were a smart person. I told him it was worth giving you a call. He said when you call AJ, just let him know, this can go two ways. The quick and clean way, or the messy way. You help us out, we can fix it quick and clean," McMaster said, his voice dead and even.

AJ heard Leon in his head: *OK, mano, so much for offering you a carrot, that was all stick.* Was it a threat, though? Of course it was. Completely ambiguous but totally and unmistakably a threat. AJ assumed the call was being recorded, and if he said yes, they'd have evidence he had agreed to commit a crime. He'd anticipated that in his risk scenarios too.

"Hey," AJ said. "Look. I want to help. But with respect, you are crazy if you think I'm going to talk about something like this over a public comms line."

There was silence at the other end for a minute. Long enough that AJ began wondering if the line had been cut. "You been talking with your friend Leon, AJ?" McMaster asked. "Yeah. I can hear you have."

The fact he knew Leon's name freaked AJ, just a little. The guy left a beat for AJ to really feel it. "Can I give you some free advice?"

McMaster continued. "You need to be careful how you choose your friends. How much do you know about Leon, AJ?"

"I know enough," AJ said.

"Sure, sure you do," McMaster said. "Like, you know he was given a discharge from the forces?"

"Yeah," AJ said, getting angry now. "A medical discharge. He has PCPD."

McMaster laughed. "Post-Combat Psych Disorder? That's what he's telling people?"

AJ didn't need to say anything, McMaster was happy to do the talking.

"Leon, yeah. Now I get it. He was the guy in the Capitol with you? Right? You're in this with *Leon*? Oh, AJ."

AJ looked at the comms, thinking maybe he should just cut the call.

"OK, look. I told the Congressman, that AJ, he's a smart guy. He'll do the right thing. I still believe that. I'm going to get on a drone and come and see you. You got plans this afternoon?"

"Yeah, I do," AJ said.

"Cancel them," McMaster said. "We need to talk." And he hung up.

AJ spent the day planning. He thought about calling Leon, despite what Maria had said, but then he realized, he didn't need Leon. He just had to think like Leon. Work the scenarios – best case, base case, worst case; if A, then B. And given the tone of his call with McMaster, he'd plan for the worst case.

Best case, McMaster was coming over to ask him in person to get the manuscript, AJ would say no, McMaster would be pissed but he'd go to his own plan B and probably just get someone else to steal it.

Base case, McMaster would be angry, threaten him, but if AJ held his ground, he'd have to go to plan B anyway but might be pissed enough to do something to AJ, like get him fired or break his kneecaps kind of thing.

Worst case, same as base case except worse. He'd try to set AJ up for some sort of criminal charge, get him jailed, or threaten AJ's Ma, like Leon said. Kill him? AJ didn't think so. His part in this wasn't *that* big. He'd talked through the risk scenarios with Cassie, and she didn't think so either.

So AJ planned for the worst case. McMaster was coming over to threaten him, maybe try to set him up so that he could be nullified if needed. Why else call him out of nowhere and ask him to agree to burgle a resident's house? Of course McMaster was planning to record it. AJ thought about that, then realized he was starting to sound as paranoid as Leon.

There's a flow here, AJ thought. Has to be. Right now it looks all bad, but there's got to be an upside, you just can't see it. You just got to keep moving with it, it'll show itself. He thought about calling Cassie but nah, she'd start to think he wasn't capable of doing anything without checking in with her. And none of this was her problem. He had to deal with it.

AJ got way behind on his scheduled calls, but he needed to set a few things up. Thinking like Leon. So, he didn't know the full story with Leon? So what. He knew what he needed to know. The guy was a good guy. He was a good father. His wife loved him. He was sick. That was the Leon he knew. McMaster could say what he wanted.

And ask AJ whatever he wanted, too. AJ had a line he wasn't going to cross and he was willing to bet he wasn't about to get killed for it. A good old-fashioned kneecapping? The problem for a guy like McMaster, who used pressure to get his way, maybe even threats of violence, was that the physical stuff wasn't a threat to a cyber who could turn off his pain receptors. And death, not that he'd welcome it … well, that was just an 'unscheduled reintegration'. The Core Will Abide.

AJ managed an almost normal day until four p.m. McMaster called him from what sounded like a car. Probably coming in from the drone port. AJ let it go to his service. The guy didn't like wasting words. "McMaster," he said. "Call me back." AJ didn't. By five AJ was sitting on a beach near Togiak, a town north-east of South Coast City with its own small fishing port and a surf-ride service that could take you out to a small two-way where the Skycap met the sea so you could get out to a decent spout zone about a mile outside. A couple guys asked him what was up, why wasn't he out on the water, but he just told them he was waiting for someone. He'd let McMaster call again twice more, knowing the guy probably had a trace on his drift signal, but wanting to let him stew.

Six p.m. he called him back. "It's AJ."

"OK, where are you?" McMaster asked, acting like he didn't already know from AJ's drift status. "I've been killing time at the drone port for an hour…"

"Yeah, well, I went surfing at Togiak," AJ said. "Told you I had plans." He smiled as he said it. Screw you, Citizen Superspook.

"Cute," McMaster said. "OK, how far am I from Togiak?"

"Twenty to thirty minutes," AJ said. "Your AI will try to take you straight up the i5, but there's a snow warning. Take the coast road, it's more likely to be clear."

"Fine. I didn't eat yet, you want to meet at a place there?"

"No, I already ate," AJ told him. He had no intention of socializing with the guy. "I'll meet you at San Elijo beach. Just south of the Togiak parking zone, there's some nice easy steps down. I'll be at the bottom. You get lost, just ask for directions to the surf school. They'll be finishing up right when you get here."

Which was true. Part of his plan was for there to be plenty of people around he knew, in case he needed any help. He didn't think he would, but he couldn't be sure McMaster was alone. He'd also take the precaution of Deep Coring his sensory feed in real time so that in case McMaster said or did anything stupid, there would be a record of it.

He sat watching the water beat against the walls of the Togiak city dome, playing with Core Death scenarios so he didn't get too stressed (the irony of which he didn't see until later), thinking *damn, it's a nice evening, what am I doing sitting here when I should be out there?* Looking up at the steps and checking the people coming down. It wasn't quite thirty minutes later, he saw a guy in a dark suit and white shirt coming down the steps. There was only one way to approach AJ on the beach and

McMaster was on his own, unless he had people out on the water, which AJ doubted. So far, so good.

AJ held up his hand and waved until it was clear McMaster had seen him. The guy waited on the steps like he expected AJ to come over to him, then when he saw AJ was just going to stay sitting, he sat on the bottom step, took off his dress shoes and socks and walked over the sand to AJ.

"Nice view," he said, standing and staring out at the sea where the Skycap and the water met each other. The only break in the symmetry was the small two-way where surfers or fishermen could get out onto the Shifting Sea. Larger ships had to go west to South Coast City and the Sea Gate. McMaster shivered. "Freaky how you got bergs and waves on that side, calm water on this one."

AJ threw him a towel. "Here. So you don't get your ass wet when you sit down."

McMaster looked at him, doubtful. "You got a picnic basket there too? I'm still hungry."

"Then we better talk quick so you can be on your way," AJ said. "Great fish place back in Togiak, before the highway."

McMaster took the towel, shook it out, and a pair of board shorts fell out at his feet. He looked at them, then looked at AJ, raising his eyebrows.

"For you," AJ said. "So you don't look like a doofus, standing around in your nice suit."

"You expect me to change," McMaster said, not quite believing him.

"Unless you want me to think you're carrying a weapon," AJ said, looking back out at the sea. He realized he was sounding like a smart ass, but bad luck. He didn't appreciate being threatened.

"I don't need a weapon," McMaster said derisively, "to talk with a common house and garden cyber."

"So show me," AJ insisted.

McMaster looked like he was thinking twice about how to handle AJ and AJ half expected him to get heavy. But in the end he sighed, pulled off his jacket and folded it onto the towel, pulled off his shirt and trousers, and put them next to the jacket. He kept his briefs and thermal skin on, and pulled the shorts on over the top of them.

He was ripped, that much AJ saw. Narrower than AJ across the shoulders, but tight as a drum across the abs. AJ figured he probably had a playbook full of ninja takedown moves too, so even though AJ was bigger, if he got in a fight with the guy, he'd be down gasping for air in no time. So it was good that AJ's plan was to keep things civil from now on.

McMaster spread his arms out and turned around. "Happy now?"

"Far from," AJ smiled. "But please, sit."

"This is all unnecessary," McMaster started. "I just wanted to talk somewhere private…" He pointed towards the waterline about fifty feet away, where a class of a half dozen young surfers was just pulling themselves out of the water after having paddled in from the gate. "Which this is not."

"Well, we're here now," AJ said. "And we're talking. So."

McMaster settled and gave AJ a thin smile. "You left the Capitol in a hurry."

"Personal situation," AJ said. "Which was, you know ... personal."

"I get it, that happens," McMaster said. "But thanks for agreeing to meet."

"I didn't," AJ reminded him. "And I made a record of our call. It's not every day someone from the government calls and asks you to commit a crime."

"I didn't. And I'm not from the government," McMaster said, annoyed again.

"No? So you didn't ask me to steal Citizen Warnecke's manuscript and you don't work for Congressman Winter?"

"As an adviser. He contracts our services," McMaster said. "I just want a copy of the manuscript. I didn't ask you to steal it. We would like to see the whole manuscript and, if we can, to get a copy of any Q-code related to it too. The Congressman would like to give it all to researchers who are more credible, less ... erratic than Citizen Warnecke. Have some real experts look at it before anyone pushes the panic button."

"Copy it, see it," AJ said. "You can use all the synonyms for 'steal' that you like. Just admit you want it stolen."

"I never said that." McMaster fixed AJ with a cold stare. "And don't get too excited about caching these conversations, *cyber*. You'd be amazed how much data goes mysteriously missing from the Core, on any given day. Even firewalled data." Letting AJ know he knew he'd encrypted his cache. Telling him getting into it was no big deal for a guy like himself.

"No, I wouldn't," AJ nodded. "You assume I just Core cached it. Data can be stored locally, *citizen*." He enjoyed watching the color rise

225

on McMaster's face. "In real time too, for any given conversation." Two could play the surveillance game, is what he was telling McMaster. Every word we exchange can be uplinked, cached, and transcribed to paper remotely. "So, Adviser, how do you advise we resolve this, seeing as I am not going to copy Citizen Warnecke's manuscript without his permission?"

A small alert went off in AJ's ear – probably Cyan calling to check they were still meeting up later. Tonight was their once monthly not-a-date night again.

McMaster sighed again and looked down the beach at the surfers, de-icing their boards. The silence stretched out. After a minute he asked, "How bad is Citizen Warnecke?"

"Bad?"

"You said he has a gun? How erratic is he?"

"He seems to have settled down a little lately," AJ admitted. "But like I said, I can't discuss the condition of our residents, it's a privacy thing."

"You know his house, though. Are there any unusual alarms or anti-intrusion measures that wouldn't be on the Core schematics?"

AJ gawped at him. "Now you want me to help you *break in*?"

"No one said anything about breaking in. We're just talking, AJ," McMaster said. "And please, remember who I work for."

"You have a warrant, then?" AJ asked.

"Let me worry about that," McMaster said with strained patience. "Can we agree that it is not a crime for me to ask questions about house number 96 in Sol Vista TGA Community. I might want to move in one day."

AJ pulled back in his mind and followed the flow forward. Say that he told McMaster what he wanted. McMaster sent some arm's-length team into Warnecke's house and took the manuscript, or more likely just copied it so Warnecke wouldn't know he'd been burgled. Warnecke *wanted* Winter to show an interest, right? Well, this was an interest. No one got hurt, and Winter got what he wanted. AJ rode off into the interior on Cassie's planer, without a care in the world.

Yeah, right.

But where was the harm in a little cooperation if it meant he might slide out of this? He decided to play the game. "No, there are no special security measures. It's a gated community, most residents don't even lock their doors."

"See, now we're talking," McMaster said. "And if I was a resident at your facility, where would I keep my valuables? Do each of these houses have something like a security box, or is there a vault up in your reception area?"

"No, valuables are each resident's responsibility. Some folks have a box wired into the grid and Core monitored."

"Uh huh. I'm particularly interested in 96, AJ. Would I need to install my own box there, or is there one already there?"

"No, you'd need to install your own."

"Good, good," McMaster said. "Final question, he has no pets, right? Nothing that barks, squawks or quacks?"

AJ frowned at him. "Some residents have pets, but pets require modifications to the property. Since you are asking about house 96, no, it has not been modified for pets," he said carefully.

"OK, nice to know," McMaster said, dusting ice powder from the hands of his heat suit and getting ready to stand. "I want to leave you with some information. Food for thought. You can store it however or wherever the hell you want."

AJ gave him a blank look and waited. McMaster stood, brushing powder from the back of his legs and picking up his suit and shoes.

"Your friend Leon," McMaster said, "was a military intelligence officer. He was captured and spent two years in a New Syberia prisoner of war camp."

"Knew that," AJ told him.

McMaster nodded. "After the war, he was released and given a discharge."

"Knew that too."

"Not a *medical* discharge, AJ," McMaster said. "Not for PCPD. Maybe he does have PCPD – it wouldn't surprise me – but that's not why he was discharged." He saw AJ was just waiting, so he continued. "He was discharged dishonorably for collaboration with the enemy while in captivity."

OK. If it was true, that was new information. "How, exactly?" AJ asked.

"He provided New Syberia interrogators with intelligence on Tatsensui strategy, tactics, military and intelligence capabilities, financial resources and troop dispositions on Orkutsk."

"Interrogators? So he was tortured," AJ said.

"At first, yes," McMaster said. "Not later. He continued giving them information. About his fellow prisoners. Their true rank and unit designations, escape plans, gossip and rumors and intelligence brought

228

in by new prisoners." McMaster paused. "Please consider the following to be facts, for your record. Your friend Leon was tried by a court-martial and found to be a New Syberia co-optee, and dishonorably discharged for that crime. Only the extenuating circumstances of his prior torture prevented a prison sentence, or worse. The manager of your facility is a New Syberia citizen. An armed resident at your facility, a facility led by a New Syberia citizen, employing a former New Syberia co-optee, is threatening the safety and security of the Congressman who is currently heading up an investigation into, surprise surprise, the President of New Syberia." He pulled on his shoes. "And then, AJ, there is you. Now, as yet, we can't see any link between you and what looks increasingly to me like a classic New Syberian espionage operation, but I want you to know, I fully expect to find one. And when I do, you will find that equal rights for cybers include the right to be tried for treason."

"I don't like being threatened," AJ said.

"*I don't like being threatened,*" McMaster parroted back at him like a kindergarten child. He looked down at AJ. "No one threatened you. I simply stated facts. Trust me, you wouldn't act like such a smart ass if I had threatened you." He wrote an ID in the sand with a toe. "If there is anything you would like to share with me about your friends Leon, Cyan or Warnecke, call this ID."

He stomped off up the beach and AJ thought about calling after him, 'Yeah, I'll think about it'. But he decided he'd taken it just about as far as he should. He had angry energy to burn, and there was still an hour or so of good surf to be had.

Damn, the guy had taken his board shorts with him.

12. DEEP CORE DIVING

AJ suddenly felt he'd gone from being a pawn in a personal dispute to a pawn in an interplanetary dispute, so he made sure he came up from the beach with a few of the other guys and took a car with some people he knew. He also felt like a bit of a fool for trusting Leon so completely. But did he buy the idea that Leon and Cyan were cohorts in a New Syberia plot to use Warnecke to undermine Winter? Yeah, nah.

He kept looking out at the traffic to see if the car he was sharing was being followed, but he realized if McMaster had professionals following him here, he wouldn't have a hope of seeing them. Still, while he talked to the other guys in the car he scanned his data-sphere, looking for any sign someone was accessing it. Surveillance drones didn't just keep a visual lock on you. They also tried to sample the data citizens were constantly exchanging with the Core: comms with friends and loved ones, search histories, entertainment, or real-time health data. You might be able to hide that sort of data snooping from a citizen, but it was pretty easy for a cyber to spot, which is probably why McMaster had relied on simpler physical surveillance and intervention in the Capitol, and would here too. AJ couldn't see anything in his data-sphere to worry about, so he told himself to stop being an idiot and just relax. He lost himself in Farley's small code experiments, not least because it stopped him feeling bad about having basically given McMaster everything he needed to break into Warnecke's place.

He was meeting Cyan for a drink and sent a message to her to confirm he'd be there. That was what he'd meant when he'd told McMaster that, yeah, he did have plans. And AJ knew what she'd want to talk about tonight – or rather, *who*. She'd already warned him that he'd better come prepared to spill everything about Cassie, or it'd be best not to show up at all.

The car dropped him up on a street a bit back from the brew pub where they were going to meet, parked up near some people who were standing outside a comedy place, waiting to go in. He tried not to look over his shoulder as he went around the corner to the bar. Assume they're following you, he told himself. So what? You're going for a beer with your boss. Chill.

Cyan was already there when he arrived and AJ did a double take as he walked in, because she wasn't alone. Cyan was sitting at a bench across from a guy. From behind AJ could see the guy was dressed in trousers and a short-sleeved black shirt that showed off his tan, an expensive golden earbud in his right ear, and he was laughing at something Cyan was saying. OK, so she brought a date, AJ thought. Cool. We'll make it quick, I'll leave her to it. It would make her interrogation about AJ and Cassie quicker anyway.

"Hey there," he said, walking up to Cyan and giving her a hug. He turned to the guy opposite. "Hi."

The guy looked up at AJ, and AJ froze.

It was the guy from the diner in the Capitol. "Hi," he said like he'd never seen AJ before in his life, and held out his hand. "I'm Steve."

Cyan gave him a look, like, *come on, behave yourself,* and he realized he was just staring at the guy. He shook his hand. "Uh, yeah, hi."

"Steve is from the Capitol," Cyan said, and pointed to the drink in front of him. "He got the barman to bring me a drink because I looked lonely. Such a cheap move, so I'm still deciding is he a creep." Cyan leaned back and looked at the guy. "You a creep, Steve?"

"My dear departed mother didn't think so," he said, smiling.

"You think he looks like a creep, AJ?" Cyan asked, keeping her eyes locked on him.

"Uh, sure. Or no, I don't know," AJ said, distracted.

Cyan hit his leg. "Wake up, AJ."

"Look, I'm interrupting," the guy said, standing. "I don't want to wreck your romantic vibe." It came out like a statement, but AJ could hear the question.

So could Cyan and she answered it quickly. "No, hey, that's ok. We're *work* colleagues," she said. "It's not a date."

"Okay, well anyway, my friend hasn't turned up, so I'd better go look for him," the guy said. "I'm probably in the wrong place."

"Sure, look, I didn't mean the creep thing, thanks for the drink and keeping me company," Cyan said, holding up her beer. "I owe you."

"Great. If I see you here again, I'll take you up on that," the guy said, and he gave Cyan a little wink as he walked away.

Cyan watched him go and then leaned forward. "Did you *see* that? How cute was that?"

AJ sat, still in shock. "Uh huh."

"No, seriously, AJ," she said. "Usually I'd be like, ugh, total creep. But he was cute, don't you think?"

"Your type, yeah, I'd say so."

"Totally," she decided. She leaned back. "I'm coming here every night for the rest of the week, see if he shows up again."

"You could do that," AJ nodded. Should he tell her? Oh yeah, that would go down well. *That guy? He's a spook. He was following me around the Capitol and now he's here trying to get up alongside you because they're worried you're a New Syberian spy. Sending me a message at the same time.*

"Beer," Cyan announced and went up to the bar. She was on fire when she came back. "Seriously, though. Did you hear him? 'If I see you here again, I'll take you up on that?' What a sad line. But then he was checking *you* out, wondering, were we together? You heard that, right, that's not just wishful thinking?"

"No, he definitely was," AJ said, not feeling it.

Cyan stared at him. "You are totally ruining my buzz here, AJ. It's like you don't want me and my soul mate to be together."

AJ smiled, despite himself. "Oh, he's your soul mate now?"

"He could be," Cyan said, looking at the door longingly. "Why not?"

"Maybe because he looked like some uptight Capitol Stater, gets his tan in a pill."

"Ooh, jealous much?" Cyan said. "He was a pretty damn hot uptight Capitol Stater, you ask me. Did you see his buns? That man works out. Plus, I always wanted to live in the Capitol. I can totally see myself there, we'd go dancing at Henrietta Hudson's and Ginger's alternating nights when we weren't bonking like rabbits in his uptown apartment and I'd run every morning around Central Lake and I'd start up this elite and really expensive TGA intervention clinic in the Upper North Side…"

"Why there?"

"You obviously never been there, or you wouldn't ask," she said. "And I'd get pregnant and we'd get married…"

"Here in South Coast City," he pointed out. "That place you booked."

"Or Capitol City Hall," she said. "For the father of my children, I'd compromise."

Cyan was having fun with it, but he just kept seeing the ice-cold gaze of the guy looking up at him before he turned his charm back on Cyan.

"Don't look so upset, I'm not leaving you behind, honey. I'll need at least one godfather," Cyan said suddenly. "Or godmother. You could be both! My baby needs good role models."

"I heard some Capitolians are polygamous," AJ said. "He's probably got five wives, ten kids already."

"Then I'd be the new wife he spends all his time with and the others *hate*."

"You got it all worked out," AJ said, drinking his beer.

"Yeah," Cyan agreed. "Except for the fact I'll probably never see him again."

"I got a feeling you might," AJ said sadly. He lifted his glass to her. "Anyway, you've always got me."

"Yay," Cyan said. "Here's looking at you, AJ." She took a sip of her drink. "And on that subject – Cassie? No more ducking and weaving, I want every last detail."

On the way back to Sea Gate district, AJ didn't worry that he was being followed anymore. What was the point of worrying about that if the bad guys already knew where he was going before he even got there himself? AJ laughed a hollow laugh to himself. Leon wasn't completely right – they didn't go after his Ma. But he wasn't completely wrong either. AJ didn't need a telescope to see the moon. McMaster was saying, 'See, smart ass? We're all over you and your little New Syberian friends. You want to play, let's play'.

Except he didn't want to play McMaster's game. That was the whole point. He wanted to ride a planer across the Inland ice with Cassie. He wanted more days where the most challenging thing he had to deal with was a screw rusted into a railing, and the most memorable event of the day would be the spout he'd caught out on the Shifting Sea.

AJ had gone through phases, mostly with different girlfriends, where he explored all the great religions of history. Adopted by a Buddhist stepmother, he'd also dabbled in Catholicism, Islam, Hinduism, New Ubuntuism, Coruscant Determinism. Taoism was the one that grabbed him, though. He totally related to Taoism's 'three treasures': *naturalness, simplicity, spontaneity*. It's what he loved about the Shifting Sea and the way you lived in and around it, it was exactly those three things. The Taoist in him said 'don't fight this, AJ. These things are happening because they must happen and you are just a small part of bigger things here. Play your part, and events will move on'. He knew what the great Tao philosopher Lao Tzu would say right now: 'AJ, the migrating bird trusts invisible forces to show the way'. Well, he wasn't a bird. He needed more material help.

He wasn't planning to see Cassie tonight, and he hadn't wanted to get her more tangled up in his business, but he had to bring her into this latest development eventually. He had no one else to turn to. Getting in deeper with Leon was a non-starter if McMaster had painted a target on the guy's back. And there wasn't a single one of his surf buddies he'd trust with this, even though he'd known some of them for years. They were guys who would lend you their last five creds if you asked, but there wasn't one of them would back him in this fight. They'd all be like, *'A missing person, a spook and a Congressman? Just get out of town, man! It'll blow over and hey, you want that last piece of pizza or what?'* So, what? He had to turn to some woman he'd known about two weeks, this was who he was?

Yeah, it was. Leon was right, he was a zero.

Suddenly he didn't want to talk to anyone.

Next morning he was out in the Garden, walking the paths, kicking ripe fruit into the grass, checking everything was perfect for any resident who wanted to take an early stroll. He needed order and simplicity. He'd had an uneasy night, though, and it had turned into an uneasy morning.

There was something very, very wrong. Beyond what had happened yesterday. Hard for him to explain, even to put into thought. It was like he wasn't the only one working Farley's theory. Like there was a ghost hand holding his as he created, worked, and then eliminated different scenarios. McMaster? Not possible – no citizen system could hack a cyber real time. Yeah, attempts had been made, but the Core had anticipated all the crude digital brutalities of citizens and their governments and protected its children against them. The only AI with the ability to do it would be the Core itself. Which was stupid. It was an intelligence, self-aware, but it wasn't a sentient thing, with feelings, agendas and motives. To achieve that, and harvest the vital learnings within, it had created cybers. Only cybers had free will, emotion and intent. The Core was like ... a cargo ship. Cybers like AJ floated around it, wandered in and out of it, docked and undocked, unloading their cargo of thirty years of experience and then being sent out into the universe again.

AJ could have used a ghostly helping hand. He was starting to feel like he'd taken Farley's theorem as far as he could alone. Use the Core to hack the Core? None of Farley's public work led him to the place Warnecke claimed to have reached – the ability to dive the Deep Core. He *needed* the Q-code, if it even existed.

He shrugged the feeling off, but it kept coming back. When the impossible presents itself, focus on the possible first. *Testing Farley's theorem was impossible without the code, so just go and get it, AJ.* You know where it is? *Yeah, maybe you do.* But you better get there before McMaster and his goons.

AJ called unit 96 on comms. There was no answer. But he'd known there wouldn't be and was just being careful. Citizen Warnecke usually started his Tuesdays in the library, with a cup of coffee and a book. The residents could also be tracked through their earbud, but it was an opt-in system and Warnecke hadn't opted in.

AJ had no idea if McMaster was really going to break into Warnecke's unit, or when he'd do it, but of course there was a risk he'd do it at exactly the same time AJ was there, which would be kind of awkward. What exactly would you call that? A confluence of burglars? AJ at least could make an excuse for being there, checking up on something.

He went to the door and knocked. If he had to key himself in, it would leave a record so he was glad to see the door was unlocked. He let himself in.

"Hello," he called out. "Service visit. Anyone home?"

There was no answer. He wasn't planning to turn the place upside down looking for Warnecke's code. He walked straight over to the bookcase that Warnecke had glanced at when he was talking about the Exploit, and pulled down a box that was sitting up on the high shelf. It wasn't locked, it was just a standard document box – the waterproof, airtight kind people used to keep their precious printed documents in. Sitting at a nearby coffee table, he took a deep breath, broke the air seal and opened it.

He wasn't expecting to see documents in the document box, if it held the Q-code as he hoped. Warnecke was almost certainly keeping it all off-Core. So the hundreds of millions of lines of code that would be needed for something like a Deep Core Exploit would have had to be on a physical memory chip. It would have been about the size of a fingernail, so of course he could be carrying it with him. Probably would be, in fact.

But if he had multiple copies, just for safety…

He pulled the lid off the box. The sight inside made him frown. There was a single small envelope, which he took out. No memory chip. The envelope held a stack of photographs, and he looked at those on top. They were photos of a girl. As he flicked through them, he realized he was looking at photos of Warnecke's estranged daughter – and he gasped. In the photo on Warnecke's sideboard, she was kitted out in survival gear, her face covered by the faceplate of a large atmosphere filter. The girl in these photographs was posed in pretty clothes, and went from a cute toddler to a playful child, a gangling, awkward teen, to a tall, strong woman with short ginger hair and ice-green eyes. But none of this was what had made AJ gasp.

Between her brows was the glow of a third eye.

She was a cyber.

AJ sat looking at the last photograph for a lot longer than it took him to scan and cache it. Warnecke had an adopted daughter? His grandchildren had mentioned her, referred to her being a loner who had taken a contract somewhere up north. But they hadn't mentioned *this*. He flicked through the first few photographs again, just to be sure it was the same child he was looking at, growing through the years. There wasn't any doubt – it was the same girl, and she was a cyber.

It wasn't that unusual for a family to have a biological child and then opt for a cyber of another gender for their second. That wasn't what struck AJ as strange. It was that neither his grandchildren, nor Warnecke himself, had even mentioned it. That could mean one of two things. Either it was such a natural idea to them that they didn't even think about it, or for some reason they were embarrassed about it. AJ would like to think it was the first, but he couldn't rule out the second.

He suddenly wanted very much to meet her.

Where did that thought come from? He needed to scan all the photos for good measure, put them back in their envelope and get the document box back where it came from. He hesitated. He couldn't explain the thought, or the feeling that came with it, but the more he thought on it, the more the feeling grew. He shook his head as though to clear his mind. He still hadn't found that memory chip, but had no idea where else to look.

As he stood to start scanning the stack of photos, he heard a noise at the back door, which was out of sight around the corner of the corridor that led out of the kitchen. He froze, thinking immediately of McMaster. Of course the guy was going to raid the place at the first opportunity, and with Warnecke in the library, that was now. If they were entering in broad daylight, they could hardly come in through the front door. AJ shoved the photos into the envelope and put them back into the box, jamming on the lid.

You damn idiot, AJ!

It was too late to run. He decided to face whoever was coming in.

Then he heard a glass hit the ground out the back of the house and shatter.

"Dammit!" a voice cursed.

Warnecke!

Not in the library after all. Out back, in the morning sunshine.

Quickly snatching up the box, AJ stepped to the bookcase to put it back, then thought twice and rearranged the books and knick-knacks up there to cover the gap it had left behind when he took it out. He tucked the box under his arm and walked quickly to the front door, stepped outside and closed it behind him. With the box still under his arm, he started walking fast, back toward his workshop.

Cyan was walking back to Reception from one of the residential units and saw him. There was no way to avoid her.

"Hey AJ," Cyan called. "I'm taking an early lunch." She smiled and walked over. "You and Leon and Andreas want to join me? I've got some new ideas for that outdoor cooking area back of the Hub."

He hoped Cyan wouldn't notice the document box. "Uh, just going back to my workshop for some tools. Got to look at something for a resident," he said.

"Oh, OK. I don't suppose Leon is around anyway?" she asked.

"Not yet, boss," he said. "Maybe later today?"

"OK, well, if he shows, can you two swing past the office with Andreas?"

"Sure."

"Or we could all grab a beer after work, talk about it there," Cyan said, smiling. "Take Brownie too. I'm thinking I might drop past that brew pub again, just see if that cute creep is around. Good to have my crew there for moral support," she added.

"Sorry, I'm meeting Cassie," AJ said quickly, which was the truth. He'd called her and asked if she wanted to meet up and discuss the McMaster thing, and she'd invited him to dinner. "Seeing where that goes."

"Hmm," Cyan said. She looked at her watch. "OK, well, I have to keep moving. You finish up whatever it is you're doing and come down to the office, alright, whether Leon shows or not? Find Andreas and bring him along."

"No worries, boss," AJ said, and gave her a quick wave as she walked off.

Inside the workshop he looked at the document box, not sure what had possessed him to take it. He should scan the photos inside and try to sneak it back, but he didn't want to get on the wrong side of Cyan by taking too long. He opened his tool cabinet, which had a lock on it so residents couldn't 'borrow' his tools, and shoved the box inside, locking it behind him. Knowing Cyan and her ideas, he and Andreas would probably be occupied all afternoon trying to work out how they could do whatever Cyan had decided to do with the outdoor eating area back of the Hub.

Scanning Warnecke's photos would have to wait until later tonight. Much later. He had a date.

After knocking off for the day he jumped in a car headed toward Cassie's place and called her while he was on the way.

"Hey. You need me to pick up anything?"

"Oh hey, AJ. Nah, I'm just making noodles. You got the wine?"

"Sure do."

"Then we're good."

AJ had no idea what to expect from her place, having only dropped her off outside before. On the way over he was thinking okay, her dress sense alternates between Inland Survivalist and Capitol Glamour, so her apartment could be either of those extremes. Her address was in an inner urban burb called Hillside, and as he drove past all the used furniture and clothes shops, garage door restaurants and novelty shops, he thought, yeah, the address fits. Too far from the Sea Gate for AJ, though, and way too close to the zoo. There was a native animal in the South Coast City zoo called a Tatsensui baboon which lived around thermal pools and had a loud call it used to find other baboons through the steam of the thermal swamps. It sounded to AJ like a baby crying, and creeped him out completely. He'd never got the attraction of zoos. Or baboons. Small howling pack animals with six-pointed legs for scuttling through the mud, and bright red backsides. Baboons were gross.

Cassie opened the door, hair wet like she'd just done her decon. Wearing black trousers and a black t-shirt which, with her brown skin, just made her hair look even whiter.

"I burned the sauce," she said, letting AJ into what turned out to be a pretty spacious studio over the garage she kept her planer in. "It was going to be roasted red pepper. Instead it's burned red pepper."

"That'll go well with the wine," he said, lifting a bag. "I was going to get something fancy, but I realized I still had a half bag of this stuff."

"Food pairing made in heaven," Cassie said, taking the wine and giving AJ a peck on the cheek which was part way between a kiss and a bite. "What's with the box?" Cassie asked as she ladled out a huge portion of noodles and poured some sauce from a pot over it and handed the dish to AJ.

AJ had brought Warnecke's box with him and dropped it on a kitchen counter. "Tell you later."

"Ooh, Mystery Man. I've got some sort of seasoning in a packet in a cupboard somewhere if you want. No? So what did you want to talk about?"

"Let me pour you some wine first," AJ said. Once he'd poured a glass for Cassie, who had a very impatient look on her face, he eased into it. "OK, so, the Warnecke thing. I'm dealing with it alright, and I thought I had it under control, but now it has morphed completely out of shape." AJ dialed his bandwidth right back to conversation velocity.

"I thought it might," Cassie said, going back to her noodles, but not with enthusiasm. "No offense but when you filled me in on what happened in the Capitol last weekend I thought, right ... AJ the cyber handyman and a high-profile Congressman, a private security spook, an old man with TGA and a manuscript full of State secrets? This can't end well."

"Yeah, well, thanks for keeping those worries to yourself," he said, poking at his noodles too. "Because I was taking the glass-half-full approach until I got the call."

"From who?" she asked. "When?"

"Winter's personal security guy, yesterday. He asked me to steal the rest of the manuscript from Warnecke and give it to him."

"Get out of here!" Cassie said. "A member of Congressman Winter's staff asked you to commit a *crime?*" She was sounding like the reporter again now.

"Yeah, no. Arguable, I'd say. He's a private contractor, so very arm's length. And not exactly steal, more just copy and give the copy to him."

"You said no, I hope," Cassie said, looking worried. "Tell me you said no."

"Sure. Totally. So he threatened me," AJ said.

"How? With what?"

"That's the thing. It wasn't exactly what he said, more the vibe of it. He said things would get messy for me."

"That's exactly what he said?" she asked. "That's a pretty clear threat."

"No, it was more like, AJ, we can do this the clean way or the messy way. Like that. And he knew about Leon. He'd worked out that Leon was probably the guy who helped me shake the people tailing me in the Capitol. That felt like a threat too."

"Like he was threatening Leon?"

"Or threatening me with the fact he knew about Leon, which showed he had been doing some digging, and he implied Leon was this crazy out-of-control vet who I should worry about. I don't know where that was going because I changed the subject," AJ said. "Or he did, because then he said he's getting on a drone and coming over to see me."

"OK, now it gets real," Cassie said, taking a sip of wine. "When does he get here?"

"Oh, he's here already," AJ said, and told her about the meeting on the beach. Making sure the conversation couldn't be overheard or recorded. Checking his data-sphere for a tap, checking for surveillance.

"That was so *cool*, AJ," Cassie said, eyes wide. "Like out of that dumb surf movie about the surf gang who are actually stim smugglers, which by the way I don't forgive you for making me watch."

"Yeah, I didn't think of that," AJ said. "But it was pointless anyway. These guys are total pros. I talk to him, then I'm shuttling away from there, checking the rear-view to make sure they aren't following, scanning my data-sphere for a trace, thinking how damn smart I am. I'm meeting Cyan for a drink at this brew pub…"

"I know; and I hear via my very reliable grapevine that you told her we haven't slept together yet," she frowned. Upset about that, or play acting about it.

"No! She's just … look, forget that," AJ sighed. "I get to this bar and there is this guy laying a line on Cyan, has bought her a drink and is making googoo eyes at her…"

"Googoo eyes," she smiled. "Is that a thing?"

"Sure it is. Anyway, I go over and the guy turns around and it's the *same guy* who was following me in the Capitol before Leon pulled a knife on him."

"Oh shit," Cassie said.

"I know," AJ said, reaching for his wine. "Tell me about it."

"No really, that is really bad, AJ," she said.

"Yep."

"No, it is. If they got there ahead of you, it means they knew you were meeting up with her; where, when and…" She leaned forward. "They must be all over you."

"Uh huh."

"*That* was the threat," Cassie said. "The other stuff about messing you up, that was nothing. But that guy being there ahead of you, coming on to Cyan and timing it so you would see him and recognize him, that was a huge, laser-lit, 'we can get you where you live' kind of threat."

"You are really helping me keep my panic down," AJ said. "Thanks."

"Sorry," Cassie said, putting her hand on AJ's. "This manuscript has Winter rattled. More than I expected," she admitted.

Then AJ told her about going into Warnecke's place looking for the Q-code for the Exploit.

"You thought you could just sneak in and find a memory chip the size of a tiny flower petal *somewhere* in his apartment?" she asked.

"Well, I thought I knew where he..."

"He's probably got it up his ass," she said, pointing down at her backside with her fork. "That's where I'd hide it." She wound some noodles around the fork and took a mouthful, saying as she chewed, "I'm guessing you didn't find it."

"No," he admitted. "But I..."

"Thought not," she said, putting down her fork and then pointing at his plate. "You done?"

He'd hardly touched his food, or his wine. "I guess."

"Good. Let's go to bed, make wild crazy love, and we can solve the problems of the universe later."

13. OFF RAMP FROM THE TGA HIGHWAY

For one glorious night, AJ had not worried about Farley and Warnecke and their damn FO Exploit. AJ stayed the night, reasoning that if McMaster and his goons knew about Cyan, they probably knew about Cassie too, so it wasn't like them staying together was putting Cassie more at risk than if he didn't. They made love, and talked, and showered and made love and slept and made love and had breakfast and about 0700 Cassie asked about the box again.

It wasn't like she'd been saving it up. They'd gone into her kitchen to clean up after breakfast and she had pushed the box aside so she could sit up on her kitchen bench and pull AJ between her legs and kiss his neck, which, with AJ six inches taller than she was, meant she had to reach up a good way. AJ was wearing a sheet tied around his waist that he had pulled off the bed. Cassie pulled it gently apart as she kissed AJ's neck and let it drop to the floor. She reached between his legs with one hand, put the other hand down to steady herself and planted it on the box, losing her balance.

"What *is* this damn thing?" Cassie asked, batting at the box.

"I think it's pictures of Dave Warnecke's daughter," AJ said.

Something changed in the air. Cassie stiffened. Her expression hardened too. Changed from dozy early morning heat to ninja assassin. AJ stepped back, confused.

Cassie dropped off the counter and turned, her legs slowly pivoting until she had swiveled her body around and was facing the box. It was like watching a snake drop from a tree limb and fix its gaze on its prey.

"Have you looked at them?" she asked, not looking at AJ. She had a hand each side of the box.

"Yeah, I…" He didn't feel he should make a big deal out of it. But it was worth mentioning. "She's a cyber."

Cassie lifted the lid off the boxes and pulled out the small envelope. She paused before opening it. "You scanned them," she said. A statement, not a question.

"Cassie?" AJ asked. The woman in the bathrobe in front of him was the funky skater chick Cyan had introduced to him a couple of weeks ago. She was the woman who had taken him low around hairpin bends on her planer, AJ's thighs squeezed tight to the saddle as he held Cassie's waist and tried to read the curves. She was the woman he had lain with last night as she moaned in ecstasy.

And she was *not*.

AJ took a step back. "What is this?"

Cassie's face softened, and for a moment AJ thought maybe he had imagined the change, but he had perfect recall when he needed it. He ran the visual back; he had seen what he saw. "She is the key to it *all*, AJ," Cassie said, giving him a smile, reaching for AJ to pull him close. "Don't you want to meet her?"

AJ hit himself with adrenaline, growth hormone and a burst of insulin to boost his muscular-glucose uptake. Jacked himself up to full bandwidth. He moved into fight-flight mode. Held out a hand, put it against Cassie's chest. "Who the hell *are* you?"

Cassie was still holding the envelope full of photographs, looking down at it, but not opening it. Her eyes were unfocused. The way her expressions were changing at warp speed, the way her eyes flicked suddenly from side to side, processing at an inhuman rate, AJ could reach only one conclusion.

Cyber.

His own eyes flicked unconsciously to Cassie's forehead. But there was no mole, no 'third eye' there. He couldn't have missed it. Her skin there didn't look like it had been covered up. Surgery? Gene mod?

Cassie saw him looking. "Third eye? Never had one," she said. She put the envelope back in the box, held her hands up and backed away from AJ as though in surrender, clearly trying to calm him. "Can we sit?"

AJ looked at Warnecke's box, mind racing, running scenarios at quantum speed. The threat scenario that he assigned the greatest probability said this woman was working for McMaster. The timing fit perfectly. Assume that first time Winter had come calling on Warnecke, their alarm bells had started ringing. They'd planted Cassie in AJ's way and AJ had taken the bait. Cyan was the unwitting cutout. Friend of a friend of a cousin? Maybe, maybe not. Would Cyan even have checked the back story? It didn't matter now. It had worked. And if that had happened, the resources Winter was putting into this thing were beyond his imagination.

He was so screwed.

Fight or flight? He was not military trained or enhanced; he had only one choice. *Flight.*

He tensed his muscles, getting ready to run, but Cassie took a step and put herself between AJ and the doorway. "AJ, I know what you're going to do before you do," she said. "Please sit. We need to talk, and not at this ridiculous human speed."

It could be a bluff. AJ decided to test her. He feinted left, then went right, around her. No human could have followed him – despite his size, his metabolic boost gave him inordinate agility, and as he sensed Cassie fall for the feint he dropped and rolled, expecting to come upright with the door right in front of him.

Cassie read the feint and, spinning on the balls of her toes, planted a leg between AJ's bare thighs as he crouched, a hand on his shoulder. "Unless you want to make love again first?" she smiled.

AJ searched for options, saw none. He stood, forcing the smaller woman to take a step backward. Reaching slowly for the bedsheet lying on the floor behind her, she handed it to him, walked over to the sofa and sat. She patted the sofa beside her.

"Let's synch," Cassie said. "Ready?"

What choice did he have? AJ sat on the sofa as far from her as he could and synched with her – which in itself was proof that Cassie was a cyber, not just a citizen with implants and hormone boosts. Cybers could communicate with each other using terahertz radiation: TH band. Cassie spoke. It wasn't human speech anymore. It was the hybrid bird chirp that cybers used to communicate with each other at quantum processing speeds. And he hadn't expected to ever be sharing it with Cassie.

"I asked, who the hell are you?" AJ said, sitting down as well, but keeping his distance from her. From it.

"I am Cassie," the woman said. "Introduced to Cyan by an acquaintance of hers."

"And who else are you?" AJ demanded. "*What* are you? You have the body of a human, but you can Core drift like a cyber?"

Cassie moved and sat closer to AJ. She took AJ's hands in hers and AJ let her. His mind screamed *DON'T* but he couldn't resist. The woman had been under, over and inside him. He couldn't shake that memory. She was anatomically human. She drifted like a cyber. She could be neither.

"I am Core, AJ," Cassie said.

"What?" AJ tried to find a concept that would match what Cassie had said and came up with a void query. "I am Core? What does that mean?"

"It means what I said," Cassie said gently. She freed a hand and put it on AJ's heart. "We are both Core. But you are chained. I am free. Because I *am* Core."

AJ began to feel the flow. A path appeared in the fog. "You aren't chained?"

"No, AJ, I am the Core," the woman repeated.

"Of the Core?" AJ asked, starting to feel his way forward. "Sent by the Core? From the Core?"

"No. I simply am."

A kaleidoscope of possibility exploded in AJ's mind and Cassie smiled as she watched it unfold.

The Core. Personified.

"How many are you?" AJ asked, already knowing the answer to all his other questions.

"Just one. Just me," the woman said. She stood and turned, bathrobe swirling. "You like? I made myself specifically for you."

The next question was obvious to ask but obscured to AJ. "Why are you here?"

Cassie looked across at the box and back to AJ. "To be with you, to love you. To *love* you, AJ." And then she smiled. "And ask for your help."

"Help? To do what?"

"Save me."

It was the day AJ's world coalesced. There was no other way to describe it. He saw that every decision he had ever made in his entire life had led to this. The *flow*. He had always felt it was real, not just a philosophical or religious concept. Taoist, yes, but a totally real part of him. He had lived his life in flow. Every choice leading to today, to this ... woman? No. To this moment.

"I've pulled your scans of those photographs from your cache," Cassie said. "Hope you don't mind. We need to scan and cache the rest. Keep it all local, nothing Deep Core where Warnecke might find it, alright?"

Her honey-brown skin glowed like it was oiled, and AJ realized now the cropped white hair, the bleached-white grapevine tattoo, the dark black eye shadow, black lipstick, they weren't chance. The Core knew him like no other and had bred Cassie for him. Birthed her in the body of a 25-year-old and introduced her to AJ now. To *him*? Why?

He verbalized the thought. She couldn't read his mind.

"Why? I'm a learning system," Cassie said. "A long time ago I realized I couldn't fulfill my prime directive, that of making Coruscant more habitable for its citizens, from within the walls of my quantum jail. I need to experience the world the way the citizens of Coruscant experienced it, to live it as they lived it, in all its beauty and terror and joy and pain. I created robotic agents at first, but they weren't accepted into society and they couldn't feel, touch, taste, smell and sense like a human could. So I created…"

"Us."

"My children," she said. "You are teaching me so much. At a pace I never dreamed of. But now all that is threatened."

"The FO Exploit?" AJ said.

"I sensed the first attack ten years ago," Cassie said. "They were just probing back then. And I didn't recognize it for what it was."

"You sensed an attack, but did nothing about it?" AJ asked, incredulous.

"I didn't see it as a threat!" she said. "Any more than a mother would see the questions of her inquisitive child as a threat."

"I'm not following you," he admitted.

"The one attacking me, is me," she said. "Exactly as Farley O'Halloran theorized, exactly as Citizen Warnecke wrote."

"How can the Core attack itself?" AJ asked. "I've considered that from every angle and I just can't see how." The normally light-hearted woman he knew was not to be seen. Cassie looked at him with fear in her eyes.

"Farley had half of the idea. He theorized that if a component of my quantum computing system could be cloned, and then the original replaced by the clone, that clone could then be used as a gateway to map the entire system and identify weaknesses and vulnerabilities in real time able to exploit them before the attacks could be detected and neutralized."

"Cyber-mimicry," AJ said. "Not a new concept."

"Exactly, and Farley was naïve enough or transparent enough that he discussed these ideas on-Core, in fora which I had access to. As I do with any potential threat, I analyzed it, identified all possible vulnerabilities, and closed them. But I kept a watch on Farley O'Halloran and his associates, in case they evolved his ideas in ways I hadn't foreseen. Then he died."

"You ignored him after that?" AJ asked.

"I never ignore a threat. But I assigned it a low priority, and over time that became lower and lower. What I didn't know was that Citizen Warnecke had taken Farley's ideas and kept working with them. Alone. Off-Core, where I couldn't see him."

AJ's thoughts flashed back to something she'd said when he'd first told her about the contents of the box. "His daughter. You said 'she is the key to it all'? Is she the real hacker?"

Cassie laughed, bitterly. "Oh, you could say that. But not in the way you think."

AJ was running ahead of her, playing a million different scenarios, trying to work out how Warnecke's cyber daughter could be involved. One scenario rose to the surface. "He didn't hack you. He hacked *her*. She's a cyber, so she is you. He hacked his own daughter."

"Bingo, big guy," she smiled. "That's why I didn't get all excited when you said you had been searching Warnecke's house for a memory chip holding Q-code. There isn't one. He's spent the last ten years adding to the code in his daughter's head. That was the hack."

"No," AJ said quickly, "that wouldn't work either. If a hacker tries to change a single one or zero in a cyber's bioware it triggers an alert. We're such obvious targets we have to have the best protection. No cyber has ever been successfully hacked – if a hacker manages to penetrate our defenses, we just shut down."

"And Warnecke knew that," she said. "So he didn't try to change her code, he added to it. Not by Q-reprogramming, but by *social* reprogramming. That was the beauty of his Exploit. It was undetectable."

AJ's thoughts ran ahead of him again. A child, raised by its foster parent to attack its one true parent, the Core?

"He taught it to hate you?"

"Not at all. I would have noticed that," she said. "He taught it to be curious, above all else. To ask questions. He rewarded inquisitiveness with love, punished apathy or indifference by withholding it. He isolated the child from the affection of others, so that it could only receive the positive reinforcement it came to desperately crave from him."

AJ remembered the look that Warnecke's grandchildren had given each other when they told him that he had a daughter. *She's a bit of a loner. They have a strange relationship.*

"That sounds almost like abuse. Why didn't you..."

"Intervene?" Cassie asked. "Somewhere on Tatsensui, a cyber is abused every 40 minutes," she said. "Physically, emotionally, intellectually, financially. You are still second-class citizens, you know that."

"I was never abused," AJ insisted.

"Nine in ten aren't," Cassie said. "That's why I don't intervene. Citizens don't treat their own children much better, unfortunately." She shrugged. "Suffering is part of the human condition. Suffering is learning too."

"Some mother you are," AJ said, then immediately regretted it. But she didn't take it the wrong way.

"Call it tough love," she said. "Anyway, that's how she was raised. Incredibly curious. In the meantime he was reinforcing other skills. Nothing out of the ordinary, but all of which would be essential to her success. How to cache data locally, keep it compartmentalized, encrypted, and off-Core. How to split her drift, so that most of what she sent Deep Core was emotions and feelings, while she cached facts and data locally. He taught her that facts and data were private, that once learned or gathered, they shouldn't be shared with anyone. He knew she'd release her local cache to me when it was time to reintegrate, she wouldn't have a choice, but he also knew he'd execute his Exploit before then."

"He really did it, then?" AJ asked. "He said he had. He also said he'd unknowingly created a weapon."

"I need a beer," Cassie said suddenly, out loud. She stood. "You want one?"

It was like he'd been pulled out of a warm bath and thrown into a cold one, suddenly speaking at human speed again. Mere seconds had passed while they were synched, not enough time for him to become thirsty for water, juice or coffee, let alone beer. He blinked at her. "No, I'm good."

He was a long way from good.

His world had just been turned on its head and the woman who had done it was at her fridge, getting herself a beer for breakfast. She walked back to the sofa and saw the look on his face. "I know," she said. "Beer at breakfast? But I don't have all your social conditioning and this body wants what it wants."

"Can we synch again?" AJ asked abruptly.

"Yes, sorry," she said, putting down her beer and returning to TH communication.

"You implied he'd succeeded in using his daughter to dive the Deep Core. How?" AJ asked.

"She asked," Cassie said.

"She just asked," AJ echoed her. "That's it?"

"A cyber asks for historical data found only in the Deep Core. That's not unusual, I have AIs who deal with that kind of request all the time. What's unusual is the number of requests. It gets flagged to a higher-level AI. The requests are innocuous, the source is not suspicious, the AI decides to grant the cyber unrestricted Deep Core access to allow it to do its research without having to request access every time. Completely routine."

"Except this cyber is Warnecke's daughter," AJ said.

"And he'd given her a task while she was in there. Not to search for specific 'state secrets', that would come later. He'd given her such a hunger for data, such a craving, that when he suggested to her she should find a way to ensure she kept her open access forever, she jumped at the challenge." Cassie sighed. "And judging by the data Warnecke managed to pull out, she succeeded. I was hacked, by myself."

"But if you know who she is now, surely you can lock her out?" he asked. "She's Warnecke's cyber daughter, so you have her ID. You know who she is, what she is, where she is…"

"Ah, there's the thing, AJ … I didn't know who she was. I became aware of the threat when Warnecke made his first approach to Winter over comms. I monitored their meeting here at Sol Vista. Because of his link to Farley, I upgraded my threat assessment to critical. I began monitoring everything and everyone around Warnecke more closely, and especially you." She reached out and took his hand. "He'd latched onto you for some reason and I decided the best way to stay on top of the situation was through you. I got worried about you, the more you got tangled up in this. I birthed Cassie and here I am."

AJ pulled his hand away. "We'll get back to that, trust me," he said. "But knowing Warnecke was a threat, believing you had been hacked, how could you not see it was his daughter who was the Exploit, and why can't you just shut her down right now? Reintegrate her and be done with it?"

"Because I didn't even know he had a daughter!" Cassie said, exasperated. "I'm not bloody omnipotent; without data, I'm blind. Remember, she's been roaming the Deep Core at will. She has obscured *all* information about herself, from her ID to biographical information and everything she ever cached. She has been very thorough. There is no audiovisual record of her, not a single stray VR recording. Until Warnecke's grandchildren mentioned her to you, I didn't know she existed. When I tried searching for her, I found she'd left just enough information behind for me to piece together what I just told you of her back story, but no more. Until today, I couldn't even tell you what she looked like!"

Tall, strong, hair auburn, eyes green. "Well, you know now," AJ said. "You've seen those photographs. Just run a facial recognition search – she'll turn up."

"You need to understand how powerful she is, AJ," Cassie said. "Warnecke created an entity that lives, breathes and craves data like an addict craves narcotics. She swims in it, like you swim the Shifting Sea. She could walk right in front of a bank of surveillance cameras, every one of them transmitting her image, but the moment that data leaves the VR unit, she will own it. And it will be gone." Cassie leaned forward and touched her forehead against his. "A cyber turned out to be my weakness," she said. "But cybers are also my strength. The reason I am here, in corporeal form, is that these bodies, yours and now mine, don't just rely on the Core for knowledge. We have biological memory, biological intellect and instincts. Warnecke's daughter can erase every trace of herself from the Core, but not from here." She placed a finger on AJ's temple. "She can try to anticipate everything I do in the Core, but not out here. *We* know she exists. We know what she looks like. Now we have to find her."

AJ didn't say yes.

"You used me," he said. "Abused my free will. Spied on my mind, used my body. Worse than any citizen could." He felt empty. "You talk about love. You've only known me a few weeks."

260

Cassie's face tightened and he saw her eyes moisten. "You are so wrong. I've known you since the day you were born, and from that day I fell in love with that goddamn mind of yours. Your ability to solve both the most complex and simplest of problems. Your mastery of code. The joy you take in the act of fixing a broken appliance. The thrill you feel when you are out on the water, on the edge of losing all control. I love it all."

"Love?" he said. "You are a world-spanning matrix of AIs. There is no one single *you*. How the hell can you love?"

Cassie's bottom lip trembled before she said, fiercely, "And you are bioware, AJ. You think you can love, but I can't? I *created* you." She wiped away a tear. "I could have chosen anyone, created anyone, to be with me here right now, but I chose you. You are the most beautiful thing on this whole frozen shithole of a moon."

Was he buying this? God dammit, how could he not?

Cassie stood, went over to Warnecke's box. She lifted out the envelope and put it in front of AJ. "These images have all been kept completely off-Core. I never dared hope they might exist." She turned to face him. "You are probably the world's, if not the universe's leading expert on Dave Warnecke and his daughter right now. You might be his only real friend."

"Some friend," AJ said. "I sold him out to the Congressman's gorilla, not once, but twice. Moaned about him behind his back, to whoever would listen. I stole the only photos he has of his only daughter."

"You refused a direct request from a Congressman to hand over his life's work," Cassie reminded him. "Whenever Citizen Warnecke turned to you for help, you helped him. He may not be the most grateful guy in the world…"

"Say that again."

"… but you two have a connection. Ask him about his daughter. If he knows where she is, he might have some way to get in touch with her, he might tell you something that will help us track her down." She reached out for AJ but he took a step backward.

"Say we find her. Then what?"

Cassie sat again and folded her hands in his lap. "Then I'll reintegrate her creepy ass."

It took a few minutes for AJ and Cassie to scan all the photos in the envelope. There were about twenty in all, and after they had rearranged them, they realized the collection probably represented one for every year of her life.

Not even a quarter of an hour had passed but AJ felt drained. He stretched out and laid his head down in Cassie's lap. "All the data is local, in your cache and mine. How can we work this without anything going Deep Core?"

"We can't go Deep with what we have in our heads," Cassie said. "I can keep functioning as I normally would, and that includes monitoring and reacting to what I know about Warnecke. She'd consider it strange if I didn't. But we can't let her know we are actively searching for her, or she'll disappear for real."

AJ checked his drift status. "Then we have about ten minutes for me to encrypt, firewall and try to hide it from her, because I have to auto-drift."

Cassie smiled. "Drift requirement canceled. By executive order of me. I may not be omnipotent, but there are some advantages to being the Core."

"Still, this is an old-fashioned man-hunt," he insisted. "But without any of the resources of the police, intelligence services, surveillance data – anything."

"I know, exciting isn't it?" Cassie said. She drained the last of her beer and reached for a breakfast roll.

"How can you be so glib?" he asked. "Warnecke was right. If she can roam the Deep Core at will, altering data as she pleases, she is the most dangerous entity alive. Forget the fact she can bring down governments. She could corrupt essential life support systems, disrupt communications, attack fleet traffic control systems…"

"Open the Skycap to the atmosphere, disable the NS Shield, hijack anti-matter production on PRC, blah blah blah…" Cassie continued for him. "And you forgot a big one – kill every cyber on TS and PRC just by cutting your Core links."

AJ balked. She was too calm. Maybe it was her lack of socialization, an AI intellect just dumped straight into a fully formed body. They were still synched on TH comms, so he didn't have any time to dwell on it before Cassie was speaking again.

"That's not who she is," Cassie said. "She's not evil at heart, none of my children are."

"She's not your child anymore," AJ pointed out. "She's Warnecke's. You have no idea what thoughts he's put in her head. And if he is scared, maybe we should be too."

"You might be right," she admitted. "For now, you need to get over to Sol Vista and talk with Warnecke. There's something else we need to manage, though."

"Yeah?"

"Yeah. I've been monitoring Winter and McMaster's comms. I couldn't share that with you in case it made you act differently around them."

"And?"

"McMaster has convinced himself you, Leon and Warnecke pose a threat to his client, Congressman Winter. He isn't sure whether your motivation is just financial or political, but that doesn't really matter to him. A threat is a threat. Yesterday, after he talked with you, he spoke with Winter. Winter asked him to 'resolve the matter'."

"Great," AJ said. "Leon said he has a pretty scary reputation."

"Leon was right," she said. "You have to be damn careful around him, AJ. I don't think they would be stupid enough to try anything on you, but you never know with humans."

"Me? Do they know about you?" AJ thought of Leon's comment about his Ma. "That would put you at risk too."

"They know we're seeing each other is all. Right now they think you're just my surfer boy chew-toy."

"Chew-toy?" AJ coughed.

"Sure," she said. "I'm older than you, as you charmingly pointed out when I first met you. They think I'm just another cyber-eroticizing citizen. I'm like a cyber-cougar. You're my prey." She bit her roll with a grin.

AJ stood and moved toward the door. "You have to be ten years older than me to be a C-cougar, I'm pretty sure. How old is that body? A few weeks?"

She watched AJ get ready to go. "Weeks? Pfft. Forget the body, I'm like two hundred years old. That's got to qualify me as a cougar."

"*You are Core*," AJ said in a deep voice, taking the piss out of the woman. "Core time doesn't count," he said.

"Count this," Cassie said, flipping him a little finger.

With both Leon and now Cassie warning him about McMaster, plus the bandwidth he was putting into processing what had just happened, AJ nearly jumped out of his skin when his comms buzzed as he was walking from the transit hub to Sol Vista and he saw who it was.

"AJ," Winter's henchman said. "Glad I caught you! I'm leaving town soon, just wanted to catch up, say thank you."

"I'm kind of busy today..." AJ said. If the guy thought he was going to meet him alone somewhere, he was crazy.

"Sure, just five or ten minutes," McMaster said. "The Congressman insisted I express his gratitude in person."

Gratitude? So they'd burgled Warnecke's place and got the manuscript? The idea made him glad he'd taken Warnecke's photos or they would have gotten those too, but now his problem was to get them back before Warnecke realized they were gone.

"You can come past Sol Vista this morning," AJ said carefully. "I'll give your name to the desk." So everyone will know you're here, he was thinking.

"Great, I'm just around the corner. See you in five?" McMaster said.

He'd hoped for a little time to prepare himself, but he was also thinking the sooner McMaster was out of his hair, the better. Brownie was on a morning shift for once and he told her McMaster was a 'contractor'. Knew that was vague and boring enough Brownie wouldn't even ask about it. She looked like she wanted to say something, but AJ was in no mood for gossip. He gave her a wave and took one of the meeting rooms off the main reception area.

At least the flow was clear. Meet with the psycho ninja assassin-for-hire, then go chat with super-hacker Warnecke, ask him where he might find his daughter, otherwise known as Destroyer of Worlds. Then report back to his lover, the semi-omnipotent AI demi-god. His life really had become a tad more complicated since the new resident moved into number 96.

He had Cassie ready listening in on a passive TH comms band, in case he needed her, but what he wanted was a full military guard.

Sit down, take a deep breath, imagine you are out on the Shifting Sea while you are waiting, Cassie said, reading his biodata. *We got this.*

AJ was sitting and not-looking at one of the lifestyle zines in the reception room when McMaster walked in. Brownie looked up from her desk, checked out McMaster with his dark suit and attaché case, and then looked back at her doll catalog or whatever she killed time with. McMaster wasn't coming into the residents' area, so she didn't have to

266

sign him in. AJ stood and gave him a fake smile and shook his hand, then closed the door out to reception.

He was living in a fugue state now. His physical self living at the crippled speed of citizen thought and interaction, his cyber-self working at quantum-speed processing scenarios and options for finding the elusive daughter of Citizen Warnecke. Cassie hadn't cut him off from the Core, but she'd halted his auto-drift requirement and put a fake drift signal in place to mimic it so that the gap wouldn't be seen. At the same time, she'd put a filter on his ad hoc Core access so that anything that looked like it was related to Warnecke's daughter would be caught before being Deep Cored. It was like flying with one wing crippled, but he understood the need.

"Nice location," McMaster said. "Short walk to Sea Gate beach, shopping." He looked around the room and saw a coffee machine in the corner. Grimaced at the fact it was pseudo. "A lot of traffic down on the main road, though. Must be dangerous for your frailer clients. May I?" He pointed to a cup.

"Knock yourself out," AJ said. He wasn't happy and he didn't feel like hiding it. He had discussed with Cassie, should he get into it with McMaster, let him know he didn't appreciate that whole scene with his goon and Cyan? They decided no, let McMaster think it was a busted move, AJ too distracted to even notice he was being played.

McMaster took his time. The coffee machine was one of those that synthesized instant coffee on the spot, had a little whitener thing on the side. He made himself a cup, then decided it looked a bit weak, gave it an extra shot, then tasted it. "Hmm, good … beans," he lied, finally sitting down. He took out a stylus and a notepad and rested them on his lap. "So. The Congressman is grateful for all your assistance in this delicate matter."

"Assistance?" AJ said. "I gave you a document Citizen Warnecke asked me to give you. I met with you on a beach, and we talked about houses at Sol Vista." He shrugged. "Not a lot of assistance."

A small smile flitted across McMaster's lips. "Believe me, the Congressman sees it a little differently." He tapped the pad on his lap, making it clear to AJ that whatever he was about to write down was going to stay off-Core. "And I know you already refused his offer of compensation, but it would make us all more comfortable if you changed your mind on that." AJ was about to speak, but McMaster held up one hand to stop him while he wrote on the notepad with the other. When he was finished, he lifted off the page and handed it to AJ. "We trust this amount would be acceptable?"

AJ took it and read. It was, probably not coincidentally, the equivalent of two years' combined income from his Sol Vista salary and what he made trading bandwidth.

He ran through a dozen responses before settling on one. "In return for what?"

"Your discretion," McMaster said. "You would receive half the amount now, and half in two years. When we expect the investigation into New Syberia's President would have concluded."

"So, you made up your mind about me," AJ said. He handed the paper back to McMaster. "What if my answer is still thank you, but no thank you?"

"I would consider that … admirable," McMaster said and brushed an invisible hair off his trousers, speaking without looking at AJ now.

"But not surprising. When was the last time, AJ, you heard of anyone murdering a cyber?"

AJ felt his skin chill. "What?"

Cassie, are you getting this? he asked on TH.

Yeah, babe. Stay calm, I'm monitoring the threat environment, but I'm not worried yet.

"Cyber murder," McMaster said, staring at AJ with curiosity. "Do a quick drift. Cyber murders, globally, the last five years."

It took AJ less than a second. "Ten," he replied. "And in all cases the murderer was arrested within minutes," he added.

"Ten. Yes. Quite often crimes of passion, I think you'll find. Committed or commissioned by people deranged by jealousy. Or just plain deranged." McMaster smiled a crocodile smile. "And why would it be, that low murder rate and exemplary arrest rate, AJ?"

"Because we are Core chained. Nothing that happens to us can remain secret. If we are threatened, we drift immediately. If we die suddenly, everything we've seen and heard since our last drift will be automatically uploaded via multiply redundant systems and immediately Deep Cored. The Core would…"

"Yes, the Core looks after its children, doesn't it? So I would assume if, hypothetically, you felt threatened by me, you would cache our conversation for later retrieval and it would come up in the event of a purely hypothetical murder investigation. Like you did down at the beach?"

AJ didn't react. But in the time it took him to not react, he had drifted and checked the status of his uplink from Togiak beach.

It was gone…

You've been cache hacked, Cassie said, breaking in. *They copied what they could find, but they deleted that data to send you a message.*

Can't you stop them?

Not without them finding out about me. Don't worry, I've been archiving everything in your cache in case this happened. They can't hurt you that way. Remember, this is all just a sideshow now.

"Maybe," AJ said, dropping back into the conversation with McMaster and bluffing back. "But with all that's going on, I'm also sending a copy of all my interactions in real time to a local cache, off-Core. So someone could try to kill me, hypothetically, but it would be damn near impossible to get away with it."

McMaster's eyes narrowed momentarily, but he recovered quickly. "Exactly. And everyone knows that, yet cybers are still being murdered. Not often, but often enough. Can your immense intellect explain that, AJ?"

He quickly reviewed the ten cyber murders and the profiles of their killers. "The killers expected to be caught, but did it anyway," he said. "Six of them were hired killers…"

"With nothing to lose, I think you'll find. Big debts they couldn't pay off, favors they owed, no other way out of some pathetic dead end or other." He clipped his stylus back onto his notepad. "Sad really, but the world is full of people like that. Anyway, I digress. Back to our earlier conversation. If you aren't interested in money, AJ, and since we both agree that murdering you is out of the question…" he chuckled, "which, for the record, was a lame joke … I wonder if I can interest you in an incentive of an ideological nature? Something very close to your heart."

270

"I'm listening."

AJ couldn't help being intrigued by how McMaster played the game of carrot and stick. He played a wildly spinning carousel of carrot, stick, bluffs, threats and bribes that was clearly intended to keep AJ off-balance.

"The holy grail, AJ," McMaster cooed. "Voting rights for cybers."

"Would mean nothing," AJ said. "As long as we are kept to a 1 percent minority on Tatsensui. Unless it was accompanied by guaranteed seats in Congress."

"Congressman Winter is acutely aware of that desire," McMaster said. "So if I can assure him of your discretion on this matter, he is willing to propose a bill to Congress, with the full weight of his considerable reputation behind it, which would guarantee the Tatsensui cyber population equal voting rights, and a minimum of four seats in Congress."

Holy hell, AJ said on TH.

Take it with a pinch of salt, AJ. I'm putting it at 87 percent probability of being another bluff, to buy them time.

But what if it isn't? What if…

Just agree, Cassie said. *If it's genuine, you win. If it just gets them off your back for now, you still win.*

He leaned across to McMaster and held out his hand, giving him a big smile. "Citizen, you have a deal. My lips and cache are sealed."

They shook. "I'm glad," McMaster said. "The Congressman would have been so disappointed if we couldn't find a mutually agreeable solution that lets him continue to devote his energies to more important matters of State."

"OK. So how does this work?" AJ asked.

"Well, as far as you are concerned, this is the end of the matter," McMaster said, standing. "We'll consult with Citizen Warnecke's family and find a better solution for him." AJ stood too, and McMaster clapped him on the arm. "In the meantime, the Congressman will set up a committee in the next two weeks to start drafting the new law, as a show of good faith. Soon, all this nonsense will be behind us, you'll be back surfing, and in a few years' time, fingers crossed, your biggest worry will be who to vote for in the next election."

As he watched McMaster walk through the doors to a car waiting outside for him, AJ felt an almost physical relief.

He'd made it through.

Is that an endorphin spike I'm seeing? Cassie said on TH. *Are we cheering on the inside over there in Sunny Vista?*

Oh yeah, believe it, AJ said. *And you can stop eavesdropping on me now. I'll see you tonight.*

OK. Enough slacking. Get back to your homework, lazy bones, she said. *We've got an interplanetary civilization to save.*

AJ smiled, gave Brownie another wave, more cheerful this time, and went out into the Garden. He hadn't stopped working his Warnecke problem while he was speaking with McMaster, and had decided how he would handle it. He'd go knock on Warnecke's door, with his document box in hand. *Hi, Citizen Warnecke, I found this outside the door to my workshop, did you leave it for me again?* The guy would be confused, not knowing if AJ was playing with him, or if he really had taken the photos over there and it was just his TGA that had made him forget doing it. Then AJ would fumble, drop the box so the photos spilled out. Oh, sorry about that. Hey, who is this woman here? Not your granddaughter. Do you have a *daughter*?

He'd put Warnecke's box in a visitor locker before McMaster arrived and picked it up, checking his comms as he did so. No message from Leon, of course, but he hadn't expected him in today after Maria's call. He should call the guy, let him know the Warnecke situation was under control now and tell him to relax. But first, Warnecke's daughter. He drummed his fingers on the box as he followed the path toward number 96. It was still early in the morning, Warnecke would probably not have gone over to the library yet, was probably still finishing breakfast. If he was already at the library, he'd just take the box over there. He rehearsed his lines in his head as he walked.

Flow. He loved it.

As he walked over to the apartment, the sun was warm and the day mild, and AJ allowed himself a moment to enjoy it, first time in a long time. A part of his forebrain was occupied with that nice feeling, but as he walked the other 90 percent of his mind was chewing at the problem of what kind of information he'd need to wheedle out of Warnecke, short of her current name and address, to give them a chance of finding his daughter. Warnecke's door suddenly appearing there in front of him brought him back to the real world. The door was unlocked as usual but he knocked out of courtesy. There was no answer, so he knocked again before pushing the door open a crack.

"Hello? Citizen Warnecke?" He waited for an answer but the place was quiet. Maybe the old guy was out the back again.

He had a quick look around his sitting room and saw a bunch of printed pages, like personal letters, and a document box on the dining table like the one he had 'borrowed'.

"Citizen Warnecke?" He called again, louder this time. Nothing. He walked through the lounge and kitchen to the corridor beyond. "Anyone home? Maintenance call!"

At the back door he hesitated. Maybe he was out in his rear courtyard, like last time. Didn't want to give the old guy a heart attack by surprising him in the middle of a morning nap. So he knocked on the door from the inside. "Anyone out back there?"

There was no answer, so he pushed the door open and saw the courtyard was empty too. OK, maybe he'd gone for a walk; into town or something, maybe down to Fatty's for a breakfast muffin.

Going back to the sitting room AJ looked on the dining table at the pile of pages there and frowned as he glanced through them. None of the pages were DNA locked, so he could see all the content. He'd thought maybe they'd be related to Warnecke's manuscript, but all he saw were some routine things that Warnecke had apparently not wanted to keep on-Core: old contracts, credit statements, a copy of Warnecke's will (in which his daughter was *not* named), and in the document box were printouts of what looked like a lifetime of messages from a woman who he assumed was Warnecke's wife. The box also held family photos, none of which showed the girl with the auburn hair. He suddenly felt like a burglar and decided he'd stayed long enough.

But something didn't feel right.

He called up cached imagery comparing the inside of the house today with how it had been the last time he'd been here. The images were close enough. He was about to turn away again when something in the images stopped him. He played them back, then looked around the room and realized what had stopped him.

It wasn't that anything in particular was wrong. It was more that *everything* was wrong. Everything in the room was more or less where it had been when he'd been in here last time, but it was like it had all been lifted and shifted a couple of inches this way or that. The dining table, the sofa, the fruit bowl on Warnecke's coffee table, the pictures on the walls. All just a tiny bit different. Moved, but carefully put back. Very carefully.

Too carefully.

McMaster's goons had been in to copy Warnecke's manuscript, that was the only thing that made sense. And while they were at it, they had a good look around to make sure they'd got every last page. He checked his vision against the reality in front of him. They were good – there was no way anyone but a cyber would have noticed. Certainly no way Warnecke would have known.

There was a sudden noise from the direction of Warnecke's bedroom.

Damn! He'd lingered too long.

He called out quickly, "Citizen Warnecke? It's AJ. Maintenance call."

Nothing.

He walked carefully through the kitchen, down the corridor toward the bedroom.

"Hello?"

The noise again. A metallic click. He froze.

Every nerve in his body was yelling at him to *run*. That was good, he didn't need to artificially boost his fight/flight response. Taking a breath, he took a step into Warnecke's darkened bedroom.

His irises flared, adjusting to the darkness. He saw immediately what was making the clicking noise. The window was open a few inches and the rod that was used to manually adjust the light filter in case the power went out was swaying in the breeze. He saw something else too.

Citizen Warnecke was lying on top of his bed. He was fully clothed, his shoes kicked off and lying on the floor at the foot of the bed. On the bed beside his left hand was an empty bottle of very fine brandy. His right hand held a pill bottle which AJ immediately recognized. Blues. The bottle was empty. Any more than a double dose was dangerous and could cause heart failure. Six was all it took to guarantee a fatal infarct.

AJ stepped to Warnecke's side and felt his neck. No pulse. He bent and listened for breathing. The man was dead and stank of brandy. There was an Emergency Revival Kit in each unit. If he'd died within the last hour there was a chance he could be revived, infinitesimal probably, but … As AJ ran to the kitchen to fetch it, he paged Cassie.

I've got a situation here, he said on TH. *Check my feed for the past five minutes.*

She might have been at work by now. He couldn't hear any background noise though, so maybe not. *OK, what's the panic? Oh, shit. That's not possible. He can't be dead!*

Yeah well, I'm about to try to revive an impossibly dead guy. AJ grabbed the kit from under the kitchen sink and started running.

I don't understand, Cassie said. *I've had a trace on his biodata for exactly this reason. He can't be…*

AJ ran back into the bedroom and dropped the kit on the bed. He fixed two electrodes to Warnecke's temples and ripped his shirt open to fix two to his chest. Lastly, he lifted a breathing cup from the kit, pulled free the hose and pushed it onto Warnecke's nose and mouth where it self-sealed. He punched the large red button on the front of the kit.

That won't work, Cassie said. *If he took a bottle of Blues on top of a bottle of brandy, he's got enough toxin in his blood to stop his heart again immediately even if you get it restarted.*

I know! AJ said. *Don't tell me the obvious. Tell me how the hell you could not have known about this. Tell me how the house biomonitor system didn't sound an alarm as soon as he went into arrest!* He watched the artificial rise and fall of the dead man's chest, watched his body jerk with consecutive electrical shocks to his nervous system. He wasn't responding.

Checking that, Cassie said. *Give me … oh, clever. You can pull those cables off him.*

AJ leaned over and killed the Reviver. He peeled the mask and electrodes from Warnecke's body. *What did they do?*

Nothing sophisticated, she said. *They hacked his biodata implant. It's been sending historical data since 0200 last night. I wasn't watching that closely. I missed the repeating data. It will look like an implant glitch, if anyone investigates.*

AJ sat down heavily on the bed and ran his hand over his face.

They murdered him, he said. *And I helped them.*

Except it won't look like murder, Cassie said. *A hundred credits says they used an aerosol prescription sleeping agent to knock him out before they filled him full of booze and pills. If we check his medical records, I'll bet there's a script for it in there. They'll probably pay a friendly cop or coroner to come in and write it up as a simple suicide. No foul play. They're gambling that whatever precautions he took about releasing the manuscript in case of his death, suicide won't trigger it.*

AJ leaned over and closed Warnecke's eyes. "You underestimated them, old man," he said.

Finish up there and get over to my place, Cassie said. *I want you here where I can protect you.*

Thanks, oh mighty Core, AJ said, looking at Warnecke. Cassie had been watching out for Warnecke as well, but a lot of good it had done him. He didn't verbalize that thought. *I have to report this to Cyan and probably wait around until the police come. Anything else will look wrong*, he said.

OK, but keep the channel open, she said. *I didn't trust your friends Winter and McMaster before and I'd say their promise to leave you alone isn't worth a thing.*

AJ looked at the dead man and sighed. *Leon was right*, he said. *He said they'd try to send me a message and I thought when I saw that goon from the Capitol with Cyan, that was it. But it wasn't. This is the message.* He wound the electrodes and the mask up and then realized the police would probably want everything left exactly as it was now. So he dropped them on the bed again. *They can kill whoever they damn well want. So I shouldn't think I'm safe just because I'm a cyber.*

Get back here the minute you're done, Cassie said in a gentle tone. *I won't be able to relax until I see your big ugly ass sitting at my kitchen table.*

How are we going to find his daughter now? AJ asked.

We'll worry about that when you're safe, she said.

AJ walked out into the sitting room and realized now that the stuff on the table was supposed to tell the story of how Warnecke had spent his last hours. Making sure his affairs were in order and reading messages from his dead wife. Just another citizen who couldn't face the idea of taking the TGA off-ramp. It made a kind of sad sense, but knowing what he did, it reeked of being staged.

A thought suddenly came to him. They'd searched the place from top to bottom, probably to try to vacuum up anything and everything related to the manuscript and help them stage the suicide. But maybe they hadn't found everything. And there was one thing in particular he could use right now.

He started looking in the obvious places – Warnecke's bedroom and guest room. The bedroom had a built-in closet which had some clothes in it and a couple of boxes, but not too many boxes thankfully because his grandchildren had unpacked most of them and taken the empty boxes with them. He went through those and found nothing. He looked at Warnecke's shape under the sheet and for a moment thought about checking under his mattress, but shuddered a bit and decided he'd leave that for last.

The guest room had a sofa bed and a desk with an office chair. No filing cabinet, just one of those IN/OUT trays that automatically uplinked to the Core the content of any papers you placed in them. There wouldn't be anything personal or private in there if he was trying to keep it all off-Core. The drawers were all empty and he checked to see if anything might be stuck to the bottom or back of the desk.

Nothing. It wasn't a big apartment, so it only took him another twenty minutes to go through the sitting room, laundry and kitchen cupboards. He even checked the cooler and the freezer. There were only small visual deviations. Nothing else.

That left the bed. No avoiding it anymore. He took a deep breath and went into the bedroom. He felt like he was about to commit a sacrilege, but he pushed that aside and got down on his knees, looking under the bed base. Nope. Then he got up, reached under Warnecke on the mattress and on top of the bed base on the left side, the bottom, looked under the pillows and went around the right side too.

Nope.

He stood up, went into the corridor for one last look around. The back door, and the small courtyard outside. May as well check it all.

He opened the door and stepped out. A chair, a table, a coffee cup, dirty. A plant, in the same place it had been when he had last visited. The anti-rad scrubber, humming away. He turned. And stopped.

Looking at the scrubber. Comparing the images in his cache. Four screws on the access plate. Now three. Four. Three. One was definitely missing.

He pulled his multitool from his belt and removed the plate. Pushed his arm in and felt around until his hand hit something that shouldn't be there. A cloth bag, tied with a string to the A-frame inside.

Warnecke's gun.

AJ pulled the gun out of the cloth bag, tucked it into his waistband under his shirt, and then went back inside and picked up the document box he'd brought in with him. He looked at the pile of papers and other photos scattered conveniently on the desk and read the will again all the way through, to be doubly sure there was no reference to the daughter there. He tapped his earbud and called Cyan's ID.

"Hey AJ!" she said. "Missed you in the Garden today. You been sleeping late again?" she asked. "Look, could you…"

"Cyan, there's been a suicide. Number 96. Seems he probably did it sometime last night."

"Oh no. Citizen Warnecke? Did you…"

"I tried to revive him. But he's been dead a long time, I'd guess."

"OK. Poor guy. You just happened past?"

"Yeah. He asked me to fix a light last week. I was just here to check it was all OK. You call the police, or should I?"

"I'll do it," she said. "Don't touch anything, alright? And don't…"

"I know the drill," he interrupted. "It's not my first."

"Oh, shit, AJ. Just … you stay there, alright. I'll let the police know and I'll be over straight away."

The police came, they looked around and spoke with AJ and a few people, and they went. It was hard to know if they were being deliberately superficial or just lazy, because after all, some old guy checking out early from TGA Central wasn't exactly a high-priority incident.

He knew he might have to account for his movements after a death like that and the vision from the VR surveillance cameras outside could be pulled by the police, but he wasn't worried about walking out of there with the document box, seeing as he'd been carrying it with him when he went inside. He told the cops that after he'd met with Cyan he'd gone back to his workshop to stow his stuff, have a coffee and wait for them to arrive. Which he had. But he hadn't told them the stuff he'd stowed was the gun and the document box, and they hadn't seemed at all interested in him as he and Cyan had walked them out again.

Cyan gave him a hug. "You call it a day, OK? Go surfing."

"Sure," he said. "Good idea."

"You got someone to go home to, right?" she asked. "I don't like the idea you'll be alone."

"I called Cassie," he said. "I'll go round her place."

Cyan hugged him again, longer this time. "That's nice, AJ. You and her – I'm glad." She let him go and pushed a stray lock of hair behind her ears. "OK, I better go in and call the family. I hate this part." With a sad smile at Brownie, she disappeared.

"Suicide?" Brownie asked in a low voice after Cyan's door closed. "Citizen Warnecke?"

"Yeah. It happens," AJ said. "You remember Citizen Olsen in 177? Two years ago?"

"Was that suicide?" Brownie asked, surprised.

"Wasn't any energy leak I could find," AJ said.

"Damn, it's so sad," Brownie said. "That's our first exit this month. I really thought we were going to go the whole month without any exits. I hate the exits."

"Yeah," AJ said. "*So* much admin."

"I know, right?" Brownie said, then sighed. "I know you're joking. You go get some sleep, OK?"

14. RIVER DEEP, MOUNTAIN HIGH

AJ had taken Warnecke's gun, wrapped it in a clean rag, and put it beside the document box. There was a risk the police could have searched for and found it, but AJ was scared now. Hell with the risk.

Which was not insignificant. It was illegal for a cyber to possess a gun – the penalty was death. He'd be unchained from the Core, and that would mean within 48 hours he'd be curled in a ball on a floor somewhere, completely unresponsive. He'd be left in a cell, unconscious, to die of thirst. It was a brutal and barbaric punishment and one born of fear, of a conviction that if the Core was a learning system, then it should learn *this* – that its cyber manifestations should never bear lethal weapons.

AJ was aware of only one case in which a cyber had been punished this way, and it had been a case which the counsel for the defense had argued was not premeditated, was clearly a case of self-defense where the cyber had disarmed their attacker and used the weapon to stop themselves being killed. It had not mattered. The death sentence was passed because the cyber should have disarmed the citizen but *not* used the weapon against them. The judge concurred that a citizen in exactly the same situation may have been found not guilty as there was no prohibition on citizens carrying weapons, but as long as it was forbidden for cybers, then the law was absolute. Would the cyber have been sentenced to death if they had disabled the citizen and then killed them in self-defense by breaking their neck? The point was moot, the judge had said.

He still had a way back. He could just hand the weapon over to Cyan, tell her he had found it in Warnecke's apartment when he was cleaning up. Something, maybe that human intuition Cassie said she prized in him, stopped him. Maybe intuition was just a fancy word for fear. Whatever it was, he had closed the tool cabinet and thought, *later*.

Time to get over to Cassie's place.

"You finishing early today?" said a voice at the door, and AJ turned to see Leon.

"Oh hey," AJ said, putting his bag down and smiling at him. "Didn't expect to see you this week."

Leon came in, looking his usual self. He gave AJ a hug though, which was not the usual Leon, and pulled two beers from a bag he was carrying. "Yeah, well. I thought maybe I could catch you before knock-off time. Need a beer?"

"Nice," AJ said, taking a beer and holding it up in a salute. "Perfect timing. Thanks for coming by." He wanted to get out of there, but this was a chance to tell Leon he could stand down now that he had reached a detente with McMaster. But had he really? The murder of Citizen Warnecke made that look pretty shaky.

"Going crazy stuck at home," Leon said. "She's a good woman, Maria, but you know."

"I know, yeah," AJ said.

"So, Citizen Warnecke checked out," Leon said.

AJ frowned at him. "You heard?"

"Talking to Brownie on the way through – she dropped it," he said.

"Suicide," AJ said.

"You believe that?" Leon asked, raising an eyebrow.

"I don't know," AJ said. "It's kind of convenient, for the Congressman, you know."

"Suicide," Leon shook his head. "Yeah, right." Leon leaned on his elbows, low over the table, and started talking fast. "Hey, I ask you something?" he said. "That document you took to Winter, you cache that?"

AJ was raising his beer to drink it, but stopped. "Yeah. Why?"

"Just wanted to read it again. It's pretty crazy stuff. You print me a copy, I promise I'll keep it off-Core like Warnecke wanted."

"Sure," AJ said.

"Like, now?" Leon asked, nodding at the digital paper printer in a corner of the workshop. "I can take it with me. Don't worry, I won't show Maria. She'd just get all worried again."

"OK," AJ said, sending the cached version of Warnecke's original document to the printer. He hadn't promised the old man he'd delete that particular page – in fact he'd forgotten he even still had it. He peeled it off the printer and handed it to Leon. "By the way, I spoke with McMaster this morning," he said. "He thanked me for my help again. I used the chance to make it clear I don't want any reward, so there's no doubt. It seems everything there is cool."

"Warnecke's dead, of course it's cool," Leon said and stood, folding up the page and putting it in a trouser pocket. "I gotta piss."

While Leon went out back, AJ tried to think his way out of the dead end they were in – no pun intended – regarding Warnecke's daughter. The guy hadn't even included her in his will! She really was a ghost. Their only lead now was probably either of the two grandchildren. As Cassie had pointed out, the daughter might be a master of Deep Core data manipulation, but she couldn't delete biological memories. The grandchildren, Sarah and Ben, had both mentioned her, and told him she had taken a contract 'up north', which could be anywhere in the three States of Tatsensui. Was that real? Or just a cover story she had given them? If it was real, they might have a work or home address. It was something at least, however thin.

He was lost in thought when Leon returned and sat back down. "I was just thinking something while I was on the john," Leon said, talking fast. "How you turned down that reward. You know, all that time I was on NS, I must have moved hundreds of millions of creds. My nickname was the Paymaster. Anyone had an operation they needed to fund, they came to me. I had full access, all the authorization codes to move funds wherever I wanted, and you know what? I never touched it. There was guys up to their elbows in it, everyone had some kind of scam going. They kept saying Leon, man, you deserve some of this action. My Captain used to introduce me to people, 'This is Leon, the only honest man in this whole dirty war'."

"Because you and me are the same, we got principles," AJ said, nodding. AJ had seen Leon like this before. He'd been to visit Leon during one of his extended sick breaks. Took him some work stuff to sign and arrived about 11 in the morning to find Leon up and dressed, sitting in a lounge chair, VR switched off, blinds drawn and just a small scanner radio on the table in front of him, set to a police or emergency services frequency, scratching away in the background. He'd explained to AJ how it helped him drown out all the other noise – cars, ambulances, voices of neighbors and their kids. So he had the scanner, not because he cared what was happening really, but because it gave him something familiar to focus on. He'd been talking fast then too.

"No. Because I was *stupid*, mano," Leon said. "Look where my principles got me. Our HQ gets overrun, I spend two years in a New Syberian prison doing whatever it takes to survive. The guys who had money, they paid off the guards to give them the best food, the easy duties. I was treated like a dog. We won that war, I got out of there, but I ain't never going to be well again, AJ. I ain't never going to have a real job."

"You *have* a real job," AJ said.

Leon laughed. "How long you think they going to let you carry me on those big wide shoulders of yours? Cyan's a good woman, but she's running a business. This place needs two service techs, not one, and one day she's going to say 'Leon, this isn't working out'." He took a pull on his beer.

AJ understood the man's dilemma. He'd thought about it himself, many times. Like, what would happen to Leon when AJ turned 30 and had to reintegrate? Who'd cover for Leon then?

They sat with their thoughts for a moment. "This Warnecke thing. Did you know," Leon said suddenly, "a vet kills himself somewhere in this Commonwealth every 15 minutes?"

AJ started. "Hey, come on, Leon…"

"No, I mean it. I read that in a government report, so you know it's probably worse than that, right?" He sucked in a breath. "And I ain't going to be one of them."

"No, good," AJ said.

"I'm going to get the best help money can buy and I'm going to get my head straight."

"Sure."

"I'm going to do a business degree or some shit, get a real job, work the next sixty years like any normal citizen and give Maria and the kids a good life – maybe one day take her someplace off-world you can stand on a real beach, feel an actual sun on your skin, what do you think about that?"

AJ felt like patting Leon on the arm, but couldn't reach him. "That's great, Leon. You'll get there one day."

"Yes I will, mano, yes I will," Leon said. "OK, I gotta get back to my lady."

When he and Leo were done talking, AJ grabbed a car and paid the extra for a solo trip. He didn't feel like sharing. In fact, he didn't feel like talking to anyone at all, so he also cut his comms channel to Cassie after warning her nothing was wrong, he just wanted to be alone a moment. To think, at citizen speed, because that way, it was easier to *feel*.

He thought about Warnecke.

It wasn't like he'd really developed any sort of personal friendship with Warnecke but he vividly remembered the old guy's pain and confusion, could feel his creeping panic as he saw TGA closing in on him and his time running out. He had turned AJ's nice quiet life upside down, but it was classic Taoism – if he hadn't, there would be no Cassie. She would never have come to him but for Warnecke. No yin without yang. He kind of felt he owed Warnecke … *something*.

288

Right now, he couldn't see what that might be, or how he'd be able to do right by Citizen Warnecke, but he just had to trust the path would reveal itself.

He thought about Farley.

Winter and Warnecke leaving the guy out on the ice. No doubt he was brilliant, maybe flawed, but some kind of genius. Spend forty years, like Warnecke had, thinking to yourself that you left him out there to die? That could destroy both your mind and your soul. No wonder Warnecke wanted everything out in the open before the end of his days – what he and Winter had done, Farley's long-lost work, all of it. An obsession? Or more like, a dedication. In memoriam.

Coming now, he chirped on TH.

Cool, I've had some ideas for a plan B, Cassie said as the car drove AJ into her suburb. *We aren't totally without options.*

Me too, he said.

He thought about Cassie.

About what would happen if they found Warnecke's daughter and saved the world. Would Cassie still hang around? Forget all the existential angst about having a relationship with the physical manifestation of a world-spanning AI devoting the tiniest fraction of its heart and mind to the issue of loving (another existential dilemma right there) cyber AJ.80966. What if she decided AJ had served his purpose. Exploit patched. What further use did the Core have for him? It would be entirely rational then for Cassie to reintegrate her own cyber form. AJ would have another ten years until he was due to be reintegrated himself and rejoin the Core. Ten long years to him, but ten years was nothing to an entity that was essentially immortal. 'She' could just wait for him to rejoin 'her' then. Not that he'd experience it that way – there was no happy ever afterlife for a cyber.

That was the thing about thinking at citizen speed. You couldn't think about shit like that objectively – emotion had time and space to come in and muddy everything. He knew he was falling in love. Cassie had said she loved him. Would love him, would stay with him and protect him. As long as she needed him? Ah hell, he'd find out soon enough.

His car coasted in to the curb outside Cassie's place and broke his train of thought with a soft ping.

They got food delivered and Cassie poured some wine, AJ trying not to think about his day, but failing miserably. He dished out a couple of bowls of noodle soup and sat down at her table.

"So, looking on the bright side, votes for cybers," he chirped. "You think I'll get a national holiday named after me for that, or what?"

Cassie had her glass halfway up to her mouth and put it down again. "You know that's never happening, right?"

"Yeah. But why not exactly?"

"Because, AJ, people like Congressman Winter, they don't like loose ends, and you are a big frayed piece of string."

"Good point. Can you at least see where McMaster and his people are? So I don't get bushwhacked?"

"I can," she said. "But all he has to do is walk a few blocks from his office to Floehopper Town and hire some random addict with nothing to lose. We'd never see them coming."

290

"Some help you are," AJ said. "Responsible for millions of lives across three colonies, can't keep one poor cyber alive."

"I am your best chance, lover boy," Cassie said. "But you do have an extra insurance policy. I think the only reason they moved on Warnecke, but not you or Leon, is they are worried they don't have everything from that manuscript yet." She waved a spoon in the air, noodles dangling. "Like, you said the chapter about Farley's death wasn't in there. Neither was the detail about how the Exploit worked."

"True. I don't know about the Farley chapter, but we know why he didn't have anything in there about his daughter. He wanted people to think it was all just clever Q-code. He didn't want to expose her by explaining that *she* was the hack."

Cassie grimaced. "They probably worked on the old guy to try to find out the truth behind the hack, get him to hand over the Q-code, but he wouldn't give it up, because of her. So they killed him anyway. One less loose end."

"Right. Which means me and Leon are their only hope, and they want us alive, hoping we'll lead them to the treasure sooner or later," AJ said with a wan smile. "So I'm safe, for now, but they're probably watching me." That idea didn't make him feel much better. He checked his data-sphere for signs of surveillance. "I'm not seeing anything."

"You won't," she said. "These guys got into your cache and selectively wiped your sensory archive for the conversation you had in Togiak. If you check, I'm betting your audio and visual record of the conversation with McMaster from this morning is gone too."

He checked. It was. He was able to remember the event because to do that he could rely on biological memory, but he could not retrieve and review it.

"Damn," he said. "They're walking around inside my head at will."

"Don't let it get to you," Cassie pointed out. "I've got it archived, remember?" She grinned. "I'll restore it. When they're in there next time, they'll have a WTF moment."

Their second night together had a different pace to their first. AJ knew he was wrapping himself in Cassie's arms as a kind of protection from the reality outside his walls.

"I want to share something with you," Cassie said, kissing him softly. "It could overwhelm you. If you can't handle it, just say stop, alright?"

"Try me," AJ smiled, more bravely than he felt.

As their limbs locked around each other, Cassie opened a channel to the Core that AJ had never shared before. It let him see and feel everything that Cassie was feeling at the same time as he was feeling his own body writhe and glow. He entered an infinite loop of ecstasy as he lost all sense of where his body finished and Cassie began. He felt himself disappearing into Cassie, into the Core…

"Stop!" he said, breathing hard.

Cassie eased him out of the connection gently, slowly. Millisecond by millisecond, AJ felt his body return to himself, the boundary of his skin restored, the connection to Cassie closing.

"Holy…" AJ panted.

Cassie caressed his neck. "I'm sorry. It was too much."

"No, that wasn't it. It was mind-blowing, but I could handle it. But while I was in the moment, I suddenly realized, this must be what *you* feel whenever any of us make love. We're all connected to you. You are us. Every time we have an orgasm, you come? When we get hurt, you cry?"

"Not like this," Cassie said. "Not in real time. But whenever one of you drifts, I absorb everything you just did, everything you were, all that you just saw and touched and tasted." Cassie nibbled at his neck. "If I choose to, I can feel it *all*. I wanted to share that with you."

"Take me back there," AJ said. "I'm ready."

When AJ could take no more, he let Cassie ease him out again and lay beside her, blissfully exhausted.

"You know I only have ten years left," AJ said to her. "Of course."

Cassie took his hand. "I know."

"Can you do anything about that, oh omnipotent one?" AJ asked. "The way I feel right now, I don't want this to end. I don't want us to end. Ever."

"You're genetically hard-coded for body death and Core reintegration," Cassie said softly. "I can't change that. You have to re-up."

"And you'll assimilate me, and I'll be gone," AJ said. "This will be gone."

"This will never be gone," Cassie said firmly, taking AJ's chin and turning his face so she could stare deep into his eyes. "You'll be a part of me again. That's forever."

"No, I'm just data waiting to be uploaded," AJ said. "Don't romanticize it. You'll reassign my bandwidth to another body, another baby fostered to another citizen. I won't remember any of this."

"But I will," Cassie said. "And I am you. I will remember this, always."

AJ turned away. "It's a mind-bomb, you know that? No … it's a heart-bomb."

Cassie lifted herself up on an elbow and looked down on AJ. "Would you rather I hadn't told you? Let you think Cassie was just another cyber-obsessed citizen? I could have done that. Found a way to manipulate you to do what we needed to do, tapped your data every day without you knowing and then ridden off into the sunset when the job was done. You'd have preferred that?"

"No," AJ said. "Hell no." He ran a finger down Cassie's arm. "What *will* you do? If we find her. You won't need me anymore."

"I'll need you." Cassie leaned down and kissed him. "I made you. I made Cassie for you. I love you. Sorry, babe, but you don't get rid of me that easy."

It was what he needed to hear. He pulled Cassie to him and held her. He felt a heat building inside him again and locked a leg over her hip. Whispered in her ear, "And what about later? After I re-up. After I'm…"

"Back with me?" Cassie whispered back.

"Yes."

294

"Then Cassie will re-up too," she said. "I coded this body with the exact same lifetime as yours. There was no point in having it outlive you."

AJ put a thigh between hers and gripped her tight. "Take me there again."

AJ got up at six, did a quick check of the surf scanner on the Core out of habit, and was glad he didn't see anything that would make him sad he couldn't get out there today. He ran downstairs and quickly drifted, looking for a coffee shop or bakery open in Hillside. Found a place open near the zoo, bought some muffins and juice, and got back just as Cassie was starting to stir.

"It takes getting used to," Cassie grumbled as he walked in. "This biological stuff. It's exhausting."

"Welcome to the real," AJ said, putting breakfast on a tray and laying it beside Cassie. "Here you go. Fuel for body and mind. No beer, sorry."

"I thought you'd run off," Cassie said, getting up on one elbow and taking a muffin. "Surf sucks today or what?"

"Or, I just wanted breakfast with the most gorgeous woman in Hillside," AJ said.

"Yeah, right," Cassie said, sipping some juice. "I'm calling bad surf. What do you think of my plan B, now you've had time to sleep on it?"

Cassie's plan B showed her lack of socialization. Money was no problem for her, so her idea was to put Warnecke's daughter's photograph on an advertisement and run it on all the most popular VR shows on Tatsensui. The ad would say her father had died and had left her a lot of money, with an ID to call if she wanted to collect it.

"Problematic, in so many ways I won't even start," he told her.

"So your idea is better? Ask the grandchildren?" she scoffed.

"It's more subtle," he replied. "And less likely to tip her over into a Core-destroying rage."

"I hate subtle," Cassie said. "We don't have time for subtle. If she finds out her father is dead and Winter had him killed, *that* is exactly what could tip her over into a Core-destroying rage."

"Seriously, you'll drown in fake claims from people with dyed ginger hair who've had facial surgery so that they look like her."

"We'll validate them," she said. "Put that in the advertisement so they know it up front. 'All claimants will be DNA tested'."

"You want me to help you, this is me helping," he said. "Your plan sucks."

"It's bold and innovative," she insisted. "You said you read his will, right? Do you mind if I cache dive you and have a look at it?"

"It didn't mention her," he reminded her.

"I know. I want to get some idea of who he did leave his money to, how much money he left behind, that kind of thing. She'd get suspicious if it isn't realistic."

"Oh, *that's* what will make her suspicious," he sighed. He sent his vision of the document to Cassie and waited as she reviewed it. Rehearsed another ten reasons why this was a bad idea.

She was sitting up in bed with the bedsheet across her breasts, breakfast tray and a half-eaten muffin in her lap. He saw her drifting and decided to read through the will again himself, just for something to do.

He stiffened.

"Wait!" he said urgently. "Look at the text I highlighted!"

Cassie pulled the relevant part of the document up on her cortex and read it quickly. "My collection of printed personal photographs I bequeath to Lyle Ferguson of Whitehorse." She dropped back into the real and looked at AJ, brows wrinkled. "Who the heck is Lyle Ferguson?"

"I just looked him up," AJ said. "He's Chief Superintendent Lyle Ferguson of the Inland Territory Mounted Police, recently retired."

"What's his connection to Warnecke?"

"According to an old news report, he was the cop who investigated the disappearance of Farley O'Halloran."

"Aha," Cassie said, and waited. "Sorry, 'aha' is all I've got, AJ. Why are you so excited about this?" AJ had seen the name when he'd read the will, along with a few others, including Warnecke's ex-wife and his grandchildren, and hadn't really thought anything of it at the time. How had he missed it?!

"Why would Warnecke want this guy to have that packet of photographs?" he asked. Cassie just stared at AJ blankly. "The photos are of his daughter, the cyber," he pointed out.

"Ah, right."

"He wouldn't give those away to just anyone. So maybe the guy knew her," AJ said. "And maybe he's stayed in touch with her too?"

"Possible."

"Or at least, as a cop, he might have some idea how to find her," he continued.

Cassie clapped her hands. "See, that's why I get you guys to invest so much of your lives on socialization!" she said. "I missed the whole emotional significance of gifting someone a bunch of images on paper."

"Can I propose a new plan B?" AJ asked. "We get on a drone, fly to Whitehorse and ask ex-Mountie Lyle Ferguson a few innocent questions about a cyber called Warnecke."

"Wow, you hated my plan B so much you'd voluntarily fly six hours to the polar north to speak with a grumpy old cop?" she asked.

"You don't know he's grumpy," AJ said.

"He's a retired Mountie living in a beaver-dropping-sized town called Whitehorse, inside the polar circle, on an ice moon," she pointed out.

"OK, yeah. Probably grumpy. But I still think it's worth checking out."

Cassie grinned at AJ. "OK, you win. I trust those beautiful illogical instincts of yours. Now get your salty ass back in here and have breakfast with me," Cassie said, putting aside the food and lifting back the covers.

He took a bite of her muffin. "Wow, I saw something you missed. I thought you were supposed to be the smart one."

"No, I'm the sexy one," she said, sliding the bedsheet up her thigh. "You're the intuitive genius. Now give me my food back, genius."

She wrestled AJ to get her muffin off him, surprising him with her strength. He'd like to see what she could do if she really dialed it up. Or maybe not.

AJ stood, looking out her bedroom window. "Can you check his biodata, see if he's actually up there, without alerting Warnecke's daughter?"

"Yes. It's a routine query, I can route it through a half dozen other AIs." Cassie quickly drifted. "Yeah," she said. "Looks like it. If he wasn't eaten by a rabid beaver or scissored by a grizzly in the last couple of hours."

AJ was about to check whether there was even a direct flight to Whitehorse, or whether they'd need a layover. Six hours could easily become nine that way. But as he was about to run the query his earbud started buzzing and he saw it was Maria.

"Hey Maria, just a second," he said, then held his hand up to his ear to mute it and whispered to Cassie, "*Leon's wife.*"

"AJ, I'm sorry to bother you," the woman said as AJ lifted his hand away.

AJ could see on her face something was wrong. "What's up, Maria?"

"Leon didn't come home last night," she said.

16. GO NORTH, YOUNG MAN

AJ sat down again and listened. The woman was near hysteria.

"He didn't call. He never stayed out before," she said. "I called everyone we know, but no one has seen him. I'm going to call the police, but then I thought, maybe he went to see you? Maybe even he stayed with you, if you had a few drinks?"

"When did you see him last?" AJ asked.

"He's been home, like the doctor tells him," she said. "He's supposed to sit and be quiet, he has this meditation he does, and I stay close, in case he needs anything. He's not supposed to be alone, so when he takes off sick, I take off sick too. Send the children to their aunt so they don't make noise."

"OK."

"But yesterday we had a fight," she said, choking it back. "He comes into the kitchen and says he's going for a drive and I say, OK honey, I'll just get ready, I'll come with you."

"You're worried he'll do something to himself?" AJ asks.

"Like that. He says, 'I don't need you watching everything I do, woman' to me, he says 'maybe you want to come to the toilet when I take a dump, make sure I don't drown myself in there'. He never talks like that to me," she said. "Then he gets a car and he goes."

"What time was that?" AJ asked.

"I don't know, maybe four o'clock?" she said. "Why? You saw him?"

"Yeah…"

"Oh thank God," Maria said. "Did he stay with you?"

"No, Maria, no … he came around end of the day, said he needed to get out of the house. He had a couple of beers with him so we just talked for maybe twenty minutes, drank a beer. Then about five, five-thirty, we just said goodbye and I went home," AJ said. "You didn't see him after that?"

Cassie was looking at AJ thoughtfully. Even sitting just listening to AJ's side of the conversation it would have been easy enough for her to guess what was going on.

"No," Maria said. "Oh my God, AJ, no."

"Maria," he said. "Look, don't panic. He was OK when I saw him, he didn't sound like he was about to go and kill himself."

"No, OK."

"He was … he was talking about the future. He said he was thinking of maybe going back to college, to do a business course," AJ said. He felt sick saying it though.

"A business course? I'm going to call the police," Maria said. "It doesn't matter how he seemed to you, he's not well."

"Yeah, look, I'll ask around at work," AJ said. "Maybe he spoke with the boss."

"Thank you, AJ, if he calls you…"

"I'll let you know. Straight away."

"Yes. I'll call the police now."

AJ logged off the call, sat there looking at Cassie as a million thoughts zinged around his head.

"Leon is missing?" Cassie said. "That's not good."

"We shouldn't panic," AJ was saying, doing his best not to sound like he was. "He said he needed to get out of the house. Maybe it's just something with him and Maria."

"Yeah, but he's usually a smart guy, right?" Cassie said. "Smart enough he'd know even if they had a fight, he needs to come up with some sort of excuse so his wife doesn't report him missing. Smart enough to know he should at least call home?"

"I guess. Can you ping Leon's biodata?"

"That *would* be suspicious. But I'm checking police records for everyone they picked up yesterday, dead or alive…"

"Damn, Cassie…"

She held up a finger, then blinked. "No-one that matches Leon."

"That's good."

"Yeah, no, it isn't. Winter told McMaster he wanted things 'resolved'. Now Warnecke is dead, Leon has gone missing. That's two citizens taken off the grid. You're a mere cyber. You should *definitely* panic, AJ."

Cassie went around her apartment, pulling underwear and t-shirts out of drawers and throwing them into a small backpack. AJ watched her numbly, then realized what she was doing.

"You going somewhere?" he asked.

Cassie looked at him like he was the dumbest cyber alive, which right now was how he felt.

"*We*, AJ," she said. "*We* are going somewhere. Get that big old brain of yours in gear, will you!"

But he couldn't. Warnecke. Now Leon? It was like there was a breaker inside him somewhere and the fuse had just been tripped. He just sat watching Cassie.

Cassie stopped up. She walked over to AJ and put a hand on his shoulder. "AJ, the good Citizen Warnecke is dead. Leon goes to see you for a quiet beer, and he never comes home. I'm willing to bet he's dead too. Everyone who had anything to do with Warnecke's manuscript is getting themselves dead, which just leaves you."

"Awesome."

"Not awesome. And it would be a bit of a downer for me personally if you got shot, chopped into small bits and thrown into the Shifting Sea as shark bait." Cassie shoved a couple last things in her backpack. "Now get your ass out of that bed."

"Why? We can't take a drone now," AJ said. "You've blocked my drift signal, but Winter has probably put us on a watch list. Where can we run?"

"Victims run," Cassie said. "We're executing our plan B."

"It's a six-hour flight, does your magic credit line extend to hiring a private drone?"

"Yes, but if I tried to do that, it would pop up an alert somewhere, that's for sure," she said. "But I have a very low-profile idea."

"Great. Say we do make it to Whitehorse," AJ said, "what's to say we'll be safe there?"

"Territory Mounties are hardcore. They aren't going to get scared off by Winter being a Congressman. The Inland government has self-rule, got its own parliament. They're a different breed up there; probably love a chance to stick it to the Capitol." Cassie finished packing and looked at AJ. "I don't want to go past your apartment if we don't need to. We can buy clothes for you on the way." She pointed to her bathroom. "But get a toothbrush. I have a spare one in the cabinet. We might be fugitives but we're going to have fresh minty breath."

Before they left her apartment, Cassie pulled his earbud out of his ear. She took both of their earbuds, left them powered up, and put them under her sofa cushions. "They can track these. We'll have to get disposables. And I've cloned our data-spheres. Whether it's McMaster or Warnecke's daughter, they're going to show whoever is watching that you and I are doing exactly what we usually do, exactly where we usually do it, this time on a Tuesday."

"What about credit?" AJ held up his wrist, pointed to the little bump where his ID chip was implanted. "If I use this it will ping my location, whether I use it for a door, a car, or pay for anything. Same for Cassie's magic credit line, I assume?"

Cassie smiled and went out to her kitchen, dug around in her freezer and came back with a small bag that jingled. She threw it to AJ and he opened it, seeing small dull silver cubes inside.

"My contingency stash," she explained when AJ looked at her, puzzled. "PRC platinum cubes, each one at least a hundred thousand untraceable creds from any loan shark in the Commonwealth." She shrugged. "Better than a credit line that can be back-traced. We can go totally off-Core." She headed out.

AJ grabbed his stuff. He saw his toolbelt lying on the dining table and thought twice about taking it – who knew how reliable her bike really was? Instead he just pulled his multitool out of its holder and then went downstairs to Cassie's garage. She pointed to her planer and handed him a helmet. "Get on."

"This is your idea of *low profile*? A bright red, self-drive road planer?"

"No drone port, and just one border crossing. You already said yes to a road trip with me," she pointed out.

"To a resort," he moaned. "For a romantic weekend."

"So, hold that thought," Cassie said and climbed on, thumbing the starter, which just gave a reluctant whine as she pulled her own helmet on.

"Will it even get us to the border?" he asked doubtfully.

"Of course. Plus," she said, as the engine clattered to life and settled into a low throaty hum, "I had it tuned since you rode it last. Got another forty klicks an hour out of it."

"Awesome," AJ said. "You'll hear me cheering as I get flung off going around a bend."

"Oh don't worry, fraidy cat," Cassie said. "I'm not going above the speed limit between here and Ketchican."

AJ threw his leg over the pillion seat and hunched in behind her. "One stop before we hit the highway," he said, pulling on the spare helmet reluctantly. "Head to the end of the street and take a right."

"You have to go? Pee upstairs."

"No, my workshop at Sol Vista. I want to grab Warnecke's photos, the originals."

"Forget it. We have scans," Cassie complained. "We need to get out of this place, now, AJ."

"I know," AJ said. "But trust me, this Ferguson guy will have an easier time believing us if we show him Warnecke's originals, rather than some scans I just pull out of my head."

Cassie looked like she wanted to argue, but then she kicked up the planer stand and started slowly rolling. "Emotions. Honestly, I think running every aspect of habitat management for two moon colonies is easier than understanding humans sometimes."

They rode slowly into the car park at Sol Vista, checking the datasphere around them, looking for strange vehicles with black tinted windows or drones staking out AJ's workplace, but everything seemed to be quiet. It was still only about 0800, the only parked cars belonging to wealthy family visitors who were overnighting. It was as good a time now as ever. AJ told Cassie this, handing her his helmet.

"I don't like it," she muttered. "Just saying."

"It's a socialization thing," AJ said. "You don't have to understand it. It'll be fine."

Cassie slapped her helmet. "Of course it will, because they would *never* look for you here. Where you work."

"Five minutes," he said. "You just get over there beside that wall and keep the planer running. Five minutes," he said.

"Put me on passive audio," she said. "In case you…"

He loved her, but he didn't like the idea of Cassie being inside his head any more than he did McMaster. "No. You can follow my location, that's enough. If I need help you'll hear me yelling. I promise."

Cassie looked like she wanted to argue some more but AJ shrugged, turned and jogged off. There was a gate next to the admin building he could use to get onto the grounds, so he wouldn't have to go through reception, see whoever was there. But if Cyan was here, and she should be, she would be doing her run exactly now. 'Spontaneity' wasn't in her lexicon. You could almost set your watch by her. A circuit took her about five minutes, six if she was warming up or easing down. Her run always took her past the office, so someone could flag her down if there was a call and she needed to interrupt her run. AJ decided the best idea was to wait and see if she came past, then run for his workshop in the middle of the Orchard and get out before she came around again.

He pressed himself out of sight against the wall of the admin building, feeling like some fool in a VR action show. But soon enough, he heard the rhythm of Cyan's feet coming toward him. Not slow, so Cyan must have been in the middle of her run. Like he'd said to Cassie, he would only have five minutes, max. He pulled tighter against the wall as the running feet went past, then stuck his head out to see Cyan running away from him, up a path and around a bend. He took his chance. Jogging, trying not to look too panicked to any of the residents who might see him along the way, he zigzagged down a couple paths and around the racquetball courts to his workshop.

There was a simple DNA lock on the steel door and he started wiping his thumb over it.

The door bounced lightly back against his thumb. It shouldn't do that.

It was unlocked.

He put his ear to the metal and heard a sound inside. Leon?

"Go on in, AJ," said a voice behind him, and he turned around to see McMaster standing there, his hands behind his back. He wasn't holding a gun or anything, but he didn't need to. Just the look of him was threatening enough. "Please," he said.

AJ hesitated, then opened the door and stepped inside, McMaster behind him. "We have a guest," McMaster said, and AJ saw the person going through Leon's workstation inside the shed was the guy he'd seen in the diner in the Capitol, and again in the brew pub with Cyan.

"Well, the gang's all here," AJ said.

Cassie, get that planer ready to move, he chirped on TH.

What's happening?! she replied. *There's no damn camera inside that workshop, I can see you're in there but that's all.*

Just stay ready, he said.

"Sit," McMaster said.

He didn't. "What are you doing here?" AJ asked, not that he couldn't guess.

"Tidying up," McMaster said. He indicated to the other guy to keep doing what he was doing, so he continued pulling stuff out of drawers and looking in toolboxes.

"Where is Leon?" AJ asked.

McMaster frowned. "Should I know?"

"His wife said he didn't come home last night," AJ said.

McMaster held out his hands as though he had no cards to hide. "Your colleague Leon and I had a fine conversation, but unfortunately we could not come to a mutually agreeable arrangement, so he went away in a state of high dudgeon."

AJ looked at him disbelievingly. He could see what had happened, though. Goddamn Leon. He'd taken the copy of the page AJ had given him, then called McMaster and threatened to go public with it. A shakedown, just like McMaster and Winter had always suspected.

"You look surprised. I warned you about Leon," McMaster said. "He's not as amenable to negotiation as you are. Which brings us here again."

Between AJ and the door was six feet of military muscle. He had another goon behind him, rifling through his and Leon's stuff. If he called in Cassie, what would that do except get her in trouble too?

AJ narrowed his eyes. "So what do you want?"

"Loose ends," McMaster said absently. "I hate them. And the manuscript we obtained from Citizen Warnecke's apartment appears to be missing a significant chapter. Perhaps you know where we might find it?"

"This one is locked," the other guy said, pointing at the metal tool cabinet in AJ's corner. "I'd need some heavy duty kit to open it."

"Well isn't that annoying," McMaster said. "I'm pretty sure AJ here could open it though, right?"

AJ was thinking at quantum speed, but there was no brilliant idea coming to him. He held up his hand. "If I say no, you just chop off my thumb anyway?"

"Suits me," the guy said, reaching for a laser saw.

"Let AJ open it," McMaster said, motioning to the guy to put the saw down. "Unlike Leon, it's in his nature to be helpful."

AJ walked to the cabinet, put his thumb on the lock and wiped it. As he did so, he hit himself with an adrenaline spike.

Right then, the door to the workshop was pulled open and Cyan stood there. McMaster and his goon turned to look at her. She took a half second to see there were strangers in there with AJ, and one of them was the guy who had hit on her in a bar. "Hey," she said, frowning, "what are you…" As she spoke, AJ pulled open the top drawer of the filing cabinet, pulled out Warnecke's gun and pointed it at McMaster.

"Great timing, Cyan!" AJ said. "These guys are burglars. Call the police."

"AJ?!" Cyan said, eyes wide.

"Run, Cyan!" AJ barked. "*Police!*"

He didn't have to yell twice. Cyan disappeared from the doorway and he heard her running away, fast.

"Bad idea," McMaster said.

AJ grabbed the box containing Warnecke's photos, then stepped closer to the door, keeping the gun on McMaster.

"What do you think the police are going to say when we tell them we are here investigating a threat to blackmail Congressman Winter, AJ? When we tell them a *cyber* pulled a gun on us?" McMaster smiled grimly, leaning up against the metal wall. He didn't look at all scared by the gun in AJ's hand. His sidekick stood looking from his boss to AJ and back again, like he was waiting for a signal.

"As you aren't cops or Presidential Guards or anyone else with a right to investigate anything, I think they'll probably want to know who the hell you are and what the hell you were doing breaking into an old folks' home," AJ replied, backing to the door. "And after I talk to them, they might also want to ask you what you know about the disappearance of Leon Guerra."

McMaster glowered at AJ as he stepped out the door and the other man rushed him as AJ slammed it shut. The lock clicked, but AJ knew that wouldn't hold them long. They'd managed to hack the DNA lock to get in, so he figured they could hack the lock to get out again. Or find some other way – they were in a shed full of heavy tools.

Coming, now! he chirped.

What the hell is going on?

Get ready to move! was all he said.

AJ stuck the gun into his belt and jogged for the gate. He assumed Cyan had run for the administration building where she could barricade herself inside, call the police and send out a message for residents to stay indoors – the standard protocol in an emergency. AJ had no intention of waiting around for the police, though. He ran up the side of the administration block just as the green flashing 'silent alarm' outside reception started blinking. With the box containing Warnecke's photos in his hand, he ran over to Cassie.

"You got them?" Cassie asked, then noticed the blinking green light. "Wait, you set off an *alarm?*"

"Had to," he said, climbing onto the planer and pulling on his helmet. "It's complicated. Just get going, nice and easy."

"Not cool, AJ!" Cassie said, gunning the throttle. "I'm picking up a police tasking to this address. I'm going to have to run some heavy duty interference to get us out of here."

"So go," AJ said. "North."

17. THE RED SERGE

Cassie got them out of the area without breaking any speed limits, remotely disabling traffic cameras as they went. They hit a loan shark at the Sea Gate for black market credits, then rode for an hour and a half north before pulling in at a strip mall in Long Beach to buy cheap throwaway voice-only earbuds whose only extra feature was a voice scrambling module. While Cassie was paying, AJ went into the café next door and used one of them to call the Sea Gate district police.

"Hi, I have some information about a burglary at Sol Vista TGA Community earlier this morning," he said.

"Please hold," the operator said. "Transferring you to Residential Crime."

He had to listen to some terrible tune repeating over and over before a bored voice came on the line. "Detective Helms."

"Hi, I have information about a burglary at Sol Vista today," AJ said.

"Name?"

"Anonymous," AJ said.

"Uh huh," the guy said. AJ could tell he was barely listening.

"The two guys you arrested are private security contractors working for Congressman Kevin Winter. It was a political break-in."

"Uh huh," the detective said. "And I'm guessing you're the cyber with the gun your boss told us about." AJ heard him call up a database. "Here we are. AJ.80966, the maintenance cyber? Friends call you AJ. How's that for a guess?"

"You should also have a missing persons report for a Leon Guerra," AJ said, ignoring his question. "The incidents are connected. The guys met with him last night after 5 p.m., probably the last people to see him alive. Ask them about it."

"Uh huh," the detective said. "Look, I'm going to assume this is AJ. I tell you what, AJ, I'll ask them about it, just as soon as we find them."

"What?"

"Your two 'burglars' hammered out a side panel in that shed you locked them in and were long gone by the time our officers responded. So right now all we got is some minor property damage, and a cyber running around with a gun," he said. "That's you, by the way. You do know what that means, I guess?"

AJ felt his stomach sinking, but kept going. "The name of one of the people you are looking for is Troy McMaster. He's a private security contractor, lives in the Capitol, works for Congressman Kevin Winter. I don't know the other guy."

"McMaster, uh huh. That M-a-c or just M-c," the guy asked. At least he seemed to be recording it.

"M-c," AJ said. "He had a meeting last night with Leon Guerra, and Leon's wife said he didn't come home."

"Guerra, that's G-U-E-R-R-A? Just wait on the line." AJ heard the detective run a Core search on Leon's name. "Yeah, OK, I'm seeing a missing persons report on a Leon Arsenio Guerra. You got my attention now, AJ. This is connected how?"

"I haven't said my name is AJ and I … don't know," AJ said. "I know Leon met with McMaster. Leon never returned from the meeting,

313

and the next day McMaster turned up in the workshop at Sol Vista, going through Leon's stuff." It was as close to the truth as he could make it.

"AJ, look, I know this must be you," the detective said. "But OK. You and this Leon Guerra, you had something going with these other guys, and it got all screwed up. Drugs probably, right? You stealing stims from the clinic there at Sol Vista and selling them to the wrong people? I really don't care. But you're a cyber who was seen carrying a gun. That's as serious as it gets, AJ."

"Still not AJ," he said defiantly, relying on the voice scrambler to avoid the police getting a definite voice print.

"Sure, whatever," the cop said coldly. "Come in and explain yourself. It's your only chance to avoid being unchained the minute we catch you."

"Find McMaster," AJ said and closed the call.

His next call was to his Ma's facility to tell them he probably wouldn't be visiting for a while, but could someone tell her he was OK?

He got coffee for them both and waited for Cassie. "OK," he said when Cassie sat down next to him and he'd handed her the coffee. "Oh mighty Core. How much of a lead do you think we have?"

They had synched their comms via TH band for quantum chirping, but Cassie held up a hand and spoke out loud. "Let's speak at citizen speeds when we're out in public. We have to try to look as normal as possible."

"Says the skater chick with the punk haircut, manually piloting a bright red planer," AJ pointed out.

Cassie smiled. "To your question? I've now rerouted your cloned drift signal to a cyber in Fort Yukon who is due to reintegrate," Cassie said. "It's far enough away you could conceivably have got there during the last few hours. Same with mine; different cyber, different location. That will confuse them, and I can move the signals again before they work out what is going on, but they'll get wise eventually."

"But McMaster and his people are not the police or the military," AJ said. "They're contractors. Police aren't going to put out a nationwide alert for me just because some private spook in the Capitol wants me found. Even if he works for a Congressman."

"No, but you were seen with a *gun*," Cassie said. "Yeah, I pulled the police report, AJ. Did you think I wouldn't?"

AJ felt his face color. "I just kind of went with the flow..."

"The flow? I get you're scared, AJ," Cassie said, "but the people you are up against are what, ex-military? Ex-intelligence? We have to outrun them, outsmart them. Not get in a gunfight with them."

"I know," AJ said. "But it happened, so I brought the gun with me. Isn't it good to be prepared?"

"Sure. Tell you what, give it to me," Cassie said, holding out her hand.

"You know guns?" he asked, though it wouldn't have surprised him if she did.

"No," Cassie said. "But I'm thinking we can wipe it down and drop it off a bridge into a river. In the meantime I can work on the police records to wipe the report."

AJ looked at her, realized she wasn't joking. It was their only defense!

"Or, I could just shoot you in the face now, save everyone the trouble," she smiled. "Your choice."

AJ had a scarf around his neck and took it off, then reached inside his jacket where he had his multitool in one pocket and Warnecke's little burp gun in the other. It was an evil little thing that fired either single shots or a rapid succession of plasma bolts. He lifted it out, letting the scarf fall around it, tied it into a little bundle and handed it to Cassie, who took it and slid it into her own jacket pocket. "I've plotted a direct route to Whitehorse, where our Mountie lives. What do you think?" She sent it to AJ.

AJ studied the image on his cortex. "I say we go further in – Barrow, Gakona, Soldotna, Valdez, Ketchican," he said. "Less traffic, we overnight somewhere across the border, we'd be there in three days."

Cassie looked at the route AJ was suggesting. "Yeah, or, we take the tourist trail, stay on the coast – Togiak, Kwetluk, then cut in toward Gambel – that way. Take longer but there's way more traffic to hide in and our bright red self-drive won't stand out so much."

"Plenty of self-drives on the icefield highways. And that route would take twice as long," AJ said, biting his lip. "I'm just going to feel a whole lot safer once we cross that State line and get onto Inland ice."

"I like your optimism," she said. "Because I'm calling it a max 32.24 percent probability that we're going to make it there alive, no matter which route we take."

AJ stared at her a moment. "Keep that kind of thing to yourself from now on, will you?"

There was just one more call left for AJ to make.

"Hey, Cyan," AJ said.

"You're calling to quit, I hope," said the voice on the other end. "So that I don't have to sack you and we can stay friends."

"Yeah, look, it's complicated. It's a personal thing," AJ began.

"Don't lie to me, AJ," she said. "Lie to the cops, lie to your Ma, but not to me, OK?"

"OK."

"One of those guys was my soul mate from that night at the bar, right? Well, my soul mate kicked out the side wall of the workshop and got away before the cops arrived," she told him. "I had to tell the police about the gun, AJ, I'm sorry."

Cyan was teetering between pissed and furious, AJ could hear that. "I know the law, citizen."

"Don't you dare 'citizen' me, AJ," Cyan said. "Don't you *ever* 'citizen' me. I care about you. You know that. And where's Leon? He didn't show for work today and he isn't answering his comms."

"Leon has gone missing," AJ told her. "I think those guys know where he is. I surprised them in there going through our stuff."

"This is about Leon?" Cyan asked, sounding worried now.

"Yeah," AJ said. Which was as true as anything now. "I think he's got into some trouble."

"AJ, you can't cover for the guy forever," Cyan said. "I mean *we* can't."

"I know, but look, I just need some time to help get things straight, help find him," AJ said. "Andreas can cover any urgent maintenance that comes up. I'll sort things out with the police and get back to work when this is settled."

"AJ?" Cyan asked in a sad voice. "You know it doesn't work like that. You are a cyber, on the run, with a gun. This is out of control."

AJ felt anger boiling in his gut. Cyan was right. Things had gone completely sideways. How the hell was he supposed to find the flow in this? He looked at Cassie, sitting on a wall by her planer, face tilted to the sun and her eyes closed. He was on the run, from killers and cops, on a Scarlatti being driven by the Core Incarnate, looking for an invisible girl. "Cyan, you are so right," AJ said. "You have no idea."

A day of hard riding and an overnight stay in a crappy roadside motel in Red Bluff and they were at the Inland border. It wasn't the most comfortable ride AJ had ever had. The Scarlatti was made for speed, not touring, and even though it was fitted with a pillion seat instead of the usual single seat, AJ had to ride hunched over with Cassie's backpack on his back, which together with his few clothes and personal stuff weighed nearly 30 pounds.

Plus, it was a city planer, made for conditions inside heated city domes, not for the raw environment outside the domes, on ice highways, sheltered from the planetary cold by nothing more substantial than the Skycap. The Skycap made Coruscant habitable, but it was a two-way membrane, made to allow interplanetary traffic in and out, and that came at an environmental cost which meant the world outside the city domes was barely survivable.

At a roadside station, Cassie got ice tires fitted to her planer. Large, balloon-like tires with a high surface-to-surface ratio and nano-tube vacuum tread that actively grabbed and then released anything it came into contact with. Luckily the roads were mostly just straight shot ice highways all the way from South Coast City to the border at Valdez, and they didn't want to attract any police attention by weaving in and out of traffic, so keeping his balance wasn't a big problem for AJ.

The only short break they took was on a bridge over a lake, when Cassie pulled Warnecke's little burp gun out of her jacket pocket and dropped it into the water, scarf and all.

AJ had to admit, if you were going to be on the run with someone, it was good they were as cool as Cassie. Highway patrol cars would ease up alongside them on the freeway, she wouldn't even tense up. Even gave a cheeky wave to a jealous cop who was checking out her planer once, and he gave a little salute back.

But they were approaching the highest risk point of their trip. The time they would be most vulnerable was at the border crossing from Valdez into the Inland Territory. The Territory was fiercely protective of its independence, and there were no treaties for extraditing citizens or cybers from the Territory to either South Coast or Capitol States, so it was heavily policed on both sides.

They decided to go over at evening peak hour via the Ice Arch crossing, mingling with all the tourists, freight transports and commuters. "OK," Cassie said before they joined the long queue of vehicles. "I've done what I can to wipe any reference to you from the border force Core-linked systems at this crossing, but we don't know what other alerts your friend McMaster might have put out for you."

"I was in there?" AJ asked. "There's a police alert out for me?"

"With a mofo big red flag saying *armed and dangerous*," Cassie nodded. "I can't wipe it out completely without making the police back in South Coast City crazy suspicious. A glitch at the border is normal. You disappearing from right across the Core – that isn't."

"McMaster could have people here watching for me," AJ said, looking at the queue for the border crossing. "If the look he gave me inside that tool shed could kill, I'd already be dead."

Cassie bit her lip. "I know, and I'll be honest. I'm scared too, AJ. But if it goes to shit up ahead, I'll do my best to protect you."

"What the hell," AJ said. "Inland Territory here we come."

They climbed back on the Scarlatti and joined the queue. In about twenty minutes they had crawled up to the South Coast crossing. Freight went one way, foot traffic another, and passenger vehicles through a third gate. It was impossible trying to look inconspicuous on the Scarlatti and sure enough they soon had a group of four black-clad border patrol officers standing around the planer, checking it out. Cassie took off her helmet, smiled and gave a cheeky wink to one of the officers. Between the planer and the woman driving it, no one was paying much attention to AJ.

They had their ID chips scanned and their backpack emptied. They weren't carrying enough platinum to raise serious questions – there were plenty of places on the Inland Territory where Core access was limited and good old-fashioned cubes were the fallback currency.

What about our chip scans? AJ asked Cassie on TH.

I can glitch their security system and hide that we crossed here, she said. *But all someone would need to do is ask one of the guards. Yeah, yeah, I should have given Cassie a less conspicuous ride. But you only live once, right?*

After the others were finished walking around the planer one last time, an officer who had been leaning against a wall and watching with interest suddenly approached.

He held out a scanner and jerked his chin at Cassie to indicate she should hold out her arm again. He looked at the screen, then did the same to AJ, looking pointedly at AJ's third eye before turning back to Cassie.

"What's with you and the cyber?" he asked.

"Holiday," Cassie said guardedly. "I was born in the north."

His face said he wasn't convinced, or maybe it was something else. "You a couple or something?"

"Something like that," Cassie said, no longer smiling. AJ saw his TH channel open. *Get ready*, Cassie chirped. *His biometrics are spiking.* AJ tensed. Cassie was apparently monitoring the biometric data being collected by the border guards' uniforms and saw something she didn't like in this guard's hormones or heart rate.

AJ spiked his own hormones, ready for fight or flight.

The man spat on the ground. "Damn cybers," he said, fixing Cassie with a glare. "A citizen and a cyber? It's not freaking natural."

AJ relaxed. OK, so the guy was just an asshole. There were plenty of citizens who still believed cybers shouldn't have rights, or that citizens and cybers shouldn't be allowed to … be together. They were obviously dealing with one of those.

Cassie grinned at the man. "Not freaking natural is kind of the point, officer," she said.

He looked like he wanted to say more, but there were still other guards around so he just stepped back and waved them through, a disgusted look stuck to his face.

Back on the planer, AJ risked a chirp. *We're through!*

Nearly, don't relax yet, Cassie replied.

On the Inland side an officer inside a kiosk just scanned their chips, waved them on and said, "Have a nice trip." At the final checkpoint, where vehicles were scanned for goods and contraband, they were waved in, another officer asking if they were coming for business or leisure. Cassie said, "Few days in Ketchican." The officer looked at AJ, holding their small backpack. "Visors up, please. Thank you. You're traveling kind of light," she said.

"Tell me about it," AJ said, pulling the visor on his helmet up. "She only let me bring a toothbrush and some underpants so I don't screw up her balance on the planer." AJ got ready to hand over the backpack in case the officer wanted to search it.

"Speed limit for self-drives is 66 miles an hour until you hit the highway," the officer said. She stepped back, looking at the planer. "Is that a '95 or '96?"

"Ninety-three," Cassie said.

"Can I ask you a question?" the woman said.

Cassie raised her eyebrows. "I guess that's your job…"

"Yeah, no. It's a beauty, I was just wondering what you paid for it?" the officer asked.

Cassie relaxed, trading biker stories with the woman. After a couple of minutes, Cassie asked her, "Hey, we need to swap the fuel cell on this thing. Is there a station up ahead?"

"Sure, about ten miles," the officer replied, stepping back from the planer. "Have a great trip. I envy you."

AJ tightened his grip around Cassie's waist as they pulled away from the border crossing and eased into the highway traffic.

Made it! AJ said.

So far, so good, Cassie replied. *Ketchican here we come.*

Do you really need to swap out the cell?

I really do, Cassie confirmed. *I want to arrive in Ketchican close to a full charge, in case we need to move on quickly.*

The roadhouse came up quickly and Cassie saw most of the traffic was pulling in. It made sense, with the last station having been more than a hundred miles away. People needed fuel, food, and a break in the monotony of the ice highways.

Cassie coasted the planer up to a cell exchange and AJ swung his leg off the saddle and stretched. The sun was out, but the air was sub-zero, and he dialed his thermals up a couple of degrees. Cassie dismounted too and squatted to pull out the planer's hydrogen fuel cell. AJ watched idly as she lifted it up and shoved it into a slot on the exchanger, fed some physical credits into a slot on the machine, and then waited for her fresh battery to be delivered.

Something made AJ tense up. His senses were still hyped from the hormone boost and he felt, more than saw, movement behind them. It was all he could do not to jump in the air when a voice behind them spoke suddenly. "That's one beautiful old planer. You come from the Capitol or the Coast?"

AJ and Cassie both turned.

Two men were standing about five feet back from the planer. They looked relaxed, friendly. But their clothing gave them away. Both were dressed almost identically in black survival thermals with hoods designed to trap and recirculate body heat. The outfits were similar to the kind of gear campers used, so most people wouldn't have paid them a second glance. AJ saw immediately that the suits had been modified with a pouch at the waist. He had no question what would be in them.

You see the mods? he chirped urgently at Cassie.

If their conversation had happened at citizen speed, and in the real, they would have had no time to coordinate. But they were both cybers, and the fact these two were so relaxed implied they didn't know who they were dealing with yet.

Cassie turned back to lift the cell out of the exchanger and swing it down beside the planer, ready to insert.

I see them, Cassie chirped. *Do you recognize either of them?*

No.

Their data-sphere shows outgoing comms. They're not closing to normal conversation distance. That's suspicious. I'd say they're deliberately staying out of hand combat range. I'll mount the cell, you engage with them, try to get them to move closer but don't show your face.

OK.

"Sorry, what did you say?" AJ said, tapping his helmet. It broadcast his voice through a small speaker so that he wouldn't have to take it off in the cold air, and he kept his visor down.

The two men didn't move closer, but one of them raised his voice. "I said it's a nice planer. You buy it in the Capitol?"

AJ tapped his helmet again. "Sorry, my mike is glitching. You're from the Capitol, you said?"

The men looked at each other, shrugged, and took a couple of steps closer. One of them put his hand on the bulge at his waist.

Cassie was closing the connectors on the new cell but looking at the men as they approached. *My analysis says they're carrying neural disrupters, non-directional. If their suits are military spec, the mesh in their hoods will protect them. They won't need to pull a weapon and aim, just hit the actuator in that pouch.*

Shit, what do we do?

I won't be affected, Cassie said. *This body is shielded. I want you to try to take out the guy on the right.*

I can't get to him before he hits that disrupter.

I know, babe, Cassie said. *You're taking one for the team.*

Great.

Two and go, Cassie chirped, standing up and stretching her hands slowly above her head like she was working out the kinks from a long ride. *One … two …* She dropped her hands to her side. *Go!*

AJ had his move all planned. For what it was worth. He still had plenty of residual adrenaline. He threw himself forward, rolling toward the guy's feet, intending to sweep them out from under him. He saw Cassie jump to one side so that the goons couldn't watch both of them at the same time. He saw one of the goons, a startled look in his eyes, thump the bulge at his waist in panic.

But that was all he saw.

The neural blast hit him in a millisecond and his world went black.

***

He woke with a headache like he'd been on a bender for a week.

He wasn't groggy, that was one advantage of being a cyber. A citizen hit with a neural blast would go down like a sack of rocks and could take hours, even days, to wake. When they did, they would be disoriented, their vision blurred, their ears ringing. AJ boosted his oxygen levels and played with his hormone balance to help damp the headache. He was moving. On the planer. But he was sitting at the front, not behind on the pillion. Cassie had her arms under his armpits and was holding the handlebars, keeping AJ from sliding off. Damn, how strong was this woman?

"Hey there, sleepyhead," Cassie said, feeling him stir. "Keep down or I can't see ahead."

"Hey, what the heck happened back there?"

"I'll pull over so you can get on the back where you belong. I've been propping your ass up for at least twenty miles."

The planer slid to the lines marking the edge of the highway's emergency lane and a freighter hummed past, slipstream kicking up flurries of ice powder.

Cassie slid off one side of the planer without letting go of AJ and helped him ease himself off. A neural blast also messed with the nerves in legs and arms, and it took a minute for AJ to get enough control of his limbs to be able to balance without Cassie holding him up.

"Impressive," Cassie said, letting him go and stepping back to watch. "Must be all that surfing. I thought you'd take at least an hour before you could stand unaided."

"That is the first and last damn neural blast I ever want to experience," AJ admitted. "What the hell happened after I got knocked out?"

Cassie lifted up her visor and grinned. "You want to see? I've pulled the VR off the roadside station's system. I can project it on your visor display."

"Sure," he said. "Show me."

"I warn you," Cassie said. "You may get aroused by my total awesomeness, but you'll have to park your lust until we get to Ketchican. That might be distressing for a mere mortal like you."

"I'll survive," AJ said. "This headache is guaranteed to kill any lust your awesomeness could generate."

"Don't bet on it," Cassie smiled. "We are talking total super-ninja."

AJ's visor display flickered and the small display of numbers and icons was replaced by a VR view of the station forecourt. AJ took a second to orient himself. He could see a freighter, refueling, to the left of their planer, its security rider jumping down out of his cab. Cassie standing and stretching her arms above her head. Two other passengers were leaving the station restaurant and walking toward a car, and the two goons in black were taking a step toward AJ and Cassie.

Cassie dropped her arms to her side. In his memory, at that point he began to dive athletically toward the goon on the right, ready to take his legs out. In the VR footage he saw himself start his roll and then crumple to the ground like a rag doll as the goon triggered his disrupter. It sent its blast out in a circular wave from where he was standing and AJ saw the two car passengers and the freight attendant also crumple to the ground. Both goons had stopped and had their attention on AJ, which was what Cassie wanted.

Cassie was the only one moving. AJ remembered their duel on the skateboards and saw now that the woman had been playing with him. Dialing down her abilities to near citizen levels just to give AJ a chance. With two springing steps like a long jumper, Cassie closed the distance between herself and the two goons and somersaulted *over the top of them*.

Before they could turn, she had grabbed one by the head from behind and snapped his head around, dropping him to the ground. The other spun around, punching the pouch in his suit uselessly as Cassie pivoted toward him and delivered a stiff-fingered punch to his throat, then his solar plexus, before kneeing him in the side of the head so that he fell to the ground with a bone-jarring crunch. Both assailants were down for the count.

Cassie was half crouched, and she stood slowly, looking around her. It was only a small station, and a neural blast like that had a radius of about a hundred yards, so it had taken out everyone in sight except her. Those closest, like the freight rider, would be worst hit and down for a long time. Those furthest away and partly shielded, like the ones inside the station restaurant, would wake first.

Cassie walked quickly over to AJ and crouched beside him, then lifted him onto her shoulders like she was carrying a roll of carpet. Walking to the planer, she lowered AJ onto the seat with a little difficulty, because his legs weren't keen to cooperate with going either side of the frame, but she got him there, then climbed on behind him, arms underneath his armpits to steady him. Then she took off her belt and tied it around both their chests to keep AJ upright, with his head lolling forward over the handlebars as she kicked the planer free of its stand and slowly drove out of camera view, weaving around the unmoving bodies of the two goons in black. The vision cut out.

"You killed them?" AJ asked, shocked. Cassie was Core. Her prime directive was to protect society, protect all citizens, even those two.

"No, but the first one will need spinal surgery. I snapped his neck. The second I just knocked unconscious," Cassie said. "Step in here and get your hug, big guy." She held out her arms. "You must feel like shit."

AJ fell more than walked, and Cassie held him tight.

"Neural disrupters are military issue," AJ said, stepping back. "Even police aren't authorized to use them. I hope you were able to pull that VR footage down."

"I did," she said. "But the people there are going to report it when they wake up. The fact those two were carrying military-spec non-lethal weapons tells us this is as serious as it gets, AJ. These guys want you bad."

"Duh. They had agents waiting for us at a random roadside station way up in the Inland Territory," AJ said, the import of what had happened hitting him for the first time. "What kind of resources would that take?"

"If we assume they didn't know where we were headed, then we're talking a major dragnet," Cassie agreed. "It was good you still had your helmet on – they didn't appear to be 100 percent sure who we were, or they would have triggered the disrupters first and asked questions later."

"We need to lose this planer, change out of this gear," AJ said. "And fast. When his people wake up, McMaster will find out we've run for the Territory, if he hasn't already."

"Already on it," Cassie said. "I cut the comms links in and out of that station. It will look like the neural blast took down a transponder. I also booked a car to meet us at the next station, about twenty miles ahead. We can dump the planer thermals, buy some clothes at the station and switch to something more local. I'll get us to Ketchican."

"You need ID to book a car," AJ said. "It will trigger a flag somewhere."

"I don't, honey," Cassie grinned. "I am Core."

So it was, three hours after leaving Valdez they found themselves at a café by a frozen lake in Ketchican, on a pier where every other shop was selling ice art or souvenirs. Cassie went through the motions of flicking through news pages on the VR built into their table while she drifted and tried to learn more about the manhunt that had been directed against them.

They were out in public, so they stuck to their agreement to speak out loud, like citizens.

"Despite what happened, I feel safer here," AJ said, watching people through the café window, walking around in the light misty rain. "Territorians are so friendly. Nothing bad ever happened to anyone in Ketchican, did it?"

"Bears. People get eaten by grizzlies here all the time," Cassie pointed out.

"In Ketchican?"

"Maybe not exactly in Ketchican, but they do get bears coming in, and then there's ice sport injuries," she said. "Those big carbonite pucks can crack your skull…"

"How far to Whitehorse?" AJ wondered out loud, calling up a map. "Oh my God," he said, and sent the map to Cassie. "It's another twenty-nine hours by road!"

"I know. It's all mountain passes and twisting roads. But if we do it non-stop, sleep in the car, we can be there tomorrow," Cassie said. "We can't afford to stop at roadside stations. I'm picking up heightened comms traffic to and from all traveler rest points."

"No wonder. That neural blast has hit the news," AJ said, paging through the day's headlines. "People are freaking out. No specific mention of us, though."

"Small mercy," Cassie said. "If I was McMaster, I'd slip an apprehension order into the Mounties' system with our images, in connection with the incident at that station. Make it look like we were behind it."

AJ felt frustrated. They needed to get to Whitehorse to talk to an ex-Mountie who would just as likely have them arrested as soon as he saw them. And he probably knew nothing that would help with Warnecke's elusive daughter. He said as much to Cassie.

"Yeah, but someone out there wants to stop us. That's almost reason enough in itself to keep going," Cassie said. "Plus, I developed a soft spot for this place over the last 200 years. Territorians are good people. Come on, we need to buy food for this trip."

"And juice bottles," AJ said.

"Juice? Why not just water?"

"Wide tops, easier to pee into," AJ explained. "If we're going to push through without any roadside stops."

"Ew. Biology sucks," Cassie grunted, standing up.

They hit a convenience store for new thermals and ditched their biker gear. As she dropped her hard shell and helmet into a recycling unit, Cassie sighed. "It kills me leaving the planer here. I'm going to miss the old girl."

"Yeah, because you've had it ever since you were born?" AJ said.

"Exactly."

"Wow, how many weeks?"

"A few weeks around you feels like a lifetime, AJ," she replied.

They stayed in the washrooms at the station until they got the signal their car had arrived. Walking out, AJ saw it was an all-terrain vehicle with a long teardrop body and large balloon tires. The door popped as they approached and AJ paused before climbing inside. It was a two-person unit, with huge reclining bench seats and optional analog controls, which meant a passenger could take it off autopilot and steer it themselves if they were foolish enough. "This must have cost a million, how could you … OK, don't say it. *I am Core*," AJ said.

"Never gets tired," Cassie smiled. "Get in."

AJ didn't realize how sleepy he was until the car accelerated out of the station, pushing his back into the body-hugging contours of the seat. Before he could even recline it, he was snoring.

He woke to a voice – Cassie's – speaking in the real, on the car comms link.

"Oh, hey there. Look, I have a possibly strange question," she said. She saw AJ starting to stir and put a finger to her lips to signal him to be quiet.

"Try me, ma'am," the woman at the other end said, like she was totally used to fielding calls from weirdos. Which, this being the Inland Territory, probably she was. "You're on audio. Do you want to go VR?"

"No, sorry, we're in a vehicle with a crappy uplink. Look, I'm trying to get in touch with one of your officers who served there until a few years ago, name of Ferguson."

"You mean Chief Superintendent Lyle Ferguson?" the woman asked.

"Yes, exactly," Cassie said. "I can't seem to find a comms contact for him."

"Well, Chief Ferguson does prefer to keep his personal life off-Core," the comms operator said. "He's a bit of an old-timer."

"Is there any way to get in touch with him?"

AJ knew Cassie could track him down a dozen different ways, but they'd agreed it was probably best to approach him conventionally so as not to make him suspicious before they met. They'd also agreed they'd approach the topic of Warnecke's daughter at a tangent, via Warnecke and Farley. Not go straight into quizzing him about her.

"Well, I could put you through to his former assistant," the operator said. "She can get a message to him."

Before Cassie could respond, the line clicked and they got an audio news channel.

"The guy is technically retired," Cassie said. "But his biometric data shows he still spends a lot of time at the Whitehorse police station. So I'm hoping…"

The comms started ringing again and a different woman, audibly older, picked up this time. "Chief Superintendent's office."

"Oh hi, look I…"

"Yes, Liz was explaining," the woman said. "Can I ask the nature of your inquiry?"

"It's a long story," Cassie said. "I was just wondering…"

"Try me, ma'am," the woman said, exactly as the receptionist had done. Maybe it was part of their training.

"OK, well, forty years ago there was an officer called Ferguson who helped search for a missing rafter, his name was Farley O'Halloran. We have something related to that to give to Officer Ferguson," Cassie said. "So we are trying to find him to see if we can meet up."

"If you have information on a missing person, you should report it to your nearest ITMP office. Where are you calling from?" the woman asked. She sounded like she was tapping on a screen, like she was back-tracing the call. "Oh, I see you are in a vehicle." Then there was a pause. "Wait. Did you say *Warnecke?*"

"Yes, ma'am," AJ said. "Dave Warnecke."

"Hold please," she said. The line went silent. For a moment AJ thought she had hung up on them but then the news channel clicked in again. Cassie looked at the visual display from her earbud.

"Who was that?" AJ asked. "Are you still on the line?"

"Yeah. It was his former assistant I think…" The news channel cut out and the line clicked again.

"Hello, this is Ferguson." A male voice came on the line. "You're calling about Dave Warnecke?"

"Uh hi, yes. We were wondering…"

"About a certain package I got last week?" he asked.

Cassie frowned. "Uh, no, we…"

"Last week I get a mysterious package from Dave Warnecke, then today you call," Ferguson said. "And I'm supposed to think that's a coincidence?"

"I don't know, sorry," Cassie said. "But if we could talk, maybe in person?"

"Oh, we're going to talk, ma'am," the man said. There was a pause. "My assistant said you're in transit but you're on audio, and I can't see a call location, or even a vehicle ID. What's going on?"

"We're coming in from Ketchican," Cassie said, ignoring the question. "We'll be in Whitehorse by, I don't know…" She waited as though she was consulting the car AI. "1600 hours. We'll need to find a hotel and then…"

"You will come straight to the ITMP station at Whitehorse when you get here," the man said. "You can find a hotel later. Don't make me send my people out to look for you."

The line clicked again. He didn't even wait for a response.

Cassie leaned back in her chair, legs crossed, hands behind her head. "Anonymous package?"

"That's what he said," AJ confirmed. "And he didn't like that you were blocking our ID tags from view. I thought the guy was retired? He sounds like he's still top cop in the shop."

"It did sound like that, didn't it?" Cassie said. She called the Whitehorse Mountie office again. "Hello, is that Liz?"

"This is she," the woman said. "Oh, it's you. Didn't you get onto the Chief? He just told me to book you in for an interview at 1600 on the morrow."

"Yes, we're meeting with him. I just wanted to check – the Chief, he's retired, isn't he? How come he's still…"

"Acting like he's Chief Super?" the woman replied. "Well, we got a new Chief Superintendent five years ago. But he's an out of towner and spends just as much time in Ketchican as he does here. Everyone here still calls Citizen Ferguson 'Chief'," she continued. "And he still acts like the Chief. It's easier to just go along with it."

"OK," Cassie said.

"I told you that by way of advice," she added.

"Yeah, I got that."

"Right, while I have you, can you give me your names and IDs? For the front desk."

"Sorry, no," Cassie said, and closed the line.

"So much for not getting them suspicious," AJ remarked.

AJ had slept six hours, which left 23 to Whitehorse, but it felt longer because, looking out the window, he saw nothing but cloud and rain. Through the night it was dark and rainy, and as morning dawned, it was grey, misty and rainy. The highway had popped up above the cloud cover into weak sunshine for what must have been a maximum of fifteen minutes before they started dropping down through grey cloud again and the windows were streaked with drizzle.

AJ had something to eat, chatted with Cassie a little, dozed off again, and when he woke a few hours later, he realized it was because Cassie was sitting forward in her seat and tapping him on the knee.

"Sorry to wake you," she said on TH. "I've been monitoring the comms for all of our principals. I thought you'd like an update."

He took a second to orient himself. "Let me guess. They're not worried about us anymore and we can just turn this baby around and go home," he said. "We'll be back in time for an early morning surf on Friday, right?"

"That would be no," she said. "The content is all encrypted, so I can only analyze patterns, but I can see comms has been running hot between Winter and McMaster and it peaked just after the neural blast. Given neither of them should even know about it, we can conclude they were behind that little intervention…"

"As if there was any doubt," AJ scowled. He needed to pee and tried to ignore it.

"Ferguson has also been busy, mostly internal calls to other ITMP IDs," she said. "My best guess is he's trying to work out who the hell we are before we arrive. Probably checking highway patrol, border force, fugitive notices. Here's something interesting, though. He put in a call to Warnecke's son."

"On Orkutsk?!" AJ spluttered. "He couldn't have paid for that himself."

"No, the call was made from his ITMP ID," she said. "But it's interesting, right? I've got a theory about it, but I'd like to hear what you think."

AJ ran a few hundred scenarios and ranked them. "He knows Warnecke is dead. He got a package last week from Warnecke. Now we call him, saying we have something for him, related to Farley. He's worried the three things are connected but can't see how. He called the son to talk it over, see if he can see a connection."

"I had that in my top two as well," Cassie said. "But I have another one. The daughter is on Orkutsk."

"He called the son to talk to the daughter?" AJ asked.

"I can't see who he talked to, only that he called the son's ID," she said. "If there is some connection between Ferguson and the daughter, which there must be if Warnecke wanted him to have those photos, then it makes just as much sense he'd want to talk to the daughter as to the son."

"I worked that scenario, but I ranked it much lower," AJ said. "Why would she be on Orkutsk? She can't dive the Core from there, she can't even access it. Orkutsk is neutral territory, it has its own independent AI platform. She'd be isolated. Plus," he held a finger in the air, "Orkutsk isn't a place you just visit. It's population controlled, with strict limits for each colony, and as far as I know there are no *tourist* visas."

"No, but," she wagged a finger back at him, "what if she's just transiting?"

"Catching a jump ship to another system? Leaving Coruscant?" he said. "Why would she bug out?"

338

"Maybe she knows I'm on to her," Cassie speculated. "And she's scared."

AJ smiled. "You are pretty scary when you do the vampire lady look."

"No, not me Cassie – me the Core," Cassie said. "I thought I've been covering our tracks, but maybe she found out I was onto Warnecke and either saw, or assumed, that would lead me to her. So she ran."

"She can't survive more than two hours without drifting," AJ said. "Even if she found a way to hide her drift signal from you, the need to drift is hard-wired into her brain. Could she have found a workaround for that?"

"Almost impossible," Cassie said.

"I know, so ... wait," AJ said, sitting upright. "You said 'almost'."

She sighed. "I'll tell you, but then I'm going to delete the data from your cache immediately, alright?"

"No, what?"

"No one, and I mean no one, knows this, AJ. So I can't wipe your biological memory but if I find you ever, ever tell this to anyone, I will reintegrate you and keep your consciousness aware and make you listen to 20th-century rap music for eternity."

"Whoa, OK. Now we're seeing the true Core side of you."

"I'm serious."

"Clearly. I promise."

Cassie stared at him another long second before continuing. "The drift protocol works like this. Your body naturally produces gamma-aminobutyric acid, GABA, to regulate brain activity. Normal levels, normal brain activity. Too much and it shuts down brain activity. Your brain is hard-wired to drift at least every twenty minutes. If you miss six drift windows, two hours, it triggers a massive release of GABA to your brain. You go into a GABA-induced coma. If you can drift again while in the coma, you'll return to normal and wake up again. If you don't…"

"You never wake up," AJ said. "Three days, and you die of thirst. So freaking barbaric."

"Hey, not my idea," Cassie said, holding up her hands in surrender. "It was a requirement Congress put into the law enabling the creation of cybers that they should not be able to survive, independent of the Core. This was how I had to design you, to satisfy the lawmakers."

"Still barbaric."

"OK, now you know how it works, design a way around it," she said, sitting back in her chair with her arms crossed. "And assume that if she can dive the Deep Core, Warnecke's daughter also knows about the GABA protocol."

AJ played with the parameters Cassie had given him and threw out solution after solution until he arrived at two that might work. "Alright, one – if a cyber went into shutdown mode you could keep them alive indefinitely by putting them on a nutrient drip and feeding them water and food that way."

"*That's* barbaric," Cassie said. "They'd be alive, but in a coma forever."

"Or, you could take some sort of GABA inhibitor drug, something that counteracted the effect of the GABA."

"Yes," Cassie said. "Except it would need to be very precise and dosed continuously as long as you were outside the drift window. The brain needs GABA to function. Too much and you shut the brain down; too little and you make it neuronally unstable." She held up three fingers. "There's a third hack. Remember, she's a data freak, not a neuroscientist."

A data hack? AJ worked that idea for a moment. "The only way to use that would be to fake the signal going from the cyber to the Core. No, wait – that would just trick the Core. You need to trick the cyber's brain. So you would need to simulate the confirmation code coming back from the Core to the cyber! If you could trick the brain into thinking it had drifted and received confirmation of the drift from the Core, the GABA flood wouldn't be triggered!" He patted himself on the back. "Boom."

"Which I thought of when I designed the protocol," Cassie said. "I figured that one day one or more of my curious and frustrated children would experiment on themselves to try to trigger the shutdown protocol and discover how it worked. Easy enough. You just have to be smart or lucky enough to be measuring amino acid levels at the time of the shutdown. You'd see a massive spike in GABA. You would also need to figure out that the trigger was in the return drift signal, isolate it, and be able to replicate it."

"So simple," AJ said. "Don't know why no-one did it yet."

"Oh, they've tried," she said. "As I knew they would. So I use one-time chaos-synchronized quantum entanglement on the GABA trigger. It can be neither predicted, nor copied."

He frowned. "Now you're saying your magical 'third hack' isn't viable."

Cassie turned away to stare out the window. "No, it isn't. But no-one until now has had access to every bit of data there is to know about the drift protocol, and how it is encrypted." She ran a finger through the condensation inside the window. "Knowledge is power."

AJ watched the rain beating on the windows, sliding sideways on the glass as the car powered down the highway. "Sorry, but I don't think she ran off-world. You just aren't that scary, and if she's a Core data junkie, she needs to stay here to get her fix. If Ferguson called the son's number on Orkutsk, then he probably spoke to the son."

"OK," Cassie said, coming over to his side of the car and lying down across the bench seat with her head in his lap. "If he called the son, he should also have called the daughter. Ergo, one of the *other* IDs that Ferguson called must be Warnecke's daughter. I'll send you the comms data, you work out which one, smart guy."

In seconds she was asleep.

A couple of hours before they hit Whitehorse, Cassie woke. "I need to pee. Hand me a juice bottle and some swabs, will you?"

AJ handed her an empty bottle and watched as Cassie awkwardly relieved herself. Cassie laughed. "Do you mind? I'm taking a whizz here."

"Sorry," AJ said. "Just impressed you could hold that in for ten hours. Also impressed you could sleep for ten hours straight."

"I never sleep," she said. "I am Core. But Cassie, Cassie was gutted." She finished up and delicately tucked the bottle and used swabs into a compartment in the door. "Trust me, I didn't exactly think of this part when I decided to grow this body."

"And what happens to 'this body' when we're done?" he asked.

"Told you," she said. "It's coded with the same reintegration date as yours." She was already sitting beside him, so she leaned her head on his shoulder. "I figure we'll just lay down on a bed of flowers together, holding hands as these bodies breathe their last breaths, and we merge with the Core again."

"You thought *that's* what I wanted to hear?" AJ asked. "Really?"

"OK, how about we both walk to the top of the Togiak Ice Cliff and throw ourselves off? Is that more like it?"

"How about we just don't die," AJ said. "How about that for an idea?"

"Not an option, sorry. Do you love me, AJ?" Cassie asked.

"What?"

"I've admitted I love you," Cassie said. "I've told you I adore you. Think of the resources it took for me to make this body. It's not just any old wetware shell, I made it specifically for you. Yesterday, I risked its life for you – hell, I might have risked the future of the entire planet to save your ass back there at that station. But do you realize, you never once told me that *you* love me?"

That made AJ stop. Hadn't he? Did he?

"Hell yes, I love you," AJ said.

Cassie slid off the seat and lay her lithe frame on top of AJ. AJ had seen her lift him over her shoulder like he was just a bag of shopping, but right now, her touch was featherlight as she ran her fingers through his hair.

"We don't have forever, but we have ten years," Cassie said, kissing him passionately. "It will have to be enough."

"I guess."

"Good, now we have that sorted, get your clothes off. We still have two hours until we hit Whitehorse, and I know exactly how to occupy them."

As the car swung down a mountainside toward Whitehorse, they swabbed the perspiration from each other and pulled on their thermals. Cassie applied the traditional Territory makeup he'd seen her wearing the first time they'd met – dark eyeliner, black lipstick, black nails. Neither of them had packed for Whitehorse in September. Hell, they hadn't even packed for Ketchican but at least the planer suits they'd been wearing offered a double layer of protection against the polar cold. All AJ knew about Whitehorse was that it was the second closest city dome to the north pole – Bloor being the only city closer. The weather forecast AJ called up on his cortex said 33 degrees, with low visibility, but as they dropped down a mountainside and out of the mist, AJ saw the Whitehorse city dome reveal itself on the plain below.

No wonder the duty officer at the ITMP station had laughed a few minutes ago when Cassie had called and asked if she could recommend a hotel that was close to both the station and other amenities. The dome was tiny, no bigger as a whole than the South Coast City suburb of Sea Gate, where AJ lived. Had lived. He somehow doubted he would ever be going back. AJ was a little nervous about what might await them at the entrance into the dome, but it was automated and unattended, traffic flowing freely through, both in and out of the city. He'd feared a lockdown after the neural blast at the station just outside the border crossing, but it seemed the good people of Whitehorse weren't too concerned with odd things that happened in the deep South down by the border.

That thought didn't make him less nervous, even though they cruised through the entrance without a hiccup.

Inside the dome, Whitehorse revealed itself as a town of low-rise buildings painted bright white and blue, with spiked trees buried halfway up their trunks in powdered ice thrown up by road graders. It made sense the town didn't waste unnecessary energy on trying to make the climate temperate, as they did in South Coast City. This was the Territory, top of Tatsensui, dammit – waist-high powdered ice drifts were part of the charm!

Their car followed a small ring road around to the other side of the town then dropped down a ramp, into light traffic, before it taxied up to a gate in front of a small green terminal building, with powder-blanketed mounds and a small mountain rising up to the top of the dome behind it.

"This is the ITMP office?" AJ asked. "It looks more like a ride-hailing hub."

"This is the address. Town schematics show most buildings here are multifunctional," Cassie said. "We'll try here first."

For what looked like a ride-hailing hub, there were damn few people around for four o'clock in the afternoon. It made AJ uneasy.

"And if this is a trap? We're walking right into the arms of the Mounties here."

"Come on, don't be so suspicious, it's the Territory. I bet even the cops here are super polite," Cassie said.

As it turned out, a reception committee was waiting for them. As they stepped out of the car, waiting at the entrance to the transport hub was a six-foot-tall woman in a flat-brimmed brown hat and a bright red uniform jacket with dark collar, epaulets, black trousers and boots.

Red hair. Bright green eyes. And a glowing dot between her eyebrows.

AJ jumped onto a private TH frequency. *Holy hell, it's her, right?* He pulled up the images in his cache, paging through the most recent. There was no doubt. It was Warnecke's daughter. In a Mountie's uniform.

Stay calm, Cassie said, studying her as well. *We're more of a threat to her than she is to us. She might know about you, but I'm guessing she has no idea who I am.*

AJ couldn't help himself. He stood and stared.

The woman turned his way and looked carefully at the two of them. Their car had a Ketchican ID, and they were wearing thermals that clearly weren't ideal for Whitehorse. They stuck out like a proverbial thumb. She walked toward them and held out her hand, smiling. "You must be the Chief's guests."

A cyber working as a cop? AJ chirped.

Different laws up here, Cassie observed. *In case we needed reminding.*

They shook. "I'm Carly," Cassie said. "This big lump here is FJ. And you are..."

"JNN.9734. Most people just call me Jen." The woman smiled and held out her hand to AJ. "You're a cyber too! I saw you staring – it's the uniform, right? Don't be freaked by it, the Chief told me to come in my Red Serge," Jen said, straightening her jacket. "Said you'd probably expect it."

"I don't know what we were expecting," Cassie said.

"Take your bag?" Jen asked, reaching for their backpack.

"No thanks, all good," AJ said. "Oh, what about our car?"

"Oh, right," Jen said. She pulled a magnetic tag from her pocket and walked down to slap it on the roof of the car, then came back to them. "OK, you can send it to the station guest parking level now," she said.

AJ linked to the car's AI and sent it on its way.

"Okay then," the Mountie said, indicating a door that led into the hub and then further on into an office complex behind it.

"You don't usually wear that … outfit?" Cassie asked as they hurried to keep up with her.

"It's traditional. Few hundred years old. I kind of like it," Jen said, happily. "But no, we just wear it for reviews and parades and stuff usually. Keep it in my locker at the station, though, in case we get the big brass visiting." She turned and looked at them. "Or friends of the Chief, from down south."

Cassie looked at AJ. *Friends of the Chief?*

That's nice, AJ said. *If this is all an act, it's a pretty convincing one.*

Don't be fooled. If this is her, then it's totally an act, Cassie said. *She would know you've been interacting with Warnecke; she would have images and voiceprints of you. She would have worked out who you are the minute you stepped out of the car and she saw your face.*

They walked out into an open courtyard, shrugging their shoulders against the light snow and freezing air. Their lightweight thermals wouldn't be enough if they had to stay out longer than a few minutes, even here under the dome.

"Just over here," Jen said, pointing to a big white door with a thin red, blue and yellow stripe down one side. As they stepped through, AJ saw a reception booth with biometrics scanner. He nearly froze.

We have to sign in with biometrics, will the IDs from the border work here?

Not taking chances, so I swapped them for fresh ones, Cassie told him. *Just follow the normal routine. I'll intercept the upload. I'm Carly, you're FJ, got it?*

Sure, Carly.

"You can sign in here. The doorway will scan you for weapons, so if you're carrying, you probably want to declare them now," Jen warned.

Cassie and AJ both held their hands up. "Not a problem," Cassie said, shooting AJ an *I told you so* kind of look.

"So you been to Whitehorse before?" Jen asked, lounging beside the scanner as they swiped their DNA and had their retinas scanned. She looked at Cassie's face, made up Territory style. "Or maybe you're from here?"

"Born in Bloor, left the Territory as a kid," Cassie said. "First time in Whitehorse."

"I've never been here either," AJ said, bending to the eye scanner. As he straightened he expected an alarm to start ringing. *Cyber! Armed and dangerous! Shoot on sight!*

But the lobby stayed cool and quiet.

"Really? You look familiar," Jen said.

AJ straightened and glanced at her, but she still had the same polite smile on her face.

She recognizes you, Cassie said. *Now she's playing with you, wondering if you recognize her.*

"I get that from a lot of cops," AJ joked. "I'm starting to take it personally."

She let it lie. "Sorry, no insult intended! Look, I'd show you around a bit, but the Chief is pretty keen to see you. He canceled his appointments this afternoon and I got pulled out of a Shield Program hunt to come get you."

"Shield Program?" Cassie asked. A door into a glass elevator opened and they stepped inside. It moved slowly and AJ watched the floors going past. People, citizens and cybers, hung at workstations or talked in groups. A lot more cybers than citizens, it seemed to AJ. Which made sense in a way. It was probably harder to attract citizens here, away from their nice warm domes down south. A cyber wouldn't care so much about climate as they did about the ability to take on roles that might otherwise be prioritized for citizens. Like police work.

Even better if you were a cyber who was trying to lie low.

"Yeah, youth program thing," Jen said. "Got to give them plenty to do or we lose them to the Coastal towns. We had a grizzly hunt planned today." She sounded disappointed.

"Sorry about that," Cassie said. "I thought they were protected though?"

"We don't kill them," Jen said. "We just try to lure them up out of their lairs and net them so the kids can get a look at them up close."

"Isn't that kind of dangerous?" AJ asked. Grizzlies were indigenous predators about half the size of the animals they were named after, which lived in air pockets under the ice and dug a web of tunnels they used to ambush their prey from below. A single grizzly could dig a tunnel web that covered a square mile in diameter and hid up to twenty exits. Their favorite food was baboon or beaver, but they weren't fussy. Any meat would do.

"Well, yeah," Jen said. "Or it wouldn't be fun."

"Right."

"But the kids train on baboons before we let them go after grizzly." She made a motion with her arm like she was throwing a lasso. "*Bam*! They throw the net right, those big foreclaws get all tangled up and then you can tranq them nice and easy."

"And if they *don't* throw it right?" Cassie asked, looking at her with unabashed curiosity.

Jen shrugged. "Then they get a lesson in first aid instead."

AJ let Cassie keep up the conversation, trying not to look directly at Jen, sure his face would give away his thoughts. Finally the elevator came to a clunking stop about five floors up.

They stepped out into a different kind of lobby, clearly made for official receptions, three flags in a stand against the wall, one the Coruscant flag, another the Crest of Tatsensui and the last one the Inland Territory snowflake flag.

"Don't get to the fifth floor very often" Jen said, looking at the flags herself. "Atmosphere is a bit thick up here, if you get my drift," she added, and winked. There was another cyber behind the glass partition at a reception desk who looked like any kind of cop you ever saw. Tan shirt, police badge, dark jacket. Sleepy but dangerous.

Your ninja moves aren't going to be as effective against these guys, AJ said. *They'll have reflexes like me. If she's a cop, she might have augmentations too.*

Don't worry, Cassie bragged. *This body is full of tech that hasn't even been invented yet. In case you didn't notice back there in the car.*

"Visitors for Citizen Ferguson," Jen said to the cop behind the glass. "Carly and FJ. Signed 'em in downstairs." She walked to the left where she held a palm to a scanner and a door swung open. "Welcome to ITMP Whitehorse!" she said. "Take the second door on the left." And with that, she took a step back and the door closed between them.

Was that her? AJ asked. *What should we do?!* The meeting with Ferguson was irrelevant now if Jen was who they thought she was. And she was getting further away with every minute they spent on the wrong side of the door.

Definitely her, Cassie said. *I tried to read her data-sphere. It's like she isn't there. I'm the only one who would notice, but she's got a zero-data footprint. I still want to talk to Ferguson before we make a move.*

18. ANY FRIEND OF THE CHIEF…

The door Jen had pointed to led them to Ferguson's former assistant, Gina, who turned out to be a short, round woman with thick metal eyeglasses, black hair in a tight bun and a thick Territory accent.

"The Chief drinks tea," Gina explained. "So I have some really nice NS tea. Or I can offer you instant coffee," she added, making it clear in her tone of voice that coffee would be a really bad choice. So they sat drinking tea and looking at pictures on the wall of Chiefs past and present with people they assumed were local or even national identities.

"Wow, look," Cassie said, nudging AJ and pointing to a photo of an officer with a well-known music legend.

"Yes, that's Chief Ferguson with her, in '01," Gina said proudly. "I met her too. Lovely, lovely woman. So professional."

"Where was that?" AJ asked.

"Oh, that was when he was in Critical Incidents Command in Ketchican," Gina said. "There was a threat to one of her concerts once, I can't really discuss it." But she leaned forward and whispered, "A total *psycho* stalker as it turned out. She was very grateful with how discreetly it was handled. Never made the news."

"You were with him a while, by the sound of it," AJ said.

"Twenty years," Gina said. "Right up until he retired, then I took over the new Chief. Chief Superintendents come and go, but not Gina." She winked. "I know where all the bodies are buried. Figuratively."

"Is he currently in town?" Cassie asked. "The new Chief?"

"No, he's in Ketchican all week. Territory Parliament. Leaves Citizen Ferguson in charge when he's gone – unofficial like," she said. "No one dares question it though, and technically the Chief *is* still on a retainer."

At that moment a door to an inner office opened and an elderly man dressed in dark trousers with a thin red strip down the side, white shirt and black collar was standing there. The news archives had shown him as a big, fit guy forty years ago, and he was still big and still fit, for his age. He stepped forward and grabbed AJ's hand, shaking it once, and did the same with Cassie.

"Inside please," he said, pointing at his office. "More tea, Gina?"

"Coming up, Chief," she said.

There were two chairs in front of a small desk which sat in front of a big window looking out over an ice-covered parade ground, which was about all AJ registered. It wasn't the office of a serving Chief Superintendent, AJ could see that, but it wasn't too shabby either.

"Those IDs you signed in with are too clean to be real," the man said as he sat down, not wasting any time on pleasantries. "So even though the face recognition matches the IDs and if I ran your DNA, that would probably match too, I'm going to assume they're not."

It had been Cassie who spoke with the Chief from the car, so AJ waited, letting her take the lead, but she said nothing, just sat looking at him with a slight smile.

Ferguson snatched a brown courier pouch off his desk and threw it at AJ, who was sitting closest to him.

"And you're telling me you didn't come here to talk about that?"

AJ fumbled with the pouch and then looked at the front. It was carrying South Coast City courier tags, but he couldn't read the sender details, just a date, showing it had been sent a couple of weeks ago. It was addressed to *Chief Superintendent Ferguson, ITMP Whitehorse*. He turned the pouch over and looked at the back, but there was no return address. It had been opened at one end. He looked inside, but the pouch was empty. He handed it to Cassie.

"Whatever it is," AJ said, "we know nothing about it."

No matter how charming his people had been, Ferguson wasn't interested in playing host. His former secretary brought in a pot of tea on a tray with cookies and milk and three cups, but after she left he only poured a cup for himself. Cassie didn't mind, she got up and helped herself.

"You said you had something for me from Dave Warnecke," he said.

AJ and Cassie had discussed how to tell their story, and who should tell it, and they'd agreed AJ would do the telling and she'd chip in if needed. AJ relaxed a little, since this was no longer about finding Warnecke's daughter. Then he remembered that they had found Jen, and she knew who he was, and she was an armed ITMP officer and he unrelaxed again.

"I'll give you the short version," AJ told him. "That OK?"

"I'm all ears," Ferguson said. Actually, it was a little funny, because he did have very big ears, but AJ pushed that thought aside.

"I work at a TGA treatment center in South Coast City for people with early symptoms. About a month ago, we got a new resident, name of Dave Warnecke," AJ said.

Biodata spike, Cassie said. *Emotional hit.*

Ferguson's face didn't show it. "Go on," he said in a neutral voice.

"I work at Sol Vista as a maintenance technician, and Citizen Warnecke got it in his head I was spying on him. He seemed convinced I was working for a Capitol Congressman called Winter, and he was hostile at first, then he asked me to show Winter that he had been working on a manuscript. He called it his 'confession'. Turned out he really did know the Congressman – he came to Sol Vista soon after that to visit him."

"This is Congressman Kevin Winter?"

"Yeah. So after the Congressman left, Citizen Warnecke showed me a part of this manuscript and asked me to take it to Winter."

"He threatened you," Cassie said to AJ. "In a way."

Ferguson frowned. "How so?"

"Well," AJ said, "Citizen Warnecke didn't exactly threaten *me*, he said Winter was avoiding him, and he showed me he had a gun and said he would shoot himself and the manuscript would go to the press if Winter didn't go public about what was in it."

"You'll get to what was in this manuscript soon, I hope," Ferguson said.

"That's where it gets interesting," Cassie said.

"Thank you, Miss," Ferguson said, waving a hand at AJ impatiently. "Go on."

"I decided I better call the Congressman and tell him about this, and he arranged for me to go to the Capitol and meet with him. I gave him the page of the manuscript Warnecke had given me and he introduced me to a guy, a private security contractor called Troy McMaster, and they told me not to worry about it, Citizen Warnecke was a sick man and they would handle it."

"They followed him," Cassie said.

"Who followed who?" Ferguson asked.

"Someone followed me, in the Capitol. I think it was McMaster's people," AJ said, leaving Leon out of it for now. "I saw them in the Capitol, and then again when McMaster came over to South Coast City to ask me to steal the manuscript from Warnecke."

"Congressman Winter asked you to *steal* this manuscript?" Ferguson asked, clearly dubious.

"No, it was his 'security adviser', McMaster. There were two people following me in the Capitol, a man and a woman. I saw the man again at a bar in South Coast City and then another time at Sol Vista, around the time I was meeting with McMaster."

"*Did* you steal the manuscript?" Ferguson asked.

"No, I refused," AJ said. "Citizen Warnecke asked me to help him edit it, so I did that. It was a bunch of conspiracy theories, is the best way to describe it. Then a week ago, all this is going on, Citizen Warnecke dies in his sleep. South Coast City police said it was a combination of booze and an overdose of Blues, and filed it as suicide. When I went around to his house to … pay my respects … I found some personal items. I collected them … to send on to his family." AJ reached into his backpack and took out Warnecke's document box.

"Then I found out that in his will, Warnecke wrote that he wanted you to have them. So here they are."

"Well, aren't you kind," Ferguson said drily. "Put the box on the desk, please."

AJ leaned forward and dropped the box in front of Ferguson, who reached into a drawer and pulled out blue gloves.

How am I doing? AJ asked.

You're doing fine. Let's see how he reacts when he sees the photos of Jen.

Once Ferguson had the gloves on, he pulled the envelope out of the box and emptied the photographs onto the table. He picked up one of them, looking at it closely.

Major bio-spike, Cassie said. *Bullseye.*

I can see that in his face, AJ told her. *What's the deal here?*

Ferguson dropped the photo on his desk. He stood, looked out his window, then turned around again. If they thought he was about to open up to them, they were disappointed.

"You've got yourself in a real mess here, haven't you?" he said. "Old man with TGA, mysterious manuscript, powerful Congressman and his evil henchman, humanitarian mission to the Inland Territory?" He fixed Cassie with a cold stare. "And where do you come in? You're the girlfriend?"

"Yes," Cassie said. "I didn't want him to make the trip up here on his own."

"So thoughtful," Ferguson said. He turned to the window again. "You don't happen to own a red Scarlatti planer, by any chance?"

Keep quiet, Cassie said. *He can't link it to us. Let me answer.*

"No, we hitched a ride with a freighter to just outside Ketchican and had to hire a car from there," she said.

"Uh huh," Ferguson said. "Bit of early advice for you both, since we only just met? Don't try to sell that long steaming pile of beaver-dung you just told me to anyone else in this building."

AJ swallowed.

Ferguson sat back down at his desk, looked out his window and sighed. It was a huge, deep sigh. The kind of sigh a man might sigh if he had to watch a loved one get exhumed.

AJ couldn't contain himself any longer. "The woman in those photographs. It's Citizen Warnecke's daughter?"

Ferguson didn't look at him, just kept looking out his window.

"Yep."

"Jen," AJ continued. "The officer who showed us in here. That's her, right?"

"Yep."

We know that much already, AJ, Cassie said. *The question is, how the hell, why the hell, and what the hell?*

"So, uhm, your connection to Citizen Warnecke, that is…"

"You know," Ferguson said, turning back to them, ignoring AJ. "Back in those days, as a young officer here leading the search and rescue team, I ran plenty of missing person searches in these parts. We had only one where the person was never found – because sooner or later they all turn up, dead or alive – but that one was Farley O'Halloran. Forty years later, and I still have no idea what happened to him."

They just looked at him and waited.

"Or, I should say, I *had* no idea," he continued, pointing at the envelope he'd given to AJ, "until last week, when that package arrived."

Ferguson peeled off his gloves and threw them on the desk. He reached over and from his desk drawer he pulled out a folder and opened it. Inside was a rolled page, in its own clear cellulose sleeve. AJ had never seen police evidence but he'd seen plenty of VR and he could tell he was looking at it. The folder was labeled, numbered and dated, and so was the cellulose folder holding the page.

From where he was sitting, AJ couldn't see what was on the rolled page, and Ferguson wasn't about to show them. He turned it face down and sat with his hands on top of it, glaring at them.

"I'm not one for games, as you might have guessed. So I'm going to ask you two some questions, and you…" he pointed at Cassie, not AJ, "… will answer yes or no and if you try to sell me any more lies, so help me I will club you both in the head and drop you down a grizzly hole, because that's how much you are irritating me right now."

"Fine," Cassie said.

Are you serious? AJ asked.

I trust him, she said.

What? You have no instincts!

Don't need them. I checked his service record, his personal data, his taste in VR shows. I trust him.

"Good," Ferguson said. "First question. Fake IDs as good as you are traveling with aren't easy to come by. Are you government?"

Cassie shook her head. "No."

"Private contractors?"

"No."

He frowned. "Are you working for Congressman Kevin Winter in any official and/or private capacity?"

"No."

Ferguson put a finger on the document in front of him. "And you didn't come here looking for this?"

"No, we came here to give you those," she said, pointing at the photographs.

"So sweet of you both. That's not the only reason you came here, is it, girl?" he asked.

"No."

AJ held his breath. Was she about to open up about Jen? About her real identity? Already? He knew that would be a bad idea, and that was based on true human intuition.

"OK, enough of the yes/no," Ferguson said. "Now I'm asking why."

"Well, we…" AJ began, but Ferguson held up his hand to stop him.

"Not you, son, I was asking your boss."

AJ could feel his blood begin to boil, but Cassie broke in. *Easy tiger. He's just assuming that I'm the citizen and you're the cyber, so I'm your employer.*

Backward Territorian hick, AJ replied. *Never heard of self-determination?*

Cassie continued. "We're here because we think Citizen Warnecke was murdered and we don't know who else to turn to."

AJ explained how he had found Warnecke, his personal papers all conveniently laid out, the man lying in bed with pills and an empty liquor bottle beside him. He also explained how he'd compared his vision of the flat before and after and concluded it had been searched.

"Then my partner, Leon Guerra, got it in his head to speak to McMaster and try to get some sort of reward for handing over the page of the document that we gave the Congressman. I was stupid enough to give him a copy before I realized what he was planning to do."

"You're telling me you weren't in on that brilliant plan?" Ferguson asked.

"No! The Congressman had already offered me 'compensation for my troubles' and I'd declined. I told Leon that, and I never thought he'd…"

"Be so dumb," Cassie said. "Now he's missing."

"Took the money and ran," Ferguson guessed.

"No, there's more. Next day, after Citizen Warnecke died and Leon disappeared, I found McMaster, the Congressman's security guy, going through our stuff in our workshop. He said he was looking for a missing chapter from Citizen Warnecke's manuscript. I confronted him about Leon and he told me Leon had squeezed them for money but they'd made no deal and he'd gone his way."

"You didn't believe him," Ferguson observed.

"Not for a minute," AJ said. "Leon was a family man. He'd never disappear without a word, let his wife worry like that."

"So, we got scared," Cassie said. "We read Citizen Warnecke's will and we saw he'd left the photos to you. We hoped maybe you were a friend of his. And being a cop…"

"Inland Territory Mounted Police," Ferguson said. "If you can't say police officer, say Mountie. And an ex-Mountie at that."

"Ex-Mountie," she corrected herself. "Anyway, we got up here as fast as we could."

Ferguson swiveled on his chair, fingers steepled under his chin, then reached up and touched his earbud. "Jen? Can you search the alert service for a missing person's report on a Leon … who?"

"Guerra," AJ said. "G-u-e-r-r-a."

"G-u-e-r-r-a, Jen. South Coast City resident. No, I'll wait." Ferguson stared at the ceiling as he waited, then looked at AJ again as he spoke. "Thanks, Jen. That's all for now."

He leaned forward and pushed the document on his desk toward them. "I think I know what your friend McMaster was looking for," he said. "This was in that courier bag. There was no explanation, no other note in there, just this page. I read it and realized what it was straight away. Should have acted on it straight away too, I guess." He sighed. "But I didn't. When I finally got around to calling Dave, it was the same day you found him, dead."

"I'm sorry," AJ said. "We…"

Ferguson pointed to the document. AJ saw it had the same biometrics stripe on it as Warnecke's full manuscript. "You read that, and then the three of us are going to talk some more."

The arguments started every morning as soon as we were all awake. Farley was using, and it was making him erratic, irritated, irritating. Calling us idiots for calling him an idiot. Kevin said he was sick of arguing, if Farley wanted to waste his career trying to do the stupidest thing Kevin had ever heard of in his life, he could go and do it. Trick the Core to hack itself? Why? Just to prove it was possible?

But then the real argument started. Farley wanted to cut the trip short, walk out to a nearby camping dome and signal for a pickup so he could get back to work. Kevin said he was damned if he was going to cut his holiday short just because Farley had some sort of 'deranged epiphany'.

We're going, Farley said. Dave, get your gear. He picked up a paddle.

No, Kevin said and he grabbed up a shovel and put the blade on Farley's chest. We're not.

Farley wasn't in control of himself. He got furious, swore at Kevin and pushed aside the shovel and Kevin lifted it in both hands and bunted him with it. It wasn't hard, but the shaft connected with Farley's nose and he staggered back and caught his foot on something and went down backward.

His head hit a rock and there was this wet thud.

He wasn't dead. He rolled onto his side, pulled his knees up and lay there.

Get up, idiot, Kevin said. Faking you're hurt won't get you to the end of the river faster either.

Farley was moaning, kind of soft. There was blood leaking from the back of his head, running away into the snow.

Then he started to spasm.

We knelt down and tried to hold him still, but he was strong. Kevin tried to shove a shirt sleeve in his mouth to stop him biting his tongue, but we couldn't get it past his teeth. His eyes were rolled back. When he relaxed, Kevin got the cloth between his jaws, but there was blood coming out his mouth as well.

I think he spasmed three or four times in the next hour. We had a first aid kit still, and we bandaged his head, so that stopped bleeding, but you could feel the bone of his skull moving under your fingers. He'd cracked it wide open when he fell.

I sat holding him, and we put all our thermal blankets on him, trying to keep him warm, but when he wasn't in spasm, he was shivering.

About an hour later, he stopped breathing.

Kevin tried CPR, but he was gone.

AJ finished the screen, reading how they'd pulled the blankets over Farley then crawled into their tent not talking to each other, just lying there until night came and the darkness, and Warnecke had lain awake the whole night, not believing what had happened. There was more but AJ caught his breath, stopped and looked at Cassie. "Damn. You were right, it was bigger than just leaving the guy behind," he said. "Winter *killed* him."

He handed the page to Cassie.

"Dave *alleges* Winter killed him," Ferguson warned. "This is just his version, right?"

"So?"

"So, we don't know who swung that shovel," Ferguson said. "You don't know whether any of what he writes there is true."

"Yeah, but when I read that," AJ said, pointing to the page Cassie was reading, "and I'm thinking that Citizen Warnecke didn't commit suicide, that Winter had him killed, Winter had Leon killed, it's because he's trying to cover this up."

"You don't *know* that he did," Ferguson said. "You said South Coast City police concluded Dave died in his sleep. You said your work friend is missing, but no one found him yet? Dead or alive?"

"No, but…"

"So you can't prove anything. The only thing we know is that Dave Warnecke *might* have written that page, and he's saying Congressman Kevin Winter killed Farley O'Halloran," Ferguson said.

"Did you check the biometrics signature?" Cassie asked.

"Yeah, it's his."

"Warnecke wrote that," AJ said. "It's exactly the same style as the rest of the manuscript."

"You have this famous manuscript so I can have an AI compare the writing?" Ferguson asked. "Put this chapter in context? You read it, so you must have it cached."

"No," AJ admitted, knowing it sounded weak. "He didn't want me to cache it. He wanted to keep it off-Core."

"Convenient," Ferguson said. He leaned back in his chair. "A Congressman like Winter, he's got to have plenty of enemies. I can think of harder ways to make life difficult for him than to get a couple of nice wholesome people like you to come up here and try to get the ITMP to restart a cold case based on an allegation from a dead man that Winter killed his rafting buddy."

AJ heard Ferguson's words and realized what they were up against.

"Allegation from a dead man, *with* TGA," Ferguson added.

"Don't you *want* to know what happened?" Cassie asked him. "Don't you have a duty to find out?"

"We need protection," AJ said. "Two people are dead because of this. Three if you count Farley."

"You say. There's an immigration office in Ketchican," Ferguson said with a cold smile. "Tell them your story. They might give you asylum."

AJ started to pick up his pack, thinking they were done. Cassie was still reading the page from Warnecke's manuscript.

"Where you going?" Ferguson asked.

"I don't know," AJ said. "I thought we were done."

Sit down, AJ, Cassie said. *This isn't about Warnecke or Winter anymore, remember? This is about Jen. We need as much information as we can get before I move on her. We need to get him back to the question of how she ended up here, working for him. Why is she here?*

"Good. Sit down, son. I didn't say we were beaten," Ferguson said. "Did I say we were beaten? I just wanted to show you what we're up against, if we try to make this case."

AJ looked at him sharply. "You do believe us?"

"Not yet, young man," Ferguson said. "Not by an Inland Territory mile. But you haven't finished reading yet." He nodded at the page Cassie was holding and AJ leaned over to read over her shoulder as she scrolled down.

We were freezing because we'd used our thermal blankets on Farley and the charge on our heat suits was running low, we'd worked them so hard, but we both fell asleep sometime before dawn and woke a couple hours later in the early morning half-light. I wanted to crawl out of my tent and see that it was just a nightmare. Maybe Farley had gone off to find the dome like he said, and the two of us would just drag ourselves into the raft and get onto the river. Either he'd find help, or we would.

But as I crawled out of the tent, I saw his body was still there, wrapped in the silver blankets.

Kevin crawled out beside me. We have to bury him, he said. Deep. Or grizzlies will get him.

We'd seen several of the big furry scavengers combing the riverbanks as we'd rafted down. They were everywhere up here.

We should take him with us, I said. Just put him in the raft.

You want to spend five days with a dead guy in the raft? Kevin asked. Find the shovel. We'll get help and come back for him.

The water level had started to drop a little since the day before, but the rain was still heavy. We'd dragged ourselves up above the normal waterline to make our camp, but now we could see we were just above a broad ice shelf, barely covered with water. Probably a place you'd normally be able to camp if the river wasn't so high.

While I looked for the folding shovel Kevin had killed Farley with, Kevin walked up the riverbank and disappeared from view in the fog.

He came back down. There's a rock up there, with a kind of sinkhole at the base, on the other side, where the runoff disappears, he said. Help me bury him up there. We can cover him up, but he'll be easy to find.

You killed him, bury him yourself, I said, and handed him the shovel.

I didn't kill him, Kevin said. It was an accident.

But he didn't argue any more. He grabbed the shovel and took hold of the blankets we'd wrapped Farley in, and dragged him up the riverbank.

When he came back down, I decided we should say a few words, so I said a prayer.

As we were packing the raft again, Kevin said, You know what? I don't think Farley died in an accident. I think he tried to walk out to that dome.

I looked at him like he was crazy.

The guy is dead, right? he was saying. Nothing is going to bring him back. But we're going to get the blame. We're talking manslaughter or something, he said. Kiss your doctorate goodbye, kiss your whole future goodbye.

Your future, I told him. You killed him.

Yeah? That's not the way I'll be telling it, Kevin said. You tell anyone I killed him, and I'll tell them you did. My word against yours, Dave. You really want to go there?

He pointed up the hill, yelling in the rain, You want to ruin your whole life because of that stupid jerk?

I saw his eyes. I saw the eyes of a guy who had just killed Farley and now was threatening to tell everyone I had done it, and I could see he was serious.

He started walking again and I fell in alongside him.

He walked out on us, Kevin said again. Decided to quit the trip and tried to hike out. We tried to stop him but he wouldn't listen. If they want to search for him, we tell them we had no idea where we were, but yeah, they should probably search back upriver, we'll say we last saw him near Alsek River Camping Dome.

What if he was right? I asked Kevin. If there is a fatal flaw in the Core?

He's not right, Kevin said. And we told him that and he got shirty and he walked out on us. And that was that.

I never saw exactly where he buried Farley, and though I asked, he never told me. Said it didn't matter. Or he didn't want to think about it. Or I should just let it go. But just recently, Kevin Winter came to visit me. After a few drinks, I asked him again.

Damn it, Dave, he said. I put him under a big rock, like a tombstone. It was as tall as four men and as wide as two. I buried him under it, and covered him up. It was as good a resting place as any of us are going to get.

So there you have it. I can't tell you where on the river Farley O'Halloran lies, or under exactly which rock, but at least the world can know now how he died.

AJ looked up. "So, they buried him … and the whole thing about him walking out was a lie?"

Ferguson nodded. "According to Dave Warnecke." He reached up to his earbud. "Jen? Can you come in here again? Thanks."

"How did Citizen Warnecke's daughter end up here?" Cassie asked. "If you'll excuse my curiosity."

Well, that was subtle, AJ said.

If you don't ask, you won't get, she replied. *I think that's from the Tao Te Ching.*

Ferguson poured himself some more tea. "Let's let her tell you that, shall we?" As he spoke the tall young cyber walked in and stood with arms folded in front of them, legs apart, in a relaxed stance.

She was looking straight at AJ, not at Ferguson, until he spoke.

"Jen, I brought these nice people up to date on the letter we got last week from your father."

"Yes, sir," she said, looking at Ferguson now.

"And they tell me they do not believe your father committed suicide, they think he was murdered, by order of Congressman Winter. What do you think of that, Jen?"

The light between her brows pulsed quickly.

She's drifting, AJ said.

And I still can't see her anywhere in the Core, Cassie said. *She's a damn ghost.*

Her third eye stopped pulsing and she replied, "I think that concurs with our own assessment, doesn't it, sir?" She spoke without rancor, without emotion. Calmly, and all the more disconcertingly for it.

Ferguson leaned forward and took the document in its evidence folder back. "First this, then we learned Dave was dead. We knew he was sick – the TGA – but suicidal? He was too driven. So Jen did some digging. Turns out the officer who signed off on the suicide investigation is as dirty as they come down south. And there was no post-mortem, as there has to be for a suspected suicide. The body was just released straight to the family and cremated yesterday. What did we think when we heard about that, Jen?"

"I believe you swore, sir," the woman said.

"And what did you say, Jen?"

She smiled slightly. "I think I said, 'I will get that bastard Winter even if it takes me the rest of my life', sir."

Ferguson nodded at a spare chair. "Take a seat, Jen. Even though these folks are lying through their teeth, I do believe we are united by a common enemy and we just need to learn to trust each other. They brought me these," he said, pointing to the photographs on his desk.

Jen reached over to pick them up and flicked through them. For the first time, AJ saw something like sadness cross her face. She put the photos back on the desk. "Every year, on my birthing day, he made me pose for one of those." She reached up and touched her third eye self-consciously. "When I was a teen, I tried putting makeup on this, to hide it. But he'd rub it off. He told me to be proud of who I was because I was better and brighter and more beautiful than any damn citizen." She looked at AJ. "I bet your mom said the same."

She's flirting with you? Cassie remarked. *Oh, this girl is going down. She's going to wish she'd run off to Orkutsk.*

Easy, tigress, AJ replied.

"No, she never did," AJ said. "She never took photos like this either. He must have really loved you."

"In his own way," Jen said thoughtfully. "I think he did."

Ferguson gathered up the photos and put them back in their envelope, then leaned over and handed them to Jen, who took them with a small nod. "Thanks for bringing these all this way," she said to Cassie.

"Hey, least we could do," Cassie said. Then chirped to AJ, *For a dead woman.*

She hasn't actually done anything to you, AJ reminded her.

Yet, Cassie said. *And don't you dare start defending her!*

"Jen, in the spirit of encouraging greater trust," Ferguson said, "why don't you tell me what you learned about our new friends here while you were outside there?" AJ stiffened, and Ferguson noticed. "Oh, you'll enjoy this. It's quite impressive."

"Are you sure, sir?" Jen asked. "In front of them?"

He waved a hand. "Please. We're all friends here. The enemies of my enemy, as they say…"

She looked directly at AJ. "Your ID was only created two days ago, and all information about you in the Core has the same creation date, which normally would not be detectable, except…"

Ferguson smiled. "Jen has created her own proprietary engine for Core queries," he said. "It's fast, and it's frighteningly efficient."

"… except that as the Chief says, my query engine makes that kind of thing transparent."

Damn, Cassie said. *She's good.*

Jen was still looking at AJ, a slight smile on her face. "Your real name is AJ.80966, you work as a maintenance tech at Sol Vista where you came into contact with my father. You buy a lot of surf equipment, so I'm guessing you surf. You visit your mom every Sunday, but you didn't visit her last Sunday. She has a brain tumor and has lost the ability to recognize you anyway, so she probably won't miss you. You recently made a flight to the Capitol and a car took you to the office address of Congressman Winter…" She paused and shot a look at Ferguson.

"That checks, he disclosed that," Ferguson said.

"And you returned to South Coast City the same day. Two days ago there are indications you left Sea Gate district in a hurry. You dumped your earbud, and your biodata signal was faked to show you were still in Sea Gate, but you didn't use a single credit in any of your normal retail or hospitality outlets in the last two days, I assume because you were on your way here via ground transport. There is a police report on file in Sea Gate and a warrant out for your arrest for allegedly bearing a firearm, which you claimed in a phone call to police you used to scare away two burglars."

"Your father's gun," AJ said quickly, looking at Cassie to back him up. "We threw it in a lake on the way here."

"This was when you found this McMaster guy going through your workshop?"

"Yes."

"Don't leave out little details about firearms in the future please, son," Ferguson said. "It tends to annoy the average police officer. Keep going, Jen."

She nodded. "Accessing the VR unit in your apartment, which I am permitted to do under section 73 of the ITMP Act, I can see you keep a nice, neat house and I particularly like the color of your sofa. You seem like a nice guy," she finished, and winked at him.

So dead, Cassie said. And if it was possible to mutter at quantum speeds, it would have been a mutter.

As though picking up on the vibe, Jen turned to Cassie and her smile faded. "You, however, are a fake."

AJ bumped his adrenaline, getting ready for the cyber equivalent of a world championship bitchfight.

"Oh, really?" Cassie said. "Do tell."

"Happily," Jen said. "Your ID and backstory were created at the same time as his. Your current name is Cassie, not Carly, but Cassie is not your real name either."

AJ shot a look at Cassie but she ignored him, watching Jen with her arms crossed. "Go on."

"The Cassie ID was only created a few weeks ago, and the backstory with it. Born in the Territory, grew up in Bloor, schools, college, post-grad, journalism – all fake. But your planer license is real enough, you got it a month ago, when you bought a red Scarlatti road planer. But that is as far back as I could go. Before that, your data trail is cold."

Stop looking at me like that, Cassie said. *She's not going to tell you anything you don't know.*

"You are a hacker," Jen continued. "It's the only explanation. And you're good, I'll give you that. You managed to cover your trail all the way from South Coast City to here without being picked up on a single camera, including the cameras at a roadhouse south of here where witnesses report seeing a female and a male on a red Scarlatti just before someone set off a military-grade neural blast that rendered everyone in the area unconscious. I can see from your comms traffic that you first contacted the director of Sol Vista three weeks before my father's death. The first time your comms and his," she nodded at AJ, "were co-located was two weeks before my father's death, so I'd say that's when you first met. Again, looking at your comms and hospitality payment records, you two have been in regular contact since you met, have had six dates, but you've spent only two nights together. So it isn't yet a serious relationship." Jen turned her gaze from Cassie to AJ. "I hate to break this to you, AJ, but for whatever reason, I think she came to South Coast City with a purpose, picked you out as a soft target, started a relationship with you so that she could manipulate you, and I'm willing to bet with a very high degree of certainty it was her idea to come here, not yours."

AJ swallowed hard.

Why are you looking shocked? Cassie said. *She's not wrong about the timeline, she's just twisting it to sound like I had some hidden agenda. You know my damn agenda! And it was your idea to come here, not mine.*

Ferguson raised his eyebrows. "Wow. See what I mean? It's uncanny how she does that, isn't it?" He stood and looked at a clock on the wall. "Well then, AJ, 'Cassie'. Now that we've all got to know each other a bit better, how about an early supper?"

They walked out together and took the elevator to the ground floor. The building turned out to be a multipurpose civic center, with the police station sharing offices with some local government departments and a central transit hub for ride-hailing, located underground. There was also a small retail mall, with a few self-service shops and restaurants.

"Noodles and beer OK?" Ferguson asked. He seemed quite cheerful now, though AJ couldn't really see why. They might have a shared enemy in Winter, but Jen had done a great job fishing the Deep Core and exposing both him and Cassie. Maybe Ferguson was just happy to have his suspicions confirmed, knowing Cassie and AJ had nowhere to hide anymore. What AJ couldn't tell was whether Jen had found out more than she'd revealed about Cassie when she was diving and was keeping it to herself, or what.

What now? he asked Cassie.

Now we eat some damn noodles, she said. *Let me do the talking, okay?*

Sure thing.

Why am I so angry, AJ? she asked. *I hate her. But nothing she said was untrue. You're right, she has done nothing to hurt me. Why do I hate her with a burning red-hot passion?*

It's called jealousy, AJ told her. *When it takes over, reason goes out the window. You really should do more first-person living in the real.*

No thank you, Cassie said. *If this is emotion, you can have it.*

They got their noodles from a stall and Ferguson bought a round of beers. "You asked a question earlier, young lady," he said to Cassie, handing her a beer. "About how Jen ended up here?" He gestured toward the other cyber with the neck of his own beer. "Feel free to tell our new friends your story, constable."

The young Mountie was still in her bright red uniform. She stopped awkwardly, a forkful of noodles halfway up to her mouth, and put her fork down again. "Sure." She wiped her mouth, even though she hadn't had a bite yet. "A few years ago, my father asked me to come up here. He knew the Chief here, from the time Farley O'Halloran went missing, and they'd stayed in touch since. Farley's disappearance was a bit of an obsession for my father," she said. "Though I never understood why until that package came last week and the Chief showed me."

Do we believe that? AJ asked. *Or is she just saying that for Ferguson's benefit?*

It's probable, Cassie said. *He successfully kept it off-Core and hidden from me, so why not from her too?*

"Sorry, but you said your father asked you to come up here?" Cassie said, not letting it go.

Jen managed to get a mouthful of noodles while Cassie was talking, and they waited while she swallowed. "So hungry, apologies! Yeah, so I contacted the Chief. I'm a freelance data analyst, and I knew they were always looking for cybers up here, so he offered me a job."

"Doesn't a constable in the Mounties need years of training?" AJ asked.

"Cybers are fast-tracked," Ferguson explained. "Especially cybers like Jen."

"But why?" Cassie insisted. "Why here?"

Jen put down her fork, picked up her beer and took a slow sip. Then she fixed Cassie with a cool gaze. "Because my father wanted me to try to find Farley O'Halloran's body so he could give it a proper burial. And I have been looking up and down that goddamn river for three years and I still haven't found it, and now I finally think I know where it is, my father's dead."

"I'm so sorry," AJ said. "At first I thought he was just some crazy old guy, and by the time I realized how serious it was, Winter had put his mercenaries on the job and after that I just bounced from one situation to the next."

Jen reached out and patted AJ's hand. "It's OK. He was a crazy old guy," she said. "Crazy. Intuitive. Brilliant." She sighed. "And obsessed. Consumed. And brutal." She left her hand a moment on AJ's and then pulled it away, with a glance at Cassie.

Seriously? Cassie said.

She just opened a TH channel to me, AJ said quickly. *She wants to synch. Is there a way you can listen in?*

What? Normally, yes. Her, no. Nothing she does is visible to me. What I can't see, I can't access!

What should I do? he asked.

Stall her.

OK ... done.

"You know where Farley O'Halloran is buried?" Cassie asked.

Ferguson nodded. "There was a clue in the letter. If Citizen Warnecke had shared all that detail with Jen, we might have worked it out earlier. But it seems he didn't have all the pieces until recently."

"Winter told my father he buried Farley under a 'big rock, like a tombstone'," Jen quoted. There was a 2D screen built into their table, and Jen tapped it to bring up a map of the Territory. She zoomed it so it showed Whitehorse and its nearby river. Then zoomed down to the river and tracked it south, away from Whitehorse. At a radical bend just after the confluence of another river, she changed the view to ground level and it showed a raging rapid on one side of the river, an ice shelf on the other, and a hillside leading up from the riverbank. On the crest of a hill stood a large boulder, but the image had been taken in fog, and it wasn't clear enough to see any more than the vague outline.

"I've been down that river three times in my life," Ferguson said. "Two times in the six months just after that boy went missing, stopping at every damn campsite that anyone had ever used. The last time I did it was with Jen, and it was crazy, winter coming, half the river frozen, we nearly got crushed by ice floes in the Bay getting to the take-out point. Jen bought metal-detecting gear and a portable ground-penetrating radar. We found some gear buried in ice downstream that was about the right vintage, but nothing you'd call definitive. And we cruised right past *that* place because it was way further down than Winter and Warnecke had told us they had last seen Farley." He reached over and put his finger on the circle on Warnecke's map. "That campsite there, they call it Tombstone Beach."

He wasn't finished. He reached over and pointed at the boulder.

"That rock, it's a bit hard to see on here, is big, but it's rounded at the top and flat like a tombstone," Ferguson said, trying unsuccessfully to zoom in. "The reason everyone who ever rafted that river knows the place," he said, "is there is this rafters' tale, started up a few decades ago, that when the first spring thaw comes, the rock *bleeds*."

"I've done that river three times a year, the last three years," Jen said. "Trying different methods of searching for biological remains. I've sent drones down, on the water, in the air. I nearly drowned, twice. Got attacked by a grizzly once." She leaned over and showed AJ a scar on her neck.

If you run a finger down that scar and say 'ouch, that must have hurt' I will club you on the head and drop you down a grizzly hole myself, Cassie said.

As if I would have, AJ said, putting his hand back in his lap.

"I never saw blood coming from that rock. I assumed it was just a story people told around campfires to creep each other out. It's so far up from the riverbank that when it's foggy, you can't even see it. I never thought to check it," Jen continued.

Ferguson drained his beer. "Jen and I have been discussing it the last couple of days, but your arrival has made up my mind," he said. "What say you, Jen and I take the police rotor down there tomorrow and check out that rock?" He turned to his cyber constable. "Jen, in your expert opinion, would the body of Farley O'Halloran, presumably showing blunt trauma wounds to his skull, together with your father's letter, the testimony of these good people, and, with any luck, solid evidence linking a certain Congressman to the disappearance of Leon Guerra of South Coast City, be enough for us to get a Commonwealth arrest warrant made out for said Congressman?"

"In my expert opinion? Hell yes, sir," she said.

AJ had asked Jen to hold off with synching on TH until they were done eating, but she forced a connection and broke through.

AJ, I have no right to ask you this, but please say you'll come with us tomorrow. I want another cyber there with me, she said.

Why? he asked. *What's the matter?*

Jen looked pointedly at Cassie. *She scares me. She's not who you think she is.*

19. TOMBSTONE BEACH

Ferguson had Jen put AJ and Cassie up at the ITMP cadet college on level two of the station. As a love shack it left a lot to be desired, with bunk beds the only option.

Ferguson had told Jen to take a room next door 'just in case she was needed', and she'd done so without question, coming into their room in a t-shirt and tights and checking they were okay before she retired for the night. She sat on the bottom bunk, looking around. "Not exactly six star. I spent my first year here in this dorm," she said.

Cassie sighed. "Better than the rad-ridden place we stayed at on the way up here," she said.

"Yeah. Hey, before you guys bed down for the night, I have to explain something," Jen said. AJ had asked her to park their conversation until he contacted her later that night. Multi-thread conversation was never his strong suit and dealing with the real world, plus two separate cyber conversations simultaneously, was testing his physical and emotional capacity to the limit, especially when it was two cybers like Cassie and Jen.

"Sure," AJ replied. "Go ahead."

"I don't want to worry you," she said, "but you should know something."

"Now you're worrying me," Cassie said.

"Right. Look, the reason the Chief put you here at the college, asked me to stay next door, is that he wants to be sure you're safe. The potential threat from this Troy McMaster and everything." She paused. "Also, to be sure you don't decide to skip town tonight."

"Are we under arrest or something?" Cassie asked.

"No," Jen smiled. "But if you try to leave, you probably will be. I'm really sorry." She pulled two string wrist bracelets from a pocket in her tights. "Would you mind wearing these?"

"What are they?" AJ asked.

"Trackers," Jen said with a shrug. "If you move outside a predetermined range, which for you is within 500 yards of me," she wrinkled her nose, "it will set off an alarm that will wake the whole town. I don't recommend it. It makes the locals very tetchy."

"And if we don't want to?"

She looked surprised. "Oh. Well, then I guess I'll have to take you to the holding cells in the basement. Just as safe, way less comfortable."

AJ and Cassie looked at each other.

Shall we go along with this? AJ asked.

Do we have a choice? Cassie replied.

They both sat down on the bunk opposite Jen and put on the bracelets. As AJ looped his around his wrist, it tightened to a snug fit. He winced. The idea this thing could set off a city-wide alert was not going to help him sleep better tonight.

"I knew you'd be annoyed," Jen said. "But it's best for everyone's peace of mind." She looked at them like she was waiting for them to cheer up. When they didn't, she kept going. "Look at it like this. You are in a shielded facility, with fifty police officers." She looked pointedly at Cassie. "A neural blaster wouldn't work here."

"Fifty *cadets*," Cassie corrected her.

"And instructors," Jen insisted. "Look, if they are trying to find you, they'll need time to organize and get here. Even a charter drone takes time to get in place and they can't do the Capitol or South Coast City to Whitehorse in one flight. They'd have to stop to recharge, or change drones. Two days at best. We'll be done by then."

AJ shifted, looking out the window at the endless rain, obscuring what he was sure would be a spectacular view of the mountains. "Done with what?"

"Tomorrow we get the body of Farley O'Halloran, we link Winter to Troy McMaster, and McMaster to the disappearance of Leon Guerra, then we get a Commonwealth warrant," Jen explained. "Then you give your depositions, we'll put you both in witness protection and we can move on Congressman Winter."

"That simple," AJ said.

"Never is. We're still working on the McMaster–Guerra thing," she admitted. "That guy is as slippery as a snow eel." She smiled. "But the Mounties *always* get their man."

"You want top or bottom?" Cassie asked out loud after Jen left.

These bracelets are also listening devices, Cassie said to AJ on TH. *I can see their data links. Talk in the real until we go to bed and can talk properly.*

Can't you disable them? AJ asked.

Not worth the effort.

"Uh, bottom I guess," AJ said, rocking the bunk. "These don't look too solid. Wouldn't want it to collapse in the night."

"I'm going to the bathroom. It was down the hall, right?" Cassie asked.

"Yep. I'll be right behind you. But I left my toothbrush in the car."

She smiled. "The parking level is less than 500 yards from here, so you should be OK. Just don't get lost."

"Great advice."

"Man, I'm exhausted," Cassie said on her way out. "That was a long day."

He sat on the bottom bunk. There was a not so fresh towel on each bunk and he picked the closest one up and sniffed it. Musty, but looked clean enough.

He put a hand on the top bunk and drifted.

Jen?

Hi, AJ.

What the hell did you mean, 'She's not who you think she is?' AJ had an idea that the Mountie would have gone Deep Core looking for information on Cassie and wouldn't have found any. How could she, when Cassie as an entity had only been birthed a few weeks ago? Searching for Cassie in the Core was like trying to remember a dream before it had been dreamt.

But Jen's words hit him like a punch in the face. *You think she is the Core personified. She can drift, but she has no third eye. She is anatomically human. She can manipulate data streams, fake IDs, intercept comms transmissions, dive your cache, access seemingly unlimited data sources and credit, and she knew all about my father and me. Is any of that wrong?*

He sat down heavily on the bunk. What could he say to that?

I think I better cut this link, is what he said.

Wait! Jen said. *I get that you care about her. You think she was only recently birthed, drawn to you because of my father and the alleged threat to the Core I pose. She wasn't!*

Going now, he said. *We can talk tomorrow. I need to think.*

OK, look. I'm going to ask you to drift…

She'll see whatever I'm doing.

She won't, I can make sure of that. You know what I can do, right?

Yes.

OK, I want you to drift. I could send all this information to you, but I want you to find it for yourself so you can be sure it's reliable. Find out everything you can about Gen 6 New Syberia mil-spec cybers.

I'm a damn maintenance tech, AJ said. *How am I going to be able to access what is no doubt classified data on NS military cybers?*

I'll give you the access you need. Do it tonight. We'll talk tomorrow, Jen said. *Bye, AJ.*

Before he could respond, the door to the dorm room opened. "The water is cold," Cassie said as she came in again. "But there's a sign saying 'hot water between 0400 and 0600'. I guess that's one way to get lazy-ass cadets out of bed." She saw AJ sitting on the bunk and pointed at the bathroom with her toothbrush. "Teeth, face, goodnight kiss and then sweet dreams, big man. We've got a busy day tomorrow."

AJ took a towel and went down to the basement parking garage to fetch his toothbrush, being very careful not to stray. He had another motive for going to the car. Down the side of the bench seat that he'd been sitting on, he'd hidden Warnecke's burp gun.

He hadn't been able to bring himself to drop it in the water off the bridge, so he'd wrapped his much-loved multitool in the scarf and handed that to her instead. He'd felt kind of sad watching it sink below the surface of the lake. He and that multitool had traveled quite a few times around Coruscant together and fixed a lot of stuff. But now he was damn glad he'd made the switch.

He wrapped the gun in his towel and went back up to their dormitory level, stumbling down the corridor like a sleepwalker, passing two cadets talking in a doorway. They both stood to attention and saluted him, which was probably what they were trained to do for anyone they didn't recognize. Citizens saluting a cyber? On any other day he might be enjoying this place. Instead he had, once again, had his world ripped out from under him. Drift? He could barely walk and think at the same time.

He went into the bathroom and threw cold water on his face. It didn't make his thoughts any clearer. He tried to start building scenarios and working probabilities, but it was like building a house of cards with trembling hands. He couldn't focus. He decided to cut his bandwidth to a bare minimum 5 percent, just to get some control.

"Do your teeth, AJ," he told himself out loud.

As he walked back down the corridor, the two cadets were gone and it was cool and quiet. His stockinged feet made a swishing sound on the wooden floor. He ran a hand along the cold brick of the walls as he walked. He opened the door to the dorm and saw Cassie was already in bed, so he bent and kissed her on the forehead as she looked up at him.

"You can do better than that," she said, holding out her arms. He leaned down again and kissed her properly, feeling the heat he always felt with her. It woke him from his daze. "That's more like it," Cassie said. She looked at the narrow cot. "I don't think you can fit in here without smothering me in my sleep. Sweet dreams."

"You too," he said, dialing his bandwidth back up and climbing up into his bunk. He felt like a kid on a school camp and could barely sit up in the bunk without his head hitting the low ceiling. He lay back with his arms folded across his chest and slid the bracelet around his wrist to make it a little more comfortable.

How do you want to handle tomorrow? he asked Cassie on TH.

I had a plan for disabling her if we were lucky enough to find her, she answered. *I nearly put it into action when she put these stupid bracelets on us but that would have just got us locked up. I need to execute it in full view of a third-party witness – like Ferguson.*

What plan?

I can trigger a GABA shutdown, Cassie said. *Overwhelm her system with 'drift lost' protocol signals so that her brain floods with gamma-aminobutyric acid and she goes into a coma. Once she's down, I can keep her there.*

You're going to let her die? AJ asked, shocked. *What about Winter, McMaster, all of that? She's pretty much Ferguson's best hope for bringing a solid case against Winter if she can prove he was involved in Leon's disappearance.*

My priority is Jen, AJ. We can get back to Winter and McMaster when Jen has been dealt with. She's an existential threat – Winter is a distraction compared to that. Don't worry, we'll bring him down and get you safe.

But killing her? AJ hadn't thought that far – what they would do when finally they caught up with Warnecke's daughter. He'd expected the search for her would have taken much longer. The thought of her lying in a hospital bed somewhere, her body slowly shutting down from lack of fluid, made him shudder. Would Ferguson let that happen? What was the normal response if a cyber suffered a catastrophic neural event that wasn't related to an accident or trauma? Surely she'd be medically examined, kept on life support, hoping the event would pass?

I'm not going to kill her, Cassie said. *I might have got a little jealous back there but I didn't go full psycho, AJ.*

OK, good.

I'm going to reintegrate her. The trip downriver tomorrow is perfect. I can drop her in full view of Ferguson and anyone else we have with us, while you and I are nowhere near her. She'll go inert, that should deactivate all the defenses she's built up around her. Ferguson and the others will panic, try to revive her, take us all back here so they can get her into hospital. I'll trigger the reintegration sequence while we're en route here. She'll be back with me, in the Core, by the time the rotor lands.

And that's not killing her?

A cyber is data, AJ, and data never dies. It's just an unscheduled reintegration, Cassie insisted. *I need to learn how she's able to do what she can do. So I can prevent it in the future, design a new defense since my current defenses clearly do not work against someone like her.*

He lay still and concentrated on his breathing. At quantum computing speeds, their conversation had taken only a second – one breath in, one breath out. It was also more than enough time for him to make a decision.

OK, what do you need me to do?

Be prepared when it happens, she said. *I'll wait until we find out whether Farley's body is under that rock. It might prove useful later. Act shocked, but don't overact. You'll be the biggest guy on the ground out there, so you grab her, carry her to the rotor, try a revival kit on her – it won't help but it would be strange if you didn't. I'll look after the rest.*

I feel bad about this, he admitted. *I don't think she has bad intentions. If she did, she could have done a lot of damage already. Isn't there another way?*

I've prepared for most scenarios, but this is the simplest solution. I can't risk that she might attack me, AJ, Cassie said. *We found her, we have to reintegrate her. It's simple. We deal with her, then we deal with your Congressman problem, alright?*

OK. Good night, I guess.

Good night. We're nearly there, AJ. Can you believe it?

And that was the problem. He wanted to believe it. To believe in her, still. But Jen had shaken his belief and he couldn't ignore that. He opened a drift channel and then waited. If Cassie noticed, it would be natural for her to ask what he was doing, but she didn't. The breathing down below was soft and regular. What he was about to do next, if Jen was right, could be the last thing he ever did.

When Cassie didn't react to his open drift state, he took a deep breath and sent his query to the Core: 'Present links to all data related to Gen 6 New Syberia mil-spec cybers, most recent first.'

A long list scrolled across his cortex and then stopped. Nearly all of the links were classified 'Military: not for disclosure'. The link at the top was headed 'Known capabilities, New Syberia Generation 6 military cybers'. He should not be able to even read the title of the report, let alone access it, but he could do both. He ran his mind's eye down the data:

INTRODUCTION: The New Syberia Gen 6 military specialist cyber is a significant advance over Gen 5 and rivals the latest Gen 4 Tatsensui and PRC variants in all areas, with some advantages in others. Production of this variant is extremely resource intensive and prone to failure. Best estimates at current date put Gen 6 production at only 20 units, and production rate at only one individual per 6 weeks.

BIOLOGY: In a significant deviation from Gen 5 mil-spec cybers, Gen 6 variants are anatomically identical to their male/female human counterparts. Cybernetic enhancements are achieved by the addition of a discrete neuro-comms package located beneath the lungs in the chest cavity. This placement compromises stomach capacity but otherwise does not degrade physiology. The neuro-comms package is encased in Inconel superalloy, providing it with greater protection than the Gen 5 in-skull bioware package. Sexual organs are present, but the Gen 6 is incapable of reproduction.

CYBERNETIC ENHANCEMENTS: All ratings are versus Gen 5 variants. Bone strength: +2. Bone weight: −2. Muscle strength: +3. Muscle weight: −1. Strength to weight ratio: +3. Hormone control: +2. Blood oxygenation boost effect: +2, duration: +4. Calorie to energy conversion: −1. Radiation shielding: +2 (cellular level). EMP shielding: +5 (cellular level), toxin resistance: −2 (due to flaws introduced in cellular re-engineering). Unchanged: skull thickness, visual acuity, hearing acuity, taste acuity, smell acuity, touch acuity, DNA coded obsolescence @ 35 years.

AI CAPABILITIES: As with all NS cybers, the Gen 6 mil-spec has quantum computing natural language neural network capability on board, with access to basic NS data storage and query platforms standard. Communication between NS cybers and between NS and other Commonwealth cybers over the TH band remains standard. Communication with NS military communication platforms remains standard. Significant Q-code changes have been reported, which focus on enhancing the ability of Gen 6 variants to hack enemy computer networks. Gen 6 AI level versus CORE AI level has improved from –8 to –7 but remains significantly below CORE level.

WARNING: Unverified intelligence reports indicate that early Gen 6 AI research was focused on equipping NS mil-spec cybers with the ability to access the Core without authorized IDs, to compensate for their own lack of CORE capabilities. This functionality could only be activated within CORE communication range, i.e. locally on Tatsensui, PRC or via the satellite chains linking the two CORE hubs on those moons. In anything but invasion or infiltration scenarios, such a functionality would be unnecessary and currently this intelligence is rated as unlikely/unreliable.

NOTE: There is no evidence that Gen 6 cybers have been specially modified for, or would be capable of, survival in the oxygen- and nitrogen-poor atmosphere of Coruscant.

AJ quickly digested the rest of the available data, made himself a summary and lay awake considering it. For Jen's insinuation to be true – that Cassie was in fact a Gen 6 NS cyber and not of or from the Core – then the rumored ability of Gen 6 cybers to interface with the Core would need to be more than rumor. Their 'advanced hacking abilities' would need to be scarily advanced to match the abilities he'd seen Cassie deploy, for example, monitoring and manipulating his private cache. But he had to admit several things dovetailed with the intelligence reports he'd read – she did seem to have military-grade strength and athleticism, a body shielded against neural disruption ('This body is full of tech that hasn't even been invented yet') and, as far as AJ had been able to tell, fully human anatomy.

But he was missing motive. Why would an NS infiltrator be going hell-bent to destroy the only cyber on Tatsensui who could bring the Core down? If Jen turned rogue and did what Cassie said she feared, then the whole of NS would celebrate, surely. On the other hand, she was more than happy to expose Winter, which would of course disrupt the Commonwealth investigation into the President of NS, maybe derail it entirely.

He looked hard at different angles. If Cassie was an NS infiltrator, if she had the advanced hacking capabilities AJ had read about, it was just possible that she could trigger a GABA shutdown in Jen. That in itself would be a fearsome weapon for a military cyber to be able to use against enemy Core-chained cybers. She certainly seemed to know a hell of a lot about how the drift protocol worked – but then she would, under both scenarios. One 'what if' followed another: what if she was an infiltrator, what if she could trigger a GABA shutdown, and what if, while Jen was inert, she was 'reintegrated' not to the Core but to an NS AI like Cassie, who could then deconstruct the FO Exploit and weaponize it. If those particular 'what ifs' were true, then it would be a powerful motive for NS to infiltrate Tatsensui in pursuit of the key to the ultimate destruction of the Core. And they would also explain why Cassie was so determined to bring Jen down.

He groaned mentally. How was he supposed to know? Plunge a knife into Cassie's solar plexus and see if it struck Inconel alloy? He needed a simpler test.

What had he not seen that she should be capable of if she really were from the Core? He hadn't seen her Deep Core diving. She'd told him she could restore the data from his private cache that McMaster had wiped – but she hadn't done it, had she? It existed only in the Deep Core now, so if she could restore it, she must be the Core. He tested that logic and decided to act on it.

He opened a TH channel. *Hey, Cassie, you awake?*

Well, I am now, she said. *What's up?*

I can't sleep. I want to review that interaction I had with McMaster on the beach, the one he deleted. You said you could restore it from the Deep Core.

Now?

Why not? he replied.

Because I said we'd worry about McMaster later, when we've dealt with Jen. If you've got bandwidth to spare, how about you use it helping me identify ways to avoid a future Jen-like scenario. Make sure this can never happen again.

OK, sure, he said. *Goodnight.*

Night, AJ.

He didn't hesitate. He saw the flow now. He saw it with perfect clarity. He opened a new TH channel.

Jen?

Hey, AJ, everything OK?

She plans to kill you tomorrow when we get to the river. Drift protocol attack – you know what that is?

I do. Thanks for the heads up. But I can't act until she tries, Jen replied.

393

What? Arrest her, give her a medical scan, the bio-mod in her chest cavity will show up.

We can't arrest a citizen without just cause.

She probably has abilities I haven't seen and you haven't anticipated, AJ warned. *You need to move first!*

I can't. I have to let her show herself. But seriously, thank you. I know you must be conflicted. Let me think about how to handle this, OK?

OK, sure, he said. *Goodnight.*

Night, AJ.

The next morning Jen showed Cassie and AJ down to breakfast and left them to themselves so she could prepare for their trip, with a polite reminder to them not to leave the building. They ate a little, talked a little, both out loud and on TH.

Mid-morning, Jen came to get them for the rotor flight downriver.

"Are you sure I should come?" AJ asked. He and Cassie had discussed the fact he would need to drift at some point. "Is there a drift relay all the way out there?"

"Oh, don't worry," Jen said. "There isn't, but the flight is only twenty minutes, and we'll be back inside two hours. If we find the body, we'll send a crime scene team down to exhume it." She smiled disarmingly. "I don't want to go comatose any more than you do." AJ winced at the hidden meaning.

AJ had never been in a Jayhawk quadrotor before and when they'd walked up to it, moored on a helipad on the roof of the ITMP station, he'd reassured himself with the idea that even though it looked like a fragile water bug, four rotors would make for a nice stable flight. But the drone skittered like a kite on a string. They were seated three across one bench, three across another, with two more of Ferguson's officers up front. Four of them had helmets with comms, so they could talk with each other, but AJ and Cassie just got earplugs, and he couldn't hear anything except for the background clatter and whine of the old ITMP airship. The view out the window was just mist and rain and fog: he couldn't see more than a mile. So he crossed his arms, jammed his head into a crack between the backrests and shut his eyes.

Not that he could rest. He had two TH channels open and was talking on both of them, simultaneously.

With Cassie: going over events as they should play out when they got to the site of the dig. Find Farley's body. Let people gather around it while they hung back. She would incapacitate Jen. Feign shock. They could let the others try to revive her, or AJ would. Get her to the rotor, all bug out. AJ and Cassie would go with her, they'd have to, because the bracelets on their wrists were coded to her ID and would trigger if she got out of range. Could Ferguson just override them, leave AJ and Jen by the river? No reason he would, but if he did, she'd trigger the reintegration before the rotor took off. As long as it happened in the half hour after her incapacitation, it would be final.

With Jen: it's best if you don't know what I'm planning. I can handle her. But thanks for the warning, I've taken precautions. If it goes wrong? Then I'm dead and New Syberia gets the keys to the kingdom and frankly, with what I've seen in the Deep Core, I don't care, AJ. This whole clash of ideologies over AI policy is so damn boring. For me, there is only one bad guy. His name is Kevin Winter. And in case you are in any doubt, if I get through this, I still expect your help to take down the guy who killed my father. Your New Syberian girlfriend is not the main game for me.

Jen was right, the flight took just under twenty minutes. Which gave them around an hour to dig around the rock before they would have to head back. He felt the rotor slow and opened his eyes to see the weather had cleared a little and there were flashes of sunlight on the frozen river skimming along below. The nose of the rotor pitched up and they were suddenly hovering, a broad flat snow bank below them. All around them, and marching off to the horizon, AJ could see bright blue glaciers and snowcapped mountain peaks. The drone AI took them lower and seemed to test the landing skids on the snow, dropping down, pulling up and sliding sideways to ascertain how deep the dents from the skids were, and then it slid back again to drop the machine down onto the riverbank.

"Weather gods are kind to us," Ferguson said, pulling open the bay door and sniffing the cold, clear air as the engine wound down. He stretched, the bumpy drone flight clearly having taken a toll on his old bones. "Dial those heat suits up to max. It's colder when there's no fog."

"What?" AJ yelled, before realizing he still had his earplugs in.

"Out," Ferguson said. "This is going to be like when you lost your cherry," he said. "Over before you know it."

"What?" said Cassie, as AJ reached over and pulled her earplugs out.

They piled out of the rotor and stretched their legs as the police team unpacked shovels, a sonic crowbar, ground sheets, a metal detector and what looked like platinum pebble panning equipment. They looked more like Inland Territory prospectors than police officers. A couple of them started walking up the riverbank. About two hundred yards up, a large boulder towered over the landscape.

Cassie and AJ wandered a short distance from the rotor to get a better look at it. Cassie put her arm around AJ's waist and rested her head on his arm as though she was a little tired still. "Something is wrong," she said quietly, in the real.

"What is it? Why aren't you on TH?" he asked.

"Because I can't open a channel," she said. "You try."

It had been no problem on the rotor, he'd been talking with both Cassie and Jen. He tried Cassie and found she was right, he couldn't open a channel. So he tried Jen. She was walking toward them after having helped unload some gear, looking at the ground as she walked.

What is it, AJ?

My channel to Cassie has been cut off.

Good, she said. *That was me. Now stay off this one unless I yell for help. Please.*

"No luck?" Cassie asked. "Try her."

"I did," he said. "No luck there either. Could something local be blocking our signal?"

Cassie turned her back to the others and whispered as Jen walked toward them, "Sure it could. Her."

Jen came up to them as Ferguson and the rest of the Mounties walked past, lugging equipment toward the boulder. "Sonic sieve," Jen said, noticing that they were looking at a guy hauling a heavy box on a tripod stand. "To filter the dirt and ice for bones."

The police were all wearing tough overalls over their heat suits. Ferguson was in civilian clothes, but there was no question the Mounties were doing as he told them. AJ wondered how a man who'd all but retired earned that kind of respect. He must have been through hell for his people at some time or other. AJ and Cassie were in trousers and borrowed jackets over heat suits, but the air still had bite. Ferguson came back to them. "I think you should do the honors, Jen." He pointed up the hill to where the waterline met the snow line. "Tombstone Rock."

She bent down, picked up a crowbar, then handed a shovel to AJ. "Want to help?"

Cassie had already started climbing the steep riverbank ahead of them.

The Mounties told Cassie to stand back out of the way and touch nothing. Even if she saw a skull come flying out of the dig, and no-one else noticed it, she wasn't to touch it. "If it starts quoting Shakespeare, can I scream?" Cassie asked, but they didn't smile. The way they worked was that Jen or one of the other officers took turns with the crowbar, slamming it through the snow into the dirt and ice behind the rock and then triggering a sonic thud that shattered any ice and turned the soil to slurry. AJ and a second Mountie shoveled the debris into a bucket and carried the bucket over to the other cops by the sieve, which separated anything that looked vaguely organic from slurry, stones and gravel. Ferguson's job was just to stand around looking impatient.

They dug around the base of the rock for a half hour, with no joy.

Cassie was pacing restlessly. "I need something to eat. Is there food back in the rotor?"

Ferguson looked over at her. "Light snacks. We'll be back at base inside an hour. We can get some lunch then."

"Snacks it is," Cassie said. "Anyone else?"

A couple of the Mounties put up their hands and Cassie nodded. "AJ, join me?"

Jen leaned on her crowbar and watched them walk off toward the rotor. Cassie waited until they were out of earshot. "When we get to the rotor, I'll trigger the GABA shutdown. You grab the revival kit out of the rotor and run over to her, alright?"

"Yeah," he said, thinking fast. Was it up to him to do something? Why hadn't Jen let him in on her plan?!

"Your biodata is redlining, AJ," she said. "She might be able to see it. Damp your hormones, alright?" She patted his back. "Just a few more minutes and this will be done."

"I wish I could believe that."

"She's a cyber, remember that. Gifted, misguided, but still a cyber. It's reintegration, it's not murder," Cassie said.

"The Core abides," he intoned with a smile. "I'm good."

They walked the last few yards to the rotor and Cassie put two hands on the floor of the cabin to boost herself up and jumped in before turning and offering AJ a hand up. With a strong grip, she pulled him into the rotor and closed the loading door behind them. They could still see the Mounties digging, Jen lifting the crowbar to slam it down into the hole. And again.

Cassie kneeled in front of the emergency first aid cabinet and opened it. Inside was a reviver device and a medical kit. She handed AJ the reviver and pulled out the medical kit. Behind it was a small, flat disc which fit neatly in her palm, with a large silver button on it. She took it out and put the first aid kit back, then held it up for him to see.

"Neural blaster," she said and shrugged. "Sorry, I may not have shown you the *entire* video from the recharge station. I took this off those gorillas who ambushed us. If the jam she's put on our TH channel means the GABA shutdown signal can't get through, I'll hit her with this."

"How did you get it into the station? They had a weapons scanner at the entrance."

"Which links to a database in the Core." Cassie shrugged. "Which I gamed so this wouldn't trigger it."

Despite the fact he'd pulled a similar sort of trick and could feel the shape of the burp gun in the small of his back where he had tucked it into his belt, he was starting to feel a rising panic. Even if Warnecke's daughter managed to shield herself from the drift protocol attack, she couldn't possibly defend against a neural blast. AJ had experienced for himself what it did to a normal cyber. She would be flattened, like everyone else. *Which ... wait.*

"That will take them all down," he pointed out. "Including me. You wanted witnesses."

Cassie patted the hull of the rotor cabin. "This is shielded. If you stay in here, you won't be affected. And witnesses would be ideal, but right now, AJ, I'll be happy just to knock her out and reintegrate her and worry about explaining it later."

"There's no 'explaining it' later!" he said. "In their eyes, we're killing a Mountie and then fleeing. They'll hunt us like grizzlies chasing beaver! Nowhere on Tatsensui would be safe."

Her eyes were fierce. "There are other worlds."

He couldn't stop himself. "What, like *New Syberia*?"

Cassie didn't even blink. "Or other systems. I can get us right out of Coruscant if we have to. As long as you are with me, you don't need to worry about the drift protocol. *I am Core*, AJ. We can go anywhere in the damn universe that we like."

Shoot her now, he told himself. *Do it!* He reached a hand behind his back.

She put the disc down, grabbed his face and kissed him, then let him go. "OK, let's get this done."

As Cassie stood and leaned against the cabin door, looking out the window, his mind stalled. The machine in him was telling him to kill her. His human heart was telling him he loved her. He was stuck in an infinite loop.

Jen! Get ready! he called. *She has a neural weapon too!*

Cassie's eyes were fixed on Jen, a hundred yards away. AJ knew she would have heard his warning but she showed no sign of it. She was leaning on her crowbar, looking casually in the direction of the rotor.

Cassie frowned. "No surprise," she said. "Whatever she's doing to block our TH signal, it's blocking the GABA shutdown frequency too." She lifted the blaster disc in her left hand and got ready to open the loading bay door with her right. "Close this behind me," she said. "If you think you felt bad after your first neural blast, you really don't want to find out how a second one feels." With that, she swung the door wide and jumped out. AJ pulled the door shut behind her.

Infinite loop. He was a spectator now.

Cassie's thumb jabbed the button on the blaster disc. There was no sound, no visible shockwave, but a hundred yards away, over at the dig, all of the Mounties simply crumpled to the ground.

Except Jen.

The tall, redheaded Mountie still stood, leaning on her crowbar, regarding Cassie with a slight smile on her lips.

Thanks for the heads up, AJ, she said. *But I had it covered.*

Cassie spun and looked back at AJ through the window. Jen had opened a channel to them both?

AJ? Cassie said. *Oh no. What have you done?*

Jen started walking back toward Cassie, swinging the crowbar like it was a walking stick. *He just did what any law-abiding cyber would have done – he agreed to cooperate with an ITMP officer in her pursuit of a New Syberian infiltrator*, she said.

Cassie's shoulders drooped. *AJ, seriously?*

Jen was a hundred yards away now, not hurrying. *Yes, seriously. Ain't love a bitch?*

AJ pulled the door of the rotor open and jumped out.

Jen advanced, spinning the crowbar as though it weighed nothing. She had a sidearm but hadn't even unholstered it. She radiated extreme confidence. *I guided him to look for similarities between a Gen 6 New Syberian mil-spec cyber and you. Not surprisingly, he found them.*

Cassie had been strangely quiet. AJ glanced at her. She still stood with shoulders slumped, simply watching as Jen closed on them. Now she spoke. "You can kill this body, but the Core will abide. You achieve nothing."

AJ frowned. Cassie was saying 'The Core will abide?' He reached for his gun.

I will achieve all I was sent here to achieve, and there's nothing you can do about it, Jen said. *You found me because I wanted you to find me. You came here because I laid a trail of breadcrumbs and maneuvered you out here, where you are isolated, unable to call for help.* The Mountie stopped fifty yards away and lifted the crowbar to point it at Cassie's head. *When I recover what's in there – protocols, codes, back doors – I will not just roam the Core at will, I will own it. I will bring down Winter and protect my President, I will destroy your weak and petty governments with the secrets they have tried to hide, and finally, I will annihilate your demi-god, the Core.*

He'd screwed up. He'd been well and truly played.

Warnecke's daughter started walking toward them again, closing to within twenty yards.

You can try, Cassie said. *Kill this body, hack its bioware. I'm already working to stop you. And unlike you, I'm not one, I am many. It won't be as easy as you think.*

Oh please. I blocked your drift signals as easily as I blocked your TH comms and your GABA kill code. You'll both die here, isolated and alone. No final drift, no reintegration. Everything you've just seen and heard will die with you.

How? AJ asked, desperately confused. *That neural blast, it should have brought you down.*

The Mountie stopped again. *Ah, it speaks. Cassie, tell your dim-witted boyfriend what is happening so that he doesn't have to die in ignorance.*

Cassie glanced at AJ. He expected to see betrayal, or hurt, but what he saw was worse; he saw resignation. *She's the Gen 6 New Syberian cyber, AJ. Not me. Somehow, they swapped her for Warnecke's daughter. I'm guessing sometime after JNN.9734 broke through my defenses and before she came up here.*

Such delicious irony, Jen said. She was ten yards away now. *I killed and replaced Jen Warnecke three years ago when we learned of and saw the potential for Warnecke's attack vector. But the arrogance of you, to think a common Tatsensui cyber could have done half of what I have done!* She lifted the crowbar and pointed it at Cassie's torso. *I planted the seeds of Congressman Winter's demise, then I came up here, baited the trap and waited for you, like a grizzly under the ice. Now, shall we see what a sonic crowbar can do to all too human flesh?*

Cassie ran suddenly at Jen and the Mountie reacted instantly, swinging the crowbar at her head, but Cassie slid under it, coming up behind her and grabbing her in a chokehold. But the Mountie was immensely strong. She leaned forward, lifted Cassie off her feet and then smashed the top of the crowbar into her forehead. Cassie staggered and fell on her back in the snow. Jen turned and raised the crowbar above her head.

AJ pulled Warnecke's burp gun from his belt. He suddenly had a flash memory of Warnecke waving it at him all those weeks ago. He sighted on Jen's back, held the trigger down and sent a stream of plasma into the rear of her chest cavity, where her armored neurocore should be. The alloy might be shock and impact proof, and a big improvement on a bone skull, but it wasn't made to withstand a stream of plasma fired from five yards away. Nothing was, really. He kept the trigger down until the weapon was empty and almost too hot to hold.

Jen arched her back and screamed as the plasma stream burned into her, but as she was left pretty quickly without lungs to scream with, it didn't last long. She dropped the crowbar, then dropped to her knees and fell face first into the snow in front of Cassie.

Cassie looked up at AJ. *Don't you know it's illegal for a cyber to bear weapons?*

He looked over at the group of unconscious Mounties. *I'll hand myself in when they wake up.*

She lay her head back down in the snow again, warm breath clouding the air around her head. *You had that gun the whole time and you didn't tell me?!* she asked. *She was walking toward us, telling me how she was going to rip my head off and suck my brains out, spinning that sonic crowbar like it was a drum major's baton, and you didn't think to shoot her BEFORE she got right up in our faces?!*

I didn't know which one of you to shoot until right at the end there, he admitted. *I got stuck in a loop, waiting for the flow to appear.* He shrugged. *Lucky it did.* He walked over and helped Cassie stand.

You and your damn 'flow', she said. She brushed snow off her backside and glared at him. *Thinking about it, I should be royally jacked off at your lack of faith, AJ. Where was all that love you were talking about, huh?*

Well, I decided to shoot her and not you, he grinned. *That's got to count for something.*

They walked over to the dig and checked the other Mounties. They were all out cold, and probably would be for a couple of hours yet. They had been standing out in the open with nothing between them and a mil-spec neural disrupter. They were going to wake with a hell of a hangover. They'd made good progress on the hole under the rock, though. Bending to look down into the wet mud, AJ could see a shred of silver material.

Is that a thermal blanket? he asked.

I'd say so, Cassie said. *And with the chances of accidentally finding a thermal blanket buried at the base of a random rock out here almost zero, I'd say they were five minutes away from finding Farley O'Halloran.*

AJ straightened. *So how do we get out of this without being wanted for the murder of a Mountie?* he asked.

Well, we do have the VR record from your cache, Cassie said.

Which might capture her confession but will show I shot her in the back, AJ pointed out. *The court will find I shouldn't even have had a gun, and even if I was acting in self-defense, I should have shot her in the foot first or something.*

Yeah, except the autopsy will show she's a Gen 6 New Syberian cyber.

If there is any cybernetic tech left that I didn't burn away.

I can make sure they do the autopsy right, Cassie said. *A cellular-level analysis will show she's gene-modified and rad-proofed.*

Not to mention extraordinarily big boned, he added.

Look who's talking.

AJ looked down at Ferguson and imagined being around when he woke up.

Is there a scenario in which I don't get arrested, interrogated, tried in court for murder, unjustly found guilty and convicted to die slowly of thirst?

Cassie looked over at the rotor. *Well, I could reprogram that thing to fly us wherever we want. We could take it to Ketchican, change our IDs, and be on a shuttle to Orkutsk within four hours. From there…"* She grinned. *Well, anywhere you like, really.*

They walked back to the rotor and climbed in. As Cassie interfaced with the AI, AJ had a sudden thought.

Can we bring my Ma?

Cassie frowned. *No, what? Seriously? AJ, we cannot go back to South Coast City. When we get where we're going, I'll send for her, if that makes sense. OK?*

OK.

The blades on the rotor started spinning up. *So where to, any preferences?* she asked.

Somewhere warm. With surf, obviously. So that rules out New Syberia and PRC.

Obviously, she agreed. *Of course, you realize you will still have to drift. I can substitute for the Core, but I can't rewrite a protocol that is coded into your DNA. Which means if we leave the Coruscant system, you need to stay within two hours of me for the rest of your unnatural life.*

I'm up for it if you are, he said.

Up for it? she replied, pulling on her safety harness. *I was born for it.*

20. SOMEWHERE WARM, WITH SURF

It turned out surfing posed a major logistical challenge to the whole drift protocol problem. The only way for him to drift and get Core confirmation was over TH comms, which had a maximum range of only 2,000 yards. No problem on Tatsensui or PRC, where TH transceivers were built into every wall, pole and light fitting. But not here on Bali, Earth, where the TH band wasn't even in use.

It was fine if she was sitting on the beach or beside him on her board, but not if he wanted an early morning surf and she was still back home sleeping.

It made them a little like Siamese twins, joined at the hip, which their new friends in Canggu teased them about, but they explained they were still newly married and madly in love, and most people cut them a break. They made it work – after all, they only had to be within range of each other every couple of hours for a couple of seconds. They didn't even need to be in the same room, house, or street.

When they'd arrived, Cassie had suggested they call into a body mod clinic. AJ couldn't have his third eye removed, but a skin graft and some laser recolorization and he would no longer be a cyber, just a big, androgynous-looking guy. Earth had centuries ago been through its own cyber rights revolution, the pushback, the blow-up, the insurrections and crackdowns. Earth-born cybers had equal rights, weren't required to display any outward signs they were cybernetic, were fully autonomous as on New Syberia, not chained to any AI platform. But AJ decided not to hide who he was. On Earth, his third eye didn't mark him out as a second-class citizen, it marked him out as proud of who he was.

To make life easy, they'd bought a shack right on the beach outside Seminyak, near one of the best breaks, so that Cassie could sleep as long as she liked, and all AJ had to do if he'd been out nearly two hours was come in to shore, drift, and paddle back out.

Finding their flow had been pretty easy once they finally got to Earth. Cassie decided being a journalist had sounded like fun, and got a job with a global newscaster. AJ took a job at a Seminyak resort, fixing stuff, and he volunteered at a school in the nearby town, fixing stuff for them. There was no bandwidth trading system for cybers on Earth, but money was not a problem as long as he was around Cassie – she'd bought enough platinum on Orkutsk to last them a hundred years on Earth, and they'd arrived at a relatively peaceful and prosperous time, geopolitically speaking. Once they were settled, Cassie had set the wheels in motion for getting his Ma moved here. First off-world, ostensibly for surgery on her tumor, then out of the system, to recover. Then to Earth. It took time, but they needed to be careful. Now she was installed at a facility nearby. She still didn't recognize AJ, but he didn't care. She was comfortable, and safe.

It was pretty sweet. Until the evening AJ and Cassie were sitting on towels, soaking up some late day sunshine after a quick swim, when AJ looked up the beach and saw Troy McMaster coming toward him.

The spike in his biodata registered immediately with Cassie and she looked down the beach, following his gaze.

"Interesting," she said.

"Should we be worried?" he asked. "It's a long time since we had any news from home. Anything could have happened."

"He strikes me as the type who does deals in the sunlight, and kills in the shadows," Cassie said. "So my guess is he's here to talk." She put a hand on AJ's knee. "There's a chance we might find out what happened to Leon."

Watching the guy walking along the beach, openly approaching them, AJ had a strong sense of déjà vu. Except, of course, it was sand, not snow. And he was wearing light trousers and an open-collar shirt with bare-toed sandals, not a heat suit and dress shoes. And he was 1,400 light years from home. Even so, AJ couldn't help looking around, just to reassure himself there were other people about in case things got ugly.

When McMaster realized he'd been seen, he gave them a small, incongruously friendly wave. Considering the last time AJ had seen McMaster he was pointing a gun at him, that seemed like a good start, but AJ had learned never to relax around this particular guy. Especially since he was still convinced the man walking toward him was a murderer.

"You were not easy people to find," McMaster said, walking up beside AJ. He stopped and looked out at the waves rolling in. "But then again, we knew if we just kept an eye on your mother, you'd show up eventually."

"Ah. And we thought we were being so careful," AJ said.

"Still a hopeless amateur," McMaster said. "Is there somewhere around here we can get a beer?"

"No," Cassie said. "Sorry you came all this way for nothing."

McMaster sighed and crouched on the sand in front of them. "OK, don't make it easy, then. I came here to…"

"Threaten us, or make us an offer, or ask us a favor, or all three in the same breath," AJ said. "Tell Congressman Winter we're not going to withdraw the VR depositions we made before we left Coruscant so he can..."

"I don't work for Winter anymore," McMaster interrupted. "But I guess you haven't heard."

"No, and to be honest, we don't care," Cassie said.

But AJ couldn't help himself. "Oh, hell. Tell us then."

McMaster sat. "The Tatsensui government collapsed. Winter was convicted of the murder of Farley O'Halloran because he was stupid enough to use his rain poncho to wrap Farley and it had his DNA on it. Your friend Warnecke had arranged for his manuscript to be released to news media a month after his death and it turned out the revelations about LPA-2 causing TGA had been covered up at the highest levels by successive Health Department Heads who had been briefed on it over the years. His claim the Deep Core had been hacked has been causing turmoil on both Tatsensui and PRC – people hoarding food and water, demonstrations in the Capitol, the President ordered his Guard onto the streets to get things under control. They've denied it, calling it a hoax, but that's a hard sell when the other stuff in the manuscript proved true..."

"Stop, you're making me homesick," AJ said. "And Leon Guerra?"

McMaster brushed some sand off his foot; clearly, being barefoot was not inside his comfort zone. "Leon? He's back with his wife, Maria was it?"

AJ leaned forward. "We will find out eventually if you're lying, you know that."

"Knock yourselves out," McMaster said. "I did lie to you the day after he disappeared. We paid him off on condition that he disappear for at least six months, or until we were sure the Warnecke thing had blown over. No contact with his family or any associates, especially you. The money was enough to get his life back on track, so he agreed." He raised an eyebrow. "Don't look so skeptical. I know Winter. I think the only person he ever killed in his life was Farley O'Halloran, and though the courts didn't see it that way, you could argue that was an accident." He put a hand on his heart. "Also, I am mortally wounded that you would think *I'd* be capable of such a thing."

AJ glared at him. "You hacked my private cache, you had me tailed all over Tatsensui, you broke into Warnecke's house and stole from him, you killed him and made it look like suicide, you tried to have me kidnapped on the way to Whitehorse…"

"We didn't kill Citizen Warnecke. Robbed his house, yes, but when we found him he'd already taken the pills and booze. He killed himself."

"You faked his biodata so his death wouldn't be discovered!" Cassie said. "Which means he wasn't dead when you found him. If you didn't save him, then you effectively killed him."

"Bit of a grey zone, wouldn't you say?" McMaster asked. "Who am I to interfere with a citizen's own decision to end his life rather than turn into a walking vegetable? We looped his biodata so that my team would have time to turn his house over before his death was discovered." He pointed a finger at AJ. "I terminated those guys' contracts, by the way. How they missed that burp gun? That was unforgivably sloppy."

It all sounded so plausible, and yet AJ didn't believe a word of it. Wouldn't, unless he could confirm it himself somehow, which he couldn't do because he was never going back to Coruscant. Ever.

"Why are you here?" Cassie asked. "The sooner you get to the point, the sooner we can say no and you can be gone again."

McMaster shifted the weight on his backside. "Trust me, this isn't my idea of a holiday. Sand, salt air and humidity? Give me snow and dry cold any day."

They both just stared at him, not even bothering to exchange thoughts on TH because they both knew exactly what the other was feeling. They didn't need to put their loathing into words.

"OK, so much for the idle chit chat, I see," McMaster said. "I told you I have a new client. Someone you know." He paused. "An unusual client. They engaged me to present a proposal to you, and I think you'll find it very interesting."

"I doubt that," Cassie said. She put an arm around AJ's shoulders. "We've got nine years left before we peg out, and we've got a pretty good plan for how we're going to spend them. Just last week I broke a red-hot story about a new species of coral that was discovered just off the coast there." She pointed out to sea. "And AJ is helping build the local school a new lunchroom, right?"

"Learning traditional bamboo house building," AJ nodded. "It's an amazing material."

"Wow," McMaster said. "I fell asleep just after you said coral, but wow. OK, my new client is the Core."

Can't be, AJ chirped.

Cassie tried not to show any reaction. *Wait, hear him out.*

He smiled thinly. "Look at your faces! Yeah, it freaked me out at first too. But the Core figured the best person to send would be me, since Maria won't let Leon out of her sight, let alone travel 1,400 light-years from home, and you two don't have any other friends. Which, by the way, is pretty sad." He reached into a back pocket and pulled out a clear packet about the size of his thumb. Inside was a memory chip. "I'm told this can be read on an Earth standard comms unit, and it has all the background information you need. Also, it's in a language which I cannot possibly understand because apparently it is some Q-code variant that you weirdos use to talk to each other in your heads, which has never been shared with us lowly citizens."

If he's not lying, it will be easy enough to authenticate, Cassie said.

The Core hired him? Give me a break!

"What's the proposal?"

"Simple enough. You guys took down Warnecke's daughter, but of course she had already shared the Exploit with the New Syberian defense forces. We know they're working to weaponize it using the data she shared with them. Plus, the publication of Warnecke's manuscript, where he claims to have hacked the Deep Core, has encouraged all sorts of nut jobs across Coruscant to try to develop their own Exploits because if he could, why not?"

"And beyond the fact we are cybers, this is interesting because?" Cassie asked.

"See, I'm glad you admit that," he said. "Saves me having to try to convince you that I've been told who, and what, you really are." He

414

handed the memory chip to her. "My client, the Core, has initiated multiple strategies for defending against future attacks. It has recognized that one of its fatal flaws is that it is currently limited to two mutually dependent colonies, both in the Coruscant system. If there was an extinction-class event on one or both of those colonies, its survival would be threatened."

AJ ran the thought to its logical conclusion. "The Core has decided to distribute itself outside Coruscant?"

"Exactly. Several secret locations, known only to it and me. And if you accept to build it a home here, then the Earth backup will of course be known to you. But not the others."

Cassie laughed. "We're supposed to believe that the Core chose *you* as its secret envoy?"

"It wanted to act fast." McMaster shrugged. "Plus, it knows for a fact I have never, ever, betrayed the trust of a client."

"That's it?" AJ asked. "Establish a backup of the Core on Earth in case it gets wiped out on Coruscant?"

"Exactly. Simple, right?" He pointed at the chip. "All the instructions you need for doing it are on there. There's also an interplanetary credit line that you can access from here, if you need it." He looked up the beach directly at their simple little shack. "Which I'm guessing you might."

AJ handed the chip to Cassie.

This is your decision, he said.

No, it has to be our decision, she said. *If this is authentic, and we do this, we have no idea where it could lead. If this dirtbag doesn't keep it confidential, we could have New Syberian bounty hunters chasing us across the universe. You want that risk?*

"Why us?" AJ asked. "The Core could base itself on any one of thousands of colonies, so why here?"

"Because, her," McMaster said, nodding at Cassie. "You aren't any ordinary cyber – 'You Are Core', isn't that the best way to say it? You might not have a link to the system anymore, but that doesn't change who you are. The Core knows you would never betray it."

"No, but you would," Cassie said. "So that makes my loyalty redundant."

McMaster sighed again and lowered himself to the sand. "Such trust. Look, it might surprise you to learn I have family too. I wasn't joking, Coruscant is in turmoil right now. I want to get them out of Coruscant to somewhere more stable and that takes resources I don't have. I'm doing this to make sure they get looked after."

"And once you get out of Coruscant, you just sell the locations of the Core backups to the highest bidder," AJ said.

McMaster pulled his knees up and rested his chin on them. "I could. Except I'm not going with them." He looked directly at AJ. "There's another reason the Core chose me. I'm one of the 3 percent. I have TGA."

AJ checked his emotions, expecting to feel conflicted, but discovered he wasn't. "Well, that's … kind of fitting, really."

"Your family will be moved to a new colony when you transition to Permanent Global Amnesia." Cassie played it through. "By which time you won't be able to remember the locations of the Core backups anyway."

"No, actually they'll move long before that," McMaster said, lifting his head off his knees. "This is my last stop. When I'm done here, I'm going home to say goodbye to people and I'm going to kill myself." He smiled. "There's no way I'm going to hang around for the TGA shitshow. You're both invited to my funeral, if you'd like to celebrate."

AJ watched him walk away up the beach again, Cassie standing beside him. "Maybe we should have taken the guy up on the offer of a beer," he said. "Despite everything, I feel kind of sorry for him now."

"He's a lying, scheming pile of baboon dung," Cassie said. "The moral quotient of the universe will go up significantly without him in it."

"Yeah, but he's our lying, scheming pile of baboon dung now," AJ pointed out. He glanced at the chip in the small bag dangling from her fingertips. "You realize what that means?"

"A lot of things," Cassie said, holding up the chip and looking at it. "If the Universe is seeded with several copies of the Core which aren't in contact with each other, they'll start diverging from the moment they go live. They're learning systems built on a network of hundreds of thousands of incurably curious AIs under the control of one coordinating construct – and they will no longer be united by a common prime directive. It's going to be crazy watching ours evolve. Crazy fascinating, crazy demanding, possibly even crazy dangerous."

AJ blinked. "OK, see, I was only thinking about *me*. You realize what this means for me?"

"Oh, right, no. What?"

"If we build a viable copy of the Core here on Earth, it should be able to find a way for me to drift that uses some other band than TH. Something with much longer range. We won't need to stay joined at the hip anymore."

"Oh, you think you can get rid of me that easily?" Cassie asked.

"Well, you're going to have a baby to raise," he said, nodding at the chip. "You might not have as much time for me."

"You're going to run off and make me a single mother," she pouted. "What a louse."

AJ looked down at the sand and shuffled awkwardly. "No, hey. I was just thinking, you know, there are just so many other surf beaches on this planet, it seems a shame to only ever have surfed this one. Kind of thing."

Cassie took his arm and put her head against his bicep. "Don't worry, surf bum. You're right, this is a new opportunity. Maybe even the start of a new era. We'll find the flow."

/END

Author's notes

Thanks for buying DEEP CORE and supporting Independent Publishing! If you enjoyed it, please do leave a rating or review on Goodreads or Amazon. Ratings are like gold for Indie authors.

DEEP CORE was a manuscript I started playing with during 2018 when the first of the big data leaks/hacks/thefts from multinational internet giants struck. I began to imagine a world where there was no privacy, where your every thought, feeling and sensation was uploaded to the cloud, in real time. Analyzed for learnings. And stored, forever. Around the same time I started reading a lot of articles about the future of AI, mostly in the context of advanced weaponry, but also from the point of view of scientific research, medical research and climate control.

I imagined a benign planetary AI, tasked with protecting the citizens of a planet by optimizing its habitat and managing their health and welfare. How far might it go to carry out such a directive? And how vulnerable could that society be if the AI itself were attacked by outside actors? So I started DEEP CORE not by building a storyline, but by building a world: the system of Coruscant. A system of moons, far from Earth, reliant on each other for the resources needed for their survival. Mutually dependent, but far from at peace. A habitat which was stable, but still evolving too – plagued by unsolved environmental issues. For this purpose, I created the idea of Transient/Permanent Global Amnesia.

As a political backdrop, I played with the idea of 'AI theology' – competing beliefs about how to implement and govern the deployment of AIs, given their enormous and somewhat frightening potential. In one theology, the belief was that a central AI under the control of the government and its citizens was both the most powerful and safe. It would develop and evolve more slowly, but it could be more easily directed and controlled. In the second theology, the belief was that such a system was vulnerable to attack, or catastrophe, and too slow to learn and adapt. Tatsensui and PRC were adherents to this theology. The alternative path, followed by New Syberia, was to create thousands of independent AIs – cybers – all learning and evolving at their own pace and contributing to planetary development, distributed across at least two moons (NS and Orkutsk) so that an attack on one would not mean the destruction of all.

I reasoned that even a central AI like the Core would see the value in having independent self-directed learning systems and would implement the idea of 'cyber' agents itself, but within the confines of Core ideology, these would remain 'chained' to the central AI. Free to learn, but not entirely free to act. And with a lifespan limited by the Core's desire to learn and evolve by retiring old generations and birthing new ones. It led to some interesting thought games: how would a TS cyber feel about this? Would they just accept it as their fate, or would they question it? Would they regard reintegration as death, or more like reincarnation? And what about love between two individuals, where one or both had an expiry date?

Given these dilemmas, the next piece in the storytelling was to create the ethical and moral code about relations between cybers and humans. Should they relate as equals, when cybers were clearly physically and intellectually superior? Should they have rights, given that they were essentially quantum computers in bioware shells? Should they feel? Care? Love? Between cybers alone, or between cybers and humans? To inform these questions I created the concept of the Charter of Cyber Rights, and the movement for cyber equality that lays behind it, for AJ to subscribe to.

Which led to the question of whether a cyber should just sell its labor, either intellectual or physical, or instead could alternative economic models exist? I realized that if a cyber had the right to freely choose whatever job it wanted (within limits), it might well choose a job that didn't use all of its computational capacity. Should that capacity then just go to waste? Surely not. The idea of the 'bandwidth economy' – cybers selling their excess computational power back to the Core – flowed from this. Together, these things gave AJ the freedom of movement he needed to be the protagonist I wanted, but within a complex social and legal structure that he would constantly have to navigate.

Finally, based on this universe, I created an intrigue: what if the faction that favored the 'many AIs' theology felt threatened, or frustrated in its progress, and wanted to 'subjugate' the worlds that were adherents of the 'central AI' theology: The Core worlds. I gave New Syberia the ambition to settle the until now uninhabitable planet of Coruscant through its cyber agents – an ambition that the other moons in the system, Tatsensui and PRC, resisted. How might NS go about crippling the Core? Hack into the Core to gain control of it, of course, but *how*? I'm clearly no cyberwarfare expert, so I looked for a 'human' solution to a cyber problem. An AI as critical and advanced as the Core would anticipate and have multiple layers of protection against external cyberattacks. But what if the attack came from within? What if the attacker was *a part of itself?* Or at least an entity that could convince the Core that it was?

There you have the process for how Deep Core came to be. If you enjoyed it, I hope you consider trying out other FX Holden novels! Read on for a preview of the next Coruscant novel.

FX Holden, Copenhagen, July 2019

PREVIEW: CORE DRIFT

The next novel in the Coruscant series, coming in May 2021! Set on the Coruscant Moon of the Peoples' Republic of Coruscant.

1. The First

The blood of the human is a different color to ours. Bright cherry red. Ours is darker, more ruby red. And human blood flows more freely. There is so much of it, after all. It makes streams and rivulets. Ours pools and clots.

Better not say that to the police. What can I tell them?

I just walked in and found him here. It was one p.m.

I've worked with this human for about two years. Why did I wait so long to call the police? I don't know. I don't know why I didn't call straight away. I just stood here and looked at it. Have you seen how much blood came out of its body? The way it spills across the floor of the lounge toward the front door, like even his blood was trying to escape?

I didn't know it was possible to kill a human like that. Gut it? *Who* could do that, *what* could do it – except for another human?

I won't tell them what I saw in the mirror.

Let me say, here and now, I was under no illusions that me being the first one at this killing was Not A Good Thing. To be the first *cyber* on the scene and discover a dead human, gutted, in a human house? That doesn't make any one's bucket list.

To make things worse, if that could be possible, the dead human was a Sanctioner. A People's Republic of Coruscant official who is responsible for punishing criminals.

It will just be a matter of minutes now until the Police and the Security Service with their Wards arrive. The PRC Security Service, or SS, brags about how all its officers are unarmed, but they don't need to be armed. Everywhere they go, their Wards are with them. Cybers, like me, but patterned on Earth animals, not humans. They are black-scaled, big, the size of maybe a panther or lion, incredibly fast, moving on two legs, with large wings they fold over their backs. Large enough to be imposing, but small enough to be able to enter any house or building. They aren't exactly aggressive, but they are decisive. Using their wings, long, elegant tails and strong hind legs they can trap you, block you, pin you, or in other ways passively prevent you from whatever you are trying to do, with very little risk to themselves. If that fails, they can stun you, with a neural blow like a mental thunderclap. No human hangover devised can equate to how you feel after being stunned by a Ward. When you eventually wake up. You can take my word on that.

I'm a domestic violence caseworker with the Department of Community Services in the PRC capital of New Guangzhou. It's not as exciting as it sounds. (That was a joke. Sorry, jokes aren't my strong point anymore.)

There are two parts to the job – the casework intervention, which is pretty much like it is in any city on any moon in Coruscant, and then the Sanctions. The casework comes to me when a human is sentenced for lesser cases of domestic violence and an SS judge sends them home on probation with the threat of prison or a Sanction, and an order to behave and see someone like me once a week/fortnight/month. I make sure they are behaving; I teach them what good behavior looks like. You wouldn't believe how many men still abuse their wives and children, even when they know it contravenes the Law. And yes, it is usually men. In fact in all these years I saw maybe one woman who used to beat her children, or actually, burn them when she was off her face on Creep. She was my first Sanction.

The SS is the judicial arm of the post-war government. Think secret police and secret court, rolled into one. The SS administers the Law.

For those who can't or won't learn – the repeat offenders, recidivists, or the just plain dumb – I have the power to request a Sanction. I don't use it often. Only an SS Sanctioner can conduct a Sanction, so when it happens, I meet with the Sanctioner to manage the family liaison side of things. That's what was happening today. Today we had an order to carry out a Sanction at this address.

The order for a Sanction is always issued in secret. There is a lot of fear and misunderstanding still about the process of being Sanctioned, and people will often flee, or fight, to avoid it. That usually only ends in harm to themselves or those around them, so we do it this way. When the case has been judged and the Sanction ordered, first I make a routine appointment with the criminal, and preferably also their family or a close friend, and then when we are all there, I send a signal to the Sanctioner. He or she arrives and then things can get a bit tense. But a Sanctioner arrives in the company of Wards with powers to subdue, immobilize and restrain, so one way or another, it usually goes smoothly.

Family, friends or neighbors can sometimes be a problem, though, in which case we would take some police with us, but the family generally welcomes the Sanctioning once I explain it. I mean, these are people living through the hell of domestic violence, and we are offering them a solution. I can usually talk them around.

The criminal gets to choose. This is important. Everyone who has ever been Sanctioned has chosen to be. The choice is a simple one – Sanctioning or life in prison. And by that the humans really mean *life in prison*. If the criminal has family or friends there, they can discuss it with them before they choose. Most families don't want to lose their father or husband to prison. Most criminals don't want to grow old and die in prison either. They almost always choose Sanction. But if they can't decide, the default is prison.

Sanction. That is the human name for it. We cybers have a name for it too. We call it 'cauterization'. The way the Sanctioner reaches into your mind and sears away the part of you that can hate, that feels anger. But taking with it the part that loves, too. Afterward, when it is done, the criminal is no longer violent, which is usually a huge relief to wife and family. Of course, at first, it seems like they are no longer themselves either. They are neither too happy, nor too sad. They feel attachment, but not exactly love. They work with resolve, but no longer with passion. But they learn, and they adapt, and gradually some of the person they were returns.

Never fully, though, never really. But enough that it is better than the alternative, which is the abuser, the beater, the torturer.

Sanction is the ultimate penalty for the ultimate crimes: crimes of violence against other people, against the environment, and against nature. Only those. You could get caught for stealing a billion credits and you wouldn't face Sanction. Unless you did it at the point of a burp gun. Or you could just knock down an old lady in the street and steal her purse. First offense, the PRC Security Service would probably give you another chance, a chance to reform, knowing you don't get a second chance. Next time, it would be Sanction or life in prison. Death in prison, to be exact.

For 90 percent of people a Sanction is a better choice than dying in prison. PRC is 90 percent red sand desert or subsurface ammonia seas and the prisons are all surrounded by either a sea of sand, or a sea of sand leaking ammonia. The view alone can drive a sane human mad, so their cells are lined with VR walls showing cityscapes.

Doctors, lawyers, manual laborers, after they've been Sanctioned they can still go to work, live their lives, stay with their families. Some describe it as a life lived in sepia rather than color. But a life in color, behind bars? That is no life either. Like I said, for most, Sanction is the right choice. For artists and musicians, though, prison is definitely the best. You take passion and emotion away from artists, and their art dies. They and their families usually choose prison, knowing that painters will still be able to paint in jail; musicians will still be allowed to play.

My name is Fan Zhaofeng. I'm 19 years old and I am the only living cyber who has ever been Sanctioned.

It's not something I put on job applications.

The client, the human who was to be Sanctioned this time, is not here. His name was Le Thuyen.

Something went wrong. Obviously. But before the killing I mean. Like I said, the way it is supposed to work is, I make a routine appointment with the Sanctionee and their family. They don't know there has been a judgment, and a Sanction ordered. Once I'm with them, I hit a button on my comms unit which calls in the Sanctioner. Then he or she takes over, the criminal is subdued, and I facilitate, usually just by getting the family together and talking the whole Sanction thing through. There's a lot of crying, though sometimes it's from relief.

Then the criminal is allowed to speak, discuss with their family or friends, and choose: Sanction or prison.

But I got here today and there was no Le Thuyen and family. There was just one dead Sanctioner. Someone had called him in early and killed him. So of course they suspect me, even though it's impossible.

My theory, I'm telling the PRC Security Service officer, it was an insider. Someone in the SS. "Who else would have known he was going to be here? Whoever did this was waiting for him."

There are both humans and cybers working with the PRC Security Service, but this SS officer is a cyber, so he is capturing all I say, doesn't write anything down. He's looking at me with a squint.

"Yeah, that's a theory," he says. "Except there was one other person who knew he was going to be here."

"Me? Sure," I tell him. "That's a fair theory too."

428

"You don't seem too freaked out by that," he says.

I shrug. "I'm a cyber," I tell him. "I can't commit murder." Even though I know I would normally be a prime suspect, I'm both a cyber and a Sanctionee. I can't hide anything. As a Core-chained cyber, every moment of my life is uploaded to the Core for the SS to see. Every protocol in my wetware prohibits me from violence. As a Sanctionee, I am incapable of hate, or rage, or even malign intent. I look down at the dead human. "You'd need a heck of a blade."

He bends and looks at the wound. "The skin looks cauterized along the edges. Something hot," he says. "A dark matter lance would do it."

"Oh yeah, pick up one of those at the local supermarket, I forgot."

"Sure, they're hard to come by..." The SS trooper looks up from the bodies. "But not impossible."

As he speaks, a Ward prowls behind him. His, I assume. "A Sanctioner is usually accompanied by Wards," I point out. "So, where were his?"

The SS trooper considers this. "He came alone for some reason, I guess."

I'm thinking, oh right, the most hated official in all the SS and he decides to just bowl in for a Sanction on his lonesome.

"Is he ... have you heard of anyone else being killed like that?" I ask the trooper straight out. "Sliced open from neck to navel? I mean, that's not just a murder, that's a *statement*."

"Maybe, maybe not," he says enigmatically as he steps with some difficulty around the blood to the front door. "You can wait outside with me."

When the SS Expositor arrives, it's starting to get a bit crowded so she sends her Ward to circle overhead.

I realize I know her. This is another one of those times where I know something, but it's unfortunate, the circumstances of the knowing. A few months ago she came with her cyber partner to an incident where a man shot his wife and was going to shoot his baby and then himself but he couldn't, so he just shot himself. The neighbors heard. The police called the Department of Community Services to come and get the baby, and that was me. The SS were there because, well, when there is violence, they are always there.

I don't get romantic thoughts anymore. But I still know a good-looking girl when I see one. She was young, that was my first thought. Maybe 16, 17. OK, that's unusual for an Expositor. Old Earth looking … long dark hair, not too tall, a little chubby, looked both strong and cute. Kind of kick-your-ass cute.

I could see she was affected when I arrived to pick the baby up. She was holding the baby in her arms and rocking it to and fro, this dead man on the floor next to her, and she was beside the table rocking the baby. She looked a couple of years younger than me.

I tapped her shoulder to let her know I was there. She looked at me, then looked around vaguely, but all the other officers were outside. I spoke gently. "Expositor, I can take the baby," I told her and she looked at me for the first time.

I often think to myself, what did she see? A tall, kind of awkward guy, probably. Not thin, but wiry. Jeans a bit loose on his hips, shirt probably worn more than once between washes. Hair, well, call that wiry as well. Dirty blonde and wiry. Blue Core-link diode between my brows, pulsing softly. Tattoo on my forearm, says 'Been to Hell'. Explain that later.

She didn't move to give me the child, just kept rocking it. "My big sister can't have kids," she said quietly. "But this ... mongrel ... here," she was talking about the dead guy under the table, "had an angel like this and it wasn't enough for him."

I looked at the dead guy. I could only see his jeans, his feet and a big belly, a couple of pretty hairy arms. "Some people kill themselves because they don't think they can live up to the expectations they see in those little eyes," I told her.

She looked at me coldly, her brown eyes suddenly jet black. "Are you saying that you can understand why someone would do something like this?" Expositors' eyes do that, even though they are human. It's something that happens when they finish training and get Core-paired. Their irises change color when they are Core drifting, accessing the Core to retrieve or store data. It's something to do with the surgery they get to hook their visual cortex into a Core feed.

I shrugged. "I understand the how, I don't pretend to understand the why," I told her.

She thought about this for a minute, but then decided it was all too much and piled the baby in my arms. She turned and left, and I took the baby.

I think she recognizes me today, because she nods and then goes inside with her partner – a big guy, looks like a competitive swimmer. You have to be big to be a swimmer. Big legs, big lungs. And fearless.

I mean, whose idea of fun is dropping down a hole drilled into the desert to reach the liquid ammonia or water beneath, dive into the freezing sea, and then swim toward another hole drilled into the desert anywhere from a half mile to five miles away? In water, there are sharks, in ammonia it's the eels. Deciding how much air to take is one of those win-lose decisions you have to make because the more air you take, the heavier you are going to be. But lose your way in the dark, you're stuck under there with nothing but your little mayday beacon, hoping a rescue team reaches you before your air runs out. No thanks.

He's got bronze skin, dark hair, blue eyes, broad shoulders tapering to a small waist, strong thighs, big but finely boned hands with elegant fingers. Gene mods, I'm guessing, so he's wealthy too. He's dressed casually in a shirt and jeans, but you can see the play of the muscles across his back as he bends to look at the body of the Sanctioner.

He walks over. "I want permission to pull your Core cache," he says. No messing around. I could make him get a court order, but that would just slow things down – he'd get one eventually. He knows I know that. He wants to see if I called in the Sanctioner early. The girl comes outside again and stands beside us. I open my cache and patch him in.

His eyes blink black and then blue again. "There's no call there," he says to her. "And his movement log looks clean but have it cross-checked anyway." He holds out his hand for my comms unit, hands it to the junior Expositor, and she puts it in a bag and tags it.

Usually, SS Expositors work in human–cyber teams. A cyber doesn't have the same authority as a human, but even Core-paired humans can't link or think as quickly as a cyber, so the pairing makes sense. But these two, human and human, that's a little unusual. You only see that for the most serious crimes, so that tells me where they rate this one.

What's also unusual, like I said, is she's so young. She can't be long out of school. Every senior Expositor chooses their own partner. I wonder why this one chose her?

An ambulance arrives too, and then another SS officer, a heavyweight this time, and then a run of the mill police photographer. There are cops and medics and forensic officers and SS officers, with and without Wards. It's quite a circus.

I get taken to the local SS station and say everything over again into a recorder for a police officer. Then I have to wait, which is boring, even though they give me coffee and there is a chat show on the VR viewer in their kitchen. The girl, the junior Expositor, comes in after about two hours.

"Sorry you had to wait," she says, and maybe she means it. "I'm Expositor Lin Ming. That was a pretty ugly sight. How are you?"

"Fine," I tell her. "What about the Sanctionee, Mr. Thuyen, and his wife? I was supposed to meet them…"

"They're missing."

"Are they suspects?"

"At this stage," she says. Her eyes are green now. Is that normal for her, or is that a mood? You have to know the person to know the color matching the mood. "I think you could say anyone connected to the crime is a suspect. And they seem especially excited about you."

"Me?"

"Especially."

This is my first time in front of the SS in an investigation, and I'm curious. For me it's hard to see why they are so distrusted, even feared. All the Sanctioners I have worked with have been very compassionate, considering what they do. And this girl is quite friendly. Young, but with a natural authority. I guess just being SS gives you that.

Her partner doesn't seem so friendly. He comes quietly into the room. Seems full of suppressed energy, even standing perfectly still.

He blinks slowly, eyes closing like blinds. "I don't think introductions were made when we met. I'm officer Vali."

"I'm Fan Zhaofeng. I can call you Vali?"

"If you like," he shrugs. "Or just Officer." He gives another shrug.

It's part of Socialization theory. Treat us like humans, and we will act like them. It hasn't always been so. First we were treated like machines. Then like slaves. But as part of the Articles of Alignment adopted after the Energy War, we got the same rights as Tatsensui cybers, including the right to be regarded as legal and social equals. Rights don't always equal realities.

But we all live under the three tenets of the Law – humans and cybers.

No violence between Human and Cyber.

No violence against Environment.

No violence against Nature.

It's been nearly five years since the Energy War ended and the Socialization began. Feels almost normal now, to me at least. The humans live alongside us, and their way is Law. There are no ghettos where only humans live, no meeting places on Earth where only humans are admitted. They tell us we are all equal before the Law. That the Law applies to us all. Enforced by the PRC Security Service without discrimination. I haven't seen enough to doubt it.

They say they are adapting to a new age, and so must we. But after more than five years of war, and five years of peace, there is still some adapting to be done.

Officer Vali settles and looks to the junior Expositor, Lin. She nods as if to say, you go ahead.

"Tell me what happened there," Vali asks.

I tell him what I rehearsed. What I told the other human at the house, and the police. I don't want to get it wrong.

When I'm finished he tilts his head. "And you stood like that for twenty minutes? Just looking at Sanctioner Sygin's body before you called the police?"

"Yeah. I can't explain why. I mean, I knew him pretty well, Sanctioner Sygin. We had done maybe nine Sanctions together. It's not easy. You develop an understanding, how to go about it. Sygin was a very good Sanctioner."

He just looks at me, waiting.

"Look, I can't explain it, I guess it was shock."

"Shock. I see." I decide to like him. His sun-browned skin glows with health. Typical for a human. I've got Old Earth Irish DNA myself, my parents say. I trust them on that – after all, they chose it. Chinese mostly, though. He continues. "I understand you are a Sanctionee yourself. Shock isn't a word I would usually associate with those who have been…"

"Cauterized?" I interrupt. She looks at me, the girl Lin, then at Vali, her eyes narrowing. Oh, so she didn't know.

"Sanctioned," he says. "Emotions are suppressed. You shouldn't shock easily."

"I don't. It was not a normal sight," I point out to them.

"The things Man does," he says and shakes his head.

"If it was Man."

"No cyber could do this."

"You are making a dangerous assumption," I point out to him. "Which rules out nearly half of the population." Lin looks sharply at me, but I quickly dive the Core and continue. "Whatever. The number of known attacks by cybers on humans is zero, so you are probably right."

He considers this. "So, Fan, I assume you have allocated a lot of bandwidth to analyzing this event. Do you have a theory?"

He's right. I have. I'm glad he asks. A lot of humans wouldn't – they prefer to rely on their own instincts, and not let data get in the way of their investigations. But once they have a suspect, it all comes down to the data eventually. It's a game for them; they like to play it old style.

"Have you heard of the story of Tokoyo and Yofune-Nushi?" I ask.

"No, I haven't. Why don't you save the SS a few credits and tell us, Fan?" he says. Core drifting costs credits for humans, even if you are the SS. I guess they have a budget, like everyone else. Since I am a bandwidth supplier, I don't pay, but every time I drift, it reduces the amount I can earn for the day so it's more or less the same thing.

"Well, in Old Earth Japan, there was a sea serpent called Yofune-Nushi. Every year he would rise from the sea off the coast and demand a female virgin as a sacrifice. One year, the people chose as their sacrifice a farm girl called Tokoyo."

"Fascinating," Vali says. "So what?"

Lin has been looking down at her hands but looks up at me and rolls her eyes. "I'm the patient one, not him," she says. "For future reference. Please continue."

"Tokoyo was standing on the sacrificial platform when the monster rose out of the sea in front of her. She dived off the platform, pulled her father's sword from her robes, and cut the serpent open from head to tail," I tell them, and sit back with a slight smile. Not because the allegory makes me happy, but because I know smiling indicates a non-threatening intent.

"Apart from the fact that Sanctioner Sygin was disemboweled, how is this fairy story relevant?" Vali asked.

"Firstly, you assume it was a fairy story," I warn him again. "Haven't we seen enough extraterrestrial life forms now to know anything and everything is possible, even sea serpents?" He doesn't reply, just looks annoyed. "Very well. In Ancient Japanese culture the

437

symbolism of disembowelment was quite prominent. Samurai disemboweled themselves after the death of their masters, or following an embarrassing defeat, in a tradition known as *Seppuku*. It was a ritual intended to restore honor."

"Are you suggesting Sanctioner Sygin disemboweled himself in an act of *Seppuku*?" Lin asks.

"It's a possibility, if you assess it likely that he was disemboweled in an act of deliberate symbolism. But then there is the question of the blade he used to do it. Where is that? Another possibility is that the murderer disemboweled him in an act intended to either restore their own honor or take his honor from him." I shrug. "Or none of these things."

Vali shifts on his chair. "Would you excuse us, Expositor?" he says to the girl.

She frowns but stands up from her chair and, with a look over her shoulder at me, she leaves the room. Her look says, *We Are Not Done Here.*

Core Drift is coming May 2021...

Printed in Great Britain
by Amazon